"Exquisite and audacious,
and highly recommended."

The New York Times

"Opens quietly with an intense, thrumming
poem from Egyptian poet Hermes, and then
ignites like the creature it profiles... a rich and
illuminating cultural experience."

Washington Post

"Seriously creepy... achingly lovely...
heartbreaking and hopeful."

Publishers Weekly

"I really enjoyed this anthology. It is—here's that
word again—gorgeous. Its thematic coherence adds
an extra element: not just the individual stories, but
their arrangement, have something to say.."

Tor.com

"A sparkling array of talent and imagination."

SFX

"Not only an anthology of short stories,
but of real narratives... Will let readers enter a
world that they have no idea about."

New York Journal of Books

"Pick it up, rub it and make a wish."
The Book Eaters

"A treasure chest of literally wonderful
and marvelous stories, with a kind of richness
that fantasy only rarely achieves."
Tim Powers

"Vivid, enthralling and endlessly varied.
A wonderful collection."
Mike Carey

"A superb collection of superior stories by
some of my favourite writers. This is the
must-have anthology of the year."
Lavie Tidhar

"A stunning anthology of multicultural perspectives
on the various lives and natures of the creatures
known alternately as Djinn, Jinn, or Genies....
Every story in this anthology is pretty much perfect."
Ganzeer

"An original take on the subject
and beautifully written."
Good Times

"A showcase of authorial skill—delicious prose
and well-crafted narratives bending themselves
around their chosen theme."
Speculative Herald

THE DJINN

FALLS IN LOVE

and other stories

Also from Solaris
by Mahvesh Murad and Jared Shurin

The Outcast Hours

THE DJINN FALLS IN LOVE

and other stories

**Edited by Mahvesh Murad
and Jared Shurin**

SOLARIS

Published 2022 by Solaris

First published 2017 by Solaris
an imprint of Rebellion Publishing Ltd,
Riverside House, Osney Mead,
Oxford, OX2 0ES, UK

www.solarisbooks.com

ISBN: 978 1 78618 768 0

A CIP catalogue record for this book is available from the British Library.
Designed & typeset by Rebellion Publishing

Printed in Denmark

CONTENTS

INTRODUCTION

Mahvesh Murad and Jared Shurin

THIS BOOK HAS been a labour of love for almost two years, supported and encouraged by our friends, a globe-spanning cohort of author-scrounging scouts and the terrific people at Solaris, especially the infinitely supportive Jon Oliver.

When we began, we had three goals:

First, to use the central theme to showcase global storytelling. We wanted to demonstrate not only how the djinn unite disparate cultures, but also how they can inspire new and old voices from a variety of genres. This is one of the reasons we didn't standardise the spelling across the book: every culture, every author, has their own djinn, jinn or genie.

Second, to showcase the djinn themselves. The djinn are an element of folklore that seemed, to us, to have immense contemporary relevance. Whether as pranksters or partners, the djinn have a role in modern literature.

We think we succeeded in both, and we know that we had a lot of fun trying. Our authors come from all around the world, and have brought to these pages a vast and wonderful variety of djinn. We have wish-granters and shape-changers, immortals and spirits, hoarders and hermits. They come in all shapes and sizes (even bottles), and are truly marvelous creatures.

Our third goal, and it seemed minor at the time, was to find a title worthy of the work. This poor anthology suffered for long months under the half-serious title of *Djinnthology*. It wasn't until Robin Moger introduced us to the divine work of the Egyptian poet Hermes, and "The Djinn Falls in Love", that everything fell into place. Hermes' extraordinary piece, straddling both tradition and contemporary twists, says everything we wanted—everything we *needed*—to say.

Most importantly, the poem captures what we *didn't* expect to find, assembling *The Djinn Falls in Love*: the empathy on display within this book. Perhaps this is the lingering impact of Richard Burton and Disney's *Aladdin* and other Orientialist interpretations, but the djinn have always been firmly portrayed as the *other*. They are the magical *not-us* that lurk and bedevil, existing to trick and be tricked. But the origins of the djinn, at least according to the Qur'an, are far more complex. When Allah created man out of clay, Allah *also* created the djinn out of fire. We may stem from different materials, but in all the ways that matter we are very much the same.

The contributors saw this too. In Kamila Shamsie's "The Congregation", the divide between humanity and the djinn is as thin as cloth, as close as a shadow. When a young boy stumbles between worlds, he finds, not monsters, but the missing parts of his own family. Catherine Faris King's "Queen of Sheba" also features a djinn as (adopted) family. As a young woman looks for magic in escapist fantasy, she discovers that the fantastic surrounds her already. In Neil Gaiman's "Somewhere in America", a stand-alone extract from *American Gods*, a visitor to one of the most bustling cities in the world finds companionship not with other people, but with an equally lonely djinn. These djinn are not the predatory devils that we've been led to believe: they are flawed, warm and human.

Several of the stories reverse the traditional roles. In Kuzhali Manickavel's elegant "How We Remember You", it is the humans that are tricksters and tormenters, poking and prodding at their companion. Is it the classic cry for help? Yet even in this—quite sinister— inversion of the classic relationship, there's no lack of empathy. Amal El-Mohtar's prose-poem "A Tale of Ash in Seven Birds" takes a more sweeping view of the relationship between djinn and human, in an epic tale of the rise, fall and appropriation of civilization. All from the djinn's perspective, it also portrays humanity as the other—it is *we* that lurk in the dark spaces.

Kirsty Logan's "The Spite House" again takes the djinn's perspective. In this clever tale—seeded with plausible false histories—the reader is introduced to the djinn's burden, the horrible loss of agency that comes not from relying on wishes, but by seemingly granting them. Helene Wecker's "Majnun" similarly shows the djinn not as a homogeneous block, but as individuals—with their own, often conflicting, motivations. *We are the chaos and release they need*, claims one of Wecker's djinn. But is that relationship symbiotic or parasitic, and what does that role mean for the djinn themselves?

Monica Byrne's "Authenticity" is the most explicit (pun intended) picture of the relationship between djinn and human; although, like many of the other stories in this volume, it is not what it initially seems. Byrne's story of experience-seeking cultural tourists juggles both empathy and shame, and its twist-ending wickedly turns the camera back on the reader.

Several of the stories combine the djinn with the tropes and settings of science fiction. E. J. Swift's "The Jinn Hunter's Apprentice" posits a space-faring far future, if one still marred by very Earthly religious and cultural divides. The troublesome djinn of the *Arwa* demonstrate that our worldly problems cannot simply be left behind—and also that the opportunities of the future belong to all of us. Jamal Mahjoub's deliciously cyberpunk "Duende 2077" is set much closer to the present, painting a bleak picture of a fractured theocracy, technological isolation and social destruction. Mahjoub's story uses djinn in the

---

abstract, the name itself evoking the rebellion hidden in dark places.

Usman Tanveer Malik's "Emperors of Jinn" explores the age-old Pakistani rural feudal system by asking questions about possession, ownership and power. Saad Z. Hossain's "Bring Your Own Spoon" moves forward in time, taking place in a subcontinent where humans and djinns must struggle for survival, both meager shadows of what they once were but now existing on the same plane, alongside each other. Sophia Al-Maria's "The Righteous Guide of Arabsat" is a pulpy, tongue-in-cheek—but also frightening—look at a man's fear of female sexuality and how that fear can be a danger to women. Nnedi Okorafor's "History" features a famous pop star who believes her own power to be enough to control where her ambitions may take her, though where that may be is influenced by greater magical forces.

A few other stories also examine the loss of agency by positioning djinn as objects. The djinn in James Smythe's cunning "The Sand in the Glass is Right", though central to the story, never says a word. Instead, the story examines the self-destructive nature of absolute power; demonstrating how access to wishes means not fulfillment of one's dreams, but descent into recursive nightmare. K. J. Parker's "Message in a Bottle" examines the role of djinn more abstractly, expanding and investigating on that single, critical moment of choice. A man—clever, self-conscious and only slightly pure of heart—is faced with a terrifying decision. Before him—in a bottle, of course—sits absolute salvation or total destruction. What does he do? What would *you* do?

Sami Shah's "Reap" also examines that moment of decision and the dehumanising effect of absolute power. In his harrowing story, drone operators—with the power of life and death from half a world away—encounter a force that they cannot understand. The soldiers' psychological detachment, the screen they hide behind, is shattered when they lose that control, when their lives suddenly become the playthings of others.

Claire North's "Hurrem and the Djinn" may be—on the surface—the most traditionally Burton-esque story of them all. This discursive, rhythmic story flows like a missing fragment from the *1001 Nights*. But despite the impressive stagecraft—with sound, fury and many, many djinn—North's story is not quite what it seems. As daunting as North's djinn may be, this is a story—again—about human beings.

Maria Dahvana Headley's wonderfully rhythmic "Black Powder" delves into the American past, with bullets and a gun as captivity for something powerful, proving that djinns really are unencumbered by culture or vessels. In Neon Yang's "Glass Lights", it is emotion and wanting that is magic enough, and not nearly enough.

These writers looked into the djinn and saw, not

monsters, but people. The djinn here are partners and family members, enablers and neighbours, friends, brothers, taxi drivers and even, as the title implies, lovers. They are the other halves of ourselves—close enough to reflect our sins and virtues, but far enough to give us the distance to see clearly.

That Allah created humans and djinn is known. That we live in tandem to them, parallel to their lives yet asked to not reach out to them, is also known. But what if those lines blur? What if, sometimes, the membrane between the worlds trembles, weakens, allows us a look into the other world; a glimpse into beings who are like us and *not* us, made of a smokeless fire that can consume us? What if, given our differences, we find that we are, even so, able to fall in love?

Editors' note

Djinn, jinn or genie, every culture
has their own interpretation.

Accordingly, we have left the choice of
how to address them—and, more importantly,
how to *spell* them—to the individual authors.

THE DJINN FALLS IN LOVE
Hermes

الجنيّ يقع في الحب

أنا جنّيّ، قد تكون أصفادي مكسورة،
لكنها لم تزل حول معصميّ وكاحليّ، كل جنيّ مملوك.
الشهب التي يتحدثون عنها، ولا يعرفون أين تسقط.
الحب الذي يتوهّجُ كفانوس على سبيل، لا يعني شيئا للخائفين،
يراهُ العابرون، كحصان، يحصّنك من السيوف والخناجر
لكنه يكشفك للسهام.
أمضي وخيالي، مربوطٌ بقدمي، الحبّ يأكل روحي كحمض
الكثبان تغير أمكنتها في الليل، دون إذني
الأسوار المحيطة بي، والحرس المتناوبون عليها
لا تمنع البدر الرائع من الوصول إلى قلبي
حتى قبل أن يشرق وأراه
وتغمر فضته روحي
ها هو بالفأس، يكسّر فيّ كل شيء.

A djinn I am.
My fetters may be broke but
still they wrap round wrist and ankle:
every djinn's possessed.

The comet they speak of and know not where it
    falls,
the love that glows like a lantern down a road which
means nothing to the fearful:
Those passing see it as a mount, which keeps you
    clear of sword and spike
but holds you up to arrows;
I pass, my shade lashed to my foot, love eating my
    soul like an acid;
The dunes change places in the night without my
    leave;
The walls around me and their guards in watches
cannot halt the full moon's coming to my heart
before it's even risen and I've seen it and
its silver floods my soul.
Here it is with a mattock, shattering everything
    inside me.

                          Translated by Robin Moger

THE CONGREGATION
Kamila Shamsie

WHEN QASIM WOKE up, the others were gone already. The ropes strung across the bed frame beside him were still swaying in the breezeless summer morning; it had only been a few moments since his father had hoisted himself out and started towards the mosque for the dawn prayer. *Why didn't they wake me?* he wondered, slipping his feet into his shoes and walking in the direction of the mosque. It was too dark to see more than a few feet in front of him, but he knew the way from memory. He stopped, looked up at the sky thick with stars. It was too early for the morning prayer. He looked back towards the house, considered going indoors to wake his mother or sister or aunt, but reminded himself he was no longer a child and walked on.

Winter had long since ended, but he still felt a chill as he passed the shrine of the Sufi saint, Gulab Baba. On one side of the shrine a graveyard had grown up.

In death the saint's followers would be as near him as in life; as the graveyard grew, it had surrounded the Tree of Blessings with its branches covered in infants' clothes, some bright with colour, their shapes intact, others little more than sun-bleached rags. Women stayed up all night praying in Gulab Baba's shrine. When they were rewarded with the child they'd previously been unable to have, they brought the clothes their infants wore in the first weeks of their lives and hung them on the branches of the tree in thanks. All this Qasim knew, though it was too dark to see anything but the outlines of branches—little torsos impaled on them, arms hanging limply. There was still no breeze.

The mosque was only a short distance from the shrine. As he approached it, he saw the men had already lined up for prayer, and ran to find a place on the carpet. It had been changed overnight. Previously it had been green with red flowers along the border; now the border was yellow with motifs of red flame, a repeating pattern of arched black doorways running in rows along it. The spacing was such that each worshipper stood in his own doorway. Perhaps news of the beguiling new carpet was what had brought everyone here, early and in such numbers—he had never seen the mosque so crowded. The thicket of men around him was so great he couldn't see the imam, but that didn't matter. He brought his hands to his chest, said the words of prayer with the men around him. When it was time to kneel he was a fraction later than the others, so engrossed was he in the new pattern of the carpet, its vibrant colours, the depth of its darkness. And so there was a moment when everyone was kneeling and he alone stood tall. Then he saw it. The feet of every man in the congregation were turned backwards at the ankles.

Qasim had lived his whole life in the village, had been born after his mother spent the night praying to a saint who knew how to speak to jinn and ask them to intercede with the angels to give her a child. So there was no fear in him, only curiosity. Here in a mosque they must be the good jinn—the Parees, the Rooh—and not the Shaitan. Though even as he thought that, he understood that the world was never so simple—many of the men who came to this mosque were steeped in evil. And jinn were very much like men in nature, except perhaps a little more fiery in temperament: they were made from smokeless fire while men were made from clay. He dropped to his knees, was lowering his head to the ground when the worshipper to his right whispered, "Don't let your forehead touch the darkness."

He turned his face in the direction of the voice and saw a boy his age, with flame red hair and eyes to match. The boy put a finger to his lips, and looked away. Qasim bent further forward at the waist, but just before his forehead touched the carpet he saw movement in the darkness of the doorway, a swirling.

He drew back a little and the carpet was a carpet again.

"What is it?" he said, softly, but the boy jinn next to him only said the words of prayer out loud, his example somehow conveying an instruction for Qasim to emulate him.

And so Qasim prayed with the congregation of jinn, whose prayer was just like the prayer of men. Each of the jinn had flame-red hair—why hadn't he seen it as soon as he entered?—and other than the boy jinn, they were taller than the tallest of men in the village. When the prayers ended, each jinn turned to embrace the jinn beside him. Qasim turned to the boy jinn who turned to him, and their arms went around each other, and Qasim hadn't realised until then that his heart had never known love—how to feel love and be loved, both. The embrace lasted longer than Qasim's whole life and still was too short. When the boy jinn drew away, Qasim wept, and the boy jinn wept with him.

"It is their time now," the jinn imam said, and all the jinn, including the boy jinn, fell to their knees and prostrated themselves one final time—and when their foreheads touched the darkness of the doorways they fell through it, every one of them, a head-first plummet. Then there was silence. Qasim was alone in the mosque and the carpet was a dull green and the flowers along the border were of a colour he couldn't call red now that he understood red.

He was standing in the centre of the mosque looking around, when the men of his village entered—his father, and uncles, and brothers, and all the rest of them.

"How did you get here? You were sleeping when we left," his father said. "Your mother said we shouldn't wake you because you hadn't been well yesterday."

Qasim looked at his father, his brothers, his uncles, all the men who made up his world. He thought of his mother, whispering prayers over him the night before while pressing a wet cloth to his forehead.

Why didn't you let me follow you? he wondered, looking at the place where the boy jinn had stood.

FOR THE NEXT few weeks he went to the mosque in the darkness before dawn every morning, but the jinn never showed themselves to him again. Sometimes from the corner of his eye he thought he might have seen a flickering flame, a movement in the darkness, but when he looked directly at it, it disappeared.

The world he had always lived happily in stopped having any meaning for him. Food was tasteless, sleep brought no rest, company was no longer companionable. One morning his mother asked him, not for the first time, what was wrong, and he shook his head, not for the first time, to say he couldn't speak of it.

"Maybe he's possessed by a jinn," his little brother said, and Qasim brought his hands to his face and wept.

"I'm not," he said. "He didn't want to stay with me."

That evening, Qasim's mother walked with him to Gulab Baba's shrine and said, "Now you need to hear the story of your birth."

Qasim had always known that his mother was not the woman who had given birth to him. That woman—his father's first wife—had died in childbirth, and her sister had married the widower and raised her nephew as her son. When she and Qasim's father had children of their own, they were Qasim's brothers and sisters, not his cousins. And so he had never missed, and rarely thought about, the woman buried in the graveyard near the tree on which his infant clothes hung in tatters.

The woman who had always been his mother sat down on the verandah of the shrine, and pulled him down beside her.

"You're old enough now to be made to understand how the world works. When we are young and strong, we raise our children; when we are old and infirm, they look after us. For a couple to be without children is the greatest of sorrows, but there are times by God's will when one or other is unable to have a child of their own blood. If the woman is at fault, the man can have other wives, and their children will be children to the childless woman too. But if the man is at fault, then the situation is much more serious. In the time of Gulab Baba, there was a man who had been to war and came back unable to lie with his wife in the way that was necessary. He went to see Gulab Baba, the most pious of men in the village, who said, my son, you defended all our lives with your valour and in return I will pray to God to send you a child. Tell your wife to come and pray with me, so that the Almighty might hear the combined prayers of his devoted servant and a woman in need. The man sent his wife, seven nights in a row, and nine months later a child was born. You understand what I'm telling you?"

"God heard their prayers?"

"In a manner of speaking. When word of what happened came about, another man, who had married three women and still had no children, sent all his wives to pray with Gulab Baba. And nine months later, all three of them had children. Soon, more and more men began to send their wives to him. Gulab Baba himself had four sons, and as he grew older it was the sons increasingly who stayed up all night praying with the women. You understand now?"

"He raised his sons to be as pious as him?"

"Hmmm, something like that. When Gulab Baba was dying, he asked for this shrine to be built in his memory. He said that as long as the men of his line stayed on as guardians of the shrine, God would continue to hear their prayers, with those of the childless women. And all these generations later, that truth still holds. In a manner of speaking."

"And I was born because of the prayers of your sister and the guardian of the shrine?" Qasim said, beginning to understand.

"No, my son. You were a different story. My sister came here, it's true, when she was unable to conceive a child. Her husband, your father, loved her beyond all measure and said he couldn't take another wife, he would rather they remained childless. Men say foolish things like that, because they know they have decades in front of them when they can change their minds. But a woman has only so much time given to her in which to become a mother. My sister was determined to have a child, so one night she asked me to accompany her here. She was afraid of what she had to do, but there was something pulling her greater than fear. I held her close before she went in, and said I would sit out here—on this verandah, right in this very spot—and wait for her. I had been here only a few minutes when I saw the guardian of the shrine run out, his eyes wild, holding his shalwar up with his hands. I put out my leg and tripped him, and when he fell I pinned him down with both my arms and said, 'What have you done to my sister?' He cried out, 'Nothing, I did nothing, the jinn wanted her instead.'

"When he said this, my bones became ice. I pushed him aside and tried to run into the shrine, but the doorway turned to fire. I tried to run through it, but I couldn't. All night the fire blazed there, and all night I tried with prayers and buckets of water from that well—there, that one—to put the fire out; but nothing I did made any difference. I cried out for help but my voice disappeared in the roar of the fire, and no one came. The guardian left, saying, 'There is nothing to do but let him finish, and hope he will release her afterwards.'

"Near dawn, the fire went out, and my sister walked through the doorway, her eyes a haze as if she had just woken from the sweetest of dreams. She didn't speak of what had happened, and neither did I. But when I touched her, her skin was hot. Not like a flame, just a warmth, as if she'd been sitting in the sun. A few weeks later, she told me she was going to have a child. I don't know what she told your father—he and I have never spoken about it—but he was even more adoring than ever before, during all those months leading up to your birth. That warmth of her skin was with her throughout the pregnancy. I knew what it was, but what could anyone do about it except hope it would go with the birth of the child? And then the midwife said there were two of you, two babies, in her womb. I was there the night you were born. The midwife, my sister, and me—only the three of us. I held cold towels to her head, her arms, her belly, as the fire which the jinn placed inside her began to consume her. She was so hot the midwife and I were sweating, just from being near her, though it was deep in winter. And in all of this, you were born, your skin cool to touch. Your mother wept with happiness, tears that sizzled on her cheeks and disappeared."

"And the other child?"

"I swaddled you up and took you outside where your father was waiting, to place you in his arms and protect you from the heat of the room—which was beginning to make my flesh burn. I stood outside just a moment, breathing in the cold night air, and when I turned to go back inside it happened again: the doorway of fire. I knew the jinn was in there with her, and this time I did nothing but hold you and watch. Your father was the one to try to run through the doorway, douse it with water, defeat it with prayers. When the fire finally disappeared, your father rushed into the room and when I heard his cry I knew my sister was dead. The midwife, too, both dead of burns. And no sign of a second child."

"I have seen him. He held me. Everything is nothing after that; even you, mother."

Qasim's mother placed a hand on his head. "Stay with me, son," she said.

He stood up. "It's too late already. I'm sorry."

HE ALLOWED HIS parents to call an exorcist, but after listening to his story the man threw his arms up in despair. "I can drive out a jinn that has possessed a boy, but what am I supposed to do about a boy who *seeks* to be possessed? Go to the fortune teller. Perhaps he can help you."

Everyone knew that fortune tellers didn't have the power of prophecy directly, but they knew how to speak to jinns, and ask them for favours. The jinns could enter the realms of angels and hear them discussing the future, and bring back news to the fortune teller of what was yet to happen. Of course the angels didn't like it when the jinn did this, and if they saw a jinn eavesdropping on them they would hurl a thunderbolt at the jinn—to human eyes, it looked like stars streaking across the skies. Qasim didn't want to know the future, but he did want to know someone who could speak to the jinn, and in the village there lived a fortune-teller who was believed to have a whole army of jinn ready to do his bidding.

So he went to the fortune-teller, who could be found sitting under an old banyan tree whose branches served as a canopy (a hundred or more jinn lived in that tree alone, it was said).

"I've heard of you," the fortune teller said. "The jinn have been talking of the human boy with the jinn brother. Is it true you were able to see him?"

"I saw the whole congregation," Qasim said. "But I only saw them once, and you can see them all the time."

"No, I can only hear their voices. The jinn blood in me is diluted—my great-great-great-grandmother lay with a jinn. She was the last woman in this area to do so before your mother. The jinn don't like it when their kind couple with ours; it gives rise to people like you and me, who break the rules that say the jinn are aware of us, but we aren't aware of them."

"So there are others like me? Humans with jinn brothers?"

"Somewhere in the mythology of all nations, the stories exist. When Sikandar came here with his armies, his people brought the stories of the brothers Castor and Pollux—do you know the story? No? There are many versions, but the one closest to the truth is this: Castor and Pollux were twin brothers, but one was human and one was jinn. A jinn named Zeus had lain with their human mother in the guise of a firebird. Pollux, the jinn, was immortal, but his brother was not. When Castor lay dying, Pollux begged his father Zeus to be allowed to share his immortality with Castor. There was enough jinn in Castor to make this possible, but the price was a heavy one: for half the year Castor lived in Hell, with the dead, and the rest of the year he was in the world of jinn."

"It's not such a heavy price. At least he had half the year with his brother."

"No, let me finish. Hell, as you know, is under the command of Iblis, the most powerful of the Shaitan jinn. He would not agree to give up someone promised to his realm without getting something in return. So for the time that Castor lived among the jinn, his brother Pollux…"

"No, don't say it."

"… his brother Pollux was in Hell, the only place in the universe where the fires can burn even a jinn. In saving his brother from death, Pollux ensured they would spend all eternity apart."

"Why did you tell me this?"

The fortune teller looked up at the stars between the branches of the banyan tree. "Do you think God, who sees everything, doesn't reward sacrifice? When He saw what Pollux was willing to endure for love of his brother, he brought them both up to heaven. Look, you can see them, the constellation of the twins."

Qasim's eyes followed the fortune-teller's pointing finger. A group of stars which he'd never before noticed detached themselves from the sky and lowered themselves until they were floating just above the banyan tree. He blinked once, and the stars become two boys, their arms around each other's shoulders, so close he could see the fire of the nearer twin's eyes. Blinked again, and they were just pinpricks in the darkness, rising back up into the sky.

"But though God had compassion for the twins, the jinn Zeus saw the power of His rage. No man or jinn should interfere with life and death—those are God's domains alone. To interfere with them by making a pact with Iblis puts the crime beyond the reach of God's mercy. And so Zeus, once the mightiest of all the jinns, was removed from existence. Only a few of us remain who even believe he ever lived. No jinn since has ever tried to make a pact to extend the life of his mortal son, and no jinn ever will."

"But why did my brother show himself to me only once, and never again?"

"A jinn's life span extends to the Day of Judgment. What feels like 'never again' to you is a speck of time to them."

MANY YEARS PASSED. Qasim became caretaker of the mosque, and learnt to be content to glimpse flutters of the jinn world from the corner of his eye, never turning to try to look at it directly. He lived the life of an ascetic, taking pleasure in nothing the world could give him—not food, not love, not the turning of seasons. Everything was nothing compared to the embrace of a jinn-brother.

One night, he woke up feverish, his body burning. He remembered it had felt exactly this way all those decades ago in his childhood when his mother had held a cold towel to his head to cool him down before he fell asleep. He rose unsteadily to his feet, and entered the prayer hall. It was no surprise to see the carpet of flame border and black doorways, exactly as he remembered it. A boy with eyes of fire stood on the carpet in the centre of the otherwise empty hall. He was only slightly older than he had been, more than forty years ago.

"Have you come to take me with you this time?" Qasim said.

"You can't live in our world," said his brother. "It would burn you."

"Then why are you here?"

"Because I'm old enough now to know how I can live in your world." The jinn stepped towards Qasim, and Qasim, understanding, held out his arms. His brother came closer, stepped into the embrace, and then deeper than that, into Qasim himself. No words have been invented to speak of that moment.

A few weeks later, the exorcist came to the mosque for the night prayer and saw the caretaker, a man he'd first known as a boy. He watched the man run a brush frothed with soap and water along the bare floor of the courtyard, and then called for his grandson, who was also his apprentice, to be brought to the mosque.

"Can you see the jinn inside that man?" he said.

The boy said certain prayers, and in the darkness the caretaker's shadow leapt onto the wall, like a fire with many tongues.

"Will you let me help you drive the jinn away?" the boy said.

"Oh, no," said the exorcist. "All he's ever wanted is to be possessed. There is no evil here, only love. God save us from a world that can't tell the difference."

Above, a group of stars detached themselves from the firmament and the sky twins bowed towards the exorcist, with their arms still around each other's shoulders in a forever-embrace. Qasim and Qasm, the twins in one body, looked up.

"Show-offs," Qasim said, and went to clean the mosque's carpet, with its border of flame and black doorways running in rows all along the length of it.

HOW WE REMEMBER YOU
Kuzhali Manickavel

WE REMEMBER THE first time you almost disappeared. You walked past the broken well at the end of the field and we watched you, unaware that we were clinging to each other. The atmosphere split and swallowed you. It was quiet, like a leaf falling or someone closing a book. Years later, Murali will think of this whenever he hears of people disappearing—he will think of the atmosphere opening up and swallowing people head first, and he will clutch whatever is near him, completely unaware of what he is doing.

The minute you disappeared, Murali wondered what would happen to you. Specifically, he wondered who would feed you, where you would sleep, and what you would do if it started raining. Long after Anandhi and I went back inside, Murali stood there, hesitantly poking at the atmosphere, afraid you would come tumbling out with your heart and liver in your hands. You came back four hours later like nothing had happened. No one else noticed you were gone. A couple of days later, Murali gave you his postcard of Sathyaraj, the one with *I LOVE YOU* written over and over on the back. We never saw it again. Murali decided that you took it with you when you finally disappeared for good.

WE REMEMBER THE second time in bits and pieces. It was at Mandaikadu, and Murali remembers the rain and how warm the temple seemed after the damp bus and the incessant chilly drizzle outside. I remember anticipating tea and biscuits at somebody's house, and how that anticipation carried me through that miserable day. Anandhi remembers the sea. She remembers how all the kids went to stand at the water's edge because we were told to, and how we stared blankly at the waves, our feet already turned, ready to go home. She remembers shoving you and saying something about your knees, when you walked right past her into the sea. For a second, we didn't do anything. The water continued to lap at the shore and it was like you hadn't gone in at all, like you had never been there in the first place. Then Anandhi dived in after you and was lost in a forest of strange legs swathed in cotton saris and frayed inskirts. She saw the hair on the women's legs move gently against the water. Scars seemed to glow in their skin, some sickle-shaped, some like tiny lost moons. She stayed underwater, even after she realized she was not going to find you, which is why that visit to Mandaikadu was always remembered as the time Anandhi almost drowned.

We all remember that it seemed to take forever to get back home. We didn't speak to anyone, not even to each other, and the adults said we were ungrateful, sulky brats and they would never take us anywhere ever again. When we got home, you were already there. You said you had snuck away to see the new Sathyaraj movie, *Villathi Villain*, and it was superb. Fight, dialogue, comedy, dance, ellamai top class, you said. You thrust the ticket stub into Anandhi's hands and told her to keep it safely. You even sang one of the songs from the movie, your heels hitting the ground hard and out of beat as you tried to dance along. But we never believed you.

FOR A LONG time, we remember you dishonestly. During the majority of her twenties, Anandhi remembers you as the son of the cook, a wiry boy with hot, dusty eyes who was clever with his hands and had a tendency to steal. She does this partly because it gives her a chance to talk about the inherent dishonesty of the working class, and partly because she doesn't know how else to talk about what really happened, and what she did. Murali used to remember you as a distant cousin, a poor relation who was left in our ancestral home to go to school and later build a life as best he could as a mechanic or a bus driver. He always remembered you as a fast runner, which gave Murali the chance to talk about the lack of sports opportunities among the poor. For many years, I remembered you as the first boy to show me his penis, even though this is completely untrue. Sometimes you were the cook's son, sometimes you were a poor relation, sometimes you were just 'some boy'; but you always showed me your penis, and I always laughed.

There are times in mixed company or on social media when we talk about you—1984, Doordarshan, Tinkle and Gold Spot—like it really happened that way. We create a memory none of us recognizes, soaked in mellow sunlight and a sweetness none of us understands. And it is the easiest thing in the world to place you there in the sun, drinking Gold Spot with us like you are just a boy, like you are as unremarkable as the rest of us. We like to say you excelled at life through hard work and determination, and you are now living in Australia with a white woman named Shirley. When we tell people this, they always believe us.

WE REMEMBER YOUR magic. Maybe that is the obvious thing to remember about you. We never tell anyone about it, though, not even each other, because it is hard to talk about now that we are older. The words don't make sense in our mouths, and once they are said, they just hang there, and they are ridiculous. It's not something you can put words to.

We remember watching your feet when you ran and the way our hearts would tilt the moment your feet left the ground. We remember cheering you, how we all jumped up at the same time, arms high, shouting like all this, the young boy tripping across the sky, the sun, the shouts in the air, all of it was ours.

We remember cajoling you to 'do something' and then crowding around you, watching the way feathers blossomed from your shoulders and chest, how they shuddered and settled once the transformation was done. Murali remembers that when he was younger, he thought it was a trick. Later, he would watch you do it and think how could I have been so stupid? How could I think this was a trick? We remember the rush of air when you took off, and how the quiet seemed to spread all around us when you were gone.

MURALI AND ANANDHI keep souvenirs. Murali collects bird figurines and when he meets small children, he tells them that they are magical stones that look like birds but can turn into anything when you aren't looking. When they ask if they can have one, Murali tells them to fuck off, they are his fucking birds. Anandhi keeps a scrapbook, filled with photos of Sathyaraj and ticket stubs of every Sathyaraj movie she has seen, even the Telugu and Kannada ones. There is one autographed picture, given to her by a friend who thought she was a huge fan. Anandhi keeps this one on a separate page with the words *I LOVE YOU* written all around it.

Murali hides tiny penguins or owls in the fridge when he comes to visit. Anandhi leaves cut-outs of Sathyaraj inside my bowls and coffee cups. I keep all of them, carrying them from one rental to another in a box I never unpack. I don't know what else to do with them.

I REMEMBER YOU honestly to strangers. I tell women in share autos that I never liked you very much, but you were comfortable to sit with and you sang well. I don't remember what you looked like, but I remember at one point, you thought you looked like Sathyaraj when he was younger and I had disagreed. I remember that your feet were always dusty and you often breathed through your mouth. Your English-speaking skills were poor; you could not add double-digit numbers in your head. You had no idea what a biochemist was. I am pretty sure that if you were still here, you would not have been good at computers. I also remember how your eyes would close as the feathers began to sprout from your shoulders and the way you threw your chest out when your feet were no longer on the ground, when you were just running, the sky opening up slowly underneath you. But I don't mention that to anyone.

I always remember the house. I think of how children just came and went, this one's niece, that one's son, all of them coming and going like the house was spitting them out only to swallow them up again when it felt like it. Anandhi said this is what happens in old ancestral houses where there are too many rooms, too many people coming and going. I always remember the house. That fucking, fucking house.

But mostly, whenever I remember you, I am sorry. I am sorry for what happened. I'm sorry for not opening the door. I'm sorry for saying that I was coming to get you and for not coming at all. I am sorry you are not here now. I am sorry for that most of all.

WE TRY TO remember this part objectively. We try to remind ourselves that we were teenagers then, and everyone is an asshole when they are a teenager. Add to this the limited financial resources, all of our parents, boredom, an unusually hot summer, the house and the fact that we kept getting dumped there summer after summer, and it is almost understandable; but not really.

Something had probably been wrong with you for a while before we arrived. I remember that you did not come out to see us, and when you did, you seemed slow and bewildered. One of your eyes had whitened and seemed to be focussing on something far away.

Murali kept saying you looked like an old man. Fine dust had settled between your fingers, under your nails and in the corners of your eyes. You said you felt cold, it was like ice was running through your hands and feet. I remember you taking my hand and pressing it against your neck and I had said you didn't have a fever, you were fine. Murali remembers that you weren't eating anything and that sounds were coming from your chest. It almost sounded like wheezing, but if you listened closely, you could hear voices, laughter sometimes. I remember we kept making you take deep breaths so we could hear it and we would imagine what was inside you. Murali thought it must be a city, and I thought it was a radio.

We all remember the day you showed us your back— it was covered in jagged, broken feathers. The scabs and gouges held swirls of black smoke that left behind a soft, greasy residue. You couldn't understand what was happening. You wanted to know if we could take you somewhere, or if there was something we could do. You tried to grab my hand again, but I stepped back, and when you grabbed Anandhi's hand, she pulled away and told you to stop it. I don't know what made you ask us for help, or what made you keep asking even when we were trying to leave.

In the end, it was Anandhi who told you to "just do something". Murali and I looked at you, waiting for some kind of magic to overflow from your eyes or burst out of your hands. You shook and coughed and I kept telling you to try harder. We spent the rest of that day telling you to do something, pushing you down each time you tried to get up, wrenching the feathers from your back whenever you tried to stumble away. You kept asking us to stop and we kept telling you to *do something*. Do something, or we will break your teeth.

WE ALL REMEMBER saying it was for your own good. We locked you inside your room, leaving you nothing but a tumbler of water and a blanket. Murali in particular thought this was a good idea, because he did not like seeing you once your back started getting worse. Even the wheezing voices in your chest had become uncomfortable to listen to, because whatever was inside you seemed to know our names now and Murali said they were "talking crap" about us. What we can't remember is how long it was. Anandhi and I think it was two weeks and Murali feels it was just a few days. However long it was, we spent the time sitting outside your room, telling you to fucking do something. We had seen you fly. We had seen you turn into a fucking *bird*, for fuck's sake. If we could do even a fraction of what you could do, we wouldn't even be here. Do something. Do something.

I remember you telling us to please open the door, you were better, you were okay now, please just open the door. At some point, you started saying you were sorry. But we kept sitting there. We asked you why you stayed in this fucking, fucking house. Why had you come back those two times? Maybe this is what you get for coming back. If it was us, if we could just disappear like you could, we would never come back.

You kept saying sorry. After a while, you didn't say anything.

THEN ANANDHI LEFT. She caught an overnight bus to Chennai, where she stayed with a friend for the rest of the summer, allegedly looking for a job, though she never found one. Murali left two days later. He just went home, saying that he had a spare key and nobody really cared where he was anyway. I stayed because I had nowhere else to go.

The day after Murali left, I stopped going to your door. I remember spending most of my time listening to the radio and reading old newspapers. I remember some distant relative coming to stay and how I lied to her, saying I was a big executive in a foreign company, that I had a car. I remember that I did not plan it, that it hadn't been something that was bothering me. But by the time I was about to leave, I remember thinking that I was going to save you. I was going to take you back with me and tell people you were my cousin. You would get better, find a job. We would hang out together and you would tell people that I saved your life, that you wouldn't be alive if it wasn't for me.

I remember how much dust was in the corridors. Even the walls were covered in a soft, grey blanket that seemed to ripple towards the floor. Lizards were sparring on your door and underneath, I could see a bar of bright light. I remember that I never said I was sorry. I just said I was going to get you out of there, that you were going to be okay. I would come in the morning, open the door, and we would leave immediately. I am going to get you out of here, okay? I said, like I was in a movie. You murmured something I couldn't understand and I said okay. You are going to be okay.

I remember, very distinctly, that I did not think of you at all on the bus ride home. When I finally did, I thought of the door, the smoke swirling up from your back, and even then, I didn't feel bad.

WE EACH MADE up our own stories about what happened afterwards. I always felt that you stayed, but you didn't make it. I don't know if you died. Maybe you fell apart or you just stopped. Sometimes when I see a movie where the demon or vampire evaporates in the sunlight, I wonder if that's what happened to you. Murali decided that you got better somehow and left, while Anandhi felt that the atmosphere in your room must have split and swallowed you up for good. They both liked to believe that things got better for you. Perhaps you had gotten a job somewhere and settled down. Maybe you were married. Anandhi hoped that you had gone back to where you came from, because she thought things would be better and easier for you there. Murali said you were probably still here somewhere. He thought you liked it here, despite everything.

WE KEEP GOING back, sometimes together, sometimes alone. The decay that was once confined to your room seems to have crept through the rest of the house, encasing everything in dust; the air is hot and hard to breathe. We walk slowly, taking our time as we shuffle through the crumbling rooms and empty corridors. In your old room, we find things we have given you: cut-outs of Sathyaraj, movie ticket stubs, small, colourful notes wishing you a happy Pongal and happy Independence Day. There is one birthday card. We have all signed it, and at the top are the words YOU ARE _____ YEARS OLD? We can't find the tumbler or the blanket.

Anandhi always stabs at spears of sunlight, dark shadows, sometimes at nothing in particular, hoping something will collapse and reveal you in a place that is bright and warm, maybe at your parent's house or waiting for a bus. Murali talks to you like you are still here. Sometimes he leaves you tiny birds made out of chocolate wrappers or cigarette foil.

I don't come here as often as I used to. It is harder

now, and anyway, I never liked this house. But when I do come, I go to your room and close the door. I sit on the ground with a tumbler of water and a blanket. And I remember everything.

HURREM AND THE DJINN
Claire North

*Throne of my lonely niche, my wealth, my
   love, my moonlight.*
*My most sincere friend, my confidant, my very
   existence, my Sultan, my one and only love.*
The most beautiful among the beautiful...
*My Istanbul, my Caraman, the earth of my
   Anatolia*
My Badakhshan, my Baghdad and Khorasan
*My woman of the beautiful hair, my love of
   the slanted brow, my love of eyes full of
   mischief...*
I'll sing your praises always
*I, lover of the tormented heart, Muhibbi of the
   eyes full of tears, I am happy.*

Poem from Sultan Suleiman the Magnificent
to Sultana Hurrem

IT's NOT MY place to gossip…

Oh, go on, then, you forced it out of me!

There was a lovely young man, dark brown hair, beautiful green eyes, came from near Ragusa, they said, stolen by pirates—or maybe claimed by the child-tax, the *devshirme*; likely, but less romantic, don't you think?

However you tell it, when he was still young enough to be pretty and malleable, he was taken from his home, educated in the ways of Islam, in Persian poetry and the philosophy of the Greeks, and raised, all in all, as our famous Kadis and Viziers are, to be a slave of the Sultan and servant of the Empire. And when he was a young man, the great men of the court came to inspect their pupils, and the bravest were sent to the Janissaries, ever-ready for battle, and the cleverest to the Chancellery to count the Sultan's tribute as it is paid by cowering Christian kings; the wisest to judge in the courts, and the most loyal to the borderlands, where they would stand against heretics and so-called Safavid kings. But this young man…

…we'll call him Davud…

…his qualities were of quite another sort, and caught the eye of one Ahmed Danishmend, of the Sultan's Imperial Gentlemen. You have never heard of this Ahmed? Do not be alarmed, it is not that your spies have been lax. His is a profession not spoken of, even here in Topkapi, where Sultans are required to murder their brothers to claim the crown, and the procession of ever-smaller coffins that followed our exalted Suleiman to the throne caused barely a raised eyebrow amongst our chattering dignitaries.

Given that a little light fratricide causes minimal distemper, I can only whisper that the work of the Imperial Gentlemen is most secret, and I urge you not to breathe a word to anyone. You promise? You swear? I believe you; truly, I do.

Do you know the tapestry in the style of the Chinese dragon that hangs near the armoury of the second courtyard... yes, there, behind that, did you know there was a door? Ah—few do, but I heard it from...

...anyway, open that door of great, black wood, that makes not a sound as it slides across smooth stone, and descend down, down, down. Once a Byzantine Emperor built a tomb there to bury his unruly wife in; another built a cistern to store cool water and fresh fish. Now descend into this sanctum, where hangs the bright blue eye that wards against evil, where sit bowls sanctified with the blood of emperors, the broken sword of Alexander, the silky web of a spider that, they say, once wove in a cave in the desert— all these things ordered on shelves and tables carved from the stone itself, between pillars of the ancient Byzantine, the paths carved through flowing water where pale fish swim. Now it is a place for the Imperial Gentlemen to practice their arts, serving the Sultan as someone must—I don't judge, you see—in the binding and commandment of the djinn.

Ah—you are fearful, you reach for a strip of sacred verse in your sleeve; yes, yes, very wise, though the djinn are not much interested in the affairs of men, to them we are as flies upon the rim of a horse's eye. Yet powerful men may control and bind these creatures, some for the Sultan, some against him, and it was in this art that Davud was raised, and achieved noted success, until the day that his master, Ahmed Danishmend, came to him with one Nizamuddin Mektubji—no, you won't have heard of him either—with a most strange request.

"Kosaca Davud," whispered Nizamuddin, a quivering fellow who resembled in his spirit the tiny octopus they say he loved to eat. "I am sent by the great men of this land—by vizier and pasha, by Aga of the Imperial Guard, by governor of far-away province and by the most mighty imams. What do you know of women who summon djinn?"

Our handsome Davud considered this question at length—the Imperial court does not teach men to rush to judgment—and at last replied, "There are none I know of, for commanding djinn requires a great many tools that women do not have access to—not without the assistance of men." These careful words Davud spoke as if to another place, for he had always been a scholar more interested in ideas than the audience that might hear them, and so it was with a start that he returned to the reality of that place, as Nizamuddin barked, "Ah—there you are mistaken! For there are witches who command djinn through gifts of their own flesh and blood, through offerings of their souls, and some, I fear, deep at the heart of our Empire! Many learned men, many—I cannot name them all—but many have looked into this matter and concluded that there is one, indeed, who even now works her magic upon the Sultan."

Davud glanced at his master, but the old man in his great red tunic and long brown gown said nothing, rather contemplated the high ceiling of the cavern as if seeking constellations in the stone. Within this quiet, Nizamuddin paced, ranting—some might say raving, I would not—as to the seriousness of the matter, the heathen women infecting the heart of the Empire, Istanbul falling to darkness, the Sultan, the Emperor, the Caliph, the…

Finally, Ahmed interrupted. "You have some request for our order, do you not?"

This reasoned enquiry stopped Nizamuddin in his tracks, and he coughed and said, "We have some notion of the chief woman who practices this sorcery. We wish you to prove her betrayal, banish her creatures, strip her of her power."

At this, Davud brightened—this was to be an actual exercise of his talents, rather than a political discourse. "Surely if she is a witch, I can prove it!" he exclaimed. "Who do you suspect?"

Nizamuddin hesitated, glancing uneasy towards Ahmed, and now even Davud sensed something of danger.

"She is within the harem; a favourite of the Sultan. *The* favourite of the Sultan."

Davud pondered a moment, before realisation blazed and he exclaimed, "You mean Hurrem?!" He flinched at the words, and all three men looked about, suddenly fearful that their voices might travel through the stones to whisper in the walls of the palace above.

Gentler now, quieter, barely above a whisper: "You believe that Hurrem, the most beloved of the Sultan, is *commanding djinn*?"

"Of course she is," hissed Nizamuddin. "The woman is a wolf who has bitten the necks of everyone in her path. She had Mahedeveran, the Sultan's wife and mother of his son, banished; she crosses Ibrahim Pasha, the Sultan's oldest, dearest advisor and friend, so that he fears his life is in danger. She commands armies like a general and viziers like a prince, and our noble Sultan is besotted with her! He has sworn off all other women—can you imagine? The scandal of it! Last night, Ibrahim Pasha dreamed of a serpent in his bed, and Prince Mustafa says he hears the laughing of ghosts. The Sultan's sacred mother once saw Hurrem scratch at the eye that wards against evil, as if she could not stand its gaze, and when she sleeps, she whispers in strange languages."

"Sir," Davud began, glancing to his mentor's stony face for some comfort, "this is not proof. If she consorts with djinn, I must have some item of hers to test the theory."

"Here we are prepared! See..." Nizamuddin produced a ring, brilliant emerald set in gold, and holding it between his thumb and forefinger as if afraid of its touch, dropped it into Davud's waiting palm. "Call on the djinn, bid them consume and devour the demons she has summoned—you will suffer no consequence if she has made a blood bargain, you will not be punished if in the course of your actions she... experiences ill-effect."

"There is that possibility, if she has offered blood, the tie between djinn and blood is..."

"No consequence," repeated Nizamuddin. "Foul women"—he stabbed the air with one drumstick finger on every word—"must be cast down."

So HE WAS given his task; so he set about his work. The ring was not his first choice of offering to any djinn, even one of lesser degree, but he enjoyed such challenges and taxed his mind now as to a most potent and complimentary binding. In the end, he chose a staff of gold to summon and command; a stick of charcoal to encircle the beast; a mask of iron dug from the grave of an ancient Celtic king to hide his face, and for the ring itself, which would be the offering—that, he folded in the leaves of the ashoka tree. This plant, said the sorcerers of India, contained the spirit of the yakshini, guardians of the treasures of the earth and creatures of amorous—sometimes wrathful—inclination. Such a djinn seemed to fit with the nature of his present task, and so it was that he now lit incense from the sacred groves of the east and, bending all his will to it, spoke in the voice of the forest.

That which came from his throat was not a human language, but was rather the sound of swirling leaves, of insects running through his lungs, branches creaking in his bones, roots running from his feet. The smoke of the incense twisted into strange patterns, burned down to ash within a few seconds, the leaves of the ashoka tree which bound the ring opened like a flower, and for a moment the emerald within the jewel blazed brightly before it went out, and the ring dissolved into the earth. Yet from the rippling earth now rose a woman—shall we call her that? A creature with anatomy—face, breasts, hips, wide feet on thick legs—but her skin was all autumn leaf, and her hair was of brambles that twisted and twined about her skull, and her eyes were the colour of amber, and her tongue dripped white sap, and when she looked on Kosaca Davud, she hissed in the language of the stalk as it rots upon the wet soil.

"Why have you brought me here, sorcerer?" she demanded.

"To answer a question and break a spell," he replied. "The ring whose light you now have within you belongs to a woman within this palace. I would know her nature, and what spirits she commands.

Tell me that, and you are free, and I give you all these offerings in thanks."

The golden staff he held in his hand was warm, growing hot beneath his fingers as the djinn, her swaying body still in the circle, explored the cavern with her eyes and her thoughts, testing the limits of the binding he had put upon her—but it was good and strong, and if he felt any pain from the heat in his hands, he did not show it.

Sensing this, the djinn turned her attention to Davud's words, and hissed, "I will do as you ask. What is this woman?"

"Her name is Hurrem, once Roxlana, the Sultan's favourite."

"Ah—a queen!"

"Even so."

"I sense her warmth in the meagre gift you gave me... she has slept with this ring beneath her pillow."

"Can you taste her, and the dreams she has dreamed, and the spirits she has commanded? What has she invoked to bind our Sultan, and with what offerings? Has she given her blood to do it?"

For a long while, the yakshini was quiet, or as quiet as any creature can be whose breath is the mountain wind, whose spine continually sprouted fresh pink flowers from within its wooden bone, which bloomed and died, bloomed and died within a moment. Then at last it said, "Those creatures she commands are beyond my seeing. I cannot feel them, or hear their song. There is only human breath on my skin."

At this, Davud felt a sudden chill, and the staff burned hot between his fingers, the creature's eyes lighting up as it sensed some waning in his concentration, for the djinn, even the fairest of them, always seek to escape a binding and have their mischief—but our Davud was quick, and quickly he brought the staff down hard upon the ground, bending the image of the flower carved into its top, and with a sacred word, he banished the yakshini back to its forests and sacred groves, its body dissolving into dust that fell upon the stones.

THAT EVENING, HE reported his discoveries to Nizamuddin and Ahmed Danishmend. "The djinn," he explained, "could not see if others of its kind served Hurrem."

Silence in the cavern; silence in the palace. The last call to prayers had been sung, the moon hung high above the heavy cypress trees, the flutes and drums were silent and the slumbering guards leant heavy on their muskets by the palace gates.

"Could not see?" muttered Nizamuddin. "*Could not see?*" He turned paler than a dead squid, and grabbing onto Ahmed's sleeve tugged like a drowning man. "How powerful must be the djinn she commands, if this forest spirit could not perceive them?"

"Indeed," he murmured. "The situation is worse than we first thought. Davud—what would you recommend as our next step?"

The younger man hesitated, looking to his master for guidance, for he was never sure of what palace politics might require from him, but seeing nothing in the fixed features at last answered, "If the djinn of the forest could not see, then we must invoke a more powerful creature. A djinn of the sands, perhaps, or of the stone…"

"Are they potent?" barked Nizamuddin. "Are they great? I heard that fire or the creatures of the first dawn…"

"Summoning such djinn is extremely dangerous. They are difficult to command, and if they escape our binding, they will do great harm…"

"Heavens protect us!" exclaimed the little man. "And you think Hurrem may control such things?"

"I didn't say so…"

"If she did, can you imagine what she might achieve?"

"To bewitch our Sultan, a lesser djinn might well serve…"

"Perhaps," Ahmed intruded gently, tugging at the curling grey hairs of his beard, "we might propose a middle ground? A lesser djinn of the sea might have some insight into this matter?"

"Indeed, but we would need something more of hers, more than a ring…"

"I will deal with that!" barked Nizamuddin. "I can get you anything you need!"

Ahmed looked at Davud; Davud looked at Ahmed—Davud told Nizamuddin what they needed.

A SHOCKING TRUTH, my friend, I think you will be quite scandalised—it turns out that the eunuchs and loyal men who guard the Imperial harem may not be entirely incorruptible. In fact, I have heard of many a man, whole or otherwise, who for a few coins or a lady's favour, will tell a tale, steal a ring, carry a message, employ a servant about some dubious business, or even—the whispers go so far—put a drop of poison in some beauty's cup, that her radiance might not outshine another who looks fair in the Sultan's eye.

Oh, the things that happen in that gilded cage, for these are mothers of Sultans yet to come—but of all their children, only one will be king. What mother would not protect her child? And so they play a game, these beautiful, graceful would-be-queens, with the savagery of the lioness protecting her cubs, and moonlight smiles.

So with some ease, Nizamuddin bribed a eunuch, who whispered to a servant, who commanded a slave, who—as the lady Hurrem was about some business—took from her closet a veil of softest Indian silk, scented with jasmine, and dropped it from a high window into the garden below, where a soldier armed with shovel and sword collected it, and carried it fast to our magical men, who set to in the summoning of another, greater spirit to uncover Hurrem's witchery.

THE VEIL WAS laid upon a bed of silver, taken from the wreck of a Spanish galleon that had sailed from the New World. Ahmed stood by, to assist Davud in this dangerous task, and the circle they drew was laid with fresh petals from the cherry tree on a bed of salt, and Davud held a rod carved from a slab of ice, brought from the north in a casket of thick metal set with delicate ivory. Yet even with all these sacred items and careful plans, there was something of the fearful which shook Davud's hands as he poured water from the sacred pool across the floor, and whispered his words in the voice of the waves breaking upon the shore, and the wind as it stirs white froth above the ocean, and the roaring of the ocean as it fills your ears beneath the surface of the raging storm.

The veil on its bed of silver melted, as if thread were a liquid thing; then the silver, too, melted, without heat, flowing into a pool that ebbed and eddied within the confines of its salty ring, until at last, with a great slither and splash of bright liquid, the djinn of the sea rose up and hissed in a mouth of foam and shingle:

"Why have you summoned me?"

The rod of ice, which had burned with cold in Davud's hand, began at once to melt, water flowing over his palm and into his sleeve, rippling away as the djinn shivered and spun within its cage.

"The woman whose veil you hold is suspected of being a witch. We command you to…"

"Command me?!" The djinn grew sudden and fast, its silver body snapping against the edge of the circle as it briefly became a rolling wave, a spilling flood, before returning again to a spinning pillar in the centre of the circle. "Be careful, mortal," it hissed, as a lump of ice fell away from the bottom of Davud's rod. "Be clear in your speech."

Davud's lips trembled, but his voice was steady as he said, softer, "Great spirit, we ask you to look at the woman Hurrem. Tell us of the djinn she commands, and the services they perform for her. Is it within your power to consume their magic, snuff out their doings and end the enchantments she has performed?"

For a moment, the djinn twisted in its spire, and still the ice melted in Davud's grasp, slippery and cracked through. Then, "I cannot break the spells she has cast; I cannot destroy the djinn she has commanded," it breathed, and at that moment the ice rod cracked within Davud's hand, and the djinn gave a triumphant roar and broke towards the edge of the circle, and Ahmed raised his hands and cried out the sacred words of banishment even as Davud threw himself to the ground, cowering beneath the might of the raging seas which…

…broke, as a wave on the shore, just water now, no longer liquid silver and silk, but salty water that knocked both men from their feet and spilled to the edges of the room, washing softly in the night.

WOULD YOU LIKE something to drink? Some sherbet, perhaps? A glass of wine—I know, I know, it is haram, forbidden, but our noble Sultan's father built up quite a wonderful reserve in the cellars beneath the palace, and it does seem a shame to let it go to waste...

...No? You're not in the mood, I can see.

Did you think that it would be simple, this business of the djinn? Did you think, perhaps, that with a gesture of their hands, our heroes would expose the evil of Hurrem, beloved of the Sultan? You have not seen my lady, as she walks through the palace, listens from behind the shuttered door. You have not seen her eyes sparkle, as I have, you do not know the extent of her power—but no matter. You are listening, I appreciate that. You will see.

So, then, this djinn was summoned, and so it was discharged, and so Davud went again to Nizamuddin, and reported what he had heard, and Nizamuddin indeed looked as if he might flee the palace there and then, rather than stay another minute within its cursed walls. But no, all these men were brave, most brave, so they took unto themselves their blessed charms and talismans, their sacred texts and hidden, potent words, and resolved one last try to end the woman's spells.

To the harem once again, Nizamuddin sent his spies, and this time they were to find a most foul and unclean thing, for I must tell you—please, do not be too offended by this—I must tell you that even in the palace, the women will bleed when their time is come, and our Hurrem, for all that she is majestic, is still a woman. From her bed Nizamuddin's servants stole her bloodied sheets, and carried them with great distaste to their master; he, nearly dead from the mere sight of the woman's blood, took them to Ahmed and Davud, who laid it in the centre of the circle with all the most potent of their offerings and artefacts, to entice and command one of the greatest djinn of all—a creature of the stormy sky.

Both Ahmed and Davud held staffs of hollow glass, into which the dying breaths of their makers were sealed; Nizamuddin cowered behind them, his face covered with the battle mask of a Visigoth king who fell by the waters of the Danube. Around the edge of the circle they sprinkled the seeds of the red lotus flower, and the blood of the golden eagle, and the ash of a mighty volcano. Into the centre of the circle they placed the sword of a crusading king, and the bones of a Chinese Emperor buried with seven hundred of his slaves, still-living, beneath a golden tomb. They laid down a perpetual ember from the fire of Zoroaster, and a single thread taken from the robe of the Prophet himself, that he wore on the night of his journey from Mecca to Jerusalem.

This done, the two sorcerers stood either side of the circle and spoke in the voice of the storm, and their breath was the raging wind that runs before the cloud, and their skin was the cold that precedes the thrashing rain, and their eyes were the flood and their hair stood all on end with the coming of the lightning and they spoke and gave command, and in doing so...

...nothing happened.

For many hours they struggled, incanted and implored, but no djinn came, their wishes were not fulfilled, until at last, sweating and exhausted, Davud said, "We need something more."

For the first time, the elder Ahmed showed some glimmer of fear, for he understood at once where this thought might lead. "It is not wise," he muttered. "It is not the way I have taught you."

"But you did tell me of it, when you taught me the ways of witches, and those sorcerers who do not have our offerings and our gifts to command," he replied. "And you know it is potent."

Ahmed opened his mouth to protest, but seeing Nizamuddin watching them still, he did not speak. Alas, what a poor teacher he proved then! But ambition, it is always ambition and the fear of failure that dogs our *devshirme* men, our servants who know that either glory or death hangs about their every deed. So he looked away, and in that looking there was perhaps an acknowledgment of what Davud was determined to do.

The younger man, seeing this, drew from his belt a little knife, and with barely a flinch, drew it fast across the palm of his hand, that the blood might flow.

Now all was fearful and hushed in the sanctum, even Nizamuddin mountain-still, watching as Davud held his hand out to let the blood drip onto the stones.

At once the djinn came, roaring out of the air itself, a great swirling that consumed all, all within its reach— bone, sword, blood, drawing the red liquid fast from Davud's hand, a tendril of black cloud twining itself around the sorcerer's wrist, pulling him to his knees so that he gasped in horror and pain. But still the circle held, and both men clung to their staffs, and for a moment the djinn raged and blazed against the world, arms and legs and claws and even, it seemed, the face of a child forming within the storm as it lashed against the circle, before at last—still holding the bloody hand of Davud within its tendrils—it subsided into a maelstrom column and breathed in the language of the shattered night:

"Why have you brought me here, little men?"

Davud—gasping for air, arm numb and skin white as, still, the creature fed on his blood—could not speak, so Ahmed blurted, "To command and dispel the djinn that surround the woman Hurrem, whose blood you have tasted and whose magic you must know..."

The djinn interrupted him with a roll of thunder that shook the palace walls, made the old pillars of the cavern shake with dust, cracks breaking in ancient plaster. "I see the woman!" it roared. "But there are no djinn in her command, no magic on her tongue! You have summoned me here to do a fool's deed, and fools you are that summoned me!"

So saying it lashed out again, and Davud screamed with a sudden new pain as if all the lightning of the world were breaking through his veins, and the djinn blazed red with his hot blood and tore against the circle. Ahmed stumbled as the staff in his hand began to shiver and crack, then burst in a shower of glass, shards burying in his hands, his skin, his eyes, so he screamed, clawing his face. With the roar of the tornado, the djinn burst free, still holding Davud by a tendril of cloud to his knees, in the eye of the storm. All around, it raged through the cavern, pulling down every sigil and smashing every sacred object; the gale grabbed the bloodied Ahmed and tore him apart like wet paper, drank in his hot blood and swallowed him in the storm, blazing, laughing in its freedom. Nizamuddin ran for the door, and the djinn cackled with merry lightning that ran through his heart, burst thunder within his skull, so that his eyes at once turned red, and still Davud screamed as the blood was pulled from him that sustained the storm. Falling now, the djinn reached tendrils upwards, upwards towards the slumbering palace above until all at once a hand caught Davud's glass staff from where it had fallen, and plunged it point-first into the heart of that raging storm. The djinn screamed, and as it did, the staff shattered, releasing the breath of the man who had made it from within; and the breath spoke calm, simple words of power and command, and the djinn raged and blazed but could not resist. It diminished, and withered, and at last, faded to a cloud, then a whisper of wind, then a stillness in the darkness, leaving only the marks of lightning and sweeps of blood behind.

Davud fell to the floor, the blood a mere trickle now from his hand, for a mere trickle was all he had left to give, his face greyer than an autumn sky, his lips the blue of a stormy sea.

The hand that had held the staff rested on a knee. The knee bent so that the one who had saved him might better look into his face. I stood behind, as my lady, veiled all in grey, smiled into the face of the fallen sorcerer and said softly:

"Kosaca Davud—I hear you have been taking some interest in my laundry."

The fallen man tried to raise his head, but there was no strength left in his body. So my lady, the great Hurrem, beloved of the Sultan, gently turned his chin so he might gaze into her shadowed eyes, and said, "When one may buy the service of a man, one must assume that they are easily bought. If they are easily bought, why would you think that I have not bought them first?"

Only breath, the broken rattle of air through splintered stone, could Davud give in answer.

Hurrem sighed, and rose again to her feet, looking

round the ruined cavern. "So foolish," she tutted. "Such a waste. It is always remarkable to me how many men fall from having reached too high. I have learned much from their lessons."

So saying, she gestured at me that we might depart, and I bowed and held the black door open for her that led to the palace. She moved towards it, broken glass and wet blood crunching beneath her feet, then paused again to look back at the fallen sorcerer. "I am not a cruel woman," she breathed. "It seems to me that the woman who saves the sickly child by her skill is called a witch, and the one who cannot save the child who is destined to die is also called the same. Success or failure, a woman of power is always prey to suspicion. This sorcery you perform seems to me a most unhelpful art, and unnecessary to my cause. The love my Sultan feels for me comes from the union of our souls, and the power I exert, I do so because I am wise, and clever, and know something of the turning of the world. You great men who wish to command the skies should look to me for a little something of that wisdom. You will do better for it. Goodbye, Kosaca Davud. I will pray for you. One way or another."

So saying, Hurrem departed, leaving Davud where he was, cold and grey, silent and bloodied, on the ruin of the world that he had made for himself. I followed my lady, and closed the black door behind us.

And that is how it happened, the night of the storm beneath the palace, the night the great men fell—but please, don't tell anyone. You know how gossip is; sometimes it's a story, and sometimes it's a weapon. But I don't like to get involved in such things, not me. It's not a woman's place at all.

GLASS LIGHTS
Neon Yang

BEFORE HE DIED, Mena's grandfather told her she was a djinn.

More accurately, he told her that her grandmother, whom she had never met, was a djinn. Mena was, at that time, eighteen years old. Her grandfather had stomach cancer, and her grandmother was gone; long, long gone. Her grandmother had been Turkish. They were married for a year, and she'd borne a son, Mena's father, before fleeing back to Turkey, never to be heard from again, her fate unknown. Mena's grandfather had bribed some official to get a death certificate issued (as still could be done in those days) so he could marry the woman Mena had grown up calling Nenek, and this mysterious vanished Turkish woman remained a spectre, unspoken of, the only traces of her remaining in the hooked nose of her son, a brief foreign interjection into their peaty Asian stock.

Everyone had constructed their own narrative to explain the shape of this happening, this flower of passion that had withered so abruptly into abandonment and betrayal. "She was a prostitute," Nenek would say. Mena's father said she was a runaway, a war refugee, and Grandfather had refused to follow her home. But in Mena's grandfather's telling, she was a djinn, and he freed her from the bottle he had bought from the Thieves' Market (back when it was an actual market, and not the tourist point-of-interest and hipster hunting ground it is now). She, in turn, had granted him three wishes, and after he had been blessed with the last one (a rice-fed, healthy son), she had vanished forever, for he no longer had any hold over her.

"You are like her," Mena's grandfather told her from his deathbed. "You are just like her. I look at you and I see her, like it was just yesterday." Of his sixteen grandchildren, Mena was the only one he'd said this to, and with her wide nose and round features she knew he wasn't referring to her looks. That old man, his mind clouded by the pressures of senescence, raving sometimes about the Kempeitai and the hunger pangs of the Second World War, looked at her and saw a swirl of smoke trapped in a glass bottle, an odd unlabeled thing unknowingly put up for sale amongst the mismatched wares on someone's dusty tarp.

* * *

THERE WAS A man who looked very much like Anthony plastered, smiling, to the convex insides of the train carriage. The ad, for a mobile app called SGLoveMatch, was of that species of seasonal offerings that burst forth everywhere you turned for weeks, and then just as quickly subsided into grey obscurity. For now, the artificially happy image of doppelgänger-Anthony, one pillar of the bliss depicted through the sun-drenched embraces of three couples, graced the tepid interior of the train every few meters. Mena, wedged in so tightly she could not raise her phone between the backs of the other faintly-sweating office workers, had nothing to do except stare up at the doppelgänger's face.

Like Anthony, he had the clean-cut, coiffed look sported by Chinese mission-school boys from good families, the good stock. The girl wrapped around him, like all the girls in the ad, was thin, Chinese, white-skinned, with perfectly tinted and styled locks that shone in the sunlight, shone like the perfect lines of her smile. The sunlit paradise of those pictures seemed impossibly out of reach for the tired faces packed into the carriage, waists padded by stress and faces lined by sleep deprivation.

A nebulous sense of discontent pressed against the inside of Mena's belly as she thought unkind things about the people in the picture. The blessed lives of model-types, banking on the envy of the unwashed populace to earn their keep. *Find love. Find life,* said the ad in looping, golden text, as if your life didn't count unless you were aping the airbrushed, carefully-lit confection they were presenting to you.

Mena's arrival in the office always preceded that of most of her colleagues, leaving her an hour of air-conditioned silence to grind her way through the inbox without the threat of interrupting chatter. At this hour, it was just her and the cleaning aunty Choo, a Peranakan woman in her late forties with a wide, gapped smile and a steady supply of sticky fragrant kuih-muih she would sneak to Mena in lovingly rumpled little plastic bags, the kind you put takeaway kopi into. Choo never had much time to chat—there was always too much carpet needing her attention—but over the course of the time Mena had worked there, the whole story of her life and family had percolated out of their brief question-and-answer sessions. Her recurring back pain, her husband's diabetes, their money problems.

This morning Choo pulled at Mena conspiratorially and whispered, her eyes all lit up, "I bought a dress yesterday!"

"That's nice," Mena said encouragingly, knowing her happiness came from places other than this.

Choo's voice dropped lower as her smile got wider. "I've dropped a dress size!"

"Oh! Congratulations." And she meant it. She was glad; she was glad that Choo was glad.

Choo's grip was so joyous, and so vital, that she ground the knucklebones in Mena's hands together.

"Not since I was a young girl. It's so good, I can't believe it happened."

Choo had the wide, starchy body of a person who had had four children, and had to provide for them. The pear-shaped lines told a story not of abundance, but of hardship, of too many fast food dinners, of too many hours spent standing on swollen ankles, of weekends spent in front of the TV or in the kitchen, manufacturing happiness out of nothing. Mena did not begrudge her the happiness she found in reclaiming some of her past, a time that, in all probability, had been fuller with hope and desire.

There was something bright and sweet about having the fervently wished-for fulfilled, and Mena relished the taste of it in her mouth, the feel of it in her chest. "I hope you're happy," she said.

"Oh, I am. Oh, I am!"

The office buzzed with unusual energy that morning. There was a meeting at 10am with their ad agency, and that meant Anthony would be gracing them with his presence. The senior project managers, both of them married, ribbed Wendy about the dress she'd put on, and the makeup: lips redder, eyes crisply lined. It was the office joke that Wendy fancied Anthony, in the warm way that friend groups will try to get their girlfriend hooked up with the hot guy. The corp comms department for their ministry was small—six of them excluding the two department heads—and it had the close-knit, conspiratorial feel of an all-woman team in a particularly male-dominated industry. The other five girls in the department giggled, put their heads together, talked about boys and TV dramas and dresses. The iron bars of a cage can be kind of a comfort when the world outside is all hungry teeth and slicing fins.

But not for Mena. You don't giggle with a girl in a headscarf, who can't watch any of the Channel 8 K-dramas you follow because she doesn't speak Mandarin. It's not an unkindness, it's just the way it is. The other five girls sat around in circles and whispered among themselves, and conveniently forgot to invite Mena out for lunch when they went, more often than not. They spoke a lingo that lay alien in Mena's ears and could never come from her tongue, and moved in circles she had no part of. What could they possibly talk about, anyway?

Wendy's exhilaration had quiet spots in it, and in those little silences Mena could sense how much she really wanted the romantic fantasy to happen.

Anthony arrived at 10.30, by which time the meeting room had already been filled to capacity with titter. He swept in with his arms bearing paper bags and his face bearing that winning, model-boy smile that let him get away with saying sharp things and dismissing them as jokes. "Sorry, sorry, I'm late, ladies," he said. The paper bags bustled onto the conference table. "Okay, to make up for it, I bought everybody Starbucks and donuts. Okay?" That was his way of things, his simple and easy charm, and the meeting room responded accordingly, with pleased noises and airy banter.

Almost everyone in the department was here, like it was a spectator sport. Wendy sat in the middle of the room, in between the director and one of the senior managers, with her laptop all prim and at attention. This wasn't even her account, but the civil service habit of having more participants piled onto meetings than strictly necessary was working well in her favour. Anthony had bought enough donuts to make sure everyone got at least one.

He looked at Mena while the girls were dividing the spoils, and warmly said, "The donuts are halal, I checked specially for you, okay?"

That was how it went. Anthony would do things like these, and Mena would feel warm inside for hours. Stupid, but soft and warm, and also full of bird wings, colorful and rustling and beating around her chest and belly.

This was the kind of happening that would send Wendy grabbing the hand of a colleague after the meeting, and they would descend into the kind of excited recounting that was the province of the young and in-love. But Mena had no-one's hands to grab, and never had. There wasn't anyone on her team, so to speak.

Anthony tactfully said nothing about Wendy's makeup, but he complimented her dress, which was always a safe bet. Wendy tried to play it cool, but the fairness of her skin betrayed the blush around her ears. She remained preternaturally attentive during Anthony's presentation, as if overcompensating. Mena could feel the strength of her desire, her own fairy-tale wishes, as they circled her in the dimmed light of the room, and she remembered the fruit-bright taste of a wish fulfilled that she had savored in the morning. Wendy's want was easy, a low-hanging conjecture, one which the universe had pushed together to make it as easy as possible to grant.

Mena thought about it, and found her thoughts wandering, straying far from the PowerPoint slides going over her head. Anthony's project was, in fact, on her account. But it didn't matter. These meetings were always a waste of time, anyway. Tomorrow there would be a one-line email from one of the big bosses, and everything would have to be changed again.

After the meeting was over, the girls asked Anthony to join them for lunch. It was one of the senior managers who made the invitation. "There's a new ramen place next door, heard it's quite good." Sure, Anthony said, in his booming way, stretching wide as he could. I'll never say no to lunch.

The ramen restaurant was not halal, naturally. It was authentic Japanese, it used exclusively pork for the soup stock. No-one asked Mena to join; if they had, she would have said she had packed her own lunch. Which she had. She had given up on being asked long ago.

*   *   *

A FOREST OF striped tarpaulin roofs strung with cheap, bare bulbs had overtaken the field next to the MRT station near Mena's house, catching the home-bound travellers with honeyed feasts of street food and rows of glittering kitsch. Like a desert mirage, the pasar malam surfaced in such intersections for a few days, an intense spot of saturated energy and color, before vanishing without a trace.

Mena loved exploring the transient capillaries of these modern day caravans, breathing in air perfumed by hot grease and savory steam, the plywood boards creaking under her feet. It let her dream of days past, of times when everything was as impermanent as these lashed-together tents, where the shape of the land followed tide and season, before rock and sand were poured into its bones. She bought a bag of steamed chickpeas and walked around with them soft between her teeth, looking at cheap knockoff T-shirts stamped with whatever the current pop culture obsessions were. Under the naked glare of the temporary lighting, they took on a stark, sharp clarity. Mena appreciated this: the copper tang of capitalism unromanticised, unapologetic in its ugliness.

At one of the stalls, its makeshift shelves stacked high with bootleg mass produce, a toddler tugged at her harried mother's shirt-hem, chubby fingers yearning for a small, stuffed approximation of a Disney character.

Her desire was that of a child's: Pure, overwhelming, and of universal importance. The strength of her want pulled Mena in, and she watched as the child's mother, distracted by some other shiny bit the next stall over, said no, in that tone that children of authoritarian parents everywhere know. The tone that brooks no dissent. The girl's lip trembled, and she stared marble-eyed at her object of desire, far out of her reach. The stall-keeper stood by and said nothing, stone-faced, unmoved by the moment.

Drawn by her nature, the nature gifted to her by her grandmother, Mena dove to one knee, unobserved, next to the child. This one was easily solved: tied to Mena's bag zipper was the genuine version of the small stuffed thing the child wanted, happily trademarked and bought from a gift shop somewhere. A beautiful cosmic coincidence. Mena slipped it from the zipper tie and pressed it into the child's hand. The girl's eyes went wide, star-filled, and Mena pressed a finger to her lips. Their secret.

Then the girl was being pulled away by her mother, down the narrow shop-alley, homeward-bound. Her eyes were still full of wonder, her hand filled with stuffed toy. How simple our wants are as children, how easily satisfied.

Mena waved to the girl as she vanished into the transient fade of the pasar malam like a curl of smoke, as if she had been lifted away by a desert dervish, as if she had never been.

By the time Mena got home, she was regretting her largesse. In that moment, dragged along by the exhilaration of fulfilling a child's deepest-held wish, she had not stopped to think of how it would look later. The mother, arriving home and finding strange, unpaid-for merchandise in her daughter's sticky fingers: What would she think? As if she would accept the girl's version of the truth, of the spirit of the air that appeared by magic and granted her her heart's desires.

Mena's mind marched in a line of colorful punishments that might await that little girl—lashing and beatings and heart-rendings, pain to remind her of the nature of this world, of the rules that bound it and bound her to it.

Maybe it was for the better. Teach them early that dreams and wishes are things that bring only pain, that nothing comes for free, that for every piece of good fortune, somehow and somewhere the universe will balance itself out with misfortune.

As the day ended, Mena found herself contemplating the sandy plains of her face in the mirror, the weathered architecture of it softened by the low light. Seeing it like this, the way other people did, made her wonder what they actually thought of her. People's desires were easy to read, clear as bottled glass and just as sturdy. Their thoughts were another thing altogether: hard and opaque and filligreed with teeth and claws.

She thought of doppelgänger-Anthony in the perfect world of the advertisement. In that small piece of paradise, seen as if through a perfume bottle, the perfect woman for Anthony had white arms and facial features exquisitely aligned just so.

Mena squeezed her eyes to slits and through that distortion saw her face elongate, her nose forming a perfect peak, her hair straightening and darkening to pitch-perfect black. She imagined her complexion flawless, the kind that would accept the right sort of foundation, turn her into one of those doe-eyed plump-lipped girls gazing out of billboards. The kind of picturesque girl that might turn Anthony's head. The kind of girl who was like Wendy.

A foolish notion. She could rearrange the sands of her face, changing the composition of the earth it was made from, but to what end? What would she be? Where would she stand, this polished implant, in the grand scheme of the universe?

Mena wondered if her vanished grandmother, the djinn, had ever thought of reshaping the world so it was more amenable to her. A world of hot wind and bursting stars, where women walked strong and brown and proud over land that sang to their bones, where the fires that burned in their veins were lights in the firmament, and not threats to be smothered into nothingness at all costs.

She closed her eyes and let the darkness behind her lids fill her mind. Pointless, to dwell on such things. The shape of the world was the shape that it was. Tomorrow Anthony would send Wendy a text asking her to dinner, and her colleague would sit at her desk incandescent with joy, unaware of the machinations that had gone on in the dark to bring her this gift of a wish fulfilled, neon-bright and ethanol-sweet. And Mena, hands in pockets and heart hot and silent in her chest, would continue walking alone down unmapped paths, surrounded by the bright lights of things wanted and things acquired, the great exchange that went on before her, just out of reach.

Mena opened her eyes, and, with a flick of her wrist, put out the bedroom light.

AUTHENTICITY
Monica Byrne

IT STARTED WITH a knock at the door. It was Abbas, holding a plate of oranges and a white plastic knife. I was glad because I was hungry. Even after the enormous evening meal in the main house, I was still hungry.

"I can't stay, after," was the first thing he said.

"That's all right," I said. "Come in."

He did, but only one step at a time, as if he were unsure how far into the room he was allowed. But my guest room was tiny, more like a cell. I let him come.

Once he got to the other wall, he turned around. "The reason I can't stay is because I have to be on set for a night shoot."

"A set? A shoot? What are they filming?"

He looked out the window into the alley below, to see whether anyone might be listening, and then said in a low voice, "An adult film."

The wind made a panel of the window spring open

and knock against the outside wall. We both jumped at the sound. I went to the window and pulled it closed, and fastened the clasp. The glass continued to rattle in its casing.

"It's like that out here, sometimes," he said, as if in apology. "I grew up in the desert. The wind picks up right at this time of year."

He still held the plate of oranges and the white plastic knife, rigid, in front of him, as if he were a statue. I wanted him to put them down so we could eat. I was also torn between the wind and the adult film, as both topics seemed worthy of comment. But I was hungry. I wasn't used to being so hungry. I put my hand on his arm and drew him to the floor, and he understood, without words, what I wanted him to do. He pushed his thumb on the white plastic knife and turned the orange in his other hand. Juice spritzed and diffused in the air as he cut. He held out a double segment for me, and I took it and ate it, and immediately wanted more. But I didn't want to be rude. I didn't know what manners were like here; it was best to go slow, not to frighten him.

"I've never met anyone who worked on an adult film before," I said, while I waited for more orange segments. "I watch normal films and think, *How could they be skin on skin like that, and not be wet and hard, doing exactly what they look like they're doing?* But in interviews the actors say, 'No, we don't get aroused. Not when there's an entire camera and lighting crew right in your face. None of our parts even touch. We bind them up in nylon.'"

"And it's true," he said, handing me another segment. "You never see scrota."

He was matching me, tone for tone, reveal for reveal, wit for wit. "But you're filming real sex," I said.

"We're filming Nilou Tar," he said.

I smiled, mid-chew. It was a clever name—suggesting both lotuses and music.

"I'd be surprised if you'd heard of her," he said. "She's only famous in some circles. She's setting up right now. I'm not needed till later."

"Digital or celluloid?"

"Celluloid," he said. "Nilou Tar only shoots in celluloid."

"How sentimental."

He looked abashed. I felt bad. I'd been hasty and flippant. I didn't want to be rude in my quest for authenticity.

"Well," he said, gesturing with the knife, "all artists need constraints, don't they? Infinite possibility is actually limiting."

Ah, so he was artist-minded, too. I'd chosen well. "I don't think so. I think infinite possibility is thrilling."

"But we don't have infinite time," he said, monitoring my reactions from beneath ropes of dust-curdled hair. "And we can't grasp infinity, not for more than a second or two. So we choose the constraints that are most interesting to us."

I was learning about him. This was turning out to be part of my work here. I willed myself to be content, to flow alongside him. "All right. Why does Nilou Tar find celluloid an interesting constraint?"

"Because celluloid is a physical medium," he said, "and so is the body, which is the most important thing in erotic film."

"So are you her partner?"

He smiled and shook his head, as if I'd made a great joke. As if to answer, he put down the knife and pulled out his phone—cracked screen, a still from *The Pear Tree*—and showed me a video. A young woman in a wetsuit sat on the edge of a dock; pale-skinned, blonde-haired, her legs open and her shoulders hunched; she looked back at the camera once and squealed. Male voices exhorted her in English off-camera.

"Is this Nilou Tar?" I asked.

He laughed, and his hand flew to his mouth, to cup a little orange coming out. He pushed it back in, looking sheepish. "No. She'd call this tacky," he said. "These are just some drunk university students."

"What is she doing?"

"She's waiting for a dolphin."

I watched the woman in the video, and the grey dolphins streaking back and forth just below the surface, and the rippling black waters beyond.

"You don't have to watch," he said, second guessing his choice to show me the video. He took the phone back, pressed a few buttons with his thumb, and then set it down again. "I was just making a visual analogy. Nilou is waiting for her partner. That's the whole point of this shoot. The plan is for her to sit just like this, on top of a dune overlooking the desert, and then…we'll just wait."

I smiled at him, which made him uncomfortable. He solved it by talking more.

"We don't know what they look like. We don't know if they'll come. We don't know if we'll even be able to see them, if they do. But," he said, dropping his voice, "the guesthouse owners said they live in a community just a few kilometers north of here. I love them. I know I'm not supposed to, but I do."

He smiled. He had one of those concave smiles with more teeth showing at the edges than in the middle. It gave him the appearance of a crazed cartoon character.

I swallowed the last of my orange and told him to close the door.

He did so.

I told him to turn off the lights.

He did so.

I saw his hands shaking a little. I wondered how experienced he was. He went to the corner and began to pile the blankets in a sort of nest. I waited. It was sweet. The orange mist lingered in the air like an incense.

Then he sat in the middle of his nest with his legs drawn up against his chest. He laughed, nervously, and spread his hands as if to say, *Well, here I am.*

I crawled to him and tapped his knee. It fell to the side, taking the suggestion. Then both legs fell open, like his body was blooming, and then his arm curled around the small of my back, and I was being kissed all over my face, as if I were a beloved doll.

How did I think it was going to be, when I first saw him? I'd been having dinner in the main house, on my third helping of everything on the table—flatbread, cream soup, khoresh, dizi, lamb kebab, chicken kebab, saffron rice, Shirazi salad, and pistachio gaz made on the premises, for which the guesthouse was famous—when I saw him at the other end of the table, admiring my appetite. I was not a normal student on holiday. He'd intuited this. I was hungry for an authentic experience. Just last week, over rose tea in our favorite underground haunt, my fellow student and I had been discussing my trip to the oasis. She understood how I craved new places, new foods, new experiences, new art, new men. She asked, as if posing the question to the cosmos, "What are the men there even like?" and I just stared at her, squinting, cocking my head this way and that, turning over one possible answer and then another.

I settled on the midpoint of the seesaw: "Strange."

"Strange?" she asked.

"Strange," I repeated.

And then we both said the word again, locked eye-to-eye, and bent our heads to the side in sync as if we were mirror images, drawing the word out like taffy.

I was half-asleep when I heard Abbas stir. I pretended to be asleep. He kissed my shoulder once. I heard rustling and shuffling, and then felt warm fabric settle against my skin where there'd been only air before.

When the door clicked shut, I opened my eyes. He'd draped the bedding all around me where I lay. The plate, the rinds, the white plastic knife were gone, but the smell of oranges lingered.

I turned over and stretched, enjoying the new aches, and then let my limbs settle into new delicious positions. I'd done well. I wanted to do that again. That was a good authentic experience. But the more I tried to remember the details, the more they slipped away—as if there was a veil in time, dividing the before and after. It bothered me. I tried to fall back asleep, but I couldn't—the exhaustion had knocked me out at first; now, it kept me awake. And the wind was still so loud, as if the guesthouse were a plane careening through the sky at a terrible speed. How could they be filming porn in this wind?

I turned on my back and blinked at the ceiling. My questions weaved together and acted as a membrane that kept me from falling back into sleep. I sat up and started putting on my clothes.

When I was pulling my door shut and locking it, careful not to wake the other guests, I saw the tiny skull of a jackal mounted on the wall. I couldn't believe I hadn't noticed it before. Had I walked right past it? I tapped the bone snout, to test for realness. Maybe it was new, something the wind had blown in. I looked into its big black eye holes and admired its little teeth. I could smell the calcium dust of old bone.

Outside, the wind pushed me sideways and forward. I had to hold my headscarf down to keep it from unraveling and blowing off. In between gusts, I could hear the snuffling of camels in the corral next to the main house, and the crow of a rooster in the palm forest. But then the stone alleys gave way to dark dunes like standing waves. Abbas had said the community lived to the north of them. I saw a faint reddish glow in that direction. That must be the set. I made for it.

The wind got quieter, but the sand got deeper. I sank and slid sideways on my sandals. I hadn't brought the right shoes. But I continued, now wondering whether I'd be welcome. Surely they were afraid of the police. I had a story ready if anyone should ask why I was there: I was curious, a progressive, open-minded film student. Which was the truth. Abbas would recognize me and confirm, having been inside me just two hours ago.

At the top of the ridge, I saw two people silhouetted black against a warm pomegranate light: a figure behind a camera, and a figure sitting on a rug. I assumed that was Nilou Tar. I could only see the back of her—she was sitting cross-legged, swathed and regal in black, on a long Persian rug.

"Stop!"

I stopped. One silhouette was marching toward me. It was a woman in a hijab—the director, I assumed. Nilou Tar remained facing the desert.

"Who are you?" asked the director.

"I'm just a guest at the guesthouse," I said. "I'm a student." I felt stupid and childish, as if caught in a lie. From what I could see of the director's face, that's exactly what she thought.

"So you're a student?" she asked with a touch of mockery. "What do you study?"

"Film," I said.

She smirked. "Celluloid or digital?"

Like with Abbas, I felt this was a test of some kind. It was only fitting to be honest. "I've only worked in digital," I said.

"Tell me why."

I felt my face get hot. "It's my native medium. I'm young," I said. She didn't look impressed. I remembered what Abbas had said, about artists choosing a set of interesting constraints. "I like how much I can do, how finely I can cut, how quickly I can move. I like that I can make quick decisions and splice segments, one into the other. I like that it moves as quickly as I do."

The director's face remained impassive. She was not convinced.

"But I want to learn other ways," I said. "I was curious. I wanted to watch, or even help."

Then Nilou Tar turned around on her rug. I could only see the shadows of her face in red and black, as if seeing the contours of an eroded goddess at Persepolis. She was much older than I'd expected—in her fifties.

"She can clear me of sand," Nilou called to the director in a voice firm as an oboe, without even looking at me.

The director nodded. Apparently it was as good as done.

Nilou turned to face the desert again, and the director started walking back up toward her camera.

I sensed I shouldn't wait for further permission. I staggered after her to the top of the dune, where the director handed me a long elegant horsetail brush in passing. I took it, felt the coarse hairs over the palm of my hand. I'd never felt such a thing. As I came closer to Nilou, I saw that the rug was laid over the ridge of the dune, which was so sharp it was almost a right angle. Her legs were dangling over the side, much like the blonde woman in the dolphin video Abbas had shown me earlier. Where was he? He'd said he wasn't needed until later; how much later, I didn't know.

I chose a position right at the outside of the pool of red light, making sure I wasn't casting a shadow or showing up in the camera's line of sight, and knelt, and shifted back and forth to make comfortable wells in the sand for my knees, and waited.

The wind gusted, like a soundtrack. I looked at Nilou, outlined in the red light. She looked serene.

She had a severe, queenly beauty, not the girlish cuteness I'd expected of a porn star. She was looking north in silence. It was hard for me to be silent, or even very still. I tried. To distract myself, I tried to remember more about Abbas. But it was as if there'd been a jump cut in my life, an edit ahead to a later time. Memory depends on the medium, I thought; brains are such imperfect recorders. I needed to see him again. I needed to remember.

The wind was picking up again. My eyes were closing of their own accord, against the wind and the red light. The sexual exhaustion that had first allowed me to sleep, and then forbade me to sleep, was now washing over me again.

Through half-closed lids, I saw Nilou sit up.

I opened my eyes fully and sat up, too. The director had gone rigid behind the camera. I looked to where they were both looking.

A male figure stood at the bottom of the dune.

I pulled out my phone, clicked it on, and—making sure that no one could see—positioned it in the sand, on its side, recording.

He was tall—almost two meters, I guessed—and wore a gauzy white shroud around his body. I couldn't see his face. He wore a mask over the top part of his face, with a long snout and big black holes for eyes. For a moment I thought he had no feet, but then he began climbing toward us, and I saw them rising and sinking in the sand. He had real feet. As he came toward us, he opened his arms and let the shroud fall on the dune behind him. Underneath, he wore a linen tunic around his waist, bands of gold around his arms, and leather straps that crossed over his sternum. He had a broad chest and round, muscled shoulders that glittered, as if rubbed with mica.

He stopped in front of the rug where Nilou sat. He looked absolutely real.

Nilou had drawn up her knees on her rug. She looked up at him, determined, but was breathing hard, which I hadn't expected. I could see she hadn't expected this. She hadn't known what to expect, but she hadn't expected this. He looked just like a real man, though bigger and smoother and with a strange sparkle to his skin. She had expected him to be incorporeal or invisible. Here he was, enfleshed. I saw his jawline beneath the mask. He looked like Abbas, but he was much bigger.

The man dropped to all fours, crawled forward, and tapped one of her knees.

It fell to the side, taking the suggestion.

Then both of her legs fell open and she fell back, like her body was blooming, and the man crawled up over her, kissing her along the way, not taking any notice of me, or the director, or the camera, or my blinking phone. I was so near to them. I told myself to watch for the signs of authenticity. I told myself to watch for any signs of trickery. She pulled back her black robes, and even in the red light, I could see her pubic hair, no nylon, nothing flattened, nothing bound. He shifted his sparkling hips to the side, and there was pubic hair there, too; nothing flattened, nothing bound indeed. Nilou reached up with both hands. I could see skin-to-skin contact. I could see him push, and I could see her draw him in, and then he moved forward and disappeared inside her, just like his foot had sunk into the sand. They were joined. It was real. The both of them closed their eyes as if falling asleep for just a moment, turning their heads, one to the right and one to the left.

But the stillness gave way to motion; human bodies can't linger like that.

I didn't move. The director didn't move.

Time went slowly.

I felt hungry again.

I had never been so aware of time.

What interesting constraints for a soul to choose: to have a body, made of muscle and bone and fat, discrete in time and space.

They seemed to be taking forever. There was no wind at all. Now more of their clothes were off, and her dress was up around her waist, and her hips were up off the rug, reaching up and drawing him down as if tugging on a kite. His hands pressed into the rug on either side of her, his knuckles pale and sparkling. They were conjoined below the waist and I could no longer see what was happening. But it was intensifying. Neither of them made any sound, besides their breathing. Nilou had her hands on his hips, now, fingernails digging into his flesh, steering herself up, eyes wide open as if angry. He looked afraid. His mask slipped. I willed it not to come off and drop on her, not to ruin her rhythm. But I could see more of his face now—more ear, more jawline, more forehead. He was indeed Abbas. But he'd grown since I'd last seen him.

Nilou threw her head back and screamed. But the scream went nowhere. It never even left her mouth. Then Abbas pushed his fist into the sand just beyond the rug, and it disappeared into it, wrist-deep.

I watched for authenticity.

I could see them pull apart. She pulled her black dress down. He pulled his white shroud back around him. Neither I nor the director moved, still, even as Nilou flopped onto her side, panting. As for Abbas, he trudged back down the dune, beyond the circle of light, until he was lost to sight in the darkness.

I turned back to the set.

Nilou and the director were facing me.

It ended with the video screen going black.

My fellow student handed me back my phone, careful not to drop it in her rose tea. Her face was just barely composed, but she was titillated, I could tell: her features oozed from human to dolphin to jackal and back again. Emotion, like memory, depends on the medium.

"He brought you oranges?" she said.

"Yes. He was a sweet one. What do you think?"

"Wipe it and shoot again," she said. "Next time I want to see more cock."

MAJNUN
Helene Wecker

THE PHONE CALL comes just before dawn, from an imam in Sidi Ali. A boy there needs Zahid's help. The imam has recited over him all night with no success, and his voice on the mobile is ragged and strained. *Can you come, Mr. Zahid? They aren't wealthy, but they can pay.* And then, as an afterthought: *It's as though it's waiting for something, but I have no idea what.*

What about the Sufis? Zahid knows it's cowardice even as he blurts it out. But already he has his suspicions. He knows what day it is; he's half-expected this call.

They're all busy with the festival. And the family would prefer someone more discreet. Less chanting and dancing. They don't want the neighbors to know.

So Zahid grabs his nylon backpack, leaves his Meknes apartment, and rides his motorbike to Sidi Ali, weaving around clogs of pilgrims and tourists. The dusty, out-of-the-way village has been awake for hours, and is now deep in preparations. Groups of musicians light braziers to warm their drumskins while street vendors hawk bottles of orange-flower water. Women sit together at sidewalk cafés, hennaing their hands.

Zahid finds the house, an old-fashioned, two-story *riad* that has seen better days. The parents meet him at the door. He talks to them briefly, then asks them to wait in the sitting room. It's an irregular request— these things are usually family affairs, with everyone crowded together, watching and praying—and they glance at each other, clearly uneasy. But they nod and leave, concern for their son visible in the way they lean into each other, the strained lines of their backs.

Alone, Zahid performs *wudu* in the courtyard fountain, the ablutions rinsing away the dust of the road. He grits his teeth against the pain of the water, watches the telltale steam rise from his skin—one reason for his request for privacy—and then climbs the stairs to the living quarters.

At the doorway to the boy's bedroom, Zahid peers inside and watches as the boy writhes on the bed, moaning, his thin nightshirt drenched with sweat. He tries to remind himself that it might only be a coincidence. It's been nearly a year without any contact. But Zahid watches the boy, and he knows.

He pauses to make his *du'a*, his supplication. *God grant me the strength to heal this boy, and to turn his tormentor toward Your wisdom.* Then he picks up his backpack, and enters.

As he nears the bed, the boy's eyes open. The face lights with a smile.

"Hello, *majnun*," the boy says.

Everything in Zahid clenches. He walks past the bed, past that smile, to the small *en suite* bathroom, and makes *wudu* again. It isn't the smartest idea—water weakens him, and he'll need strength—but it brings him back to his purpose. He needs to concentrate on the boy. Ignore the smile, ignore the endearment he never quite liked but still yearns to hear again. *Majnun*, crazy man, possessed one. Her little joke.

He dries himself, waits for the last of the steam to disappear, and hangs the towel back on its bar. The silence from the bedroom has turned anticipatory. He takes a deep breath—he doesn't need to, but it makes him feel better—and goes back in.

The walls of the bedroom are plastered with football posters and photos of the boy's friends. The air is uncomfortably humid. As the boy watches, Zahid crosses to a window and opens it. The cloudless sky tempts him for a moment, but he steps away, feeling the relief of a breeze on his neck.

The boy grins again and makes a show of stretching, arching his back before settling into the bedclothes. "You made me wait," he says. "How unprofessional of you."

Zahid ignores him. From his backpack, he extracts a plastic bag full of short lengths of string. He lifts the boy's hands and ties a string around each finger, tight but not too tight, between the first and second joints. He finishes the hands and moves down to the feet, cinching strings around each toe. The boy complies with an indulgent smile, playing along.

Next to the bed are a small table and a wooden chair. The boy's well-thumbed copy of the Quran rests on the table, gold embossing on its blue cover. Zahid sits in the chair and picks up the Quran, trying to anchor himself in its familiarity. He recites the *adhan*, the call to worship, then turns to the *Surah Al-Fatihah*, the first surah, which the Prophet once called the cure for every poison. *You alone we worship,* he recites. *You alone we ask for help. Guide us in the right path.*

The boy sighs. "But this is exactly what the other one did. You know it's me, so *talk* to me, *majnun*. I didn't come all this way to be prayed at."

Zahid snorts, incredulous, and lets go of the illusion that this will proceed as usual. "You came for the festival, Aisha, not me. Speaking of which, shouldn't you be on your way? The procession will be starting soon."

The boy shrugs. "There's plenty of time. And the festival will happen with or without me."

"As though you'd miss it."

"To be here with you, after so long apart?" The boy lifts a languid foot, angles it towards the inside of Zahid's knee.

Zahid shifts out of range. "Stop that."

"Spoilsport. By the way, I noticed that the boy's parents aren't here with us. Was that your doing? They must've found that odd. Who knows *what* you might be getting up to in here?"

"Yes, I told them to stay downstairs," he says. "I had a feeling it was you."

"You see? Admit it, you miss me." The boy rolls onto his stomach, props his chin on his hands, gazes at him through string-ends and lashes and sweat-matted hair—and Zahid has to look away, because he can see her glowing deep in the boy's eyes. *Lalla Aisha*, Lady Aisha Qandisha, the famous *jinniyah* of Morocco, who possesses human men and drives them mad with lust. No one knows how old she is, least of all Aisha herself. Her appearance suggests a beautiful young *jinniyah* of perhaps two or three hundred years, but her legends go back for millennia. Some believe she's descended from Astarte, or that she *is* Astarte, in a smaller form for a modern age. She's the closest the jinn of Morocco have to a queen, and for over a century Zahid was her consort, her special favorite, until the day he left without a word.

"Of course I miss you," he says. "But there were other ways to get my attention."

"Should I have rung you on your mobile? Arranged for a chaperoned date at a café, like some timid young *muslimah*?"

"For instance." She never would, of course; it would mean meeting him in his own territory, and in all things Aisha Qandisha prefers the upper hand. "But that's not the point."

"Then what is?"

"The boy, Aisha. The boy is the point. Please get out of him."

The smile shows teeth. "Or what?"

He sighs. "Or I'll do what I came to do."

"Do you really think you can?"

"I'm good at my job."

"I'm sure the Quran has something to say about boastful speech."

"It's not a boast. It's the truth."

The boy's eyes roll in open disgust. He drops the coy pose and sits upright on the bed, authority in every graceful movement. "Tell me, *majnun*, how many jinn have you exorcised since you deserted me?"

"Roughly a dozen." It's nine, but he decides to round up.

"And how many did you possess in your time as my consort? Was it hundreds, or thousands?"

"I didn't keep count. Thousands, probably. I'm not a hypocrite, Aisha, if that's what you're insinuating. I try to live by my beliefs, and I've come to believe that possession is a sin."

"Even when we bring pleasure instead of pain? Or is pleasure a sin as well?"

"Only pleasures that harm."

"There are few truly innocent pleasures, *majnun*. And who determines which is which? God? You?"

The boy shakes his head. "Do you know why I chose this young man? He's sixteen, and he has a terrible stammer. He worries that he'll never talk to a girl who doesn't laugh at him, and his parents will have to find him a wife. I came to him in his sleep, and I offered myself. You've never seen such a willing soul. In one night I've given him more ecstasy than he might find in the next sixty years."

"And how much heartache will that night cost him? Will he ever be satisfied with anyone else, after you?"

The boy shrugs. "Then I'll come back. He's very sweet."

This, Zahid thinks in frustration, is exactly what he'd warned himself against. Not once in a hundred years did he ever win an argument with Aisha Qandisha. She'll evade, cajole, proclaim, pout. She'll wear him down, and it will end as it always did, in a maelstrom of lust. Already it feels inevitable. "Why are you really here? And don't tell me the boy, or the festival."

The boy's eyes are steady and sure, and she burns in them like a candle at the bottom of a well. "I've come to bring you home."

"Aisha, for heaven's sake."

"I'll forgive everything. Just renounce this zealotry and come back to me."

"I *can't*. This is my life now."

"But what sort of life do you call this? Living like a hermit, injuring your fellow jinn. Are you happier, like this?"

I'm lonely. I hate hurting my own kind. I miss you terribly. "It's a different sort of happiness. It's hard to explain. But I feel more whole now. I have a sense of purpose."

The boy sniffs. "I'd have thought that being my consort would be purpose enough. Or did you secretly resent me, for a hundred years?"

"Of course not. When you chose me, I thought I'd never know a greater honor. I wanted nothing more than to please you."

"Which is why you slunk away in the night, like a criminal. I thought you'd been trapped! Or killed!" Anguish fills the boy's voice, bathing Zahid in guilt. "I sent out my spies, and they came back to me saying *he lives as a human, he's converted to Islam, he took another name.* I don't like it, by the way. 'Zahid.' It doesn't suit you."

"It's my name now. It suits me well enough."

The boy waves this away like an errant thought. "When the rumors began that you'd become an exorcist, I didn't want to believe them. But then your victims came to me, and showed me their wounds. Saying *it was him, he did this to me.* And all I could think was, all those years I called him *majnun*, and now it's finally come true."

He tries not to cringe visibly. "I didn't know how to tell you. I could barely make sense of it myself." *You wouldn't have listened anyway,* he thinks. *You would have shredded my resolve with a fond look and a laugh, and opened your arms and taken me to bed. And that would've been the end of it.*

"Then tell me now! Don't I deserve to know what happened, why you changed?"

"It's hard to explain."

"You said that already. So *try*. Make me understand."

She wants to draw him out, to keep him talking, so she can twist his words into a leash and lead him back to her side. And at any moment the family might creep up the stairs, and hear them. But she's right about this, at least: in leaving her, he traded one type of faithlessness for another. She deserves an explanation.

He starts slowly, searching for the words. "It started a few years ago, during an exorcism. Nothing out of the ordinary, just a man in Tangier, I can't even remember why he'd angered me. A few Sufis came. They started chanting, I fought them as usual. But then, for some reason—and I honestly don't know why—I started listening. *Really* paying attention, not just trying to gauge their attack. And as I listened to the verses, I started to feel better. Which was strange, because I'd felt fine to begin with—or at least, I'd thought I felt fine."

The boy's eyebrows rise at this, but he says nothing. Zahid goes on, afraid now to stop. "I was so surprised, I forgot myself and let go. The Sufis were delighted with themselves, of course. I flew home to you, and tried to tell myself that it had been some new kind of trick. But deep down I knew.

"I looked forward to exorcisms, so I could feel that peace again. I started reciting the verses to myself, for comfort. And after a while, I decided I wanted to become a Muslim. But how could I possess others and live as your lover, and still accept the truth of the Quran? I tried to make it right with myself, but couldn't. I didn't want to possess anyone anymore, even when I thought they deserved it. And being your consort started to feel…" *Shameful.* "Uncomfortable. I tried not to let it show, but then when you didn't notice, I felt like shouting it at you. You'd call me *majnun*, and I'd want to laugh, because it really did feel like madness.

"Then, one night, we were traveling through Fez and we saw a drunken man stumbling down the sidewalk. He passed an old woman, a hunchback, walking with a cane—"

"I remember." The boy has been so quiet that Zahid startles at the voice. "He bumped into her, and nearly knocked her over. She yelled at him to be more careful, and he laughed and said, *Ya Lalla Aisha, it's your own fault, you bewitched me with your beauty.* You hesitated, but then you flew after him. I'd never seen you balk at your duty before. That's why I remember."

He nods. "I told myself, if anyone deserves it, it's this guy. That God must have put me there to witness his transgressions, against the old woman and against you. I would deliver his punishment, and remind him that Lalla Aisha Qandisha walks in the world unseen, and will not be insulted or ridiculed. So I followed him home, and knocked his head against the floorboards for a night and a day, and tried to be happy about it.

"Then the exorcist arrived. He wasn't a Sufi, or even an imam. Just an old man, a neighbor. He asked how the man had wronged me, so I told him. The exorcist said he wasn't surprised, that he'd known the guy for years and thought he was a red-assed monkey with a mind like a shoe. *But Ya Jinni*, he said, *you've answered a wrong with a wrong*."

Here Zahid pauses. The next part is important; he wants to get it right. "When he said it, it felt like a holy judgment. The words were a whip, and he'd flayed me open and exposed my soul to God, every hidden corner. I sobbed for a while, and confessed to every sin I could think of. Then I asked if he could recite a few surahs for me. Not to drive me out, but just so I could listen. He was a little surprised, but he recited for hours without stopping. By the time he finished, I knew without a doubt what I needed to do. I had to leave you, and I had to become an exorcist. I'd never been so certain of anything in my life."

He glances up. The boy is frowning at the wall, a portrait of stoic unhappiness. Zahid looks down at his hands, fighting embarrassment. What did he expect, cries of joy? A spontaneous conversion? He knows how these stories sound to unbelievers, dull and absurd and all the same, like a human describing a dream. *I went to school, and you were there, but it wasn't you. You ate an orange, and I started crying.* Pointless even to try.

"Anyway," he mutters. "I prayed with him for a while, and then asked how to go about becoming a Muslim. He told me about an abandoned *masjid* he'd heard of in Meknes, where jinn meet to pray and study. So I thanked him, and left. And then I left you."

He trails off into a heavy silence, unsure what to say next.

After a while the boy says, "Do you regret your time with me, *majnun?*"

It's a question he's asked himself, and he knows his answer. "You were my world, Aisha. I regret my sins, but they were mine, not yours, and I made them of my own free will. Who knows? Maybe I would've sinned more if I hadn't been your consort. So, no. I can't regret it. But I can't go back, either."

The boy leans towards him, eyes wide. "I can make you, you know," he whispers. "I'll turn this young man into my new favorite, my home away from home. Cast me out, and I'll come back, again and again. There's bound to be damage to him eventually. And in a way, it will be your fault."

A cold touch of horror goes through him: would she, truly? But he shakes his head. "You wouldn't."

"Oh? Why not?"

"Because I've never known you to be deliberately cruel. You told me once, *We are the chaos and release that they need, the necessary balance to their rules and rigidity. They know this, even as they drive us from their bodies.*

"I don't believe that anymore. But I know that you do."

An offended snort. "I see. Your eyes have been opened, and now in your wisdom you are above Aisha Qandisha. I am just another of God's deluded creatures to you. I suppose now you'll go and tell the Sufis to stop the festival, to put away their drums and banners. Are they deluded too? Why would all of Sidi Ali parade through the streets chanting my name, if they don't value what I bring them?"

He sighs. "They do value you, Aisha. They love and fear you, just as I do. But they think a little of you goes a long way."

The boy leans on one arm, considering him. "You would never dare talk to me like that before."

"I know."

"So many things you know, these days. Do you also know that I haven't taken a new consort?"

His brow furrows in confusion and surprise. Can it be true? He's never known her to lie outright. But the thought of her without a consort barely makes sense. "Really? Whatever for?"

The boy shrugs, one finger tracing the bedpost. "For the novelty, maybe. Or maybe I just miss you that much."

"Aisha."

"You were so very good at your duties. So immensely skilled at pleasing me." The boy raises a hand—the nails bitten, the knuckles sprouting their first hairs—and gently touches Zahid's cheek. "Please, *majnun*. Come back. I am begging you."

He closes his eyes, fights the desire that sweeps his body, the jolt that comes from hearing Aisha Qandisha beg for anything, least of all him. "*I can't.*" It comes out strangled, a question. "Please, Aisha. If you ever loved me, don't ask me again."

A long moment passes. Zahid wills himself not to move, not to feel the boy's breath on his throat, the heat that radiates from the thin frame.

"All right," the boy says at last. "You win." He draws away from Zahid and lies back on the bed, his face dull and stony.

For a moment Zahid has no idea what he's doing. Then he realizes. "No."

"Well, exorcist of nearly a dozen jinn? What are you waiting for? Is your faith not strong enough?"

"Don't do this. Just leave him. Just let him go."

But the boy says nothing more, only stares at the ceiling, and Zahid sees that he's already lost the fight. This is his punishment, his penance. There is nothing he can do.

Feeling cold and sick, Zahid opens his backpack again and takes out a small vial of olive oil. He mutters a prayer over it, then rubs a few drops on the boy's forehead. The boy shudders once, and closes his eyes.

The exorcism itself is straightforward, even textbook. She uses no feints or trickery, no clever dodges to make him think he's weakened her or cast her out. She merely holds on, fighting him for every inch as he batters her with verses, pushing her out of the boy's mind and down into his chest. It takes nearly an hour to herd her along the boy's torso and into the arm that's closest to the open window. At some point it becomes clear to Zahid that he will succeed, that he's strong enough to do this; and he knows that she must realize it too. *It's over*, he thinks desperately. *Just let go.* But still she fights him.

More verses, more surahs, and his strength begins to flag. But she falters first, her grip slipping. The boy's hand starts to tremble. Quickly Zahid reaches across and pulls the string from around the boy's forefinger. One last recitation—and she flies free, hovering before the window.

Zahid almost cries out at the sight of her: at her beauty, newly shocking after so long away, and at the ugly marks of his exorcism. He wants to throw himself on the floor beneath her, to whimper and crawl and beg her forgiveness.

"Farewell, Zahid," she says, and flies away.

Zahid sags against the window frame and watches until she disappears. Then a noise behind him makes him turn.

The boy on the bed is stirring. The eyes flutter open. He rubs his face as though coming out of a dream, then startles and jerks his hands away, staring at the strings. He looks around, panicked, searching, but sees only Zahid. His face begins to crumple.

I'm sorry, Zahid wants to tell him. *It has to be this way. It's for the best.* But the boy has turned away from him, and is weeping into his pillow.

BLACK POWDER
Maria Dahvana Headley

THE RIFLE IN this story is a rifle full of wishes. Maybe all rifles seem to be that, at least for a moment, when they're new, before any finger has touched any trigger. Maybe all rifles seem as though they might grant a person the only thing they've ever wanted.

At the beginning of this story, there are no bullets. At the end of this story, there are no more bullets *left*. In the middle of this story, there are enough bullets to change the world into something entirely different.

This rifle is full of anything anyone could want, each bullet a captive infinity, each an ever after.

Bullets may be made, in the old way, of a thin cylinder of any animal's gut packed full of black powder and attached to the back of the projectile with glue. They may be made of bronze points, of buckshot, with tiny arrows—flechettes—embedded in them to maximize damage on entry. Rifles may shoot anything from orbs to thorns, which may be propelled, in antique weapons, by a mixture of charcoal, potassium nitrate, and sulphur, or, in certain situations, by the motions of something else entirely.

Thus may one fire a wish. Thus may one shoot a star.

That's a story people tell, in any case. Like all stories, this one contains lies, and like all old rifles, this one contains the dust of its history.

Perhaps the story begins with a kid behind the wheel of a truck, this same stolen rifle beside him.

This kid—call him the Kid, why not?—has big plans. Here at the base of the mountains, he's been looking up too long, seeing only girls who want nothing to do with him. He stole the rifle from the dumb old man at the pawnshop, who never even saw him coming.

The Kid shot the rifle once, and then—

The Kid's nothing special. He's gangle, denim, pustule and pouch. Back pocket of his jeans is full of stolen chew, and his hands are covered in corn chip ashes like he's been elbow deep in a Dorito crematorium.

Something weird happened when he pulled the trigger, something he's not thinking about.

Something asked him a question.

The something is in the back of the Kid's pickup truck now, on the dog's blanket. Maybe real, maybe imagined, maybe a flashback to some cartoon reality seen when he was little. He's decided not to think about it.

Out here, near the remnants of the reactor, there's a marker for a massacre of trappers, and there's a historical designation for the place, their possessions enough to identify them.

In the summer, poison mushrooms leap from the shadows, shape of skulls. The spot is surrounded by cliffs that glow green at sunset, and the hollow in the center feels seen. It's been declared safe enough, the radiation dispersed, though most people would never come here. It's a bad place.

The Kid imagines the fire flooding up from it; pictures the pale blue sky when the meltdown happened, tree branches shaking, studded with black squirrels. The way ash fell from the heavens, and his mother walked out from the trailer and filled her hands with it, filled her mouth with it, rolled in it like a dog in snow.

"I didn't know no better," she says. "Lot of people didn't. We thought it was some kinda miracle."

Then she was pregnant, and she swears she doesn't know how it happened, doesn't know who the Kid's father ever was.

He veers left on the highway and drives on the wrong side a while, singing along with the hum inside him. In the seat, the rifle sings too, bullets rattling, each a distinct tone.

The Kid feels stars inside his chest, burning novas, sparks flitting through his body. He's a man on a mission, to spread the word of the dead.

He thinks about his future: a hero's journey through the flat earth of high school. He's readying himself to graduate from childhood and into legend.

DROP BACK IN time to another part of the story, a hundred and fifty years ago, long before the Kid's even born.

Out here in these woods, at that time, there's a notorious freetrapper who takes all the pelts and all the women. He pays in plague as well as in tradegoods, taking the beaver, the mink, the wolves, taking the daughters of chieftains, and the wives of warriors.

He's a bringer of disaster, and in the years he walks the woods, he takes wife after wife, never for long. Some die in childbirth, and some die in rapids, and some die by bear. One leaps from a cliff. They walk ahead of him, and ride behind him. They are the starwatchers he uses when he can't see a way out of the wild, and the warmth he relies upon in winter. The animals hate him, and the wives hate him, and he carries a black powder rifle, an axe, and a bottle of whiskey. Anything else he needs, he steals. Every time he takes a new wife, he's cursed by all the inhabitants of the places he passes through. There are babies left behind after each wife dies, and he gives some to the animals, and puts others out to be collected by anyone who lives in the trees. The trapper wants only wives, not children.

The rifle in this story is the one that once belonged to this trapper.

DOWNWIND AND UPRIVER of the trapper's territory, there's a pack of company men with a bag of sugar and a bag of tea, a pile of pelts tied to horseback, the riders chewed over by the tilted teeth of the mountains. Each green cliff glints with ghosts, and each new place is written on a map of the men's making.

Silk has not yet taken over the world. It's the trappers' mission to bring back fur and carry it into drawing rooms where the pianos are made of wood from other conquered places. At night the men circle, make their fire, boil the river, steep tea leaves, drink it hot and sweet, the only rightness, their ragged remnant of civilization. It's a strange civilizer, the drinking of brackish water.

They write journals of their expedition into forbidden country: caverns narrow and full of black wings, pine trees sharp as knives pressed into soft bellies. Each man has his spoon. Each man has something gold hanging under his shirt. If they chisel into the stone they find only dark muddy green, stone the color of swamp, no emeralds. Above them, mountain lions stalk the white bone knobs at the back of each man's neck.

One of the men's got a monkey with him, the only source of comedy, brought from his lady at home, and he sets his monkey off into the woods. The monkey chitters high and holy, telling him where the beavers are building their dams. That trapper comes back rich in oily pelts, the decapitated heads of beaver strewn on the path behind him, ghost tails slapping the water while the men sleep.

One day a woman appears at the edge of their camp. She carries two pistols and wears trousers made of leather. Her eyes have tattoos of treelines along the lids.

Call her the Hunter.

With her is the French Canadian freetrapper, whose legend the men all know. He's the Bluebeard of the Rocky Mountains, and his tales travel, but something's wrong with him. He rides on the back of her horse, sidesaddle. He sucks at the insides of his cheeks, spits in the dirt, and bows his head. He wears a brilliant blue blanket around his shoulders, and shivers, even when he's near the fire. His beard's gone half white.

The trappers decide he's no longer a man. Something's gone wrong, and whatever it is, they won't ask. They decide never to speak of him again. Bad luck.

"What are you doing here?" the leader of the company men asks the woman. "What are you hunting?"

He's already given her all the tobacco they've brought, though he doesn't know why.

"What do you think I'm hunting?" she asks. "Don't you know where you are? What do *you* call these mountains?"

They tell her their name for them, and she laughs. "That's not their name. I've been following them around the center of the world. I've been hunting a long time.

"Let me tell you a story," she says.

The men carefully fail to listen. The only stories to tell nine months into a trapping are *about* women, not *by* them. *Girls on their backs, girls on horseback, girls in horsehair.* No man wants to risk drawing the attention of his own ghosts, not this far in. The longer they travel in this country, the more fear travels with them. The women in these mountains are dangerous if they exist at all, and the men pretend they don't, in favor of the few women working up in the gold veins and silver valleys outside the tourmaline range. The men make progress toward them, gathering pelts for payment at bars and brothels.

The story the Hunter tells them is something about a magical creature in the trees, left here by an earlier expedition, offloaded from a wagon and chained in a room made of metal out in the woods, all alone.

"I ran up on the last man from that expedition, and he told me they put their monster where nobody would ever find it," she says, and the men shudder.

"Next time I saw him, he was turned innards out," she says, "and hanging from a tree. He was missing all his mains. So I guess they didn't cage it well enough, now, did they? You haven't seen it?"

They haven't seen it.

When she rides away, the freetrapper looks back at them, and they pretend not to notice. All is well. Pelts and then home.

One morning, though, the men come upon a gathering of the dead, skeletons sitting in a circle, drinking tea. Cups shattered in the snow, gilt-edged smiles, brown stains in the ice. All the dead are dressed in furs, layer after layer of them, beaver, bear, and wolf. The skeletons are wearing the claws of the animals, the teeth of the animals, the tails of the animals.

The monkey leaps from its man's shoulder and runs to one of the dead. It shrieks in recognition.

One of the living men kneels beside one of the skeletons, and touches the skull with his fingernail, tapping it. With that touch, the skeleton blooms, regaining all its lost flesh, young and strong and fat with feasting. It is a body full of brilliant blood. It is a familiar body. Each man sees himself there, and shudders in time, himself living, himself dead, all in the same moment.

There's a whipping wind now, and hailstones. The fire rekindles in green flames, and there is a voice, and the voice tells them to eat.

There is the Hunter with the trees tattooed on her eyelids too, but she doesn't arrive until somewhat later, and by then, the thing she's hunting is gone.

* * *

WHAT DO WE hunt but each other? A hunter might go on an expedition, might map the forest and mountains, but what they're truly looking for is their own broken heart hidden inside an elk, their own lost lover hidden inside a wolf, their own dead child hidden inside a bear. A hunter is always looking for wishes to come true, and if it takes blood and rending to get them, then it does. There is a magic in the explosion, in the black smoke cloud, in the way whatever one is hunting runs off, the way the hunter is left standing there, inhaling powder.

All most people wish for is *more*, wishing forever until tongues are parched and hearts are tired of beating. Love is a kind of wish.

Wishing for love is the same as wishing for more wishes.

SNAP FORWARD IN time again, a hundred and fifty years. Now there's a pawnshop down a dirt trail, deep in the woods, near the spot where the trappers died.

There's a man named Yoth Begail behind the counter, scraggle jaw and white yellow beard, tin of chew in his front pocket and stretched tendons in his neck giving him the look of a scarecrow gone sentient. There's pawned-off precious in the glass cases, dust on everything thick enough to epic it. These are the gun hoards of suicides from the local police repo, snuck out by janitors looking to buy other things, trading them over to Yoth Begail for the time being, taking his cash off to dealers and alimonies.

Yoth's been out here sixty-five years, give or take. Pawnshops are robber beacons, and people come in a couple times a year to gunpoint Yoth, who pulls his own weapon from undercounter, no hesitation. Yoth's got no town rules to live by. He sells things no one else can sell.

Got a case of stones brought in by the woman out near the reactor. Bunch of folks that way went to Heaven and left their blood behind, crystalized into little geodes, and the woman, only one still out there, has been selling them for years. They left bones that look like milk opal too, centered with garnet marrow and Yoth's got some of those as well. The woman tried to sell him a skull, but he didn't want that glittering thing around, the stony brain visible inside the opal casing. All of it was like to get him sick. Rest of the stones out here are hunks of green tourmaline, but the muddy kind, and tourmaline is rough luck.

Oh, Yoth's got the usual pawn glories too. All the things people come to him to forget. He's like a confessor in that way. Bingo-bought prizes and family heirlooms, forlorn valuables traded for canned-good grocery dollars. Pearl necklaces bought in Tahiti on the only vacation, engagement rings wrung off arthritic fingers. Televisions and trophies, couple of gold bars somebody brought in from a hoard, pennies on the dollar, cause you can't spend gold at the Walmart. He's got a gunshop license, and he can sell whatever he wants, to anybody he likes. These guns have been used to kill all kinds of things: animals, trespassers, ownselves.

Up high on the wall, there's a glass case containing Yoth's best rifle. It's a black powder model, so in federal terms it's not even a firearm. It can be sold to anyone, held by anyone. Black powder doesn't need a license. When Yoth's in the mood, he turns out the lights in the pawn, drinks a beer, and lets the rifle shine. Under the fluorescents it looks like any old firearm, dents and pits, but it came with weird copper-cased bullets, and the bullets are hot to the touch, even now, unfired since the 1800s.

Or rather, fired only once, by Yoth himself, and he got what he needed.

It's not for sale, but the pawn ticket's out there still. Brought in by a young woman with tattoos on her eyelids, who said there was no place out far enough that she could be sure people wouldn't find it, so she was entrusting it to Yoth Begail and his pawn palace for the time being.

"Welp," said Yoth, who was familiar with people trying to keep their fingers on their valuables from afar. "I'll take it off your hands, then, ma'am."

"You have to keep it safe," she said. "It's a damned old thing and it's been in some trouble."

"Nothing's damned without it's had human hands on it," Yoth said. "That's just a black powder rifle. It's the man with bad aim that's the problem."

"So you say," she said. "But you'd be wrong. I'll be back for it. I haven't slept in a while, and it's that thing's fault. Every so often, I need a rest bad. There has to be a bargain made."

Yoth considered that. He was a young man then, and he thought for a moment he could consider a wife like her, if he'd consider any wife, but in her stare, he saw nothing he liked. Woman looked like a wild dog, and when she shut her eyes she looked like a rattler. She was wearing clothes so old you'd have thought she lived in a cave, and she had white fur draped around her shoulders, fur of some animal he didn't know. Leather pants so filthy she might've been an animal from the waist down.

"You a hunter, then?" he asked.

"Am that," she said. "Been hunting in these woods years now. Trapping too."

"Why haven't I seen you before?" asked Yoth. She couldn't have been much older than he was.

"I was out a long time, this last one," she said. "Years. Got any tobacco? Can't smoke when I'm hunting these."

"Animals don't care," said Yoth, passing her a cigarette, lighting it for her. This was before he took to chewing, safer in a pawnshop.

She looked at him and laughed. "What I'm hunting likes the smoke. If I smoked, it'd find me before I'm ready to be found."

The tattoos on her eyelids were faint enough to

be scars, but Yoth could tell someone had inked them in. Treelines on top of the mountains out here, recognizable peaks. A map. He looked at them secretly as he wrote out her pawn ticket.

"You keep that rifle for me," she said. "I'll be back. Don't fire it unless you want to call up trouble."

He peered out the window to watch her go. She was on horseback, the horse draped in an unlikely blanket the color of bluebells, a piebald black and white mane. Her mount moved like someone dragged up out of an armchair to dance to a song he'd never heard before. There was a little monkey in a vest sitting on the back of the saddle. The woman, the horse, and the monkey disappeared into the trees, and not long after that, snow piled up against his windows. Time he managed to dig himself out, Yoth Begail had decided to forget about the strange tracks her horse had left, nothing like hooves.

That was sixty years ago. Yoth keeps the glass of the case clear, and the rifle oiled, but otherwise he leaves it alone. It's loaded, unlike the rest of the pawnshop guns. It's always been loaded. He took the bullets out once and held them, but he got a terrible feeling, and when he put them back in, there were burns on his palms. They took weeks to heal. That time he went to a doctor, who gave him some goat-shit-smelling ointment and told him not to play with matches.

At night he can hear singing coming from inside the rifle case, but he's no fool. He's not tempted.

Yoth's four drinks into the dark when the Kid comes through the front door, slipping in without ringing the bell, loping over to the desk where Yoth is sitting. The Kid says, "Old man, give me your best shooter."

"You're not old enough to own a gun," says Yoth. "I only sell to people old enough to aim."

"I'm older than I look," says the Kid. "And I'm not what you think. I want me some magic."

Yoth eyes him.

"Mind out of here now, kid," says Yoth. "I got the right to refuse service."

Yoth Begail is eighty-six years old when the Kid steals the rifle off the wall of the pawn palace and shoots him dead.

THE HUNTER WAKES with a start in the middle of a blizzard, her cave filled with grey light. She's been sleeping a long time. Her hand is clenched around a slip of paper, and her mouth is dry.

Her heart starts up again, and she waits as blood circulates through her body, locks opening to let salmon through. Now the fish are running, red and pink and silver, bright fish in a bright river. Her horse is there in the entrance of the cave, his blue blanket over him, his mane whiter than it was when she was last awake. She shoves her boots on. The cave is lighter now, and icicles fall from the entrance, spearing the snow, cracking and groaning as they give themselves over to water again. Outside, flowers explode. The Hunter stretches her arms and checks her weapon. Her pawn ticket is still legible.

"Up, horse," she says, and the horse stands, and shakes himself. She straightens his blanket. "Up, monkey," the Hunter says, and the monkey comes out of the saddlebag and looks around, eyes shining.

"It's hunting season," she says.

ANOTHER STORY FROM the history of the rifle: Yoth Begail fired this rifle just once, twenty years after he received it, into a stick-'em-up who'd opened the door of the pawnshop while Yoth was on the can. He grabbed the rifle without thinking, and pulled trigger into the robber.

By then Yoth was forty years old and in love with the priest from down in the river valley, the one who traveled cabin-to-cabin spreading God like margarine.

Yoth had his own secrets, and his own once-a-year trip away from the woods to a city where there were bars to drink in, and men to drink to, even if he had no way with words. Sometimes he opened his register and looked at the ticket, and wondered if the Hunter was ever coming back. Yoth was starting not to sleep for thinking of the black powder rifle, worrying that someone would steal it, and he wondered if what she'd told him was true, if it was the thing's fault, or if that was just his mind running wild.

The priest—let us call him the Priest, in the tradition of this kind of story—came to the pawnshop one day in spring and knocked on the door. When Yoth opened it, he was startled. Man of God. There was no God out here. That was *why* he was in the woods. There was only the new reactor, fenced and barb-wired, patrolled by trucks, and the old places, the missionary buildings going to crumble now, nobody worshipping in them anymore. Hunters holed up eating beef jerky in the wood churches these days, pine needles and pitch, rabbit bones splintered beneath the sign of the cross. Piss graffiti on the walls. Yoth himself had spent some time with a smokejumper in one of those shacks, before he stopped that sort of thing cold. Mob of neighbors at the pawn, that was what his kind of love led to, and he didn't want it.

"Heard tell you were up here alone, Yoth Begail," said the Priest, and smiled. He was a rangy man a little younger than Yoth, wearing a string tie and a black suit, and holding a bible in his hand. His face had an openness normally found in fools, but there it was, on him, a man with a clean shave, nicked jaw, and eyes that showed evidence of a history other than prayer.

"Am that," said Yoth.

"Heard you might be looking for the Lord?"

"Heard wrong," said Yoth, who could hardly speak. His throat had a lump big as a cocoon in it, and he had no idea what wanted to emerge. Words he'd never say. "You're new out here," he said instead.

"I came from Missouri," the Priest said, with palpable awe. "On a train. I'm the new man of God out here."

"You are that," said Yoth. "Got a name?"

The Priest blushed from beneath his collar, his face heating to the color of a coal in a woodstove. Yoth felt himself blushing too, but he was in the shadow.

"I'm Weran Root. Not 'the Priest.' I don't know why I said that. This is my first assignment. I've never been to a place like this before. It's far between people. I've been walking this mountain since yesterday looking for you."

Weran Root came in uninvited and sat down at the jewelry case, gazing in at twenty years of Sunday best. He picked up a red stone and held it to the light.

"What kind of gem is this?"

"It's from when the reactor melted down," Yoth tells him. "Twenty years ago. All over the news. You remember."

Yoth could hear singing coming from the rifle. The jangling noise of a wedding in the wood, a charivari. Coins thrown into the apron of a bride, groom lifted and shaken upside down, laughter, fiddles and howls, whistles and shrieks of ecstasy. He tried to ignore it.

"What's that on the radio?" Weran Root said. It was a Sunday, but there was nothing church in the song. He looked up at the case on the wall in wonder.

Yoth looked at Weran Root in similar wonder.

Everything was new.

Six months later, when Yoth was grabbing the rifle from the case in the dark, he heard the singing louder still, and as he fired, the singing reached a pitch of tambourine and cymbal, rattling bells, all that louder than the noise of the shot itself.

"Wait! I'm here to save you from the Devil!" cried the intruder, reaching for the barrel, but Yoth's aim was true, and it was already over.

The smoke was dense and final, a black cloud in his eyes and lungs underlining each cell, a fog like a forest fire. It took a moment to clear, but by the time it did, Yoth already knew what he'd done.

He'd put a bullet in the heart of the thin man in the white shirt, string tie, and black suit, a bullet from a singing rifle pawned over by a hunter. On his back on the floor lay the love of one man's life, his heart something unclaimable by ticket.

Out of the bullet casing came the singer Yoth had been listening to for twenty years, smoke like a roomful of pipes, and in the center of it—

Yoth fell on his knees as something, some*one*, expanded from out of the wound in the chest of Weran Root, toes still in the place where the bullet had entered, fingers stretching long and gleaming, body undulating up.

"Are you the Devil?" Yoth Begail whispered. "Am *I* the Devil?"

He was weeping, his hands full of bent wedding rings and crushed cash from the box, things to bribe back his beloved from the land of the dead.

You get one wish, the smoke said.

And so Yoth wished.

FORTY YEARS AFTER Yoth Begail's wish, the Kid drives down the highway. All he can think about is lack of love. He tells himself a story a night. Girls walking past him in the hallway of the high school. When he prays, he prays to the God of lost causes. He's a lost cause himself, born bleak in a trailer out in the woods near the reactor, and his mama is a scavenger of skeletons. She smashes them up and makes craft glue mosaics out of them. He wishes she'd smashed and glued him into the shape of some other creature, but she didn't. Now he's this. It's her fault. Their trailer is surrounded by fake white wolves made of cement and paved in mosaics of glass and bone.

Everyone living left this area after the accident that didn't happen, the fire that wasn't. He and his mother stayed. Some people make peace with disaster, and his mother's that kind. Maybe the Kid's not, but he was doomed before he was born.

The Kid thinks fondly back on himself now, before innocence became experience, before he knew there'd never be any forever for him. He used to walk up and down the road, picking up souvenirs of crystal bones, and holding all that hard blood in his hands, counting it up like he could build something out of it. He had visions of everything, back then. Now no-one notices him.

Girl's eyes slant away under lashes, electric blue liner, and who's that for? Their skin under tight jeans, and who's that for? It must be for someone. Why not for him? Not for him, because it's never gonna be him. The Kid's got no future. He's only past. There's nothing for him but hands out in the parking lot of a gas station or in the urinal, head against the wall, looking for salvation in a hot air blower and any drug buyable from anyone who'll sell to invisible boys.

Magic doesn't make anyone love you. All the Kid can do is start a fire in the palm of his hand and that's a trick he ordered from the back of a magazine.

Something offered him a wish after he fired that shot in the pawn shop. He's thinking about it.

THE FOREST IS deep winter now, and the caves are full of sleep. Animals uncurl from corners, bears in the backs of mountains and bats in the tops of caverns. Out in the ice where the reactor was, there's a hot, sulphurous spot, and beneath it there is a sound like coins in the pockets of the world. Steam rises from the cut into the frozen air, a cookpot. Out around that spot in the ice there are three black wolves, sitting on their haunches, their winter coats full and their bellies fat, unlike the other wolves in the area. These wolves are fed.

Wolves are only recently back out here, after years of ranchers and strychnine, and years more of rumor. Wolves speak in howls, and when one is killed the rest know it and walk at night, grieving past the bodies on the fences, past the tufts of fur caught to the barbed wire. Now there are twelve wolves running over this mountain, living on deermeat and rabbit. They eat hot-blooded things, and an occasional bone, brought to them in payment. In the place where the reactor was, there's heat and smoke, but the ice hides it.

THE MOTORCYCLE THE Hunter's riding is gleaming black with white trim, a blue blanket stuffed in the gear bag. The monkey clings to her shoulder, its own little helmet buckled tight. There are rotting snowdrifts in the road, and fallen trees, and sometimes a dead animal starved and picked clean. A recently done deer looks reproachfully out from the roadside, flies hatching in her nostrils. The Hunter rides along this highway with its silver stripe down the center, her bag jingling as she goes.

When she gets to the pawnshop, it's full dark, and there are no lights to say this is a palace. The spot sings out with heat, though, and she has no trouble finding it. It's loud as a wedding in the woods, if it's what you're looking for. She dismounts and takes the monkey in with her, steps over the rubble and rank, the pool of blood, and finds Yoth Begail on the floor.

The monkey hops down, stands on the man's forehead, and peers into his mouth. It knocks on Yoth Begail's chest and his heart resumes beating, like an engine that's got too cold.

"You're not dead," the Hunter tells Yoth Begail. "You just think you are. Where'd it go?"

"Who?" asks Yoth, bleary.

"The one who came out of the bullet," the Hunter says. "I see you got shot. Did you shoot yourself, or did someone shoot you?"

"A kid shot me, and took the rifle when he went," says Yoth.

"Did he make a wish?"

"I don't know," says Yoth. "Boy was a strange customer, and I was well and truly dead. I regret I didn't see him coming."

She goes. The bike growls, and leaves tracks like a man running barefoot, like a horse galloping in gypsum, and then the tracks are gone again, white hollows in an evening world.

Yoth turns his head to look at the vision beside him, a tall man in the string tie. All the gemstones that were in the case are on the man's fingers, and all the music in the shop is played by his hands, and if he is not quite visible, if he lives in the crack between night and day, it's no huge matter. The shop is as fine a place for shadows as anywhere.

Yoth's wish was a switching of places, his dead beloved for the living djinn. He was left with a lover made of smoke.

"I thought I was over with," Yoth Begail says.

"I thought so too," says the man who was Weran Root. "But you're not, and I'm not, and here we are, in the dark, without the devils."

"The rifle's with the Kid," says Yoth.

"If I were still a praying man and not this, I might pray," says Weran Root. "He's going to shoot till he's done. That's his notion. It was written all over him. But *we* have a wish too. I planned for this. We don't let boys bring down the universe."

"We?" says Yoth Begail.

Weran Root opens his hand and reveals a bullet, the creature it contains still singing from inside it.

"I took this one years ago," says Weran Root, with the peaceful Missouri certainty he's always had, from long before he was a djinn. Weran Root never worried, even when love took him over and remade him. When he was changed from flesh into smoke, the love continued, blazing through Yoth Begail's lonely life, making the entirety of it bright. Yoth looks at his husband, and feels his own heart beating. He takes the Priest's hand in his own.

"The legends lie. Wish granters are not only makers of palaces full of beautiful girls, and of forests in the desert," Weran Root says. "Wish granters sometimes reverse things."

*   *   *

THIS IS THE beginning of this story.

Backward in time, a thousand years. Here's a girl in the desert, enslaved to a sultan. She wanders in and out of the shadows of a roomful of oil lamps, stepping on a stool to reach the highest ones and bringing them all down at once for polishing.

She knows what they are. She knows what she is and is not supposed to do with these lamps. She doesn't care.

She sets everything free at once. Why should they not be free? Why should *she* not? She frees herself from the job of story. She's been the girl who tells tales nightly, the girl who memorizes the histories of every star and whispers them into the ears of the sultan in hopes of keeping herself from death. She frees herself from the job of guiding men through the dark.

Forward in time eight hundred years, that same girl, now a woman, walks the woods of this part of America. She runs into a trapper, wearing a blue blanket stolen from his last wife's people. He's drunk, and he's been traveling alone too long. He's a man in a pile of pelts, bear and wolf, beaver and mink, all the heat of their fur divorced from their blood, and she has no use for him.

"I need a woman," he shouts at her across the snow. "My woman died."

"I don't need a man," she says, and keeps walking.

Deep snow and snowshoes, leaving tracks like she's two flat-tailed beavers walking side by side.

"You need *me*," he insists, but she keeps walking.

He runs up behind her and grabs her by the hair, pulling the braid away from her skull, tearing the roots, and she feels her own blood sizzle on her cold skin.

That's all he gets from her. Her heart is a copper lamp, and inside it is black smoke.

She made a wish a long time ago, and it was granted. She walks in safety.

THE HUNTER'S EYELIDS are marked with the trees from a smoke tower, the place she sees if she looks over the woods and watches how they turn to words written on white snow slates. Everything is written somewhere, and all the languages of the world are here, in the bird tracks and the wolves dragging bloodied rabbits.

She should have buried her captives when she needed to sleep, not pawned them, though the old rules said the pawn should have kept them safe. She should've left them alone in the metal house in the woods, far from anyone, but last place like that, she found empty. A thousand years of searching for the wishes she set free, and now she only wants to find the last of them. They don't stay caged in copper.

She wonders. Maybe the things she hunts, if she left them to their own devices, perhaps they'd carry the old to their beds and the dying to their graves. She's been hunting too long to tell if the world is worse without wishes than with them. She's seen some wishes made, though. She feels guilt for her part in history, and so she hunts the djinn, trying to bring them back into captivity.

The Hunter rides past the site where the expedition ate itself. There they were, their hands full of blood, their mouths full of bone. She rides past the reactor she didn't keep from melting down. It wasn't her fault. She was sleeping, and she didn't know what was living inside it.

She's behind a truck now, on the highway, her motorcycle whining, the monkey's paws twisted in her hair. Rifle rack on the back of the cab, and the Kid's driving on the wrong side of the road.

She can hear the radio, the Kid playing loud to drown out the noise as he heads toward the high school floodlights in the middle of the field, the peeled paint coming off trucks like onion skin, the smell of metallic sweat, sleep and chemistry labs, the smell of the reactor's effects continuing into the future, each generation on fire, brightness continuing through them, turning the children into something other than children. Now she knows that wishers are everywhere.

The Kid turns in at the high school. As he does, he looks to the thing in the back of the pickup truck, and makes a wish.

* * *

THERE ARE REACTIONS and reactors and spills in the river, there are trees growing up out of white dust, and children born dazzled, with hearts full of black smoke. There are wishes inhaled in first breaths and exhaled in final ones.

THE KID HAS barred the door of the high school with an axe handle, and no one knows it yet. He is walking into the cafeteria, his denim making the rustle of rough animals brushing against one another in a pasture.

But outside the cafeteria, Weran Root, a priest made of wishes, cracks open the casing of the bullet, releases the djinn inside, and makes a wish, calling a reaction from the reactor.

In the woods, there's light around trees, and heat steaming from the earth. There are three black wolves, and with a howl and a leap they fling themselves into the sky and become birds. Out of the reactor emerges a djinn, hidden in this place for a hundred and fifty years.

The Kid is walking toward the girls. They're seated in a row of shining ponytails and for a moment he thinks he's walking toward a stable, and then—

Girls on their backs, girls on horseback, girls in horsehair. Old stories from an old expedition. Stories he's told himself about happiness, all of them failures, all of them involving being lost without a guide, wandering helpless and hopeless, lonely forever.

I need a girl to look at me, he tells himself. That's his wish. It's a wish many have made before him, and it's never turned out well.

The cafeteria is, in an instant, full of wild horses, snorting and prancing, galloping, chestnuts and dapple grays, blues and reds. The Kid stands in the midst of all these girls who are no longer girls.

There's only one real girl left in the cafeteria, and the Kid, despairing on his mission, his legend shrinking, raises the ancient rifle, and balances it on his shoulder. He's surrounded by horseflesh, the smell of horses wearing drugstore perfume, horses with hairspray in their manes, horses stepping around him and treading on him, rearing up, neighing.

The girl has tattooed eyelids and a monkey in her arms. She looks at the Kid. He's crying. He has his finger on the trigger. The Kid is somebody's wish, somebody's son, with his hardening blood and brightening bones.

"Come over here, now," the Hunter says.

Around him the horses of the high school spin, about their own business. The Kid is constituted of despair. He aims the rifle, shaking, at her.

A cloud coheres, standing between the Hunter and the Kid.

The Hunter looks at the smoke, her old companion.

"There you are," she says. "I heard you melted something down. Heard you made some things."

This djinn, the first to emerge a thousand years ago, has been lonely a while.

I heard my son was up to bad wishing, says the smoke.

The Kid looks around, bewildered as the smoke wishes him backward in time, sends him back to his childhood, to his mother, to the mosaics in the yard made of bones.

He flickers for a moment, in his denim and misery, and then he's gone.

The room is full of stampeding horses and then the room is full of stampeding daughters, and then the room is full of the children of this part of the mountains, all of them made of magic, all of them the drift that comes of wishes falling from the sky like snow.

"Come with me," says the Hunter to the smoke. "At the end of every story, there's another story. I've been looking for you a long time. This is the story after the hunt."

The smoke regards her.

There's a world inside every wish. There are miles inside every lamp. There are places in these mountains where everything may dwell at once, guarded by wolves.

The two of them, old lovers, old stories, a Scheherazade and her secret, leave only a scrap of paper, a ticket exchanging one thing for another, and a little monkey that springs up and drops a handful of copper casings on the ground as it departs for the forest.

YOTH BEGAIL IS driving out of the woods, and beside him, covered in a cloak to keep him in shadow, is Weran Root. Yoth's eighty-six years old and recently dead. Death doesn't bother him. He's smoking a Cuban cigar brought out from someone's humidor, a pawnshop perk.

"Remember when I was the Priest?" says Weran Root. "Remember when I held the word in my hands and tried to put it around your finger?"

"Yep," says Yoth Begail. "I remember." He passes Weran Root a brooch made of blood and bone, and the old man made of smoke causes it to appear and disappear in his fingertips.

"What did you wish for?" Yoth Begail asks Weran Root.

"No one tells their wishes," says Weran Root. "Those are the rules of this kind of story."

They are two old men in love, freed of their obligations, in possession of every ticket for everything left in their keeping. They are driving out of the mountains, and toward the sea.

THE KID IS wished into another story, a hundred and fifty years before the beginning of this one. Now he's a newborn baby found in these woods, the forest bending to look down at him. He's the child of a dead woman, and his father is a freetrapper, but none of this is his pain.

Someone who will love him picks him up. She carries him away from the ice and into the green mountains, holds him beside a fire, sings him a song that tells a story about spring. Now he's raised with love instead of fury.

The wishes in this story are wishes built the way wishes are always built, and the way bullets are built too, to keep going long after they've left the safety of silence. Each person is a projectile filled with sharp voice and broken volume, blasts of maybe.

The hands outstretch, the hearts explode. The chamber is the world and all the bodies on earth press close around each bullet, holding it steady until, with a rotating spin, it flies.

Everything living is built to burn, of course. After the close, dark chamber comes the cold, bright world.

And after the world?

After the world is a cloud of smoke, and in the center of the cloud, a whispering flame.

A TALE OF ASH IN SEVEN BIRDS
Amal El-Mohtar

WE FALL AS cinders, scattered on the wind. We fall as leaves, a bruising brightness—land lightly on foreign shores, foreign ports, foreign parts. Our shapes unseamed, our mouths untongued, we swallow our burning into new bodies. We break space around our hearts, keep our memories nestled in the hollows of bones built from the outside in.

There is room left over.

The shores, ports, parts, they challenge us to battle. We are weary; we surrender. Nations are great magicians; they pull borders out of hats like knots of silk. *Here,* says the wizard-nation, *here are the terms of a truce: be small, be drab, above all be grateful, and we will let you in.*

We bow our heads, and change.

*   *   *

Sparrow

You keep your head low. You are small, but you are fast; no moment, no movement is wasted. Work, work, work, work, work: forage food, busy yourself with branches, sing in sixty languages the wizard-nation does not understand. The wizard-nation only has one language, and all its words for you are ugly.

You fan the spark in your bones, build your fire, pour it out of you into an egg. But the wizard-nation stalks your nest in cat-shape, grooms itself in studied nonchalance. It wants you small for a reason; wants to fold you into the sac of its stomach, wants to build its muscle from your meat. It chooses its moment.

So do you. As it closes its mouth around you, you hatch from your egg, larger, fiercer, sharper, darker, and croak the wizard-nation's language until it yowls away.

Crow

You suck the light into your feathers, fly fan-tailed into the sun. Your darkness makes the wizard-nation nervous. Because you speak it, the wizard-nation changes its language; it teaches itself to read ill luck in your appearance, teaches itself to despise the gloss of your wings, the sound of your voice. It hates, above all other things, when you speak to other crows: *seven*, it hisses, *for a secret*, and you are not allowed those.

The wizard-nation stalks you in eagle shape; it flies above you, keeps you in its shadow until you lose all sense of the sun. But there is water beneath you, and outwith the eagle's shadow are sparks that remind you of being born.

Angling its wings, the wizard-nation swoops in to hang you on its talons' hooks.

You breathe deep, sleek your feathers, furl your wings tight against your body, and dive.

Cormorant

THE SHORELINE IS a difficult place.

It, like you, is many things at once: a border blurred, a body ambiguous. You swim, you fly, you walk along it; you skirt its dangers, feed mostly on fish. Your diet is varied because you are always hungry. You never take more than you need.

With each dive you bite the river-bottom, carry mud in your beak, break the surface. You try, where you can, to build beaches: bit by bit, a place to rest, a place to nest, a place the wizard-nation can't drive you from.

(Cormorants: you get the job done.)

You make an island. Saplings grow on it, bind the mud together with roots. Here is a home, now, for gulls and ducks and sandpipers, creatures who are many things at once, whose languages are amphibious.

The wizard-nation is furious. It stalks you in raccoon-shape, makes meals of your eggs. You cannot nest safely; you dare not hatch chicks, though the spark of you burns, flickers, longs to spread and give heat and light. The raccoon washes its hands in the river while watching you, for the wizard-nation is nothing if not fastidious, is nothing if not next to godliness.

When you are wearied and miserable, when your neighbours have all fled the wizard-nation's teeth, you feel the raccoon's shadow smother your own. In the seconds before it tears feather from flesh, you fold yourself inward, swallow your languages, turn yourself inside out.

Swallow

YOUR TAIL SCISSORS ribbons from the sky. You remember mud and roots, build sturdy clay nests. You are dark above and bright below, and you wear your spark in iridescence. You are fierce in flight, swift and agile, and you are a knife defending your eggs, swoop and sweep unflinching into faces, strike fear into your foes. Your wings are scimitars. You will keep your children safe.

The wizard-nation stalks you in cuckoo-shape.

It mimics doughty sparrowhawks, throws its voice, sows confusion among your kind. While you fight the air, search eagles to mob, the wizard-nation slips into your nest.

Did you lay that mottled egg, you wonder? Could such a thing have come from you? But it is in your nest, and you must protect it, you must hatch it, and when you do the wizard-nation mewls for your protection and succour. *Me, it says, look at me, love me, give everything to me and I will love you back,* while it thrashes and smashes your eggs to bits.

Your heart breaks with them, and you change.

Hummingbird

YOU SPLIT YOUR tongue in two. You learn to fly backwards as well as forwards, straight up and down—you can stand on anything, even air. You have made yourself small and fast, and your eggs are tiny, your nest too small for a cuckoo to hide inside. Your mouth is a needle and a sword. You shine, still.

And the wizard-nation seems to love you, now, at last. Perhaps you have found the right balance of beauty and fierceness, size and speed? You are at home anywhere, you cannot be said to take anything from other birds, for you have learned to drink strength from flowers.

The wizard-nation stalks you in mantis-shape.

The wizard-nation is pious. The wizard-nation is holy. The wizard-nation makes a flower out of the dead bodies of ancient creatures and fills it with red sweetness for your sake.

The wizard-nation stands still, lies in wait.

When you see the flower you think, how generous. When you see the flower you think, how kind. You approach the flower to sip—hardly even out of hunger, but out of deep, genuine gratitude for this gift, this effort expended on your behalf—bend your head to the bloom.

The mantis preys. Its arms fall like scythes into the flesh of your impossibly small bright body. It stills the throbbing shimmer of your wings. It pulls you close enough to kiss.

You are so, so tired of being eaten.

You stab your beak through the wizard-nation's face, and change.

Great Horned Owl

YOU ARE AN apex predator. Nothing can hurt you now.

You have embraced silence. Your wings make no sound. Language is for prey, for what the wizard-nation hunts. You are not prey, not anymore.

Sparrows, though. Crows. Cormorants. All these will fill your belly now, and it's their own fault. All their own fault for not choosing a shape the wizard-nation cannot hurt, their own fault for being small or loud or trying to build communities of which the wizard-nation disapproves. You have learned the wizard-nation's way, and you will be able to stay, now, forever.

You are an indifferent parent. You lay eggs; some will hatch. You never look too closely at the results. Sometimes you eat them too.

The wizard-nation stalks you in fire-shape.

Small things catch at first. Dry leaves. Tall grasses. Then twigs; then bark. Animals scamper through the undergrowth and scream.

You think, but I am become like the wizard-nation. You think, what shape has it taken to hunt itself, to break itself? What shape is this that, finally, spells the wizard-nation's end?

You smell burning and remember being a spark. You smell smoke and cough and remember falling as cinders, scattered on the wind. You breathe pain.

You set yourself on fire, and change.

Phoenix

WE RISE AND our wings are flame. We rise and our food is air. We rise and we are heat, and we are light, and we are dark and we are bright, and we lick the wind with our thousand fiery tongues. We rise from the wizard-nation's wreck.

We are magnificent.

We seed the sky with embers. And still we rise, we onyx, rubies, garnets, constellate in burning jewels. *There is the Hunter, there the Bird.*

We nest in renewal.

We may fall as cinders, scattered on the wind. We may fall as leaves, a bruising brightness. Or we may not.

Death is a memory we keep in the broken space around our hearts.

There is always room left over.

THE SAND IN THE GLASS IS RIGHT
James Smythe

I am closer than I have ever been. I am, it is safe
to say, within a finger-tips grasp of the vaunted,
the desired. It is sweltering with the heat, and
I cannot quite control my own heartbeat with
the excitement, but I can tell how close the
lamp is, now. It is behind a door, and we have
dynamite. There are structural considerations,
but they are perhaps not to be worried about,
as when this is completed, of course there will
be nothing left here to see. We have spoken in
the past of chasms of humanity where the dead
were ritualised by the insecure, the untrusting
of their own humanity. Of seeing the tombs,
seeing those shrouded corpses encased in stone
so thick they were never meant to be found;
of eyepennies and the collapsed skeletons of
guard dogs, having picked apart their former
masters in desecrated tombs; those graves,

dug deep, piled with stick men; the habits of witches, still wet to the touch after all this time. I have been to all of those, yes, and reported them to you with the diligence that only family can muster and record. But, finally, here I am: the tomb of a God itself.

SAM, RUB IT, she says to me. She tells me. She says, You've seen the movies. You've seen that cartoon, with the monkey. With the talking bird, and the man with the depression. She makes a face, like, aaah, this is so sad. To remember a man like that. Makes me think of my own grandfather now: his sunken eyes, and the doctors saying, Well, in a younger man, maybe we could have done something. But, you know. *You know.* An incentive that wasn't there, perhaps, because why save something which simply cannot be saved? And this is my choice. My father's dead. He died a few years ago. Destroyed my grandfather. Destroyed me. Now there's a grave down the road, Denny Bond, lived and died. My grandfather is too frail to visit the stone.

Instead, he sits and stares at the lamp.

Ellie tells me to rub the thing myself, the lamp—not a lamp, not a lamp, more like a box, despite the hole, despite the stench of incense, of old, that comes out of the hole when you even so much as look at it. Ellie says, It's a genie, that's what his old books say. You've read them. I know I've read them, I tell her. I know, I know.

But: the stories never end well. They never go to places that you want them to go. It's like the monkey's paw, you know? You'll wish for a thing, and the jinn—genie, she interrupted me—Whatever, the jinn does something that's technically correct, but still. It'll mess with you.

You're a coward, she says. She reaches for it, and I swat her hand away. Coward, she says again. She's an actress from some movie in the 1940s, overacting. Melodramatic. She starts to cry, and I say to her, There's something wrong with this. With what's happening here. With us. She says, What's wrong is that we could have anything, we could use this, and you won't. I can smell the incense.

What is it that my grandfather's notes say? Absolute power corrupts? They say that he will be careful. That he won't rub it until he's sure.

It's not mine, I tell Ellie. It's his. I pick it up. So firmly that I can't accidentally rub it. I don't want it. It's not mine. It's his.

I carry it to him, and I take his hand—the veins on the back like pale troughs—and I push it to the side of the lamp. Go on, I say. Go on.

Two years scant seems enough time to plan for what could actually happen. I can still smell the whiff of dynamite on the box, even through the enclosure I have designed for it. Thick glass, the thickest I could find. I do not want to touch it, even though it calls to me. Have you read the myth of the siren? This is that very box. It calls to me, you see, when I am near it; and even when I am not, when I am asleep, so it wants me to come and lay hands on it. I have no concept if I should, I must admit. Would it be so bad? Would the outcome be so flawed that I could not live with myself? But I have suffered addiction before, as you know, and I have come through the other side of that; just as I will endure with the box.

The pull: there is something inside it of which I have no real concept. I will touch it, my fingers on it again—and still I remember the coldness of it, and the sense that, somehow, it was touching me back, despite what it is; etchings on some metal that I simply cannot identify—and I will move my thumb back and forth. A simple movement; a pleasure on skin, a tickle. What comes out of the hole? What will I see?

My readings assure me that this is as close to the genuine as I have ever contemplated. It is the third such jinn I have discovered; or the third such that purports to be so, the other two both, as I am sure you will remember, failures, washouts of such proportions that I nearly couldn't forgive myself, the time and money spent on obtaining them. I cannot tell, of course, until I rub the damned thing. But then there will be no retreating, and my choice will have been made. Will I be forced into making a wish, such as they are? Is there a countdown? No, I must wait until the time is correct. Until I know that I should actually touch it.

It is tempting, though. The glass is locked, bolted. Tomorrow, a man will come to seal the edges, to create a cube I cannot enter without shattering it. This is like any addiction: you lock the temptation away, put barriers between yourself and it. Force yourself to address it, before it encompasses you entirely.

MY FATHER'S ENTIRE wealth comes down to the one box, he always told us. As much as we had rooms full of gold, of treasures, of antiques; as much as my mother was able to do, to buy, anything she wanted; and as much as my father's own declining health meant he was, in his madness, able to afford the best of everything for himself, or we were, in proxy, signing for doctors and lawyers and healers from the world over. As much as all of that, still that infernal box. My child, my love. The one thing I have achieved, he said, his voice croaking sad bitter from his throat. Sad, sad bitter. A jewel-lined room, and, Protect this, with the alarms and the guards and the dogs whose balls were allowed to swell—unlike the house dogs, clipped and neutered to placid—so that they might really embody the rage he felt was necessary for protectors. Everything about the protection was temptation and greed and anger: line the room with rooftops and trim taken from 16th-century Italian churches, from 18th-century French stately manors, wring everything in velvet plush and gold-leaf, hang a Mondrian against the wall, hang a Picasso, a Perry vase, pedestal a first edition of Cervantes, of Dickens, mount the Cullinan, the Sancy, the Koh-I-Noor on pedestals. Make this place one that anybody would want to rob. And yet there, in the middle of it all, pride of place, there on the pedestal: the box that looked like nothing, that stank of old churches and dirty hands, that begged you to touch it. Ask any robber what they would covet from that room, and their answer would change once they were inside. The guards were never allowed inside, the dogs kept on leashes around the perimeter. But you could see them: pressing their faces to the doors, lusting for what lay behind them. No keys, of course. My father paid for DNA locks, for retinal scanning, for a room that only he could enter; or, that only he could open. And then he would say, Come, come. His children—the ones that in his madness, in his later years, he would disown, howling, You are not who I made! You are not what I remember!

Where is my Denny, my son?—he asked to come with him, to see it. Look, but don't touch, he said. This is precious. Do you know what made me who I am? Do you understand? How I nearly lost everything? Then, now, he sees me and he screams, because he says that I am not his child; that he never had daughters, only a son. This Denny. I do not know Denny, but my father seems to. Then he asks for his grandchildren; only my sister and I remained childless, because he was so worried about what might happen were we to invite people—men—to share in our family's fortunes; and I remind him of this, in the most bitter tone I can conjure. You, father, you sickened old man, you twisted old wizard, you made this. You wrought this. You trapped the house in chains and vines, and you taught us from home, hiring teachers, nursemaids, specialists; and you surrounded yourself with people who nodded at you, who protected you, until your own mind gave way under the weight of your own pig-headedness. His hands rise and they shake, and he says, Would that I could do it all over again! And I reply to him, That is not the way that the world works. The world works on finality. The things you have done can never be undone. The egregiousness you have committed: it is eternal.

Now, in his room—oh, the bed, the four-poster, and the history in this bed; the fact that he has writings about it, taken from the past, as if owning a bed that created a good person, or in which a good person slept, as if that plays any part in the life of a good person themselves!—he mutters, and dribbles. His doctor calls it drool, but a *baby* drools. This fool of a man, this selfish hole of humanity, he *dribbles*. It is the action of a feeble weakling. A failure. He says, Come, to me, beckons me with fingers like wisps of pale white smoke, and he asks me to come close. I can smell the box on him. I realised that they are the same smell, the exact same. Churches, pious wood.

He used to say: it is the smell of God.

What is the box? I would ask him. He wouldn't tell. I assumed, therefore: an Ark of the Covenant, a piece of the Cross, a box of Mary the whore's balms. A worth without actual worth; a worth only to those who see it as such.

Do I believe in God? he asked me. But I did not know. Not his God. Not the same God. So now, he beckons, and the stench of his age, of the box, of his beliefs and his troubles and the past he has struggled to foist upon his family—his own petard—fills my nostrils, and I think, I would that he would die.

He says, The End is near for me. He quivers. Oh! How I have been here before!

Shut up, I say. Shut up, shut up, shut up.

Take me to the jinn. To the lamp, to the box. Take me to the box.

So I wheel him. His wheelchair not the best model, not the one that the hospital tried to give him, but some chair from the Second World War, an archaic, rumbling thing of frailty and iron ache—pushes against me, but he cranes forward. Those smoke-fingers outstretched, the bone almost visible through his skin. Out of the house, across the grounds. The dogs are sleeping, and they do not wake. The guards shake themselves off. Nobody comes here. Their backs are pressed to the walls, to get as close as possible. I think: you will kill me, and him, to get to this. But I will not give you the chance. I have lived too much to let you, when I suspect—were I to believe in a God, this would be prayer—that my father is close to his own end.

The eyes are scanned, pressed open, malignancy rife in them, clouded but still his; and his DNA is approved, even as his body seems to have changed so much that it seems it should be unrecognisable. The doors part as I push him through. I spit words at him.

You abandoned us. Your vanity; your lust. Your greed, for all of this. Look at you, in your golden room, in your palace of dismal self-reflection. Look at what you have made.

The box! he yells. I push him, harder, forward; and his legs, his body, his antique chair that was used by soldiers who actually endured, they all collide with his pedestal—2nd-century Roman—and, in turn, to the ground they all fall. To dust, the plinth, the glass shatters into shards and lumps, and my father throws his hand out to what is truly important to him. The box in his grasp, he rubs his thumb against it. Gently,

gently; and I remember him, when I was a child, so young, that same thumb on my forehead, that same skin on the curls there, and him saying, This is a prize, a reward, a thing which I will never, ever forget.

These letters must gall, my love; for I know you wish you could be here, but my work is such that it would simply be irresponsible of me. I am so busy, so taken with my choices regarding the jinn, that I simply cannot afford to risk anything. The possibilities! I have done my diligence, as you know—and I thank you for your own research, the texts you have forwarded to me have been invaluable, as I'm sure you are aware!—but the words I speak to this creature must be worked, thought, considered.

A creature! To think of it as such. A creature, if indeed that is what inhabits the box. Of smoke, or flesh? A demon, so many of the texts say. I am learning to read so many languages through the work of my translators, as the myth of this *thing* exists in cultures as far branching as the Orient, as the Arabics, as the Eskimo. Variations on a theme, maybe, but still; and all are agreed that these things are tricksters. Devils, manipulators. Far from human, and yet to read about them in the more famous tales, one would think them jovial. They are imprisoned. They are vengeful. I must play their game as well as they will play mine. I must—*must*—choose my words carefully.

And still the box, behind the glass. A simple partition. I have thought about putting up a curtain, to hide it from my sight, though I suspect that the lure of it will prove too great even for that.

I will arrange when it is best for you to come and visit. Perhaps to bring the children, but even then, I worry: what if Denny were to touch the thing? What if his hands were to succumb, to find the box irresistible; to stroke it twixt his fingers, and to find ourselves the victims of his wish? We might find ourselves surrounded by sweets, or toys! Or, worse yet: we might ourselves be removed from this world, were he so inclined, and in such a mood.

MY FATHER'S ALWAYS been an asshole. Ask anybody: he's hated. Everybody knows. I never had a mother, because—apocryphal myth, sure, but there's truth in fire—he chased her off, or had her killed. That's what Denny and I decided, when we were twelve. She served a purpose. Who else would sleep with him? Who would *want* to? He says that our mother died in childbirth. Our mother. Such a lie. Everything a lie.

He looks at my hair now, at my clothes, and he says, This would never have happened. This should never have happened. This is a world that doesn't—

Shut up, I tell him. You don't know.

He says, I have seen this. I have seen this decade. We will be at war with Argentina soon, and then the country will slip, our money—

We have enough money. You've made sure of that. You're part of the problem.

He is silent. He has too much power, too many people asking him what he needs. Telling him what they'll do for him. He has a vault, and there is only one thing in there. A box, a small black box that smells like the aftermath of a bonfire. When I was young, I would set them, in the grounds. I would sneak out with Denny, and we would set fires. We would build them up from the things that father kept sacred; not in the vault, but around him. Newspapers. Key events, because he was tracing them, tracking them. And I hated him, so I burned them. Myself and Denny, holding hands even though we were too old for that, but he was my brother. Nine months between us. Took me my youth to work out that we couldn't have had the same mother. Took my dates and newspapers, and wondering why our father didn't lie to us better. We would never have known.

He made newspapers. He decided that this was the way to future: tell the present to the world. He was there, waiting. Escalating print runs, this curious prescience of the world. Knowing what would happen enough to make sure that he was there. And I remember, one day, Denny asked him how he knew, and he said, Power gives you answers.

He was fucking loopy, my father. He spent his younger years as some Indiana Jones dude, found this tomb when he was nineteen. Nineteen, straight there. First thing he did, first dig, and he found this box. No idea what it's worth, not a clue. But it's weird. Strange. You *want* to be near it, that's the shitty thing about it. You want to be close to it.

Denny wanted to be close to it. That's when bad things happen. My father wasn't the same after that.

He asks me to help him. Says he's got something he wants to do. Says that he's been regretting things, and he knows, now, finally, how to put it right.

He says, Sometimes you're on to a loser from the beginning. Sometimes—and I say this, he tells me, with the clarity of a man who has seen too much—sometimes you need to know when to quit. When to fold.

Shut the vault doors, he says. I have a Walkman, The Clash in my ears. London's Burning, it plays. He says, Lock them after me, and don't come in, whatever you hear.

What am I going to hear? I ask.

I don't know, he says. Under his breath, like I won't remember, he says, Never you mind. You won't remember.

Because I'm me. I'm drinking, and I'm smoking. And he says, Those things will rot your guts, your liver, your lungs. You'll die a vegetable.

What do you know of death? I have asked him.

I've lived it, he says. He's incoherent, babbling at times. Like it gets to him. Like he can't quite control what he's remembering.

Denny used to say he was schizophrenic. He calls me by names I've never heard.

Not Denny, though. He always got Denny's name right.

Lock the door, he says to me. I get a glimpse into the vault, as his fingers—long fingers, like twigs from some gnarled, ruined-up old tree, frazzled by the sun that tweaked its branches—wrap around the door. The door is iron. The room is dark, cold. Empty, like some safe. Just, in the middle, this box. The smell of familiar old afterburn.

The door shuts of its own accord, and I stand there. I can see a light flash as it shuts. I lean in, to lock it.

Hello, old friend, my father says. This is the last time?

I think: Are you sure you don't want to change, this time?

But I don't know where that thought comes from; and when I stop thinking it, I am pressed to the door, desperate to get inside, and Joe Strummer is singing in my ears about how we're all lost, we're all lost; and I shut my eyes.

*   *   *

You have left me, as of course you were always
going to. I cannot pretend that I will not miss
the occasional companionship you provided,
nor that I won't miss seeing Denny in those
infrequent visits that he was allowed; but he
and I will endure, by letter, if need be. You
said, in your last missive, that we should all
be together. That my pursuit of this folly—and
oh, how that dismissive word stings!—was the
thing that would ruin me.

I want you to understand: this is important.
If I should get this right, then we will have
this time again, only better. I will be assured.
I have been making notes, mental notes.
Remembering everything. Trying to assess
the chaos that can be caused by getting this
wrong, but equally weighing up the good I will
create should I get it right.

That good, of course, will benefit you; and it
will benefit our son. I am sad that he will never
know—or, at least, will not know in this life—
his father as the man I know I am, I can be, but
I will change that. In the next.

You say I talk in riddles, but I have found
the answer to the world's greatest riddle. What
do you ask for that cannot be twisted? That
cannot be a trick? That leaves you in control? I

have spent years wondering. I have my answer. And when this is done, when this is over, I will make it so.

MR BOND IS the hardest man I have ever worked for. I've tried to make it easy for him, but he doesn't make it easy on himself. Everything in his whole life has been some insane quest. I've read his journals. He was obsessed with a woman, back when he was twenty or something. This was, I don't know, fifty years ago? Some woman called Delia. He was in love with her, totally nuts about her. But you read it, and it's like he's a stalker. There's actual madness there. I wondered if it was fiction, for a while? But he picked out this woman, and he said to her—actually said to her—We're going to get married, we're going to have a son called Dennis, we're going to X and Y and Z and money and fame and wars and blah blah blah. Some stuff in there that's terrifying. So he told her this, and she wanted nothing to do with him. He was locked up, for a while. Sent him to Douglas, and this was in the '60s, so they were still, you know. Ice pick through the eye. Wiped him out. So then his books— he kept writing them—they're, like, gibberish. These bits sewn together. Don't make sense.

He asked me, a few weeks ago, in that slow, lingering way he asks things, if I would take him on holiday. Where? I asked. He told me, and I laughed. You don't have the money for that, I said to him. But he did, full credit. He had a bank account, few thousand in there. Marcus G, he said I should take it. Nobody would know. Guy's crazy in the coconut. But, you know, I think my mum would be disappointed in me. That's as good a motivation as any. And he said I'd get to go, and I'd never even left the country. Not gone anywhere. Scared of flying, but we had enough for first class. Thought it was as good a time as any to start.

So we land, and it's sand for days, sand and sun and not a beach in fucking sight. I lead him, and he says, We have to find some people to do a job. What sort of job? He wants—no fucking joke—he wants a hole blown in the side of a fucking mountain. There's a tomb in there, he says. His mouth drools. There's a tomb, and there's a box inside it. I want the box. He says, Don't worry about having money left over. I can spend it all. This is a man who I've wiped his face, I've wiped his arse. He's gone weeks where he barely says a word to me, and then now he's here, and he says all this stuff. Lucid, like. Like he's suddenly back in his own brain, where he hasn't been for years.

Come on, he says, we don't have all day.

I take his money and I find some people. They laugh when I tell them what I want to do. I say, there's something buried out there, all that, and they say, There's nothing in the desert. The old man, he insists. He's got a shopping list, as well. Expensive stuff.

Dynamite, and I've never seen a stick of it. It's like in a cartoon: like a big red candle. Costs so much, and it's hard to handle. Got to be careful, and that means he has to pay the men he's hired even more.

His money. His to waste.

We get out there. There are no markers, no idea where to go. He struggles. Says, get my notebooks, and he's had them packed, and he gives them to me. There's a bit in them, from when he was young, where he talks about how there's this place, all this jazz. Stuff about a genie. And I read them and thought he was being a kid, writing this shit down, but it's here, where he's describing is right here, right now. This place is, like, *exactly* it.

So we travel across the desert—he says it was on horses, in the notebooks, but we're in jeeps. And he leans in to me, and he says: I will pay you so much money, everything I own. I have more than you know. You just need to do one thing for me.

He tells me about a lamp. I say: like in Aladdin?

Nothing like Aladdin, he says. Nothing like it. You imbecile.

I can go home, I say.

No! No, no. He begs me. Just: wish for me to be as I was. Before this.

It isn't real, I say. The company isn't paying me enough to wipe his arse and pretend that magic is real.

You don't understand, he says to me. I have been here before. I have lived this before. Three times. I found the perfect phrase, the way he couldn't trick me. But he tricked me.

Don't—

Do not interrupt me. Please. I beg of you. This one thing, for me. I will leave everything to you, give you everything.

This isn't right, I say. I feel like I'm taking advantage.

Marcus G, he would say, Fuck it. Take advantage. Like that's his motto.

All you need to do is this: pick up the box we will find, and we will find a box, and say, Put Simon Bond back the way he was before he found you. Say that. That's it. Say that, and this will all be over. You'll be rich. I swear it.

He looks into my eyes. His body is rotting, and there's this smell to him. Somewhere between piss and fire.

I don't know, I kind of think, Whatever. This is bullshit. Might as well benefit from it. He'll do it without me.

So the men blow the hole in the rock. He tells them where. He's got notes, and it takes a few tries, but we've got enough dynamite.

Boom, and we're in. It's like a burial chamber or some shit like that. All this collapsing rock and inscriptions on the walls.

The old man says, I never came here in this life. I was always meant to find it; nobody else. And so it was never found.

There's a stink in here, of something nasty. Like the old man, weirdly. Like he's been here before, waiting this out for centuries.

There, he says. His eyes can't see for shit in the darkness. He points to something, this little black box. Pick it up, rub it. Say what I told you to say. You know what to say?

Put him—

Say my name.

Put Simon Bond back to the way he was before he found you.

The old man nods.

Go on, he says. Just rub it.

Under his breath, he says the same name, over and over. Denny, over and over.

I pick up the box, rub it. Say the thing, just like he said.

The stink is ridiculous.

I have left a will. I have told everybody what I am to do. This life was never about this life. It was about the next, and the next. I am prepared.

I remember the day that I found the jinn. The hole, in the cave. I felt like a boy adventurer, like in the stories. In my mid-twenties, and I remember telling myself, I will find this faster, next time. No sense in hesitating.

Now, my grandson leads me to him. I have

kept him safe enough, I think. Out of reach. Next time, I will build a vault.

My grandson pushes my hand to the lamp's side, and I rub it, and the jinn appears.

You're new, he says. When he speaks, the room filled with the reek of his fire. What do you want?

And I say to him, I want to live my life over again. Knowing what I know now. The perfect phrase, untrickable. Unflawed.

He nods, and it is done.

SAM, RUB IT, she says to me. She's so bossy. She says, like in the films. You've seen that Disney. With Mork. She makes a face, like, aaah, Mork is so sad. To remember a man like that. I look over at my own grandfather: his sunken eyes, and the doctors tell us, Well, in a younger man, maybe we could have done something. But they won't do anything, will they? No incentive to, not when you're that old, that broken. Everything in the family falls to me, now. Since my father died. Only person who was as ruined by it was my grandfather, and now I don't even know if he remembers. He doesn't visit the grave. No more mourning for Denny Bond.

Instead, he stares at the lamp.

I've read his notes. Found it when he was in his mid-twenties. Obsessed with it. He was lucky, I think, because nobody found it before him. If it does anything. Ellie's a nightmare, telling me to rub it myself. She acts like she's Marlene Dietrich, and I hate this. This melodramatic bullshittery.

It's not mine, I tell her. It's his. I pick it up. I don't rub it. Hold it firmly, not too firmly, but make sure my fingers don't rub it. He's been waiting his whole life to do this.

I carry it to him, and I take his hand—the veins on the back like grey trenches—and I push it to the side of the box. Go on, I say. Go on.

I watch as the thing appears. Bigger than the room. Bigger than I imagined. The smell of something awful, something I've smelled on my grandfather for years and never understood, a smell of rot and death and eternities of trickery and torment.

I can't contemplate the creature's eyes. My grandfather looks up at it, and there's a sadness there; a realisation, I think. That's the only way I can describe it.

Hello, old friend, the thing says.

The stink fills the room to choking.

I miss him. I miss the sounds that my boy made; the way he screamed. He cried a lot, which I didn't... I assumed he wanted the breast. The doctor said that it can start young. The sickness. Were he older, there might well have been help he could have found. But no remedy for an infant. He never crawled. Didn't want to. Barely walked. We tried, with the doctors. Urged him. Nanny tried, and Mama. But no avail. They said that he was wrong.

He drew me a picture, the day of... Denny, he wrote. Denny, across the top. And a picture of a boy, about his age. He was good at art. Preternaturally.

Old enough to open the window. We never assumed he would...

I will have no more children. His smell, so exact; I could not bear to smell it on another, not as long as I live.

REAP
Sami Shah

MAYBE IF KARRY had agreed to live on the base, things would be better, easier. But he doubted it. I'll go bugfuck crazy, she'd said. I'm not gonna be one of those dumb bitches who keep the house clean until their man comes home, then fucks them and goes to sleep. I need civilian friends.

So they lived in Alamogordo and she worked as a nurse, and they barely saw each other because their shifts never quite aligned.

The drive to Holloman Air Force Base took fifteen minutes, the city ending abruptly as the New Mexico desert opened around him. The light from the city was swallowed by the emptiness before the light from the airbase appeared. At night it was like driving along a thin sandbar surrounded by ocean.

Security at the airbase did their required checks, then waved Grant through. He sped past the suburban grid housing most of the base staff. He wondered if

Karry had found those civilian friends she was after. She hadn't mentioned any.

Grant parked in the lot, jogged across to the command building, changed into his flight suit, then made his way to the glorified shipping container he would sit in for the next twelve hours. He rapped on the door. Locks clicked and slid, then Chuck was letting him in.

Mornin', Chuck said, Briefing notes on your seat. Ess Ess Dee Dee.

Copy that, Grant said, saluting him.

Ernesto and Sian sat towards the far end, facing a column of screens. Ernesto was the pilot, his shift beginning same time as his. In a few seconds Grant would take Sian's place as the sensor, swapping in. Sitting behind Ernesto was Anna the Analyst, and oh, boy, did she hate being called that. Squeezed in next to her was where Chuck would sit, once he came back inside. He'd taken the opportunity afforded by Grant's arrival to step outside for a smoke. No one begrudged him the cigarette; the tobacco stink was actually a relief from the miasma of flatulence, B.O., and minty-vomit air freshener that clouded the container. The rest of the container was filled with shale formations of humming servers.

Relief on deck, Grant said, snapping off another salute for Anna the Analyst

God bless you, Sian said, pulling off her headset and standing up. She stretched her back, wincing as it cracked, and said, I left a welcome fart for you to warm up in. Hope you're grateful.

She's a real lady, said Ernesto, never taking his eyes off the monitors. He made an incremental adjustment to the joystick, and two seconds later the footage in the monitors shifted slightly.

For seven weeks they'd been surveilling a cluster of houses in a village in Pakistan's north-west region. They were keeping track of the number of inhabitants of each, and the patterns of behavior the residents exhibited when visible. They used a MQ-9 Reaper Drone, serviced and housed in an airbase a few hundred kilometers away from the village being observed, just across the Pak-Afghan border. Ernesto's job was to keep the drone aloft and out of visibility. Grant analyzed the footage being beamed back to them, studying the distant lives of heat signatures.

How're things? Grant asked, fitting the headset in place and settling in to take control of his displays.

Reap's good for another 10 hours, Ernesto said, Weather's clear too, so it's a good day for sightseeing.

Sian gave Grant a more detailed briefing. In the months since first being assigned the observation, the two of them had developed an intimate understanding of the lives of those being watched. They knew how many people lived in each household, what their routines were, and what motivated deviations from those routines.

They knew an old couple lived in House 2, the ones they'd nicknamed Grandpa Joe and Grandma Josephine. Grandpa Joe would go for a walk every evening after dinner, picking his way across rocky desert for an hour until he reached a stream a few miles away. He'd sit beside it for a few minutes staring up at the darkening sky, then walk back.

Grandpa needs his exercise, Sian had said the first time they followed his trek.

More likely, he just needs to be away from Grandma for a little while, Grant had thought. Running out the clock on his life. He'd seen his own father do the same thing. Just walk out every evening to the edge of the garden and stand there staring at the place where the grass ended and pavement began. When asked about it, the old man had said he was just clearing his head. It gets full up, y'know, he'd said. I like to let all the stuff inside evaporate, so there's space for tomorrow.

They knew that eleven children lived in House 4, each a year apart. They'd given them all names as well, and could tell them apart just by how they moved. Grant took attendance whenever they left for school in the mornings; Mickey, Mikey, Molly, Marty, Mel, Micah, Marcus, Mario, Milo, Miriam, and Ray. He hoped they'd be at school on the day he was asked to laser-light one of the houses, targeting it for a Hellfire missile.

He and Sian knew which houses would be the cause of an attack, if one was called. House 1 was where the local Taliban commander lived, with his family of two wives and four children. It was where he held meetings of the local Taliban shura every fortnight. House 3 was different; a single man lived there, young and alone. He kept to himself and didn't interact with his neighbors very much. Given that the local Taliban were notoriously paranoid, that he had not been killed on suspicion of spying meant a great deal to Anna the Analyst.

He's either under their protection, she'd said, or he's come to an arrangement of some kind. Either way, that puts him on our shitlist.

They'd named him Jeffrey, as in Dahmer, because he was a creepy loner.

Jeffrey's been gone a few hours now, Sian briefed Grant. Left after first prayer on his bike and hasn't been back since. He's on priority watch for return. Tommy the Talib is taking a sick day. He's been shitting himself since dinner yesterday. Runs to the outhouse on the hour. Surprised the heat signature off that place isn't brighter than the sun. And the eleven dwarves are due back from school in about fifteen minutes. Say hi to Mario, Milo and Miriam for me.

No love for Ray? Grant asked.

Ray's a monstrous shit who broke Miriam's bike this morning. *She* got smacked for chasing *him*.

You guys get way too emotionally involved in this shit, Chuck said, stepping back inside.

I don't, said Ernesto.

Gotta have feelings to feel, Grant said.

Sian left, and Grant focused his attention on the displays. There were six cameras on Reap, each one outputting to a different monitor. The largest screen attended whichever camera Grant cycled to as his primary. They all showed a world entirely in greys. Light-grey rocks casting dark-grey shadows on an even-grey landscape, broken up by intermittent growths of near-black foliage. The houses were all squat, pale-grey boxes, and their inhabitants appeared most of the time as grey-black forms. If he zoomed in enough he could see their individual expressions, divining moods from the shifting patterns of highlights and shade. Only when it was night there, or when the drone switched to targeting mode, did the heat signatures of each person glow phosphoric white.

How's things at home? Ernesto said in a low voice, free hand covering the mic positioned an inch above his chin.

Great, whispered back Grant, Really great.

That bad, huh, said Ernesto.

It was getting into late afternoon in Pakistan and there was little activity on the ground, the summer heat driving everyone indoors.

Grant had grown used to the slow dilation of time that drone operators experience: 12 hours spent watching blandly monochromatic lives, with all the tedium that daily life brings. He knew the toilet routines of everyone they watched, the drone had relayed hours and hours of footage of people shitting and pissing. He'd seen the parents of the eleven kids—nicknamed Daisy and David—have sex on their roof, while their large brood slept underneath. He'd felt guilty watching them, hating himself for taking their brief moment of privacy.

The kids were coming back from school, not walking back single file the way they did every day, but running. The eldest two—Mickey and Mikey—had just entered his view and it wasn't just that they were running, but *how* they were running. He switched to Camera 3, giving him a wider peripheral field. All the kids now, scrambling in a mad dash over the rocky terrain, towards home.

A year before, Grant had been sensor for a drone over Iraq. He had sighted a long procession of men crossing a ridge, carrying weapons. They had been deemed active-targets by someone higher up his chain of command, Anna the Analyst gave independent confirmation, and Grant used the drone's targeting system to aim the Hellfire missile that awoke, somewhere far away. The men had heard its impending arrival and tried to run, practically leaping with every step, but it was too fast, their reaction too late. The missile struck and a flash of white filled his screens, resolving into a mass of flames, flickering like broken pixels.

Grant remembered the way those men had run as he watched the children. It was the same panicked dash.

Something's up with your kids, Ernesto said.

There's one missing, Grant noted.

There were nine children. There should have been ten: Mickey, Mikey, Molly, Marty, Mel, Micah, Marcus, Mario, Milo, and Miriam. The youngest, Ray, was still at home. Miriam was missing. Grant scanned the landscape with his cameras, then zoomed in close enough to see the faces of all the kids as they tore towards home. They were all screaming, their mouths stretching and snapping over and over.

Their mother appeared at the door, wrapping her shawl around her head. She was elbowed out of the way by their father, just as the eldest of the kids reached the house. The neighbours were also starting to appear, drawn by the frantic activity.

What's happening? Anna the Analyst asked.

Miriam isn't back with the other kids, Grant said, and I think something's happened to her.

The kids were all clustered around their father, pointing back the way they had come. Grant, with eyes that could see farther and a vantage point that allowed a wider view, was already scanning the landscape. He had no way of alerting anyone on the ground if he did see Miriam, nor of helping her if she needed help.

Chuck was standing right behind him now. Nothing? he asked.

Nothing, sir, Grant said. A donkey grazing, trees, scrub, becoming bright spots of light as Grant cycled through to infra-red, hoping to pick up any heat signatures.

Well, shit, hope she's okay, said Ernesto.

I didn't know you cared, Chuck said. It's not exactly a great place to be a little girl anyway.

Grant scanned one last time, then returned to the primary zone. The father, David, had set off with his elder three children in tow, retracing their steps. The rest had gone back inside. The excitement had clearly been too much for Tommy the Talib's bowels to contain and he was back in his outhouse, light flaring out from under the edges of the wooden shack.

There was almost no more activity worth noting for the remainder of the shift. David and his sons were out of observable range, and Grant logged all of Tommy the Talib's entrances and exits.

Jeffrey's back, Ernesto said.

Grant focused the cameras, bringing into view a man pedaling across the desert. Jeffrey was thin and wore giant spectacles. He didn't wrap a turban around his head when he went out, like David and Tommy the Talib did. They didn't know why, nor did they know much else about him. He had always lived alone and seldom left the house. When he did leave, he went to the bazaar a few miles away, returning with just enough food for one. He barely spoke to the others and they gave him a wide berth when possible. His house was the one all the children visibly feared approaching. Cricket balls landing on his roof would signal the end of play, as no child would knock on the door to ask for its return.

He's scared. Or anxious. He's something for sure, Chuck said, leaning over Grant and pointing at Jeffrey's face.

They could read emotion through thermal imaging, had been trained to do so. When a subject was experiencing heightened stresses, the blood rushed from certain parts of the face, or filled it more. The tip of the nose was the giveaway, glowing brighter when angry, or embarrassed, dulling when frightened, or surprised. Jeffrey's face was almost as grey as the surrounding countryside.

How long was he gone? Anna asked from her perch.

Grant consulted Sian's notes. Seven hours and thirteen minutes.

She made a note of that. Grant imagined some nerd in the Pentagon would use that to extrapolate where Jeffrey had gone, and what he had done while gone.

He's been rolling around in mud, it looks like, Grant said. Then he zoomed in some more. No, that's not mud. It's got a mild heat sig. Very mild. But it's there.

Blood? asked Anna.

Could be, said Grant. I think—yeah, he's definitely wearing his clothes inside out. His top. Whatever the stain is, its not visible to the eye, but we're picking it up. So it must be inside out.

Hunh, said Ernesto.

Yeah, said Chuck.

They watched Jeffrey cycle furiously up to his home, skidding to a stop and almost falling off at his front door. He unlocked it, shoved the bike inside and dove in after it, the door slamming shut so hard Grant could almost hear it.

Well that's not fucking suspicious at all, said Chuck.

Grant felt bits of intuitive data grow connective tissue. David and the boys weren't back yet, which meant they hadn't found Miriam. Dried blood. And no one else had seen Jeffrey indict himself. No one on the ground, at least. Not Miriam's father, probably not her mother, none of her siblings, not even any of the neighbors. It was almost sunset in Pakistan, the dulled visibility was why they were on thermal imaging and had seen the mild heat from the splatter on his clothes. That meant that anyone who was indoors was praying. Tommy the Talib would usually be at the mosque at this time, but he hadn't left his home, likely afraid of soiling himself when he prostrated to Allah.

Grant switched to the side cameras, searching the periphery. In the distance, he picked up the flitting signature glows of David and his two sons coming back, defeat writ in their postures. He watched them head home, David pausing to look back out over the desert before entering.

Too dark to keep searching, Grant said. Then, You know, Reap's due for refueling in two hours. We can take a roundabout way home, see if we pick up anything?

Chuck considered this. As commanding officer on

deck, it was within his purvey to okay it, but he'd also have to explain higher up. Grant turned to look up at him.

It's Miriam, Grant said. We've watched her for months. I'd spot her in a crowd.

There's no crowd around, said Chuck. If she's out there, she's likely dead. Which means she isn't giving off any heat. And say you do find her? What then?

Grant cursed. Chuck was right. There was no way of notifying anyone on the ground in that small village in rural Pakistan—they didn't even know they were being watched.

Grant was about to concede the point, when Ernesto spoke up. What's that? he said.

Grant turned his attention back to the screens. In the distance—the direction the children went to school in, that David and the boys went searching for Miriam, that Jeffrey had come back from in panic—a single flare of brilliant white glowed, a blade of light slicing its way across the desert.

How far out is it? asked Chuck.

Grant did some quick math, About four klicks, heading towards the village. It's fast, too. Should make contact in eighteen minutes.

What is it? asked Ernesto. His main screen was filled with the same visual display you'd get in a jet HUD, his view oriented directly below the drone. He kept glancing over at Grant's screen. The light had narrowed into an ivory pillar, still moving steadily.

I can't tell. Too bright to be vehicular, even if it had a coal furnace. That much heat can only be... I—I don't know.

Chuck was leaning over him now. Close the aperture, I think I see something.

Grant typed out a string of commands, and the screen darkened, visibility dropping away. The speckled starlight given off by wildlife scurrying across the desert floor faded into uniform blackness. Even the blaze from the object dimmed, until it was little more than a low flame. At its base was a child.

It was still too far for Grant to be sure, but it seemed to be the same size as Miriam, and had the same scrawny build. At first he thought she was crawling on her hands and knees, then he realized that was an inaccurate description. She was propelling herself only with her hands, legs stretched limp behind her, slithering from side to side as she lurched forward.

It's her, said Anna the Analyst. Right?

Yes, ma'am, said Grant. It is. I'm pretty sure.

The girl was speeding towards the village.

How is she moving so fast? Chuck said.

This is fucking weird, Ernesto said.

Grant ignored them all. He was panning the cameras to keep pace with her. As they watched, the girl sped over rocks, across a narrow gulley, and moved so fast across flat ground she was almost leaping. The heat from within her was fierce, even with visibility reduced to almost nil.

As she grew closer to home, they were able to discern details; her clothes were torn, ragged patches hanging on her frame, and her legs were streaked with blood, the feet twisted almost entirely around. Grant zoomed in on her face and from next to him Ernesto said, Oh, Jesus.

It was definitely Miriam; they could all recognize her despite the distorted mouth. Her lips were pulled back in a grin so wide it should have split her cheeks. The long teeth glowed with the same interior light. Her eyes, however, were dark holes in her face.

She was almost at her front door now, gliding up the dirt path to her home. She stopped there, legs still stretched uselessly behind her. Then, as Grant and the others in the container watched, she turned her body sideways, tilted her head back, and stared straight up. At them.

Pinpricks of light flared in the hollow gashes in her face that should have been where her eyes were. White petals climbed out of each eye and unfurled across her face.

It's fire, Grant heard himself say. Oh, God, it's fire.

Is she fucking looking at us? Chuck was saying.

Then the feed from Reap cut out.

As GRANT DROVE home, he kept thinking about what had happened.

Okay, tell me again, Sian had said.

Chuck was red in the face then. Beyond red. The red was being consumed by furious white blotches.

Nothing. Fucking. Happened, he said.

Grant had tried to speak but Chuck cut him off.

Malfunction. That's all. Nothing fucking happened. We got it? Chuck said again, jaw clenching so tightly his voice was mostly hiss.

Grant ignored him. She looked up, he told Sian. She looked right at us. Then Reap went dark.

They had lost more than the cameras. Reap was on autopilot for a full five seconds. There were standard operating procedures for loss of contact with the drone. The software in her guts would fly her back to the hangar, and they would follow certain steps to notify the chain of command and attempt to reestablish contact. They had done none of those things.

Instead, for the full five seconds it took before the screens flickered back to life, all four occupants of the container remained utterly still. Even after Reap began sending data again, they took several more seconds to react. Ernesto was first, making heading adjustments, seeing them enacted, then initiating a full systems check. The others stayed focused on the house. Miriam was gone. Whether inside the house or away, they couldn't see. There was no other movement on the surface.

Anna the Analyst had spoken first. She looked up at us, she said. Then Chuck had said, It was a glitch, and,

Not possible, and, It's just an error, and, That's it, no more talking about it. Grant joined Anna the Analyst's side of the debate, and Ernesto focused on piloting quietly. It was how Sian found them an hour later.

Once Sian promised to keep him updated if anything happened and Chuck had threatened to punch him if he didn't leave, Grant left.

He drove beneath a bruising sky towards Alamogordo, the city's lights glimmering ahead.

I know what I saw, Grant said aloud. It was something he did, mostly voicing rebuttals to arguments he had already lost to Karry earlier. Chuck could pull rank and let his face turn as many colors as he wanted, they all knew the little girl had looked up. At Reap. Chuck could say she was looking at the moon, but Grant knew the moon was behind her then. She'd looked directly up.

And then her eyes had burned.

She hadn't had eyes at first, the sockets had been empty. He considered whether the heat sensitivity being as low as it was just made it appear that way, visually carving dulled areas out of her face. But he was adept at reading low-sensitivity footage. They had been empty sockets, aimed upwards. And then the cameras had shown flecks appearing in that darkness, growing into flame.

I know what I saw, Grant said to himself again.

A car appeared ahead, its headlights growing as it neared, then passed.

Yeah, kinda like that, Grant said, seeing the afterimage of the headlights dance lightly in his vision. Then he slammed on the brakes.

Miriam was in the road. Her legs were stretched behind her, body arching upwards as she rose up to stare at him. Bloodied patches of skin showed through where the uniform was tattered. The eyes were tacks of light aimed straight at him.

The car skidded to a stop, Grant struggling to keep it straight. He flicked on the high beams. A coyote stared up at him, its rear legs crushed almost into the road. It was struggling to lift itself on its forelegs, bleeding out fast.

Fuck, Grant yelled. He accelerated hard, swerving around the dying animal.

A MIGRAINE HAD begun burrowing through him by the time he reached home. Karry's Mazda was in the garage. He parked behind it and got out, looking up at the bedroom window. It was dark, which meant she was already asleep. Grant considered the risk of waking her—and the screaming that would inevitably ensue—and collapsed on the couch instead.

The phone trilled, bungeeing him out of a dreamless sleep. An hour later, Chuck was letting him in. Ernesto was in his seat already, Sian still in hers. Anna the Analyst was standing behind them and Chuck maneuvered back to her, motioning for

Grant to join them. All of their attention was on Sian's screen.

What is it? Grant asked, trying to look over Chuck's shoulder.

She's been like that for an hour, Sian said.

It was night in Pakistan, their view rendered entirely in milky white. The drone cameras were focused on three houses: Tommy the Talib's, Jeffrey's, and the one Miriam shared with her large family. There was a tree next to Tommy the Talib's house and it gave off a mild heat signature, represented in a faint green glow. But Miriam wasn't inside her house; she was perched on Jeffrey's roof, radiating heat so intense she was encased in a blot of darkness.

That's her? Grant asked.

Sian zoomed the camera in. Wisps of ink drifted off the girl, the air around her shimmering. She was crouched on all fours, torso pressed so low her knees and elbows jutted out like a mantis' limbs.

She moved, and they all inhaled simultaneously. Miriam scuttled across the roof, trailing black vapor in her wake. They watched as she reached the edge of the roof, then swung down, disappearing into a window that should have been too small for her to fit through.

Jeffrey's home, Chuck said. He hasn't left since he got back yesterday.

For half an hour nothing happened. Then Jeffrey's door swung open and Miriam emerged, walking upright. With one arm she was dragging Jeffrey's corpse, so empty of life it registered as an absence. He was torn open from crotch to throat, guts trailing like streamers behind him.

The occupants of the container in the New Mexico desert watched as a little girl in Pakistan, engulfed in white flame, dragged a body all the way to the tree between her house and the neighbors'. She climbed up the tree, pulling herself through the branches with one hand, dragging a fully-grown man's body up with the other. She draped him over the highest branch and swung back down. Then she walked back to her home, letting herself in through the front door.

What the fuck? said Ernesto.

She's a little girl, Grant said, how did she—?

Zoom there, Anna the Analyst said, leaning over Sian and tapping a corner of the screen. Sian twisted the control knob and the camera zoomed down, stopping on a window in Tommy the Talib's house. There, faintly visible behind a curtain, was the glow of a human being.

Whoever that is, they saw it all happen, Anna the Analyst said.

Sian swapped out with Grant, refusing to go home, napping on one of the seats behind them. In Pakistan, night brightened into day, their view switching from green thermals to ash grey. Grandpa Joe was the first to discover the body. He trudged to the mosque for Fajr prayers before anyone else, the journey prolonged by stiffened joints. They watched him exit his house and set off down the pathway that led directly past the corpse-laden tree. Watched as he stopped abruptly, noticing first the dangling innards, then looked up. He staggered backwards, his mouth widened in a scream. A few seconds later, Miriam's father, David, came rushing out of his house. More men from other houses followed; they got Jeffrey's body down, untangling intestines from the twisting branches. Some of them went into his house, but were soon back out, retching as they stumbled out the door. The body was carried to the local mosque, and once there, the crowd dissipated. Younger boys stayed a while longer, showing each other where and how the body had hung and daring one another to enter the house.

At one point Tommy the Talib was visited by some local tribal leaders. They drove up in a Hilux, guns slung over their shoulders. He escorted them to the tree and they had an animated discussion around it. Then Tommy the Talib pointed at Miriam's house.

It was him watching last night, said Grant. The rest remained quiet.

Four Taliban leaders walked up to the house and banged on the door. David attended it, flanked by his eldest three boys.

What'll they do? Sian said from over Grant's shoulder.

The discussion lasted several minutes. It seemed to remain civil. David stood with his arms firmly crossed in the doorway, his sons peering out from behind him.

Tommy the Talib was taking the lead, pointing past David into the house repeatedly. Whatever point he was making seemed to be breaking against David, who said almost nothing in reply. Once Tommy the Talib was done talking, David turned his back and went back inside the house, the door shutting behind him. The Taliban men walked away, climbing back onto their Hilux and leaving, Tommy the Talib with them. For the rest of the shift nothing happened.

KARRY WASN'T HOME when he got there. Grant took a shower, then padded into the kitchen, hopping into fresh clothes as he did. There was a container of Chinese leftovers in the fridge, and he popped it into the microwave and watched it rotate. It beeped completion and he pulled out the steaming food, turning towards the cutlery drawer. Framed in the entrance to the kitchen, on the other side of the kitchen counter, was Miriam.

Grant stood stock-still, staring at the little girl. She was squatting, back towards him. Under the bright kitchen light her white clothes looked blue, tangles of dirty black hair looping almost to the ground. Grant couldn't see her face, just the back of her head, bowed low.

She's holding something, he thought. She was too plainly visible and physically present to be an aberration. He tried saying her name. Wanted to say, Miriam, what've you got in your hands. Except, another part of his brain said, her name isn't Miriam, not really. You don't know her real name. Besides, nothing came out of his mouth. He spoke wordlessly, silently. And then she shifted, just a little, moving her shoulders as though struggling with whatever she held. And Grant heard a child's pained cry, from her arms. His voice came out then, a moan, choked and barely audible. And then she wasn't there, just him alone in the kitchen.

Grant ran, food spilling as the container tumbled off the edge of the counter.

SHE WAS IN my fucking house, he screamed at Chuck and Anna the Analyst.

You're fucking hallucinating, now lower your goddam voice, Chuck growled back. The three of them were standing outside the container. Sian was still on shift for a few more hours, inside with her co-pilot. A haloed moon leered from above.

You dreamed it, Anna said, touching Chuck lightly on the wrist.

Look, I know a dream—or a hallucination—when I have one, okay. I'm telling you, she was there. And she had a fucking baby with her. Where is she now?

They went into the container, the blast of air-conditioning almost unbearable without his flight suit.

What's going on, Sian asked, craning her neck to look at him.

Sian, what's Miriam's last location? Chuck asked.

She's been inside her house since the thing with Jeffrey. Hasn't come out.

Go. Home. Chuck said.

Wait, Sian said. Something's happening.

It was Tommy the Talib's wife. She was outside, without her shawl. She pulled at her hair with one hand, grabbing fistfuls and yanking. In the other, she carried her child. The head rolled from side to side, disjointed from the neck. Miriam's parents had come running outside, then retreated back under the force of whatever accusations she was hurling. Soon more villagers began gathering, surrounding them. The wife's accusations seemed to be gathering support: some of the others were gesticulating towards the house. Daisy spun and fled towards home, so suddenly it took everyone around her a moment to react. Then they grabbed her, men from neighboring houses holding on to her, others forcing David to the ground. Half a dozen men charged inside.

Chuck was saying something, Grant realized. He forced himself to look at his command officer standing next to him. Chuck was staring unblinkingly at the screen, just saying Fuck, again and again, over and over. Anna the Analyst had a hand over her mouth. Sian and Ernesto were quiet, focused on keeping the drone steady and its cameras aimed.

We have to do something, Grant said. Except he knew already there was no way to do anything at all, except watch.

The men re-emerged, with Miriam held between three of them. The others were fending off her siblings, who were throwing themselves at the attackers. Miriam was carried outside, a man on each arm, one on each leg, her small body facing down. As they brought her to the tree where she had left a disemboweled man just a day before, the Hilux carrying Tommy the Talib pulled up, a rooster tail of dust in its wake. He leapt out the back, surrounded by a few more armed men, and pushed through to the center of the crowd.

There, from high above, Grant and the others watched him snatch the dead child from his wife's hands, then start to beat her with his fists. She fell to the ground under his punches, and he dragged her by the hair back to his house, throwing her inside the door and pulling it shut after her. The other men, meanwhile, established a perimeter around Miriam, centering her alone in a crater of space, walled by the angry mob. Tommy the Talib walked back into the space, his gun raised and aimed at Miriam.

He's going to kill her, Sian said.

It's not her, Grant heard himself say. It's something else.

Miriam raised her head. Sitting on the ground, with a gun aimed at her temple, she looked straight up at the drone, at them. They saw her face framed in the camera's eye and Grant was right; it wasn't the face of a child at all, but the face of something old. There were no eyes, just those burning holes, glowing like flames inside caverns. It grinned up at them, lips pulling back to show long teeth.

Oh, fuck, Ernesto said.

What just happened? Sian screamed.

In the container, a familiar siren began to sound, one that Grant hadn't heard since the Iraq surveillance. From a base, miles away on the Afghanistan side of the border, a missile had launched, aimed at whatever their drone was watching.

Who launched it? Chuck bellowed. There was no command. Who fucking launched it?

It just went live by itself, Ernesto yelled back. The lights in the container had turned red, klaxons going off from every computer system. A missile was soaring through the skies.

ETA thirty-four seconds, Sian announced.

Who launched it? Chuck was still demanding.

Anna the Analyst was clutching a cross that she wore around her neck, praying softly.

Look, Grant said.

They watched as Tommy the Talib executed Miriam. His gun jerked, then her body did, and she fell over. The black heat that had pulsed from her all this time began to dissipate.

ETA twelve seconds, Sian announced.

Chuck opened his mouth, then closed it, then Grant saw him close his eyes.

Contact, Sian announced.

A black rose blossomed on the screen, petals growing outwards to smother everyone huddled around the dead girl. Black debris flew in every direction, dead pixels representing chunks of rock and parts of bodies. Then it dissipated, and all that was left was unrecognizable splatter on the desert floor. Grant turned and walked out. No one said anything as he did.

He stopped outside the container. On the concrete ahead lay a dead bird; a raven, its wings ragged and torn. It was only when he got closer that he saw it was a girl's dress, charred black. Grant picked it up. It was still hot. Without even realizing he was doing so, Grant pressed it to his damp cheeks. Then he looked up.

QUEEN OF SHEBA
Catherine Faris King

IT WAS CHRISTMAS Eve, 1953, and the radio was singing about snow, snow, snow.

Outside the window, Los Angeles remained cold but dry. Wishing for snow in Los Angeles was like wishing for wings and a crown—the province of kiddies too young to know better. Juanita, as she plugged in the iron and unfolded the tablecloth, did not wish. She remembered.

In her very first Christmas memory, there had been snow in the Esparza backyard… and Auntie Opal had been there, too.

She could remember the flakes falling, just as they did in the movies. And she could remember hugging Auntie Opal tight, the smell of Turkish cigarettes that always clung to her, the vertigo as Auntie picked her up and swung her round. It felt like a dream, but Juanita knew it had been real.

Auntie Opal was not really a relative, just an old

friend of the family's. She was always smiling at odd things, always knowing things she had no reason to. But then again, she did work with Daddy as a detective. Border work, whatever that was.

Auntie Opal often passed hours with Abuelita, talking in Spanish, and as far as Juanita could tell, their every other sentence started with "*¿Te acuerdas?*" Do you remember? Which was strange, because Abuelita had to be at least ten years older than Auntie. At least.

But then again, how old was Auntie Opal?

Juanita was not going to waste time wondering. She had a job to do. The iron was finally hot enough, and she smoothed down the tablecloth on the ironing board.

The tablecloth gleamed white. It was only used at the holiest times of year—baptisms, weddings, and Christmas. Tomorrow it would support Christmas dinner, but today it wore the wrinkles of a year in storage. And Juanita, for the first time, was going to iron it to perfection while the little children slept. And when it was time to go to Midnight Mass, Juanita would drink coffee with her parents so she would be awake to greet the baby Jesus. She was a young lady, now. She was twelve. And her parents trusted her.

She could barely wait for that coffee. She hoped she would be tough enough to take it black and unsweetened, just like Papa.

As Juanita hefted the iron and bent over the board, she remembered—with a stab of guilt—the battered paperback of *The Queen of Sheba* hiding behind her bed. Juanita had borrowed the book from a girlfriend at school, and she fell deeper in love with every page. Mama would have called it 'trashy', but Juanita thought it was wonderful. She opened the book and dove into a world of heat and perfume, intrigue and thieves, riddles and beauty. The book was a ticket to the world of adulthood.

She just didn't want anyone else finding it.

She pressed the iron to the tablecloth. She pressed, and smoothed it out, and moved the iron inch by inch. Just enough heat to smooth, not enough to scorch... Careful judgment, minute by minute.

There was the sound of someone coming up to the front door. Juanita, listening, heard Mama open it, and her welcome. Juanita heard Auntie Opal's serene alto voice saying hello.

Juanita would have liked to run in and hug her, but she was going to finish work on this tablecloth. She could picture them in the living room, anyway— Auntie would leave her Christmas presents for the children under the tree. Juanita's present would probably be a nice blouse. Auntie always bought Juanita nice blouses. Not that Juanita complained. It was nice to have some things to rely on.

After a few minutes, Opal entered the kitchen, led by Abuelita. Opal made to taste one of the sauces cooking on the stove, and from what Juanita could make out of their Spanish, Abuelita was scolding her, saying the sauces were perfect, and *get your spoon out of there!*

Opal laughed and said something about having been a cook in a palace kitchen, so she knew what she was talking about. And then Abuelita was laughing, too, and told Mama to pour them some coffee.

Juanita was still intent on the tablecloth. She passed the iron over a stretch of it, and—

She saw something on the weave, as clear as a film. She glimpsed a large kitchen, a fireplace big enough to hold a car; a chef chatting with a laughing spirit that sat in the fireplace, cradling a massive cauldron, in the heart of the flames. The spirit didn't seem bothered in the least.

Juanita stopped in her motion, and the glimpse disappeared. She jumped, pulling up the iron before it scorched the fabric. She looked at the tablecloth again.

What had she seen?

"*Feliz Navidad*, Juanita. What are you looking at?"

Juanita looked up. Auntie Opal was smiling down at her, from her looming six-foot height.

"Nothing, Auntie," Juanita said. "¡*Feliz Navidad*! It's good to see you."

"Just dropping in between calls. It's a very busy time of year for your father and me."

Juanita frowned, and bent to press the iron against the tablecloth. Enough heat to smooth... She said, "Auntie, what exactly is border work? The border with Mexico is hours and hours away."

"You're thinking of the wrong sort of border. Your Papa and I go after the ones that mess around at the border between humans... and fairies." She grinned.

Juanita scowled. "Be serious, Auntie. I know fairies aren't real."

Auntie shrugged. "You always seemed to like that *Arabian Nights* book I gave you."

"That's not *fairies*, that's genies and efreets. And they aren't real either."

"As you say. Are you enjoying your winter break?"

"Oh, yeah. It's fun."

"Plenty of time for reading."

Juanita nearly jumped. Auntie couldn't know about *The Queen of Sheba*... she couldn't possibly know...

She glanced up again. Auntie's grin had a trace of mischief to it. "You always love to read."

Juanita grumbled a 'yes.' Auntie changed the subject, saying, "You're old enough to stay up 'til midnight."

"Yes! Twelve, the oldest, and mature for my age, Mama says." Juanita smiled over the ironing board.

"And yesterday you were a baby..." Auntie's voice was sad, but Juanita lost patience with it.

"Why do adults always have to say that? Last year I was eleven. I wasn't a *baby*. I don't understand it!" She quieted; now Auntie would upbraid her for talking back. But after a pause, all Auntie said was, "The cookies smell good."

"I'm sorry I yelled at you, Auntie."

Juanita pressed the iron over another expanse—and she saw, again, an image that should not have been there. It was an old Spanish town—though how she was sure, Juanita could not say—and now she could hear something: church bells ringing. As the bells rang, tolling Vespers, a figure fled the city. She was made of dimming fire, losing her human shape in her flight. Juanita, confused and compassionate for the creature, wanted to watch further, to see her find safe haven. But the image faded. And the iron—

The iron had rested too long on its patch of tablecloth. With a little shriek, Juanita lifted it up, and saw a hideous scorch mark steaming away on the tablecloth.

Her hand shook as she set the iron back. Her eyes filled with tears. She pressed her mouth shut and realized that a responsible daughter should tell her mother what had happened, but she was too afraid to...

"Hey, what's that?" Auntie Opal asked. She looked at the spot, and then at Juanita. "Don't cry," she said, and then she pressed her hand to the scorch mark. Juanita was about to protest, but steam rose up around Auntie's fingers. With two brief sweeps, she wiped the mark away. The fabric gleamed like new fallen snow.

Juanita looked up at her Auntie. Auntie just met her eye, and smiled. Behind her, Abuelita called that the coffee was ready. Opal turned around to talk to

Abuelita. Juanita didn't relax. She kept looking after Auntie Opal, until Mama caught her eye, and Juanita set herself with taking up the iron again—now with more care and attention than ever. She wanted to go into the living room and listen to the adults talk, but no. She would not be sloppy again. And she would not think too hard about... whatever it was that Auntie Opal had done.

It took a long time, but the tablecloth was finally finished, every inch pressed and warm. Juanita set the iron back and permitted herself a break. She still had piles of napkins to do, but first she took the tablecloth up and carried it into the dining room with all due pride. That done, she grabbed a cookie from the rack and sat on the edge of the living room couch. The radio was playing and Papa and Abuelita were telling stories—or, they were interrupting one another in the attempt to tell the same story, according to their very different viewpoints.

Juanita smiled as she nibbled at the cookie. Mama had heard this story before, and got up for the kitchen. As she just passed the threshold, the phone rang.

Papa dropped his hands and said, "That'll be us." Sure enough, Mama called for him, and he hurried into the kitchen. Auntie nonchalantly got to her feet. Now Abuelita was talking in Spanish again. While Opal bent to talk to her, Papa re-entered. "It was the Chief," he said. "Border work."

"You stay at home, Juan, I'll take care of it."

"No, Opal, we're a team."

"I can manage one case without my partner. You ought to be home."

Was Juanita imagining it, or was Opal's face sad as she looked at him? In the light of the Christmas tree it was so hard to be sure, yet Juanita could have sworn that for a moment Auntie looked very old, and very sad...

The point was, Auntie was going to leave. And Juanita hadn't had time to really talk to her.

She looked down at the crèche, displayed proudly on the side table. The angel had been added just the night before; Juanita stared at it a moment while gears turned in her head. When she looked up again, Opal was hugging Mama goodbye.

Juanita darted into the kitchen. She seized a paper napkin and piled a handful of cookies into it. She ran out to the driveway, where Auntie Opal was getting into her car.

"Auntie!" she called. "Wait a moment!"

Auntie paused, but she was clearly in a rush. The door was open, the keys jiggling in her hand.

"Auntie," Juanita started, in a hurry, "I was remembering the Christmas just after Cisco was born. There was snow. It wasn't a dream, Auntie, it was real and you were there. And I think you were making it snow."

Auntie buried her head in her hand. "I'm in a hurry..." she mumbled.

"Auntie, are you an angel?"

The tall woman started at that. She stared at Juanita, and then she laughed. "No, I'm not an angel. What's that you've got in your hands?"

Juanita hurried around the car to meet Auntie at the door. "Some cookies. Christmas cookies."

"Honey, I'll be at your dinner table tomorrow."

"Still... Auntie, that snow..."

"I'm not an angel."

"But you're not human."

Auntie paused. She closed her eyes. "I'm not. You're old enough to know."

"Then what are you?"

"It is a long story. I will tell you tomorrow."

"That's not an answer!"

"No, it is not." She took the cookies from Juanita's hands.

"I..." Juanita wanted, very badly, to swear for a minute, but she bit the urge back. "Drive safe," she said, instead, as the car door shut.

"Thank you."

"Enjoy the cookies."

"I will."

THE INSIDE OF her own living room seemed unfamiliar to her. Papa and Mama were talking on the sofa, and Juanita did not wish to eavesdrop. She had stepped out of a novel, a fairytale. She numbly knew that she needed to finish her ironing, so she entered the kitchen. Abuelita had settled herself at the table there to mind the sauces.

She said something to Juanita. Again, Juanita did not quite understand, except that it was a question about *Tia Opal*. Automatically, Juanita replied, "*Si, Abuelita*."

It was inadequate, but Abuelita nodded and returned to her paperback. Juanita wondered, fleetingly, what the novel she was reading was about. Was it a story of perfume and riddles, following a someday queen through a desert palace?

Juanita shuddered again, and she did not know why.

She took up the cloth napkins and set them on the ironing board. Time to undo the work of a year. Time to apply heat very, very carefully. Later tonight, she would don her best dress, and drink coffee, and kneel and sing at Midnight Mass.

JUANITA FEARED FOR Auntie Opal all through Christmas morning. Twice, in *The Queen of Sheba*, a character, laden with secrets, had sworn, "I'll tell you all, when next we meet," only to meet a sudden death mere pages later, usually in dramatic fashion. Juanita worried that something dreadful must have happened to her Auntie. She tried her best to distract herself by working her hardest—preparing the divinity, reheating the sauces, deviling the eggs, and laying it all out in picturesque fashion on the tablecloth that Juanita had ironed to perfection.

When the feast was all laid out, Mama hugged Juanita around the shoulders, and said that this was a fine Christmas, and she was so proud of her young lady for helping. She had kissed Juanita's forehead, and at that minute Cisco and Marco had run into the room, screaming for attention, so—as had happened since the moment of Cisco's birth—Mama left Juanita to chase after her brothers.

So it went. Juanita sighed, and took advantage of the reprieve to sneak into her room and steal away one or two more pages of *Queen*.

When the clock chimed, she dressed quickly, did her makeup without any help from Mama, and was pulling on her shoes when she heard the doorbell ring. Juanita paused, holding her breath, then finished pulling on her shoes and darted for the living room.

Auntie Opal was standing there—always the first guest to arrive. Cisco ran up to hug her, and when Marco toddled to her, she picked him up with a laugh. She met Juanita's eye, and said, "Juanita! Merry Christmas!"

"Merry Christmas, Auntie! Thank you for the blouse."

"You're welcome."

Auntie sat down, still holding Marco on her lap. Papa chatted while he put on a record, and he thanked her again for taking on yesterday's call. Mama turned to get the appetizers, but Juanita stopped her and said she would get them. On her way to the kitchen, she paused at the fully set table. She had an idea.

She picked up a napkin and looked at it closely. She waited—she waited—but all that happened was that Mama asked her what she was looking at and Juanita put it down, blushing, and hurried to the kitchen.

When Juanita returned with the appetizers, Abuelita had arrived, and took her traditional seat, with her lace shawl around her shoulders. She was speaking to Auntie Opal, and keeping an eye for upcoming guests. Juanita positioned herself behind Abuelita, in case her grandmother should need anything. But Abuelita seemed quite content, talking with all the dignity of a queen while she held the squirming baby Rosa in a tight grip of love.

Juanita's eyes fell on Abuelita's shawl. She focused. She hoped...

Something flickered in front of her eyes. A bread box? No—it was a ship at full sail, a Renaissance kind of ship, and Juanita heard the sailors wishing each other *Feliz Navidad*...

"Juanita?" Auntie Opal's voice cut into her thoughts. "What are you looking at?"

She shuddered, and broke out of her trance. There was no iron for her to pore over here. But Auntie Opal, and her parents, were looking at her in such an odd way. Juanita jumped to her feet, made an excuse, and fled.

She found herself in the kitchen again. She leaned

against the counter and rubbed her eyes. Humiliated! Staring! Going loopy on Christmas day!

And... for what? For a few seconds of some B-movie?

She heard footsteps behind her.

"Juanita," said Auntie Opal. "You wanted to talk to me yesterday."

Juanita didn't answer. She couldn't think of what to say. Auntie cleared her throat.

"There are some things now that you are old enough to know."

The girl turned around slowly. "What are you talking about?"

Auntie beckoned with her fingers. They sat in the dining room. Juanita picked at the tablecloth. Auntie, too, took up the embroidered hem in her fingers. "You acted a bit odd ironing this yesterday."

"I..." Juanita thought of a way to hide this, but decided it was pointless. "I was seeing pictures on the cloth. Weird pictures."

"It's the second sight," Auntie said. "Your grandmother and your father have it, too."

Juanita lifted her head. "What?"

"I had hoped you could... well, no matter. Your sight will be very strong."

"But—what was I seeing? I saw—I saw a fire spirit, sitting in a kitchen, and running out of a Spanish town, and a ship under sail..."

Opal nodded. "That was me. That was my history."

"I don't understand," Juanita said.

Opal took Juanita's hand. "Look at the tablecloth," she said, "and tell me what you see."

"Why the tablecloth? It's stupid," Juanita said, turning crass to cover her confusion.

"Some people see in water. You apparently use cloth. Be glad it isn't animal entrails." Juanita turned to the cloth—an empty space between two dishes—and focused. Opal squeezed her hand gently—and suddenly, Juanita *saw*.

She saw a Mission bell tower, rising over the fields. She saw, standing in its shadow, two figures. One was an old woman who looked a bit like Abuelita. The other was the girl of fire.

"A genie," Juanita heard herself say.

"*Djinni*," Auntie Opal corrected, a thousand miles away.

The *djinni* was weary, bent, and broken, kneeling on the ground while tears like glass fell onto the sand. There was a word: "*Si, si.*" Yes, yes. No other sound, but a sense of immense responsibility and weight, falling into Juanita's consciousness as sure as a church bell's toll.

Juanita did her best to describe it. Her faltering words seemed to get the main point, because Auntie Opal was nodding.

Seeing her, sitting there so calmly, just *unflappable*… something boiled up inside of Juanita. She jerked her hand away. "What does it even matter to you?" she demanded. "What did I see?"

"You saw a turning point in my career." Opal leaned an elbow on the table. She suddenly seemed old—ancient, and exhausted. "You've studied the Missions in school, yes? Established by wise men, who sailed all the way from Spain?"

Juanita nodded.

"Those ships had their fair share of artifacts from the golden age... from when Spain spoke Arabic. I—or rather, my home—was one of them. I—the sole *djinni* on the ship, on the continent—I was there to grant wishes. And the wishes..." She sighed deeply. "I'm sure you've studied that time. Or read about it. Always reading." She coughed. "It was a cruel time. An unjust place. A wise woman found me, and she made a wish that eclipsed all the others. She wished that I would serve justice in the *pueblo*. For as long as one stone stands upon another."

"Justice?" Juanita repeated. Opal nodded.

"Wouldn't you know it, the stones are still standing. The *pueblo*..." she gestured towards the window. Los Angeles, the flat, delicate whole, flickered in Juanita's mind. "I'm still working."

Juanita's mind tried to pick this apart, starting at something she knew. "Border work," she said. "Then, yesterday, you weren't joking?"

Opal shook her head. "Borders are very tricky places. But I have an aptitude for them. And so does your father. And," she added, "so do you."

Juanita shook her head again. "I don't want it. I

want..." She rubbed at her forehead, trying to focus on what she did want. She wanted the soft, yellowing paper of *The Queen of Sheba*, she wanted the thrilling, dangerous, but ultimately just world within. That was the adulthood she wanted. This was piling up on her too fast.

"If it helps," Opal said, "you won't be alone. You have me, and your family. And there's many more of us. Lots of *djinn* work in the film industry."

"I thought you said that you were the only one!" Juanita knew how whiny she sounded, but with all of these questions, what else could she do?

"I was the only one then. Now, I am the first."

"What else? Who else?"

"The world is bound with secret knots," Opal replied. "Vampires in West Hollywood... hungry ghosts in Downtown... The list doesn't seem to end. Honey?"

Juanita hugged herself. It was too much, she was too young to deal with it. "I think I need to sit down for a while."

"Of course." Opal tugged her hand as the girl stood up. "If you want to talk, I will be here."

Juanita nodded, meeting her eyes. It was good to have some things to rely on.

She headed for her room. She could hear the other guests arriving. Her family would be kept busy—and she had a few minutes, at least, before duty clawed at her conscience again. The light was dim in the morning, but there was enough to read by. She sat on her bed and reached, her eyes closed, for *The Queen of Sheba* in its hiding spot.

Juanita found her book, and she dug it up with one hand. She curled closer into her sheets. She caressed the cover, with its picture of a woman laden with jewels and robes of many colors. The pages, having been read so much, were turning wavy and yellowed. Juanita breathed the scent—and pictured the story. The Silver Palace. The swaying caravans. The face of the heroine.

It was still there, for her, but dimmed, like a watercolor where it had once been an oil painting. Compared to a laughing spirit in a palace kitchen, and the weeping *djinni* in the shadow of the Mission...

Juanita closed her eyes, and remembered snow. Well, that was something to be sure of. A memory, not a dream. It had been a wish granted—so the snow was gentle and sweet in its chill, nothing frightening at all. And the coffee before Midnight Mass seemed to linger on her tongue—bitter but strengthening. That was something else she could be sure of.

She opened her eyes, kept one ear tuned to the noise of guests arriving, and began to read.

THE JINN HUNTER'S APPRENTICE
E. J. Swift

THE JINN HUNTER was late, and not what was expected.

Bukhari had been waiting in the arrivals lounge for over four hours with nothing but Martian coffee to combat his exhaustion. He watched the torrent of human cargo coming and going, greeting and parting. The thought of extending the *Arwa*'s stay for a single day longer gnawed away at him. Even worse was the prospect of the mission being cancelled altogether.

Of all the ports they could have been stranded, it had to be Shanghai Hóng. The place was a certified congestion zone. Connecting local flights to interplanetary, this lounge alone saw a daily footprint of fifty thousand travellers, all of whom appeared to be crushed into the same hot, noxious space as Bukhari.

He was interested in only one of them: Aamir Ridha Ajam, a venerable, respected man with a proven success rate in dealing with cases such as his.

But Ajam did not arrive. What came instead was a shabby woman on a third-class flight from the Moon. She was wearing sunglasses, and her head and neck were swathed in greyish fur, in the style of a hijab. As she drew closer, the fur uncurled and Bukhari saw the 'hijab' was alive. The woman was carrying a ring-tailed lemur.

A port official introduced them.

"Captain Bukhari, this is your… guest."

Even in the overcrowded lounge, the official managed to keep her distance—the way everyone did these days—and hurried off at once.

"What happened to Ajam?" he demanded.

The woman pushed back her sunglasses, but did not look at him directly.

"He was busy," she said at last.

"Busy?"

"Occupied."

"I'm aware of the definition," he said testily.

She dug in her pocket for a piece of dried fruit, and fed it to the lemur.

"You got me instead."

"And you are…?"

"Fahima."

She blinked across her papers. He scanned through, checking the signatories closely. The paperwork said she was Earth-born, twenty-nine years of age, apprenticed to Ajam for the last three. Her parents were unknown.

"I've not been to Mars before," she said. *I can tell*, thought Bukhari. *What kind of idiot brings sunglasses to Mars?* But he restrained himself. He was still a captain, a leader, and a servant of God. He hadn't entirely lost his dignity.

The lemur reached out and tugged at his uniform lapels. He slapped its fingers away. The woman gave him a proper look, then, a nasty one.

What a fuck-up, he thought. This voyage was meant to be the apex of the new renaissance, and here they were in the hands of an apprentice hunter and her glorified rat. Three months, his ship had been grounded. They'd missed the media slots, sponsorship from Earth was threatening to pull out, rent on the berth was spiralling and his crew—Allah deliver them—were halfway to mutiny. They refused to sleep on board. Maintenance was carried out by a skeleton party. Since the last incident, a few were refusing to do their duties altogether.

The crew now haunted the port in pairs, refusing to venture out alone. Some of them prayed, some of them drank themselves into stupors, and some of them no longer had the capacity for either.

He blinked away the papers to find the woman watching him. Her irises were different shades: one brown, the other green. There was nothing reassuring about her presence, but perhaps that went with the trade. Immersion in the world of the spirit was bound to affect your social skills in earthly matters.

"All in order?" she asked.

He nodded.

"Let's see it, then."

THE MAIN HANGAR was a vast construction, but so dense with activity that it appeared small. Tagging each other nose-to-tail, shuttle after shuttle skimmed inside, alighting like dragonflies on a pond. Announcements boomed across the hangar as engineers and robots rushed to unload cargo and refuel ships. But one part of the hangar was inert. Like a lone tree blasted by lightning, the dark, silent shell of the *Arwa* sat within an unspoken quarantine. Even the robots avoided her.

The ship should have been a source of fascination. Pride of the Basra shipyards, the two-kilometre vessel was an architectural triumph inside and out. It had been designed not only for scientific research, but to host guests when it eventually reached its destination. The *Arwa* was to become Ganymede's first permanent outpost, a fitting tribute to the Yemeni queen for whom the ship had been named.

"We have research labs on board, exploration shuttles, mining and construction robots," Bukhari explained. "The AI system is second-to-none. You have to understand, this mission has attracted some of the greatest minds in the system. It cannot be allowed to fail."

He looked pointedly at the apprentice, who made a vague noise of assent.

"The Chinese want us to go into orbit," he said. The *Arwa*'s continued presence was costing the port. Soon those costs would be passed to Bukhari's employers, and Bukhari would be in the firing line. He wiped his brow. The perspiration no longer itched, but he knew it was there, leached from his pores with every moment the *Arwa* was in sight. The ship was steadily dehydrating him. He looked to Fahima. Her skin was dry.

"Can you feel it?" he asked.

"Have you considered that one of your crew may be possessed?"

"At least one of them was."

"How many do you think there are?"

"Isn't that your job?"

She shrugged. "The more information I have…"

"At least three. Maybe four."

"And they are not benign?"

It felt like bad luck to speak of bad spirits. Bukhari chose his words carefully.

"There have been…" he hesitated. "Incidents."

"They like space."

Fahima's gaze rested on the ship, unflinching. The *Arwa* had fully engaged her attention where Bukhari had not. He hoped she was seeing through that beautiful hull, tempered like the armour of a Saharan silver ant, to the heart of the things that lurked inside. He hoped she would deliver them.

The lemur pawed at Fahima's cheek. She gave it another piece of fruit.

"Can't blame them, really," she added. "*We* colonized it. Why shouldn't they?"

The lemur spat out a seed, narrowly missing Bukhari's shoe. They had been in one another's company for less than thirty minutes and already he hated the animal.

"What happened to Ajam?" he asked again.

"He was diverted."

There was no way of checking. Ajam lived on the outskirts of the Arabian Desert, divorced from any form of digital communication. He could only be contacted in person.

"So how long will it take? The cleansing?"

"Do you think I can answer that?"

Her abrasiveness wounded him. If nothing else, he expected sympathy. He blinked across the reports.

"You'll want to read these."

"I'd like to interview some of the crew myself."

He sighed. "I can arrange appointments, though I doubt you'll get anything more out of them. It's all in there."

THE LOCAL COFFEE was an abomination, so Fahima settled for a pot of rooibos tea. She buried her nose in its steam, letting the fresh aroma clear her sinuses and her mind. Listening. Past the hubbub of the café around her, the relentless chatter of the port beyond. There. A tug of something. A thread. *Thud, thud, heavy as mud*—It had been there, as they stood surveying the ship. It—they—were still there.

Her first interviewee arrived. A stocky, muscular man with a shaven head, he could have made an imposing figure. The effect was diminished by his movements—furtive, like those of a small animal—and the alcohol on his breath. He scanned every corner of the café before easing into the seat opposite.

"Captain said you wanted to see me?"

"You're Faris Darzi, the technician?"

"Yes…"

"Fahima," she introduced herself. "You know, Faris, if a spirit chooses to appear to you, it will not do so behind your back. Would you like some tea?"

Faris shook his head, then yelped as the lemur's head popped up above the table.

"What the fuck's that?"

"A Madagascan lemur. You've never seen one?"

He glared at the animal. "I'm Mars-born. Local boy."

"Tell me about the cryopods. You were on duty that day, yes?"

"That's right."

Faris struggled to recover his composure. The faulty pod had been discovered through a routine maintenance check, the day before the *Arwa*'s scheduled departure. As usual, a monkey was placed inside one of the units, its stasis set for an hour. When Faris returned, the monkey did not revive. The pod was checked, first by other crewmembers, then by external engineers. It had not malfunctioned. The monkey was examined by the ship's veterinarian. It had not suffered a heart attack, or any other form of trauma. There was no reason the monkey should not have woken.

"It didn't make sense," said Faris. "If it hadn't been for the eyes, I would have said it was sabotage. There's plenty of people'd like to see this mission fail, I can tell you—"

"The eyes?"

"Yeah."

He tore his gaze away from the lemur. She noticed he had started to sweat.

"Its eyes were open, you see. When I started the stasis, they were closed. When I came back it was staring straight up at me, and the look on its face—I've never seen anything so evil. At first I thought it had woken prematurely. But it didn't move. I checked the life signs and it was dead."

The lemur mewed. Faris squeezed his hands tightly together. It was clear that all he wanted to do was get up and run until his limbs gave out.

"That's when I know it was a spirit," he said. "It was right there, behind the eyes. It knew I could see it. It wanted to be seen."

"And after that?"

"We checked the other pods. Three of our monkeys survived. The others—well, I suppose you'd say they were sacrificed. We checked everything. There was nothing to choose between the pods. But of course, they had to be replaced."

"Of course."

"Then the other stuff started."

"And there's no question in your mind it was a spirit?"

"Listen. I—" He glanced around, leaned in close. She could smell the sourness of alcohol. "I was never what you might call a devout man. Done my duty, but the minimum, right? Since this started, I've been in the mosque five times a day, I've prayed and prayed and prayed and I tell you, there's nothing in this world or the next that would get me back on that ship. It's cursed."

THE CRYOPOD COMPANY had recalled all machines from the same production line, although no other malfunctions had been reported; many of them were in use, their occupants drifting millions of miles away. The company directors were furious over the loss of income, but what choice did they have? It was a matter of reputation.

Whilst the crew waited, a spate of minor thefts and pranks rippled through the ship. At first it was childish in nature, almost playful. Socks and underwear were switched. Chilli powder was rubbed into bedsheets. Zero gravity activated at mealtimes.

Inevitably, the thievery escalated. Personal possessions disappeared. One copy of the Quran vanished, another was desecrated with illegible scribblings and drawings of genitalia. A cherished ring was stolen from the research team's petrologist. The ring had belonged to her father, who had died in the south Martian mines, and its value was immeasurable.

Only after a military-grade spacesuit went missing did the port police agree to take action. Local thieves were interrogated, and some incarcerated. The police advised Bukhari to increase his ship's security. But by then the murmurs could not be quelled. None of the stolen items were recovered. It was clear the jinn had taken them to their own realm.

Bukhari received word that the new pods had been dispatched. The thefts abated, a cautious departure date was agreed, and for a few days it felt like things were back to normal.

Then a junior chef was discovered screaming and delirious in his bunk. He had woken in the night to find a dark figure standing over him. Gripped with terror, he had been held in its presence, unable to move or even to cry for help, for several hours.

Sleep paralysis, said the doctor. But the condition spread like a plague. Within days, at any one time six or seven crewmembers were frozen in their bunks, rigid and petrified in the conviction that they were not alone. Someone—some*thing*—was in their cabins with them.

THE IMAM HAD the look of a woman whose serenity had been snatched from her in the night, although not without a battle. She sat erect and proud, ignoring the clamour around them and appraising Fahima openly—although what conclusions she came to, the jinn hunter could not say.

"You've been on the ship since it departed Earth?" Fahima began.

"Yes, I was present for the blessing."

Fahima offered her a cup of rooibos. The imam accepted. She had slender, delicate hands, at odds with the sternness of her expression. Every minute or so, a tremor ran through those hands. The imam ignored that too.

"And you were amongst those who suffered sleep paralysis?"

"We all did—all except one. Have you experienced it yourself?"

"No."

"Imagine you are awake, in the safety of your own bed, but there is an entity in the room with you. Sometimes it stands at the end of the bed, sometimes it sits upon your chest. Your lungs are crushed. You can barely breathe. You have never known such terror. Your rational mind knows this is the torment of malignant spirits, but you cannot bring any part of your body to move. You are, in short, at its mercy." The imam paused. "Do you mind if I smoke?"

"Be my guest."

"One does one's best not to indulge vices, but…"

"You told Bukhari the jinn were breeding."

The imam lit her cigarette. "The doctor and I were in agreement on that. It was the only explanation for so many concurrent cases of paralysis. And then there were the voices."

"Your second pilot."

"Yes. Dima." A brightness rose in the imam's eyes; she blinked it hastily away. "May her soul find peace."

THE VOICES WERE benign at first. Surprising, because Dima had never experienced auditory hallucinations, but benign. The voices commented on what the pilot was doing at any given moment, from cleaning her teeth to deep-level navigational immersion. They joined her in her prayers. They offered compliments. How marvellous, said the voices, to lead an expedition to Jupiter's fabled moons! How she would be celebrated, what feats she would achieve—why, even the great Saga Wärmedal could not compare! At mealtimes in the canteen, the second pilot gained a new lease of energy. Where she had been taciturn, she was ebullient. Her talk turned boastful, packed with accounts of past glories, but the rest of the crew forgave her because she told her tales with such verve and wit. With the unspoken weight of the cryopod situation hanging over them, everyone was in need of entertainment.

After a few weeks, a new voice insinuated itself with the others. This voice was less complimentary. It had questions, doubts. A tendency to sneer. Why was Dima, with her qualifications and experience, only second on the pilot's register? In years to come, who would remember *her* name when all the credit would be attributed to another?

Dima tried to argue. The voices weren't right, she knew that, but every time she thought about telling someone, they began to sing in the most exquisite chorus. It's not about the glory, she told them. We're all pioneers. But even to her ears, the statement sounded false. Pathetic, really. Everyone knew the name Neil Armstrong, but who remembered Michael Collins, the first man to see the dark side of the Moon? Was it enough, for only Dima to know the truth of her worth? Could she live with herself, knowing she had not fought for what she deserved?

There was a way, the voice suggested, that this oversight could be overcome.

"YOU WITNESSED THE attack."

"Myself and fifty others. It was at breakfast, and most of the crew were present. Dima was telling stories as usual—some Moon exploit or other." A tremor caused the imam to spill ash on her saucer, and she looked for a napkin, irritated. "I give every woman and man the benefit of the doubt, but by then it was difficult to know what to believe with her. Anyway, Joumana, our first pilot, asked her to clarify something, I can't remember what it was. And Dima attacked her."

"Physically?"

"Oh, yes. It was extraordinary to witness. The others were trying to pull her off, but she had gained such strength. I heard her break a man's arm like a twig."

"Was Joumana badly hurt?"

"Did you not read the reports? She required an eye transplant, and cranial reconstruction. Yes, I'd say she was badly hurt. Bukhari and I visited Dima in hospital afterwards. Sedated, obviously. Bukhari knew he had to ask her to leave, but she'd come to that conclusion herself. 'There are malign spirits on board this ship,' she told us. 'And they will not leave, so I must.'" The imam sighed. "The poor woman."

"She believed she was possessed."

"She knew she was." The imam gave Fahima a penetrating look. "Not every crewmember is a believer. I am there for those who are. Dima was one of them. She would not have harmed a soul."

"Why didn't you speak to her sooner, when the changes began to manifest?"

"I tried." Her face grew troubled. "Perhaps I could have done more. But the harder I pushed, the more she distanced herself. I prayed for her every day. In the end, the creature was too strong."

The second pilot had departed for Earth, and everyone was deeply relieved. It was a dreadful business, but better for all concerned if she were possessed elsewhere, preferably on another planet, and in a remote location where she—or rather, the spirit—could not assault anyone.

"One more question. You said there was a crew member who didn't experience sleep paralysis. Who is that?"

The imam lit a second cigarette.

"That would be Dr Samara."

FAHIMA ASKED THE café to connect her to Bukhari.

"Yes, what is it?"

"I assume your crew underwent a full psychiatric evaluation before you departed Earth?"

"Of course they did. Do you take me for a fool?"

"Just getting the facts. I've been called in before for cases of mass hallucinations that proved to be no more than that. Strange things happen in space."

"This isn't one of those cases," he said, and cut the call.

* * *

HER FINAL INTERVIEW was with a young astrophysicist on a post-doctoral placement. He refused the tea, but ordered a slice of carrot and cardamom cake, his appetite evidently unaffected by recent events.

"Tell me about Dr Samara."

Raheem nodded enthusiastically. "Incredible scientist. I'd wanted to work with her ever since I entered the field."

"And how was she? To work with?"

"Strict, I suppose. She wanted everything done just so. But very fair. She always gave me credit for my work. Not everyone does that. Some of them want all the glory for themselves."

"You spent a lot of time together."

"Yes. The others started living off-site, but all our equipment was on board, so we stayed." He paused, fork halfway to his mouth, a smear of buttercream on the mouthful of cake. "I don't know what to say. There was no warning."

Dr Samara had not displayed any signs of instability. Alone amongst the crew, she was not tormented by sleep paralysis. She continued her research as she always had, remained stoic in the face of delays (the pods had not yet arrived; the first pilot was recovering from major surgery), and quietly optimistic about the voyage ahead. When others expressed doubts or fears, Dr Samara was always ready with a bolstering quote: she spoke seven languages, and anything from the Quran to Ibn-al-Nafis to Malala Yousafzai would do.

One morning, the physicist took herself to the decontamination chamber and removed all of her clothes and her shoes. Naked, she stepped inside the chamber, where she locked the doors and activated the chemical decontaminant. It was hours later that her body was discovered. The engineer who found her could not prevent himself from vomiting on site. Such was the extent of the damage, it was not until a register of the crew had been taken that it was possible to identify the corpse.

The physicist had left a message in her cabin:

> *The life of this world is nothing*
> *but the enjoyment of deception.*

She had deleted her database of research. A virus was squirming its way through each of its backups. The impact to the scientific community would be devastating.

That was when Bukhari requested the services of Aamir Ridha Ajam.

"SHE LEFT NOTHING for you, Raheem? No note or explanation?"

"Not a word. Look, I'm not religious myself. I always look for a scientific explanation, and so does—I mean, did—Dr Samara, and she was a Muslim. But I've never known anyone who loved their work as much as she did. Even if she wanted to kill herself, she wouldn't have deleted the work."

"I understand."

Raheem scooped up the last few crumbs of cake.

"I was so excited about Ganymede," he said. "When I got the confirmation—I can't tell you how that felt."

"Well, the *Arwa*'s mission is only postponed."

"Kind of down to you, isn't it? Isn't that why you're here?"

She sensed the curiosity behind his words. The young researcher would love to analyse her, to extract a scientific explanation for her work. She smiled, deflecting his interest.

"I suppose it is."

"I'll still go," he said. "With or without jinn—if that's really what this is. Ganymede is worth the risk. But not many of us would say that."

FAHIMA STOOD IN the shadow of the ship's hull, the lemur's tail wrapped around her throat. She thought of the long journey to Ganymede, the ship a mere speck hurtling through the vault of space. The arrival. How would it feel to look upon an untouched moon? To hold its landscapes in your gaze, and know that its secrets were yours?

The lemur was agitated, mewing continuously as they approached the boarding ramp. She reached up to stroke his head, and ran her hand along the animal's spine.

"I know, I know."

She felt his fur separate into ridges against her palm.

"I can hear it too," she said.

ON BOARD, THE sensation of both presence and absence was stronger. Without its crew, the ship was a network of veins drained of blood. It contained the most advanced technology in the solar system, but it felt like an antique.

Fahima made her way to the bridge and stood where she imagined the pilots might, looking out towards their destination. A shuttle blinked overhead. Fahima watched as it moved away from the port, growing steadily smaller until it vanished.

It was widely acknowledged that Mars was infested with jinn. Allah might have made the red planet specifically for them; they loved its dust, its volcanic landscape and boundless plains. Earth had become too crowded. What was left of the rolling sands, the desert caves that cooled with the lowering sun? The jinn have been squeezed out, she thought. Chased from one world to the next by an insatiable human race; little wonder that they, too, have turned their gaze to Ganymede.

Or perhaps they have been here all along. Perhaps this territory rightfully belongs to them, and can only be taken through war. Perhaps they have ambitions to reach beyond this system, to inhabit other, more isolated planets, places that could never be conquered by the physical realm.

Humans misunderstood jinn; they regarded them as childish and chaotic because the consequences of their actions could be childish and chaotic. In reality, the jinn had a design to their work. The choice of this ship was intentional.

Fahima remembered the swirl of desert sand, the lustrous music of the wind as it sang through her hair. She remembered Aamir Ridha Ajam, and the words she had whispered in his ear. Then she banished the thought of him altogether.

HOW EASY TO *slip through the seams, unnoticed, and if you are noticed, to quickly revert. Easy to hide when you are slim as smoke. As fast as light. As slippery as— aaaah. There goes one of the earthbound. Thud, thud, heavy as mud. Heavy, even when they creep. We are no weight upon the earth. We dash and dart, we flip and fly! We are the voice in your head, the holes in the wiring. We are the unseen, the invisible, the invincible.*

FAHIMA LET THE lemur clamber from her shoulder and down her leg. He crouched on the floor, orange eyes alert, striped tail flicking back and forth.

"Go," she said.

The lemur ran. She closed her eyes and entered his.

Through the lemur she saw the obsolete cryopods, disconnected and sealed shut prior to replacement. She saw the crew's lockers, emptied of possessions, and the rows of spacesuits, with one conspicuous gap. She saw the bunks inside the cabins, sheets tucked in at the corners as though they had never been used, never been slept upon. She saw the prayer room where the imam had kneeled and faced east. She saw the office where Bukhari had paced, day and night, night and day. She saw the decontamination chamber. She felt the shiver that raised the lemur's fur, could feel the terrible death that had happened there. Was the physicist's soul trapped on board, or had she journeyed on?

She saw the lemur freeze, and his ears went back.

SLIP, SLIDE, SNICK, *snack, here we are in the dark and back. Oh, she's watching. Yes, she's watching. Why has she come, my dears? Why can't she leave us* alone? *Why won't she? It's so* selfish. *This is such a nice cave.*

WHEN THE LEMUR returned, Fahima sat on the floor of the bridge, her legs lotused, her hands resting palm-up in surrender. She shut her eyes and let her breath flow freely. Some minutes passed before she felt it; a gathering of the air, a tightness in her lungs as though the oxygen content of the room had suddenly dropped. Fear gripped her. They were here. Left to their devices, they had grown, gained in strength. They had tasted autonomy, and found it to their liking.

She forced herself to absorb the fear, to ride the wings of her terror. If they sensed weakness, they would defy her. She felt herself unfolding, reaching out into the corners of the room, and beyond its walls, expanding along corridors, through doors and shutters and hatches and into berths where the traces of dreams still lingered upon pillows. Now she occupied the ship in its entirety.

Come, she said. *Come, my children.*

They began to move.

She knew them, every one.

She had come back for them.

Something distracted her. A niggling, small but insistent, and close, very close indeed. She opened her eyes. Flash of shadow, quick as light. A mouse shot out across the floor and froze. She felt pressure against her shoulder—the kick of hind paws—saw a blur of black and white. The lemur had pinned it.

She extended her hand.

"Bring it here."

The lemur was reluctant to part with his prize. The primates were not hunters, but he had taken on something of her nature. She held the mouse between cupped hands, feeling the vibrations of its tiny body against her palms.

"Yes," she said. "You will do."

THE JINN HUNTER exited the ship carrying a small plastic box. Bukhari could see something quivering inside.

"Are you done?" he asked.

She lifted the box.

"Yes. I got what I needed."

She had used a mouse, she said. Trapped the jinn inside its body. Bukhari didn't want to examine the mouse closely, in case it looked at him like that diabolical monkey in the cryopod. He transferred the agreed sum and bid her a hasty farewell.

As soon as the jinn hunter had departed, the ship felt lighter. He touched his fingers to his forehead. They came away dry. They're gone, he thought. He boarded the ship and made his way tentatively to the bridge. For the first time in months, it felt empty. A sob ran through him; he collapsed to the floor. They were gone. They were finally gone. He lay there for a moment, allowing himself to enjoy the sensation of peace. To be completely still. Then he prostrated himself, and said his thanks to God.

After a while he sat up. They were gone. He would find his crew in the local mosque or one of the portside bars. At last they could return to the ship, restore their belongings, and set a departure date for Ganymede.

* * *

As BUKHARI MADE his way back through the port, he spotted one of his junior officers weaving towards him, accompanied by an elderly man in a white thoub.

"Sir! I was looking for you everywhere. Allow me to introduce Aamir Ridha Ajam. He's just come off the Earth flight."

Ajam smiled and bowed. "Peace be upon you."

In his confusion, Bukhari failed to return the greeting.

"But your apprentice has already left, she's cleansed the ship—"

The old man peered at him curiously.

"You must be mistaken, Captain. I have no apprentices. I work alone, I always have."

"Then who...?"

There was an itchiness at Bukhari's scalp. He raised his fingers. They came back wet.

He felt his chest constrict. Ignoring the protests of his officer, he began to push through the crowds, searching for the unmistakable figure of the young woman and her lemur. But the flight from Earth was disembarking. The port was at its busiest, full of people rushing to greet one another, chattering excitedly after months or years of separation, and the jinn hunter's apprentice was nowhere in sight.

MESSAGE IN A BOTTLE
K. J. Parker

ONCE UPON A time, there lived a scholar in the city of Perimadeia. Opinions are divided on this man. Some say he was the most evil man who ever lived. Others maintain that he was a saint, a visionary and the father of modern science. There's an abundance of sound evidence and convincing arguments on both sides. I've been studying his work all my adult life, and I have to say I'm undecided. I'm almost inclined to add that it doesn't really matter, to me; I study the work, not the man, and the work is brilliant. The truth, after all, is neither good nor bad; like a billet of steel or a length of wood, it's raw material. And Antigono Scaevola had a gift for nosing out the truth, no doubt about that. They say he kept a demon in a bottle, who told him everything he wanted to know, but that's just ignorance and superstition. Would it were that easy.

*   *   *

THE GOLDEN SCALES monastery is not my favourite institute of learning. They collect manuscripts, preserve priceless documents that would otherwise have been lost centuries ago, and what do they do with them? They lock them up, not allowing anyone to see them—because, they say, these papers contain dangerous learning, facts and data inherently pernicious; 'guilty wisdom' is the term they use, bless them. Their argument seems to be that some information—some manifestations of the truth—is so negatively charged that it can't be allowed out. They can't bring themselves to kill it, by tearing, burning or composting, so they lock it up in prison, indefinitely, in solitary confinement. This is their mission, and they're fanatical about it. And one of their prisoners is Scaevola's *Concerning the Plague.*

The Abbot led me down six flights of narrow, winding stairs—I'm not good with stairs, I get vertigo, and there wasn't even a handrail. There wouldn't be; the stairs and passages in the Golden Scales were built to be defended, in case someone came along with an army, to steal the weapons-grade learning by force. At the foot of the stairs was a long, narrow gallery, with iron gates every five yards; at each gate, a fully-armoured porter with a crossbow. Directly overhead was the River Auno; if an attacking army got beyond a certain point, the plug would be pulled and four miles of underground passages would be flooded in a minute. The books, of course, are up four flights from the end of the passages, so they'd escape the deluge. That's Golden Scales thinking for you. You can see why I'm not keen.

Scaevola was in a cell on his own, with an iron door an inch thick. The guards are lay brethren, traditionally No Vei, fearless, incorruptible and certified illiterate. They have orders to shoot on sight anybody who appears before their outer gate who isn't accompanied by a senior member of Chapter.

From all this you don't need to be Saloninus to figure out which side the Golden Scales is on in the Scaevola debate. Personally, if I have an opinion, I incline marginally towards the opposite view. I wasn't about to say so in this company, however.

WHEN YOU ACTUALLY get in there, the Scaevola archive is disappointingly small. It consists of one book—the autograph manuscript of *Concerning the Plague*, the only copy in existence—and a bottle.

The book is interesting. Scaevola didn't write on a parchment roll, like you or I would do. No, he had a proper codex book made up and bound, its pages pumiced smooth and blank, for him to write on. Clearly he was confident that he wouldn't have to make many corrections or alterations. By the same token, he was confident that his work would merit preservation, and would be consulted regularly. His handwriting is classic Archaic cursive miniature, supremely elegant, beautifully clear and neat, with wide margins, the words precisely and amply spaced, every letter the same height. He did his own illumination; only the capitals, in an austere but attractive abstract style, using reds, blues and the very occasional blush of gold leaf. When you look at a page of his work as an object, an artefact, it conveys a sense of great calm, detachment, a beautiful mind, an almost inhuman timelessness. You'd expect a god to write like that, causing the words to appear on the parchment without the involvement of pen or brush. Let it be written, he commanded; and it was so.

The bottle, by contrast, was just a bottle. Three inches high, cylindrical, of dark green glass, stoppered with a circular glass plug and sealed with pine-pitch. My father used to dig up bottles like that all the time, when he was a gardener at the Conservatory. In terms of style and fabric it was exactly right for Scaevola; two hundred years old, unmistakably Mezentine. They made millions of bottles like that, and sold them right across the world, sometimes empty, more usually containing perfume, arrow-poison or fermented fish sauce. The glass is so opaque that you can't see what's inside, but there's a little scrap of a label, glued on with rabbit-fur gum. It reads *For the Plague*.

I'D BEEN GREETED at the water-gate by the Abbot himself. He was a big, burly man with a neck like an ox, massive broad hands (like my father's); hard to imagine those fingers turning pages or cradling a pen. He had a high, sharp voice and exquisite vowels. I don't think he approved of me. It was raining, and his hair was plastered to his head.

"Under normal circumstances—" It was the fifth or sixth time he'd said that. "Under normal circumstances, we would never entertain such an application, not even with lives at risk. There have been outbreaks of plague before; undoubtedly there will be again. That is not our fault."

We were walking across a quadrangle so fast that I had to trot to keep up. I knew I was expected to say something at this point, but I had no idea what. So I said, "Absolutely."

"An explicit request from the Chancellor, however—" He shrugged, without slowing down. "And I grant you, the situation is exceptionally grave, unprecedented. Accordingly, I felt I had no alternative but to put my own reservations to one side and agree to this—" He frowned, unable to come up with a category that my visit fell into, or a word to describe it. "You may have full access, subject to supervision. I trust that will be acceptable."

He made me feel as though I'd got his daughter pregnant and then asked the size of the dowry. "Thank you," I said. Let the record show, by the way, that nobody had thanked *me* for anything, at any point in the proceedings; none of my superiors at the

Studium, nobody in the civil government, certainly none of the Golden Scales mob. I, of course, was the poor sod who was going to save the City. Or wipe out the human race. One or the other, anyhow.

A LITTLE CONTEXT. There are, of course, two main varieties of plague; the Red Death, which kills one in five, spreads at roughly walking pace, and burns itself out within a month; and the White Death, which travels faster than a greyhound can run, kills one in three, and can last for over a year. The outbreak reported in the City was almost certainly the Red Death; the milder form, but still no laughing matter in a city crowded to bursting with refugees and liable to be besieged at any moment. Quite apart from the humanitarian considerations, a twenty per cent mortality rate would reduce the garrison to the point where the City couldn't be effectively defended. Without the City, the source of nearly a third of its revenue, the Council simply couldn't afford to continue the war.

Hence the urgency.

Opinions, you see, are divided. Some authorities, reputable and credible, believe that Scaevola found a cure for the Red Death, but died before it could be tested during a major outbreak. The opposite view—the most-evil-man-that-ever-lived tendency—maintain that Scaevola studied the Red Death all his life with a view, not to curing it, but to improving it; and that the fruit of his labours was the White Death, which occurred for the first time in the same year that he died. A subsection of that party goes further and asserts that the White Death was merely a prototype, and that Scaevola died, ironically of his own plague, after he had perfected but before he released the final version. My job was to examine the evidence and decide—before the outbreak took hold, and before the Duke's army reached the City—whether the famous bottle stored in the vaults of the Golden Scales and helpfully labelled *For the Plague* contained the cure or the hundred-per-cent effective Mark II.

No pressure.

ANTIGONO SCAEVOLA: BORN in an obscure village in Aelia, uncertain when; took his vows at the White Bone monastery (at that time a lowly provincial priory) in the year that Gaiseric died; moved from the White Bone to the Arrowhead at some unknown point in his career; recorded as precentor of the Arrowhead in AUC 667, though the reference may just possibly be to his cousin, Antipholo Scaevola, also a monk in the same order; died at some point after AUC 682, probably. All his life he studied the plague, drawing on the extensive medical library of the Arrowhead and his own field work among the peasants of the Hugin valley during the devastating outbreaks of the 'sixties and 'seventies. Along the way, he invented what we now call the 'scientific method'—hypothesis, enquiry, experiment, proof, review; laid the foundations of modern medical alchemy; identified the seat of the choleric and sanguine humours; from his notes are drawn the cures for such now-extinct monsters as marsh fever and Aelian dropsy, though he lacked either the time or the inclination to bring the cures to usable form himself. There are hundreds of thousands of people alive today who'd be dead if it wasn't for Scaevola, and large parts of Moesia and Blemmya would be uninhabitable.

His own writings fall into two parts. The scientific works—*Origins of Diseases, Investigations* and *Concerning the Plague*—are sober, scientific and impersonal; bare records of facts and data, accounts of experiments, cautious drawing of guarded conclusions. His other writings, the *Melancholia,* are in a rather different vein, ranging from biting satires on worldly manners, institutions and conventions to what you can really only call passionate love-songs to Truth, Purity and what he chose to call the Quintessence. I have to say, the satirical bits are much more entertaining than the soppy stuff, which is mostly unreadable or unintelligible; though you have to bear in mind that he lived during the heyday of the Mannerists, and tastes change. Suffice it to say, you wouldn't read the *Melancholia* for pleasure, though some of the invectives against lust and debauchery enjoy a certain popularity with first-year Philosophy students. He's not a comfortable personality to spend time with, as I know all too well. The conclusion you come away with is that he doesn't think much of the human race as it stands. What's less certain is whether he believes it can be fixed by medicine—physical or spiritual—or whether it'd be better in the long run to throw it away and get a new one.

So THERE I was, in a cell (both meanings of the word apply), as close as I'd ever got to my lifelong companion, Antigono Scaevola; my only other companion a water-clock, to remind me that time was very much of the essence. The decision was mine; to uncork the bottle, or not. Nobody was sufficiently qualified to help or advise me. All the tools and materials that might possibly inform my decision were in front of me on the table, or in the notebook I'd brought with me, or in my head. For a man whose most momentous decision up till them had been which shoes to wear to Chapter, it was all a bit much.

CONCERNING ME. LIKE Scaevola (probably) I'm a poor man's son. My father was a gardener, and before their marriage my mother worked in the hospitality industry; quite probably, the first time they met, money changed hands. I got my place at the Silver

Lily because of my singing voice, which broke six months later, but by then I'd impressed my teachers enough to secure a scholarship to the Studium, which is where I've been ever since. I haven't seen my family for thirty years, I don't know if they're even still alive, and to be honest, I'm not all that bothered. As I see it, I'm a moderately successful and useful collaboration between the Studium and myself. Most of all, I am by nature, upbringing and inclination a person of very little importance. As for the greater world outside the monastery walls, I bear it no ill-will, but what did it ever do for me?

"I'VE READ THE manuscript," I told them.

They were watching me, like dogs watch their cruel master, ready for the first signs of a kick, ready to outsnatch the others if a reward gets thrown their way. "Well?"

I took a moment to pull myself together. I can't explain clearly when I'm shaking. Can't breathe properly. "There's no doubt in my mind," I said, "that Scaevola found a cure for the Red Death. He deduced—quite brilliantly, I might add—that it's miasmic in origin, being engendered by decay and corruption and spread through the air in the manner of pollen or spores. He stated that he tested this hypothesis by brewing an antidote, which he dispersed in the same fashion as the disease itself propagates. He left detailed notes and case studies. There was a minor outbreak of Red Death in the Cunossa district in AUC 670—I can verify that, from my own researches. It was remarkably short-lived, and abated with an abnormally low death rate. I now know that Scaevola cured that outbreak. He found a cure, and it worked."

Short pause, to let all that sink in. They were so quiet, you could hear the mice behind the wainscot. "So the bottle—"

I held up my hand. "Nowhere in the manuscript is there a formula for the cure," I said. "Either he didn't record it, or he wrote it down somewhere else, and it's lost. Now it's entirely possible that the bottle contains a dose of the cure. If so, all we have to do is uncork it downwind within ten miles of the City, and the City will be saved. The label says, *For the Plague.* There is, of course, no reference to the bottle we have in the manuscript."

The Abbot looked as though he'd been holding his breath for a long time. "Go on," he said. "I take it there's more."

"More data?" I shook my head. "No. The rest of the manuscript is a sequence of alchemical experiments and calculations. It's unfinished. My guess is, he died before he was able to complete the project, or write it up. The only way to ascertain the meaning of all that would be to replicate the experiments, step by step; my guess is, that would take between nine months and a year, before we could actually venture an educated guess as to what the procedure was actually designed to achieve. Whatever it was, it occupied the entirety of Scaevola's thoughts and energies, from 670, when he came up with the cure, until his death, when it was probably unfinished." I paused for breath, and went on, "Whatever it was, clearly Scaevola reckoned it was more important than curing the Red Death, which I think, though I can't be sure, he regarded as just one step along a greater way. In other words, the cure was a by-product, not the end in itself."

Someone I didn't know interrupted. "I know you can't say for certain, but you can guess. What do you think he was really after?"

I took a deep breath. "I can't decide," I said. "There are two possibilities, and the evidence for both is equally strong. Either he was on the track of an elixir of life—believing, falsely, as we now know, but didn't then, that decay and entropy are miasmic rather than endemic, and can be cured like any other disease—"

"Or?"

"Or he was trying to breed a perfected form of the plague; one that couldn't be cured."

Dead silence; then a lot of angry shouting. What was said doesn't reflect well on the Order or scholarship in general, so I won't bother with it. After a while they calmed down a bit, and someone asked me, "So what are you going to do?"

"On the basis of what I know? I can't possibly make that decision. I need more data."

The Abbot scowled at me. "Where from? There's no-one left to ask."

The moment I hadn't been looking forward to. "Actually," I said.

NECROMANCY IS FROWNED on, to put it mildly, in our profession. We teach our students that it's impossible, explaining why, with irreproachably convincing arguments—it's magic; magic doesn't exist, it's just silly superstition; we're scientists, not wizards.

That's not strictly true. But only about six of us at any one time have the necessary qualifications, licenses and faculties to do it, and there has to be a resolution of the Grand Chapter, with a four-fifths majority, before the actual procedure can be carried out. Convening a Grand Chapter takes between six weeks and three months, depending on the time of the year and the state of the roads; quite apart from anything else, it costs a fortune in heralds' fees, travel and accommodation expenses, the cost of having five hundred copies of the required documentation copied and illuminated, hire of the chapter-house at the White Cross (because we haven't got a functions space big enough at the Studium); it's a lot of fuss and bother and expense in order to do something that nobody wants to do and which is never necessary or justifiable.

And quite right, too. It's a singularly repulsive idea,

and nobody in his right mind would want anything to do with it. And that's assuming it is actually possible—which may not be the case at all. There are no known instances of a raising being scientifically recorded and written up in a book. It's one of those things we don't talk about.

It's typical of my luck that I happen to be one of the six. I studied—oh, for crying out loud, the M word—not because I'm remotely interested in all that junk, but because it's an area of metaphysics that happens to coincide with the genuine, real science that I specialise in. Accordingly, I learnt how—in theory—to summon spirits from the vasty deep, turn milk sour, raise tempests at sea, cure warts with kisses and (so help me) raise the dead.

In theory. I'd never actually tried it, of course. I'm a scientist, not a wizard.

THE FACE IN the mirror blinked, pulled a sad face and gazed at me. "Who the hell are you?" it said.

"Nobody you'd know," I replied. "More to the point, who are you?"

The face in the mirror was mine, of course; every familiar line and wrinkle, the soft little chins in stepped progression, like stairs. "I'm Antigono Scaevola," said my face, and a wave of panic washed over its idiotic features. "What am I doing here? What's happening? What are you doing to me?"

"It's perfectly all right," I lied.

"It *hurts*."

"It's necessary." No lie this time. "You are the ghost of Antigono Scaevola. I need to ask you some questions. The quicker you answer them, the sooner it'll be over, and you can go."

He—I—looked scared to death. "You can't do this," he said. "It's obscene."

"That's rich, coming from you."

One of the Brothers was a soldier before he left the world and took Orders. He told me, in a battle, hand-to-hand fighting, you look into the eyes of the hideous monster who's charging at you screaming and trying to kill you, and what do you invariably see? Terror. They're scared to death, just like you. "What do you want?"

I held up the bottle so it showed up in the mirror. I assumed he could see it. "This," I said.

"Oh, that."

"What does it do?"

My eyes went blank, and that fatuous stupid look that means I'm up to something covered my face. I'm a hopeless liar. "It's the cure."

"It cures the Red Death."

"Yes."

When I was a novice, the other novices loved playing cards with me. They always won. "You're lying."

"Why would I want to do that?"

"You want me to uncork the bottle."

"It's the cure."

I thought for a moment. If I was him, what would I do? What would I be thinking? "I don't think so. I think it's the perfect plague."

"No. It's the cure."

"I think," I said to myself, "that *you* think, that if I'm here and I've raised you from the dead, things must be pretty serious. There must be a bad outbreak of plague, bad enough to take this risk. If I open the bottle and it's the cure, tens of thousands will be saved. But you're the most evil man who ever lived. You only found the cure so you could make sure the improved version was incurable. If this bottle really contains the antidote, the last thing you'd want would be for me to open it. So, you say it's the cure, and the look on your face makes me think you're lying."

He stared at me, then burst out laughing. "Are you serious?"

I looked deep into my eyes, trying to see something there I could set foot on, like you do when you're up to your knees in soft mud. "Are you the most evil man that ever lived?"

"You're the expert. You tell me."

It hurts. *What* it hurts, given that the dead are insubstantial, we have no idea; but all informed authorities agree, it hurts. Time, therefore, was on my side, not his.

"I'm not a cruel man," I said. "Unlike you, I don't enjoy inflicting pain."

He grinned. "This hurts you more than it hurts me? I doubt it."

"So do I. And I can keep it up for a long time."

"Time has no meaning, where I am."

"That's fine, then." I leaned back and crossed my arms. He didn't. "Let's just relax for an hour. What's the weather like on your side?"

"What makes you think," he said, "that I'm the most evil man who ever lived?"

"You cured the Red Death and kept the cure to yourself. You invented the White Death."

"Don't be ridiculous. The White Death killed me."

I shrugged. "You're careless as well as evil."

"The White variety was a mistake," he said. "It was a side-effect of the cure. I created a vaccine—do you know what that means?"

"No."

"It's a sample of the disease, modified to cure it. Fire drives out fire, that sort of thing. But one of my early attempts to make a vaccine went wrong. Instead, I accidentally bred a more virulent strain. I tried to contain it, stoppered up in a bottle clearly marked *Do Not Touch*, but some clown of a novice opened it. I died as a result. So yes, I created the White Death. I was punished for it, though not nearly enough, I grant you. But not maliciously, believe me."

"Sorry," I said. "I don't."

"On what grounds?"

"I don't know."

I gave me a contemptuous look. "How scientific."

"A hunch," I said. "Based," I realised as I said it, "on an inconsistency. You found a cure for the Red Death, but you never wrote it down. Therefore, your motive—"

"Of course I wrote it down."

I blinked first. "You did?"

"Of course. I called it *A Cure for the Plague*. I wrote it out and filed it in the library."

Now there he had me. Tradition says that all of Scaevola's works were preserved in the Arrowhead library, but the actual index for the period in question is lost. "Did you?"

"Of course I did. It's still there. Isn't it?"

Raising the question, what happened to the index? When was it lost, exactly? I'm ashamed to admit I didn't know, though I should have found out. "No," I said. "There's no record of anything by that name written by you."

"Oh, for—" He seemed genuinely upset. By then, I was working on the assumption that he was a far better liar than me, but that was just an assumption. "In that case, isn't it lucky that I know the formula off by heart? You've got a pen and something to write on."

"Yes."

"Splendid. Now, then. Take one part sal draconis. Now it has to be absolutely pure, handle it with gloves, because the slightest trace of sweat on your hands will spoil it. Add one part—"

"Let me stop you there."

"Are you mad? This is the formula. One part sal draconis. One part aqua regia fortissima. Add the salt to the acid, not the other way around, if you value your eyesight. Add one part—" he stopped. "You're not writing."

"I have no way of knowing," I said, "what you're giving me a formula for."

"Idiot."

Fair comment. Writing it down couldn't hurt. "One part sal, yes. Go on."

I took dictation. When he'd finished, I cast an eye over what I'd got; and yes, at first glance, from what I knew about the subject, I could see, it could well be a cure for a miasmic infection. In fact, it was brilliant, inspired, pure genius. It would cure the Red Death, and with a bit of work it was a foundation for a cure for the White Death. At first glance.

He was looking at me. "Now do you believe me?"

"This formula," I said, "takes about nine months to prepare."

"Yes, about that. So what? It can't be made any faster than that. Not possible."

"I think you're rather clever. I think this is the genuine cure. I think the bottle contains the new, incurable plague. I think you gave me the cure to fool me into opening the bottle."

"Oh, for God's sake." The image in the mirror jumped to its feet, an angry, histrionic gesture. I did the same, by instinct or mere symmetrical attraction. Which one of us knocked the bottle off the table I really don't care to guess.

It fell. I watched it fall. It broke.

I'M WRITING THIS, so you can figure it for yourself. The bottle, *For the Plague*, did not contain the spores of a new, incurable epidemic. By the time I'd registered the smashing of the bottle he was gone, and I was too exhausted and traumatised to get him back.

On a sheet of paper on the table was the formula, a cure for the Red Death. Probably genuine, certainly useless, since by the time it was ready, the whole City would be dead. I had released what was presumably the antidote to the Red Death, but too far from the City for it to do any good. Wasted. Ah, well.

Needless to say, I didn't dare go back. I made my excuses to the Abbot, some rigmarole about having to look something up in a library somewhere, and rode as fast as I could in the opposite direction. I crossed the Vesani border just before nightfall. You don't want to come in here, the border guard told me, there's plague in Cortis Maior. I'm afraid I laughed at him.

IF I WAS the most evil man in the world, and possibly I was for a while, this is what I'd do. I'd brew a bottle of the cure, leave it in plain sight, properly labelled. I'd use it to cure an outbreak. I'd then publish the formula for the incurable strain, the one that starts off *take one part sal draconis,* and say that was the formula for the cure. Simultaneous release, everywhere. That's what I'd do. I think.

The plague, Red and White varieties, continues to rage through the civilised nations of the Middle Sea. I heard the other day that it's spread as far as the savages, the Arinholet and the No Vei; clouds and silver linings, I guess, though maybe that's a trifle unfeeling of me. People—scholars, informed opinion—are starting to talk in terms of a level of mortality from which there can be no recovery; the end of civilisation as we know it, the end of Mankind.

Maybe I have the cure, here, in my hand. Maybe withholding it will make me the most evil man who ever lived. Maybe every word he told me was the exact truth; I have no proof whatsoever that it wasn't. I have all the ingredients laid out on the table, ready. They've been there for five years. The alchemical skill required to brew the formula is not great.

I look at myself in the mirror, and ask myself: what would you do?

BRING YOUR OWN SPOON
Saad Z. Hossain

HANU SAT BEFORE his stove, warming himself. It was cold outside, and worse, the wind scoured away the nanites, the airborne biotech that kept people safe. He had seen more than one friend catch death in the wind, caught in a pocket without protection, their lungs seared by some virus, or skin sloughed off by radiation. The thin mesh of packsheet formed a tent around him, herding together the invisible, vital cogs. Shelter was necessary on a windy night, even for those with meager resources.

He was cooking rice on the stove, in a battered pot with a mismatched lid, something made of ancient cast iron. In some retro fashion houses, this genuine pre-Dissolution Era relic would fetch a fortune, but Hanu had no access to those places, and wouldn't care either way. A pot to cook your rice in was priceless, as valuable to a roamer as the tent or the solar stove.

He measured the quarter-cup of fine-grained rice into the boiling water, added a bit of salt, a half stick of cinnamon and some cardamom. The rice would cook half way before he added onions and chilies, perhaps a touch of saffron. In a way, Hanu ate like a king, although his portions were meager. He had access to an abandoned herb garden on the roof of a derelict tower, plants growing in some weird symbiotic truce with the nanites warring in the sky, nature defying popular scientific opinion. The rice he got from an abandoned government grain silo, sacks of the stuff just lying there, because people feared contamination. Almost everyone in the city ate from food synthesizers, which converted algae and other supplements into roast chicken at the drop of a hat.

He let the rice cook until there were burnt bits sticking to the bottom of the pot. The burnt bits were tasty. The smell filled the tent like a spice bazaar, and he ate from the bowl using his wooden spoon. No one disturbed him, for which he was thankful. It was difficult to find a square inch empty in Dhaka city, but it was a windy night, the pollutant levels were on orange alert, and most people were indoors.

He was in the fringes of the river side area of Narayanganj, where the alert level was perpetually screaming red due to unspeakable life forms breeding in the water, a sort of adjacent sub-city swallowed by Dhaka a hundred years ago, a pustule avoided by even the moderately desperate homeless, one step away from being cluster-bombed into oblivion by the satellites above. Thus he was able to finish his meal in peace, and was just contemplating brewing some tea when a gust of wind knocked the tent askew, and a lumpy black dog nosed in.

Hanu sighed, and gave the dog a bit of rice. It ate directly from his hand, thumping its tail in appreciation. Hanu got out of the tent, to prevent the creature from breaking it. Where the dog roamed, its master would not be far behind.

"You're corrupting my hound," a voice said. In the shadows a slow form materialized, a man-like thing extruding a field of disturbance around it. It was the djinn Imbidor, an ancient creature recently woken from centuries of sleep, diving again into the cut and thrust of mortal life, puzzled somewhat by the rapacious change in humanity.

"He's a mongrel, Imbi," Hanu said. "Even more bastardized than you."

Imbidor frowned. "Are you sure? The one who sold it to me, that man by the sweet shop with the bird cages, he said that it was a pure breed Mirpur Mastiff."

"Mirpur Mastiff?" Hanu laughed. "Cheeky bastard. Mirpur Mastiff is a euphemism, for the most mangled blood line possible. Your hound is descended from the original street dogs that roamed Dhaka, before they started injecting turtle genes into them."

"Oh." He scowled. "Humans are always ripping me off."

"You want some rice?"

"With cardamom and saffron?"

"Of course."

The Djinn took the pot and ate the last of the rice. He had his own spoon, a silver filigreed thing which no doubt came from some kingly horde. "Thanks, Hanu. You're a good cook, I always say."

"Not much demand for cooks, these days," Hanu said shortly. His father had been a cook once, long ago, before the banking cartel had pushed all the Cardless out of the better neighborhoods into the subsidized boroughs, little better than feral slums. There had been a time when there was apparently a 'middle class' sandwiched between rich and poor.

He shook his head. His father had told a lot of fairy stories. Then he had fucked off. "Plus it's illegal to use real plants. They'd probably arrest me. Endangering the cardamom or something."

"Well, for the Fringe, then," Imbidor said. "We should have a restaurant. Something like the old days, a place for people to gather. Plenty of the Fringe would like it. Even some of the citizens."

The citizens were general populace without capital, whose main contribution to society was the biotech their bodies spewed, adding to the mass of benevolent nanites fighting the good fight in the sky, scrubbing the air, killing disease, controlling the microclimate, forming the bubble which protected Dhaka from the big bad world outside. The Fringe was a subset of the citizenry: the homeless, the drifters, the thrill-seekers, the darker edge of the maladjusted. And djinn. More and more often, djinn emerged from slumber, found a world near wrecked by hubris, found that the lonely places they favored despoiled, unlivable. Many returned to sleep right away. It was rumored that djinn did not age while they slept, that they could afford to while away centuries waiting for a better time downstream. Of course there was no guarantee such a time would come.

"I would cook and you would serve," Hanu joked. "We could call it 'Bring Your Own Spoon.'"

"And the hound would be the lookout," Imbi said, enthused.

"We already have everything. The tent, the stove, the pot."

"The mosques give away free bowls," Imbidor said. "Their food is some horrible grey sludge, but the bowls are good. I've collected a stack of them since I woke up. And we'd give *real* food. No discrimination against the Cardless either. Pay however you can."

"Why not?" Hanu said, suddenly struck by the thought. "Why can't we do it?"

"That's what I've been saying!" Imbidor shouted. "Come on Hanu! I'm so *bored*." Boredom was the reason the djinn went to sleep so often in the first place.

"Okay, I'm in. We have to find a good place to set up the kitchen. And food suppliers, well, I know a few. Benches? Clean water? We'll need a place without the cameras, if possible…" The possibilities seemed endless. Problems jostled in his mind, shifting in priority as solutions clicked into place. It felt good to think again.

"Come on, let's go," Imbidor said. "I know the perfect place."

He extended his distortion field around Hanu like a ragged cloak, keeping out the bad stuff in the air. Hanu stumbled from the slight vertigo it caused, felt that familiar tinge of nausea brought by proximity to the field, but in truth Imbi's power was tatty, weakened from some ancient conflict, his touch feather-light compared to the great djinn. Once Hanu had seen a marid with a field so powerful it was opaque, reflecting the sun, a solid fist that rammed through the crowd unheeding, had seen a man caught in its center pulped to death by unimaginable pressures.

Djinn did not officially exist, although the Fringe knew perfectly well they were there, often out in plain sight, going about their business. There were rumors that great djinn lords ruled human corporations, wielding terrible power from the shadows. Imbidor was not that kind of djinn. He had no *dignatas*, the peculiar currency the djinn traded in; he commanded no respect, had no followers, no wealth in either world. Even mighty djinnkind had the indigent.

THEY WORKED THEIR way ever deeper into Narayanganj, Hanu suppressing the atavistic fear of the bad air. The street was still lined with shanties, extruded sheets lashed together with adhesive bands, cheap stuff which could be printed out by the many blackmarket operations found in greater Dhaka. Here the people seemed sicker, farther away from the center, and their progress was tracked warily, with more than one weapon being raised, although the djinn was recognized and allowed to pass. People moved here out of desperation, for though the main boroughs of the Cardless were crowded, at least the air was good, basic supplies were provided, and there was work. Here by the river the town was semi-abandoned, and as they got closer to the water, the citizens became more furtive, many carrying deformities, the scarring of errant nanites. The big pharmas liked to experiment their new designs on high-density populations, beta-testing algorithms on live users—for good nanites, of course, never anything weaponized; that would be immoral. There were always side effects, though.

"Here we are," Imbi said, stopping.

It was a six-storey shell of a building, built in the old style with concrete and steel, the bricks, wires, windows, doors, anything electrical looted long ago. It was near the river bank, close enough that Hanu could feel the cool air stirring, and his instinctive fear of the water made him cringe.

"Smugglers," Imbi said, knocking on the door of a makeshift room.

A man with an electric sword came out and watched them without speaking. Hanu glanced at him disinterestedly. The Fringe was full of smugglers with swords.

"We want the empty room," Imbi said.

"For the night? Or do you actually intend to live here?"

"More than a night," Hanu said. "We want to try something out."

The swordsman shrugged. "The djinn crashes here sometimes. I'm okay with that. I give him electricity and he sweeps for bad bugs with the distortion thing of his."

"It's a pretty good spot," Imbi said, embarrassed by his poverty. People who lived riverside were the scum of the earth. "I can clean the air, at least enough for us few."

"You don't get sick here? No black lung? None of the skin stuff?" Hanu stared at the smuggler, trying to spot defects.

The smuggler turned his sword off. "Not so far."

"How?"

"There's a lot more people living here than you think," the man said. "The djinn cleans the air and we have a nanite replicator. It's old, but it helps. What business did you say you were in?"

"Hanu Khillick," Hanu said. "Restaurateur."

The smuggler burst out laughing. "Karka. Riverboat smuggler and pirate."

"Imbidor of Gangaridai," said Imbi. "Djinn. Professional giraffe racer. Ahem. Of course, there are no giraffes left."

"Come inside," Karka said. "Let's get you set up. I'm not going to charge you rent, as long as the Djinn helps out. Once in a while surveillance drones show up. You have to take care of those fast, or corporate security will send someone down to investigate."

Inside was a sparsely furnished space, well swept, covered with the blackmarket geegaws of the smuggler's trade, and a few solid pieces—a power generator, an ancient nanite replicator, and a squat printer with its guts out. Karka was well-set-up; no wonder he survived out here. Hanu wondered what he smuggled. Karka motioned them to sit on the futons covering the floor.

"I will be most happy to help," Imbi said.

"You guys need anything else, you're gonna have to pay. Air scrubbing for three ain't cheap. You got any money?"

Hanu shook his head.

"I am the descendent of an ancient empire, known as the first city. I have lived hundreds of years, I have looked into the void of the abyss, I have seen the dark universe of the djinn, I hold over three hundred patents currently pending litigation in the celestial courts..." Imbi said.

"So no cash, I guess?"

"Er, no."

"Any sat minutes?"

Hanu shook his head. Sat minutes were hire time from the satellites, a secure pin which activated the chip in your head for a designated time, showing you the vastly expanded VR universe the rich people inhabited. Everyone got chipped, for consumer tracking and census purposes, but very few of the Cardless ever actually got to walk the VR world. Bandwidth was jealously guarded. Sat minutes were the way, a brief glimpse into paradise, a ten-minute birthday treat for a child, a wedding gift, a de facto currency, hoarded but never consumed, a drug for the VR junkies, news, communication, vital information, everything rolled into one.

"Do I look like I have sat minutes? I'm a cook. I'll cook you food."

"I got an old vat maker," Karka said, looking at him dubiously.

"Chinese or Indian?"

"Post crash Malay."

"Everything tastes of coconut, right?"

"Haha, yea, I don't even know what coconut is. Some kind of nut?"

"There were big trees once, and these were the fruit, kind of like big balls full of liquid."

"Yeah, well, that's fucken food for me, coconut seaweed."

"I'll make you rice right now that will make you cry."

"No, thanks." Karka looked queasy. "I already ate. Look, man, don't worry. I'll help. Imbi sorted me out a couple of times with his djinnjitsu."

Hanu scrounged in his bag of provisions and brought out something he had been saving, a rare find. It was a raw mango, from a tree near the red zone which had miraculously survived all these years, and now had suddenly given fruit. No one touched them, of course, fearing some hideous mutation; even the street kids stayed away. They had all heard stories of trees bursting open to release deadly nanite spores, of the terrible Two-Head Disease, which caused a bulbous protuberance to come out of your ass, or of the Factory Germ, which slowly hardened your body into metal. Hanu's father had taught him to forage, however, as the very poorest must do, and this foraging had given him an instinct for what could or could not be eaten.

He sliced the mango with his knife, letting the slivers fall inside his pot, careful not to lose the precious juice. Then he brought out a small lemon, nursed carefully from his errant herb garden, cut it and squeezed half of it onto the fruit. Salt, pepper, turmeric, mustard seed paste and chili flakes followed, a little bit each because the flavors were intensely different from vat food, almost alien. He mixed it together by hand, till the slices were covered, glistening. Karka and Imbi had gathered around, mouths open, inhaling the smell of raw cut mango and the sharp tang of mustard, drawn to it.

"What the hell?" Karka lowered his head involuntarily, breathing in the smells.

Hanu ate a piece, showed it was safe. "It's good."

Imbi, who had largely bypassed the Dissolution Era, had no such qualms and quickly forked a third of the mango onto his palm.

"It *is* good," Karka said, unable to resist a slice. He looked entranced. "It's damn good. You *are* a cook."

"You in?"

"You seriously want to open a restaurant."

"You've got a perfect view of the river."

"You realize they call this the river of the dead?"

THE NEXT MORNING they got started, Karka joining them for a breakfast of rice, the last of Hanu's hoard. Afterwards he handed over a key for the spare room, and a handful of electronics, a solar battery, some basic furniture. He dragged out the air scrubber and put it between their doors. "I eat for free. Plus Imbi does his shit. We share the air. If it runs out, we split the costs."

"Deal."

They dispersed, Hanu going on an herb run, Imbi dispatched to spread the word and hunt for sources of raw material. It was, after all, useless to have a restaurant without any food. Hanu knew this was the biggest hurdle. He expected the dream to end soon, for where on earth would Imbi find so much real food?

Nonetheless, he set up his station on time, arranging his supplies of herbs and spices, warming up water from the ancient ion filter, even setting up a bench for the customers. If Imbi came back, they would open for lunch. By eleven o'clock, hopeful looking-people invited by Imbi were ambling around, steering away from the glaring Karka, maintaining nonchalance. Hanu studied his prospective customers, and had to conclude that they hadn't a penny to their name collectively. He might as well have started a vat kitchen, feeding the homeless, like the mosques.

"This lot couldn't buy crabs from a brothel," Karka said, sword hilt at hand. "If Imbi's not back by noon, they're going to start looting."

"The road is my home," Hanu said. "I am not afraid." *People always assume that poor people are dangerous. They wouldn't be here, if they were.*

Imbi staggered in half past noon carrying a large burlap sack. There were a solid dozen customers still loitering, despite Karka's best efforts. The three of them gathered inside the room, where the Djinn threw open his sack with obvious pride.

"What the hell is it?" Karka recoiled with disgust.

"It's a fish," Imbi said. "From the river."

It was, indeed, an enormous fish, scales glistening, gills still flapping for air. Hanu remembered his father bringing one home once. Karka had never seen one, was clearly repulsed with the whole idea of eating something from the river.

"Look, there's a dozen people outside, and we have to feed them something," Hanu said. "I know how to cook this, I remember."

"What's wrong?" Imbi asked Karka. "We used to fish from the river all the time…"

"That was two hundred years ago, Imbi," Karka said. "We don't touch that shit anymore…"

Hanu ignored them. He had a fish to scale, and he'd only ever seen it done as a child. It took rather longer than an hour to get it right, the pieces prepped, somewhat mangled, but soon thereafter the smell and sizzle of grilled fish permeated from the pre-fab, and his customers sat down and waited in an almost hypnotized state, so docile and silent that even Karka had no complaints.

WHEN HE WAS ready, he brought it out, fifteen pieces of grilled fish with crispy skin, flavored with ginger, garlic and chili, with little balls of rice. He had used up everything. They took their portions solemnly, signifying the importance of the moment, ate with their hands along the makeshift bench, with all the dignity of a state banquet. There was no hesitation, no question of what they were ingesting. It simply smelled too good. Karka ate the last piece, his resistance melted away.

"God, this is a good way to die," he said.

It started up the conversation, rounds of introductions, stumbling praise for the food, old recollections of when they had last seen food like this, of the myriad turns of their lives that had left them Cardless and desperate on the streets. Imbi sat amongst them, extending his field for them, and they marveled at the distortion, wondered aloud that such a powerful creature should be wandering the road with them. And then, by some unspoken consensus, it was time to leave, and they began to make their offerings. A knife, much handled, the last thing a man would give up; an old card for sat minutes, so old, so carefully preserved, to receive a call that never came; a silver locket with the picture taken out, a book of short stories, an ancient watch. The last lady stood up, her hands empty.

"I have nothing," she said. "But there is a place with birds… chickens. If I bring them, will you cook?"

"Yes, of course," said Hanu. He looked at the small pile of treasure, and tears leaked from his eyes.

"Hanu and Imbi," the Djinn said, sweeping his hand back towards the establishment. "We are open for business."

OPEN THEY WERE, for six months and more, feeding crowds, sometimes with feasts, sometimes with nothing but onions and rice. Their customers scavenged, bringing food from unknown places. There were unspoken rules. Everything was eaten. No one was turned away. At first, Imbi kept his field up like a tent, kept the bad air at bay, visibly exhausting himself, burning surveillance drones out of the sky. When their accrued wealth piled up, Karka could afford to charge up his replicator, spewing out the good nanites, and people stayed by the river out of faith, adding their bodies to the critical mass required to power these things, the human fuel which made their community work.

The river kept a tax. People sickened from its bounty, one died from intestinal rot, but the people who roamed here sickened and died anyways. There was no noticeable drop in custom. Imbi wandered far and wide, bartering, gossiping, marketing, and returned with useful things—water filters, glasses, proper cutlery, utensils for Hanu's kitchen. It would have been safer to move around, but they couldn't, people relied on them, the gangs left them alone, it was a safe spot, blessed by the river gods.

"Look what we've done!" Imbi said, proud. "I told you it would work."

"It can't last," Hanu said.

ONE DAY MEN from the high city swaggered down, uniformed, with their rented armored car and their mercenary badges. Private security. They didn't like activity in the orange zones, and the river was an atavistic boundary, a dread zone which company men like this avoided at all costs.

"DISPERSE! DISPERSE! RED ALERT! HAZARD! HAZARD!" the armored car was going mad with panic, its blaring voice rising in pitch as it twisted its way through debris. Karka came out with his sword behind his back, Hanu with his cleaver and a decapitated fish head. The score or so people dozing in the sun after lunch sat up blearily. The car louvered open and two men came out in full combat gear, faces hidden inside command helmets, a swarm of sparrow-sized drones buzzing in the air above them. The models were six seasons old, a tried and tested method of crowd control. The new ones were apparently mosquito-sized, and just as lethal.

"Gathering in a red zone," the company man said. "What for?"

"Easy, we're just squatting," Hanu said. "Cardless, see?"

"What is this place?" the security guard walked around, touching the benches, the bowls, the cardboard box of scavenged cutlery.

"Shelter for the poor," Hanu said, trying to cut him off from the kitchen. "Look, we're just feeding them. Hungry, homeless people, for God's sake."

The company man touched him with one gloved hand, the powered suit amplifying force, and Hanu went stumbling back, a deep bruise forming on his chest.

"Food? This is no vat kitchen. You have set up a micro-climate here. We saw it from above." The security stared into the kitchen interior, face unreadable. "Why is there a micro-climate in the red zone?"

"It's not a crime to stay here," Karka said. "What laws have we broken?"

The company men looked at each other, not answering. They were not unduly worried. In reality, laws only applied to those who could afford lawyers. The swarm shifted a bit towards Karka, the machine whine rising an octave. They had already noted his sword, deemed it next to useless in a fight.

"I don't understand what this is." The first man said, knocking down the fab sheets walling the front of the kitchen. "What is this organic matter?"

"Why it's food, friend soldier," Imbi said, beaming. Hanu suppressed a groan. "Would you like to have some? Fishhead curry, with brown rice. A princely meal! In my day policemen always ate free! Come, friends, eat a plate, rejoice in the bounty of the river!"

The man took the plate and his helmet became transparent, revealing a face inside. He stared at it, fascinated, and Hanu could almost see the neurons in his brain put together the contours of the cooked fish head with the scraps in the kitchen, with the shape of an actual fish, which he must have seen a hundred times in pictures as a child. A flood of emotions flitted across his face—curiosity, alarm, wonder. For a second Hanu dreamt that he would actually take off his helmet and try the food. Then his face turned to revulsion, and it was all over.

Imbi was standing there, beaming with good will, when the plate struck him across the face. Drones punched into him, tearing out chunks of meat, sending him tumbling back, before his distortion field finally flickered to life, cocooning him. Karka gave a samurai yell and charged, sword up in high guard. The drones were slow to react, confused by the djinn's quantum field. They finally lunged at Karka, but he ignored them, letting them have their pound of flesh, flying through that mist of his own blood and tissue, terminal grace, and his ionized blade somehow hit the command helmet in the neck join, shorting it out, sending the astonished company man down to his knees.

Abruptly, half of the drones stopped short, hovering uncertainly. The other half of the drones, unfortunately, were not so confused. They slammed into Karka with lethal force, shredding the smuggler like paper. The armored car, programmed to be cowardly, was blaring incoherent alarms, already backing away from the fracas. The second policeman hesitated, then dived into his vehicle, his drones folding neatly into a pocket somewhere.

"*YOU HAVE ALL BEEN MARKED FOR TERMINATION!SATELLITESTRIKEIMMINENT! INNOCENT BYSTANDERS ARE REQUESTED TO VACATE! VACATE! VACAAAAAATE!*"

And they were gone, leaving their fallen behind.

"I don't think I can put Karka back together," Imbi

said, tears in his eyes. He was trying to collect the pieces of their friend.

"Never mind. We have to leave. They will destroy this place," Hanu said. He looked at the dozen or so patrons still left. "We all have to leave. They've tagged our chips for death."

But they all knew nowhere was safe. Tagged for death was death in truth. It was just a matter of how long till the satellites cleared their backlog.

"Load everything into the boat!" Hanu shouted. "Everything! We have to go across the river. Into the country."

They stared at him, unconvinced.

"Look, there's fish in the river. That means there's food outside, you fools! There must be. We can survive! They won't hunt us out there." He turned to Imbi. "Imbi is djinn! Djinn! He can clean the air for us, we can gather others, make a micro-climate like we did here. They don't know he can do that."

IMBI STOOD UP straight, spread his arms out wide, dripping the blood of Karka, and his distortion field rippled out, encompassing them all. It was stronger than before, colored with rage and sorrow.

"We should leave," he said. "We should follow Hanu, who gave us food from nothing. I have slept a long time. I remember when they used to chain you to the earth and force you to work, to force your children and their children to the same labor. Now I am awake, I see they have taken your flesh too, they have herded you together like cattle, and living or dying, your bodies are little factories, cleaning the air for them. Your chips are your collars. They kill you without thought. You fear the air, the water, the trees, the very ground you walk on. What more can you lose? Why not leave this place? Let us go forth into the wilderness, where they dare not follow."

When they heard the djinn, they grew calm, and gathered their meager things. It was resignation, perhaps, or hope. Hanu freed the boat, pushing off into the river, and the poison water splashed over him, but he did not care. It was cool, and dark, and it washed away the blood.

SOMEWHERE IN AMERICA
Neil Gaiman

Reprinted, with permission, from American Gods

NEW YORK SCARES Salim, and so he clutches his sample case protectively with both hands, holding it to his chest. He is scared of black people, the way they stare at him, and he is scared of the Jews, the ones dressed all in black with hats and beards and side curls he can identify, and how many others that he cannot? He is scared of the sheer quantity of the people, all shapes and sizes of people, as they spill from their high, high, filthy buildings, onto the sidewalks; he is scared of the honking hullabaloo of the traffic, and he is even scared of the air, which smells both dirty and sweet, and nothing at all like the air of Oman.

Salim has been in New York, in America, for a week. Each day he visits two, perhaps three different offices, opens his sample case, shows them the copper trinkets, the rings and bottles and tiny flashlights, the models of the Empire State Building, the Statue of Liberty, the Eiffel Tower, gleaming in copper inside; each night he writes a fax to his brother-in-law, Fuad, at home in Muscat, telling him that he has taken no orders, or, on one happy day, that he had taken several orders (but, as Salim is painfully aware, not yet enough even to cover his airfare and hotel bill).

For reasons Salim does not understand, his brother-in-law's business partners have booked him into the Paramount Hotel on 46th Street. He finds it confusing, claustrophobic, expensive, alien.

Fuad is Salim's sister's husband. He is not a rich man, but is the co-owner of a small trinket factory, making knick-knacks from copper, brooches and rings and bracelets and statues. Everything is made for export, to other Arab countries, to Europe, to America.

Salim has been working for Fuad for six months. Fuad scares him a little. The tone of Fuad's faxes is becoming harsher; in the evening, Salim sits in his hotel room, reading his Qur'an, telling himself that this will pass, that his stay in this strange world is limited and finite.

His brother-in-law gave him a thousand dollars for miscellaneous traveling expenses and the money, which seemed so huge a sum when he first saw it, is evaporating faster than Salim can believe. When he first arrived, scared of being seen as a cheap Arab, he tipped everyone, handing extra dollar bills to everyone he encountered; and then he decided that he was being taken advantage of, that perhaps they were even laughing at him, and he stopped tipping entirely.

On his first and only journey on the subway he got lost and confused, and missed his appointment; now he takes taxis only when he has to, and the rest of the time he walks. He stumbles into overheated offices, his cheeks numb from the cold outside, sweating beneath his coat, shoes soaked by slush; and when the winds blow down the avenues (which run from north to south, as the streets run west to east, all so simple, and Salim always knows where to face Mecca) he feels a cold on his exposed skin that is so intense it is like being struck.

He never eats at the hotel (for while the hotel bill is being covered by Fuad's business partners, he must pay for his own food); instead he buys food at falafel houses and at little food stores, smuggles it up to the hotel beneath his coat for days before he realizes that no one cares. And even then he feels strange about carrying the bags of food into the dimly-lit elevators (Salim always has to bend and squint to find the button to press to take him to his floor) and up to the tiny white room in which he stays.

Salim is upset. The fax that was waiting for him when he woke this morning was curt, and alternately chiding, stern, and disappointed: Salim was letting them down—his sister, Fuad, Fuad's business partners, the Sultanate of Oman, the whole Arab world. Unless he was able to get the orders, Fuad would no longer consider it his obligation to employ

Salim. They depended upon him. His hotel was too expensive. What was Salim doing with their money, living like a Sultan in America? Salim read the fax in his room (which has always been too hot and stifling, so last night he opened a window, and was now too cold) and sat there for a time, his face frozen into an expression of complete misery.

Then Salim walks downtown, holding his sample case as if it contains diamonds and rubies, trudges through the cold for block after block until, on Broadway and 19th Street, he finds a squat building over a laundromat and walks up the stairs to the fourth floor, to the office of Panglobal Imports.

The office is dingy, but he knows that Panglobal handles almost half of the ornamental souvenirs that enter the US from the Far East. A real order, a significant order from Panglobal could redeem Salim's journey, could make the difference between failure and success, so Salim sits on an uncomfortable wooden chair in an outer office, his sample case balanced on his lap, staring at the middle-aged woman with her hair dyed too bright a red who sits behind the desk, blowing her nose on Kleenex after Kleenex. After she blows her nose she wipes it, and drops the Kleenex into the trash.

Salim got there at 10:30 a.m., half an hour before his appointment. Now he sits there, flushed and shivering, wondering if he is running a fever. The time ticks by so slowly.

Salim looks at his watch. Then he clears his throat.

The woman behind the desk glares at him. "Yes?" she says. It sounds like *Yed*.

"It is 11:35," says Salim.

The woman glances at the clock on the wall, and says "Yed" again. *Id id*.

"My appointment was for eleven," says Salim with a placating smile.

"Mister Blanding knows you're here," she tells him, reprovingly. *Bidter Bladdig dode you're here*.

Salim picks up an old copy of the *New York Post* from the table. He speaks English better than he reads it, and he puzzles his way through the stories like a man doing a crossword puzzle. He waits, a plump young man with the eyes of a hurt puppy, glancing from his watch to his newspaper to the clock on the wall.

At twelve-thirty several men come out from the inner office. They talk loudly, jabbering away to each other in American. One of them, a big, paunchy man, has a cigar, unlit, in his mouth. He glances at Salim as he comes out. He tells the woman behind the desk to try the juice of a lemon, and zinc, as his sister swears by zinc, and vitamin C. She promises him that she will, and gives him several envelopes. He pockets them and then he, and the other men, go out into the hall. The sound of their laughter disappears down the stairwell.

It is one o'clock. The woman behind the desk opens a drawer and takes out a brown paper bag, from which she removes several sandwiches, an apple, and a Milky Way. She also takes out a small plastic bottle of freshly-squeezed orange juice.

"Excuse me," says Salim, "but can you perhaps call Mister Blanding and tell him that I am still waiting?"

She looks up at him as if surprised to see that he is still there, as if they have not been sitting five feet apart for two and a half hours. "He's at lunch," she says. *He'd ad dudge.*

Salim knows, knows deep down in his gut that Blanding was the man with the unlit cigar. "When will he be back?"

She shrugs, takes a bite of her sandwich. "He's busy with appointments for the rest of the day," she says. *He'd biddy wid abboidmeds for the red ob the day.*

"Will he see me, then, when he comes back?" asks Salim.

She shrugs, and blows her nose.

Salim is hungry, increasingly so, and frustrated, and powerless.

At three o'clock the woman looks at him and says, "He wode be gubbig bag."

"Excuse?"

"Bidder Bladdig. He wode be gubbig bag today."

"Can I make an appointment for tomorrow?"

She wipes her nose. "You hab to teddephode. Appoidbeds oddly by teddephode."

"I see," says Salim. And then he smiles: a salesman, Fuad had told him many times before he left Muscat, is naked in America without his smile. "Tomorrow I will telephone," he says. He takes his sample case, and he walks down the many stairs to the street, where the freezing rain is turning to sleet. Salim contemplates the long, cold walk back to the 46th Street hotel, and the weight of the sample case, then he steps to the edge of the sidewalk and waves at every yellow cab that approaches, whether the light on top is on or off, and every cab drives past him.

One of them accelerates as it passes; a wheel dives into a water-filled pothole, spraying freezing muddy water over Salim's pants and coat. For a moment, he contemplates throwing himself in front of one of the lumbering cars, and then he realizes that his brother-in-law would be more concerned with the fate of the sample case than of Salim himself, and that he would bring grief to no one but his beloved sister, Fuad's wife (for he had always been a slight embarrassment to his father and mother, and his romantic encounters had always, of necessity, been both brief and relatively anonymous): also he doubts that any of the cars is going fast enough actually to end his life.

A battered yellow taxi draws up beside him and, grateful to be able to abandon his train of thought, Salim gets in.

The backseat is patched with gray duct tape; the half-open Plexiglas barrier is covered with notices warning him not to smoke, telling him how much to pay to the various airports. The recorded voice of somebody famous he has never heard of tells him to remember to wear his seatbelt.

"The Paramount Hotel, please," says Salim.

The cab driver grunts, and pulls away from the curb, into the traffic. He is unshaved, and he wears a thick, dust-colored sweater, and black plastic sunglasses. The weather is gray, and night is falling. Salim wonders if the man has a problem with his eyes. The wipers smear the street scene into grays and smudged lights.

From nowhere, a truck pulls out in front of them, and the cab driver swears in Arabic, by the beard of the prophet.

Salim stares at the name on the dashboard, but he cannot make it out from here. "How long have you been driving a cab, my friend?" he asks the man, in Arabic.

"Ten years," says the driver, in the same language. "Where are you from?"

"Muscat," says Salim. "In Oman."

"From Oman. I have been in Oman. It was a long time ago. Have you heard of the City of Ubar?" asks the taxi driver.

"Indeed I have," says Salim. "The Lost City of Towers. They found it in the desert five, ten years ago, I do not remember exactly. Were you with the expedition that excavated it?"

"Something like that. It was a good city," says the taxi driver. "On most nights there would be three, maybe four thousand people camped there: every traveller would rest at Ubar, and the music would play, and the wine would flow like water and the water would flow as well, which was why the city existed."

"That is what I have heard," says Salim. "And it perished, what, a thousand years ago? Two thousand?"

The taxi driver says nothing. They are stopped at a red traffic light. The light turns green, but the taxi driver does not move, despite the immediate discordant blare of horns behind them. Hesitantly, Salim reaches through the hole in the Plexiglas and he touches the driver on the shoulder. The man's head jerks up, with a start, and he puts his foot down on the gas, lurching them across the intersection.

"Fuckshitfuckfuck," he says, in English.

"You must be very tired, my friend," says Salim.

"I have been driving this Allah-forgotten taxi for thirty hours," says the driver. "It is too much. Before that, I sleep for five hours, and I drove fourteen hours before that. We are shorthanded, before Christmas."

"I hope you have made a lot of money," says Salim.

The driver sighs. "Not much. This morning I drove a man from 51st Street to Newark Airport. When we got there, he ran off into the airport, and I could not find him again. A fifty-dollar fare gone, and I had to pay the tolls on the way back myself."

Salim nods. "I had to spend today waiting to see a man who will not see me. My brother-in-law-hates me. I have been in America for a week, and it has done nothing but eat my money. I sell nothing."

"What do you sell?"

"Shit," says Salim. "Worthless gewgaws and baubles and tourist trinkets. Horrible, cheap, foolish, ugly shit."

The taxi driver wrenches the wheel to the right, swings around something, drives on. Salim wonders how he can see to drive, between the rain, the night, and the thick sunglasses.

"You try to sell shit?"

"Yes," says Salim, thrilled and horrified that he has spoken the truth about his brother-in-law's samples.

"And they will not buy it?"

"No."

"Strange. You look at the stores here, that is all they sell."

Salim smiles nervously.

A truck is blocking the street in front of them: a red-faced cop standing in front of it waves and shouts and points them down the nearest street.

"We will go over to Eighth Avenue, come uptown that way," says the taxi driver. They turn onto the street, where the traffic has stopped completely. There is a cacophony of horns, but the cars do not move.

The driver sways in his seat. His chin begins to descend to his chest, one, two, three times. Then he begins, gently, to snore. Salim reaches out to wake the man, hoping that he is doing the right thing. As he shakes his shoulder the driver moves, and Salim's hand brushes the man's face, knocking the man's sunglasses from his face onto his lap.

The taxi driver opens his eyes and reaches for, and replaces, the black plastic sunglasses, but it is too late. Salim has seen his eyes.

The car crawls forward in the rain. The numbers on the meter increase.

"Are you going to kill me?" asks Salim.

The taxi driver's lips are pressed together. Salim watches his face in the driver's mirror.

"No," says the driver, very quietly.

The car stops again. The rain patters on the roof.

Salim begins to speak. "My grandmother swore that she had seen an ifrit, or perhaps a marid, late one evening, on the edge of the desert. We told her that it was just a sandstorm, a little wind, but she said now, she saw its face, and its eyes, like yours, were burning flames."

The driver smiles, but his eyes are hidden behind the black plastic glasses, and Salim cannot tell whether there is any humor in that smile or not. "The grandmothers came here, too," he says.

"Are there many jinn in New York?" asks Salim.

"No. Not many of us."

"There are angels, and there are men, who Allah made from mud, and then there are the people of the fire, the jinn," says Salim.

"People know nothing about my people here," says the driver. "They think we grant wishes. If I could grant wishes, do you think I would be driving a cab?"

"I do not understand."

The taxi driver seems gloomy. Salim watches his face in the mirror as he speaks, staring at the ifrit's dark lips.

"They believe that we grant wishes. Why do they believe that? I sleep in one stinking room in Brooklyn. I drive this taxi for any stinking freak who has the money to ride in it, and for some who don't. I drive them where they need to go, and sometimes they tip me. Sometimes they pay me." His lower lip begins to tremble. The ifrit seems on edge. "One of them shat on the back seat once. I had to clean it before I could take the cab back. How could he do that? I had to clean the wet shit from the seat. Is that right?"

Salim puts out a hand, pats the ifrit's shoulder. He can feel solid flesh through the wool of the sweater. The ifrit raises his hand from the wheel, rests it on Salim's hand for a moment.

Salim thinks of the desert then: red sands blow a dust-storm through his thoughts, and the scarlet silks of the tents that surrounded the lost city of Ubar flap and billow through his mind.

They drive up Eighth Avenue.

"The old believe. They do not piss into holes, because the Prophet told them that jinn live in holes. They know that the angels throw flaming stars at us when we try to listen to their conversations. But even for the old, when they come to this country we are very, very far away. Back there, I did not have to drive a cab."

"I am sorry," says Salim.

"It is a bad time," says the driver. "A storm is coming. It scares me. I would do anything to get away."

The two of them say nothing more on their way back to the hotel.

When Salim gets out of the cab he gives the ifrit a twenty dollar bill, tells him to keep the change. Then, with a sudden burst of courage, he tells him his room number. The taxi driver says nothing in reply. A young woman clambers into the back of the cab, and it pulls out into the cold and the rain.

Six o'clock in the evening. Salim has not yet written the fax to his brother-in-law. He goes out into the rain, buys himself this night's kebab and French fries. It has only been a week, but he feels that he is becoming heavier, rounder, softening in this country of New York.

When he comes back into the hotel he is surprised to see the taxi driver standing in the lobby, hands deep into his pockets. He is staring at a display of black-and-white postcards. When he sees Salim he smiles, self-consciously. "I called your room," he says, "but there was no answer. So I thought I would wait."

Salim smiles also, and touches the man's arm. "I am here," he says.

Together they enter the dim, green-lit elevator, ascend to the fifth floor holding hands. The ifrit asks if he may use Salim's bathroom. "I feel very dirty," he says. Salim nods. He sits on the bed, which fills most of the small white room and listens to the sound of the shower running. Salim takes off his shoes, his socks, and then the rest of his clothes.

The taxi driver comes out of the shower, wet, with a towel wrapped about his mid-section. He is not wearing his sunglasses, and in the dim room his eyes burn with scarlet flames.

Salim blinks back tears. "I wish you could see what I see," he says.

"I do not grant wishes," whispers the ifrit, dropping his towel and pushing Salim gently, but irresistibly, down onto the bed.

It is an hour or more before the ifrit comes, thrusting and grinding into Salim's mouth. Salim has already come twice in this time. The jinn's semen tastes strange, fiery, and it burns Salim's throat.

Salim goes to the bathroom, washes out his mouth. When he returns to the bedroom the taxi driver is already asleep in the white bed, snoring peacefully. Salim climbs into the bed beside him, cuddles close to the ifrit, imagining the desert on his skin.

As he starts to fall asleep he realizes that he still has not written his fax to Fuad, and he feels guilty. Deep inside he feels empty and alone: he reaches out, rests his hand on the ifrit's tumescent cock and, comforted, he sleeps.

They wake in the small hours, moving against each other, and they make love again. At one point he realizes that he is crying, and the ifrit is kissing away his tears with burning lips. "What is your name?" Salim asks the taxi driver.

"There is a name on my driving permit, but it is not mine," the ifrit says.

Afterward, Salim could not remember where the sex had stopped and the dreams began.

When Salim wakes, the cold sun creeping into the white room, he is alone.

Also, he discovers, this sample case is gone, all the bottles and rings and souvenir copper flashlights, all gone, along with his suitcase, his wallet, his passport, and his air tickets back to Oman.

He finds a pair of jeans, the tee shirt, and the dust-colored woollen sweater discarded on the floor. Beneath them he finds a driver's license in the name of Ibrahim bin Irem, a taxi permit in the same name, and a ring of keys with an address written on a piece of paper attached to them in English. The photographs on the license and the permit ID do not look much like Salim, but then, they did not look much like the ifrit.

The telephone rings: it is the front desk calling to point out that Salim has already checked out, and his guest needs to leave soon so that they can service the room, to get it ready for another occupant.

"I do not grant wishes," says Salim, tasting the way the words shape themselves in his mouth.

He feels strangely light-headed as he dresses.

New York is very simple: the avenues run north to south, the streets run west to east. How hard can it be? he asks himself.

He tosses the car keys into the air and catches them. Then he puts on the black plastic sunglasses he finds in the pockets, and leaves the hotel room to go look for his cab.

DUENDE 2077
Jamal Mahjoub

THE IRON HANDS had long since fallen away, leaving a blank space where time used to be. The clocktower was retained as a token of what had once been, a pagan icon from a forgotten era. A punctuation mark that closed the book on Christian hegemony and ushered forth the new, bright era of the Rashidun Caliphate.

History books chronicled the decline of unbridled capitalism, how it spiralled into social anarchy, chaos and moral bankruptcy. The illusion of unlimited wealth projected onto a world that experienced only increasing poverty and destitution, diminishing natural resources, industrialised slavery. One day it all imploded. The Caliphate flooded into the power void.

DHAKA STEPPED AWAY from the window. The room was nice, if a little claustrophobic. Heavy damask drapes and high divans, the heady scent of patchouli oil, myrrh and sandalwood. Sensuality was a big deal to whoever lived here, though you wouldn't know it to look at him now. Stretched out on the bed, naked. His head, or what was left of it, was shaven but for the bushy beard—dyed henna red. The yellow silk sheets were sprayed with crimson.

One killer or two? Dhaka knelt by the door, ignoring the clamour around him as he recreated the scene in his mind. The victim had been sitting on the edge of the bed, the killer behind him. Standing or kneeling? The slash to the neck had released a spray of blood so powerful it had left an arc across the Japanese cherry tree print on the walls. He'd tried to stand then, one hand to the neck, probably not believing the wound was fatal. A bloody smear on the high lacquered chest where he tried to balance himself. That was when the shot was fired. One high-tensile round. The force of it knocked the victim back onto the bed. The bullet went through his right eye and took off most of the back of his head.

Moving closer to the wall, Dhaka sought out a hole in the paneling with a pen. Flecks of bone and brain matter circled the spot, resembling an exploding star. He moved closer, picking up a strange, familiar smell that he couldn't place. Why shoot a dead man?

"Forensics?"

"Don't hold your breath."

The sullen, overweight figure of Kara Murat stood by the window, smoking an illicit cigarette. Murder was one of the great taboos of the Caliphate: in the perfect Islamic state, there was no homicide, no need to allocate resources. No need for men like Dhaka.

"Call me when they get here," Dhaka said. He knew he'd be lucky if he heard anything back.

The street outside was hot and humid. Autumn, and yet the temperatures were so high it could have been midsummer. The rain was so fine it flowed directly into his sweat. Dhaka longed for a deep lungful of clear air; what he got was a damp fistful of liquid smog. Realising he hadn't eaten, he trawled the riverside stalls and settled on dumplings and some kind of Uyghur soup, an unpalatable grey colour. He suspected it was dog meat, but it was spicy and hot and restored some semblance of life to him. He listened to the rain hitting the tarpaulin over his head as he ate.

"Mulazim Dhaka?"

A small, South Asian woman wearing a non-regulation hijab over her uniform stood beside him. The ideogram in her palm told him she was ISD. K.S. Munzari. Internal Security Directorate. He guessed the K stood for Khadija, beloved wife of the Prophet.

"I am to accompany you to the Majlis."

"Why?"

Her face was emotionless. "I don't question orders." And neither, clearly, should he.

He eyed the last grey dumpling floating in the soup and decided maybe he'd had enough.

"Transport?"

"Naturally."

It wasn't a given. They might have expected him to walk, or commandeer a *rucksha*. She had a *kalesh* and no driver, which said something about her, but Dhaka couldn't figure out what. He wiped his mouth and reached for a toothpick. The interior smelled of jasmine air freshener and disinfectant. Dhaka recalled the smell he had picked up in the apartment, and remembered where he knew it from. The distinctive scent of burnt almonds. Munzari swiped a finger across her wrist console and the engine came to life. The dull flash of red and blue lights reflected exhausted faces trying to get out of their way; in short order, they were sweeping along the riverbed, the lights of other vehicles flashing by.

The bridge was packed with *dhimmis* making their way home on foot. The lucky ones had bicycles. Public transport in Londonistan had collapsed years ago. Most lived outside the Separation Wadi, a barrier of walls and moats filled with electrified water that ringed the city. Once this was a green and pleasant land; now it was ash grey and dusty. Smoky columns rose over the skyline from incinerators that ran twenty-four hours a day, burning trash to create energy. The furnaces produced a wet, sulfurous heat and a blanket of smog that hung over the city all year round, blotting out the sun. A rain of grey ash fell over the city like snow, summer and winter alike.

Thin slivers of lightning threaded through the clouds, filling the air with an electric hum.

His wrist console buzzed and his eyescreen showed Kara Murat, looking greyer than ever. Dhaka touched his earpiece. He didn't want to be overheard.

"We found something. Or rather the tech squad did."

"I'm listening."

"It's a hologram." Kara Murat's usual bored tone had given way to something that could almost be described as faint interest. "Iridium traces in the wall."

"Can they reconstruct it?"

"They're working on it."

"I need to know the moment you have something."

"Sure," Kara Murat grunted. He sounded as though he had countless more important things to do. Dhaka glanced over at the woman, but she was staring straight ahead, pretending not to hear. They were already approaching Abbassiya Square. Glowing over the old sandstone building of the Eastminster Majlis was the 'Onion', as it had been irreverently dubbed, a tulip bulb of enameled glass and gaudy chrome. The glassmakers of Damascus would spin in their tombs. To Dhaka it resembled a bathroom ornament, but perhaps that was the idea. The insult of all insults: turn the infidels' symbol of democracy into a toilet. The usual crowd of protesters clamoured around the landing pad, but Munzari must have signalled ahead because a path opened up before them. Dhaka left his gun in the guardroom and followed her through the building.

A long hallway led past a succession of murals, vast oil paintings of dubious artistic merit, depicting key moments in the Great Victory. A sequence drummed into every schoolchild's head: Dhaka saw battlefields, jihadis in headbands brandishing weapons, Muslim women and children behind barbed wire in the internment camps of the Cataclysm. The war of liberation was not a pleasant memory for him. Through the panelled windows, the thin rivulet of Wadi Tanzim was visible. Once known as the Thames, it had withered to a flurry of dark mud. The gigantic silver tail of an airliner jutted out of the sludge like a prehistoric fin, left as a reminder of the anarchy and despair that ruled before the coming of the Caliphate. Cyberwarfare had brought down global computer systems, sending aircraft crashing from the sky.

The fat, pampered members of Parliament were sprawled on the carpeted floor of the Majlis. Dhaka could barely conceal his loathing. Eastminster had a reputation for corruption of the soul. Nobody came here willingly, and those who did could hardly wait to leave. Exit visas were much sought after, and impossible to get without the assistance of one of these overfed buffoons.

A spiral staircase brought them to a deserted upper gallery. A solitary figure stood at the far end. Munzari remained by the stairs. The man did not turn as Dhaka approached. No introductions were needed.

"Your reputation precedes you."

"The honour is all mine." Dhaka gave a cursory bow. Colonel Asgari was tall and slim, his body encased in a black robe that fell to his shiny boots. A black turban covered his head. Bony cheeks rose above a trim beard.

"You are investigating the murder of Sanjak Sanbura."

Barely an hour had passed since Dhaka had visited the crime scene. Asgari probably knew more about what was going on than Dhaka himself did.

"We are still conducting preliminary tests."

Asgari gave the mere hint of a nod. There was something Mongolian about his features, his face hard and tanned like old wood.

"I don't need to tell you how sensitive this is. He was a wise man, with somewhat particular tastes." Dhaka presumed this was a reference to the dead man's bedroom habits. "What is your initial analysis?"

"It's too early to say much." Dhaka shifted uncomfortably.

Asgari leaned closer, his voice a harsh whisper. "What do your instincts tell you?"

Dhaka glanced back in the direction of Munzari, who remained out of earshot. "It looks like an assassination. Whoever planned this managed to get through the security screen with a weapon."

"A weapon?"

"His jugular vein was slashed with a piece of glass, but they put a hologram through him for good measure."

"What?"

"Unnecessary, so I assume it was a message of some kind."

"A message to whom?"

Dhaka shrugged. "That's what we don't know. It's being reconstructed now."

"The weapon?"

"It's highly specialised. High-tensile crystal matrix bullet fired by a 3D projector."

"Correct me if I'm wrong, but aren't such things still experimental?" Dhaka nodded.

"Possibly."

"I want you to take charge of this investigation."

"You want someone else. This is a matter of Umma security." Dhakka nodded towards Munzari. "It should fall to ISD."

"I am aware of the protocol," purred Asgari.

Dhaka didn't like the sound of this. Crossing lines of protocol was a sure means of finding yourself on the list for a Friday beheading.

"I need someone I can trust." Asgari left the words hanging. "Your record speaks for itself. A decorated war hero. True, you've had disciplinary problems, but you've proven your loyalty." The Colonel lowered his voice. "You report directly to me. Speak to no one else of your findings."

"And her?" Dhaka nodded towards Munzari.

Asgari glanced over at the ISD officer. "She will accompany you, for official purposes, but she remains subordinate to you."

THE SHUTTLE WAS already warming up when Dhaka and Munzari arrived at Hijazi Station. The old curved railway lines could still be glimpsed beneath the launch ramp.

"This must be like going home for you," said Munzari as they strapped themselves in.

"It's almost twenty years since I left," replied Dhaka. "I imagine things have changed." He was aware that K.S. Munzari had never left Eastminster, which made her a strange choice for Colonel Asgari. Or maybe not.

Whatever she said in reply was drowned out as the automatons ran through their useless emergency procedures. The engines were already starting up; the launch platform rose until the shuttle was tilting towards the sky. Then the engines kicked in and they were thrust back into their seats. Defense flares dropped slowly in their wake, like flowers opening up their petals to the sun.

The flight to Hurriyet Station took less than half an hour. Almost as soon as he closed his eyes, Dhaka felt the floor tip as they tilted forwards and began to plunge back towards the Earth, the cabin heating up as they skimmed the atmosphere at re-entry. As they rattled towards the ground, it felt as if the entire airship was in terminal decay.

Hurriyet Station was one of the most outlandish corners of the planet. Once a glittering symbol of oil opulence, an oasis of obscene luxury where the super-rich swanned around in an artificial paradise of desert islands, indoor ski slopes and everything in between, it had since become a cesspool of human detritus, a bubbling cauldron of discontent. The Endless Jihad which followed the war had left it in ruins. The skyscrapers, the shopping malls, the marinas: all had been crushed, leaving a radioactive wasteland inhabited by the scarred and the diseased. Every vice known to man flourished here, including rebellion. It was in a state of perpetual emergency, patrolled by paramilitary forces night and day.

DHAKA MANAGED TO persuade Munzari to remain inside the security compound at the hostel where they had secured rooms. It was basic, but at least it was relatively clean. You could sleep in there and know you weren't going to be murdered in your bed.

The Sea of Pleasure was buried in the old salt caverns on the outskirts of town. Once, men had hauled buckets of saline water up to the surface to dry in the sun. It seemed ironic. Nowadays, fresh water was more valuable than the oil that once flowed here. The club was full of freaks, but the wealthy kind, the ones who could afford expensive treatments and cosmetic surgery to hide the ravages of radiation sickness. They thrived on the iodine tablets that sold like cocaine once had.

It had taken three hours of wandering through smoky rooms, breathing the heady mix of narcotics and rotting flesh before he found her. Dar Firket was not an easy woman to see, but Dhaka had an advantage, one that he was in no doubt Colonel Asgari had been aware of when he picked him for this assignment: a history. A leper beckoned with the remaining two fingers on his left hand and Dhaka was led into an inner chamber. The air was infused with the harsh smell of sulphur.

"How have you been?" she asked. He could only glimpse her silhouette through a translucent curtain. Opium smoke wafted up to the ceiling in a lilac haze, and Dhaka felt his nostrils twitch. Old habits, like a forgotten nerve, resurfacing from somewhere deep inside.

"I never thought I'd see you again," she said.

A part of him wished she would pull back the screen; another was terrified she would.

"I wasn't sure I would be able to find you."

"And yet here you are…" There was a longing in that husky voice which made his heart tense.

"Unless I'm mistaken, you knew I would be coming."

She laughed at that. "Poor old Dhaka, always too perceptive for his own good." Her voice sounded low and breathless, and he tried to work out just how sick she was.

"Times change. People don't. You know why I'm here."

"Of course," she laughed lightly.

"The hologram was a message for me."

"I thought you'd like that."

"But *why*? Why now? Why me?"

"You know the answer to that, better than anyone. Time is running out."

The smoke changed colour and she vanished in a saffron haze, leaving the faint scent of burnt almonds in the air. A scent he had always associated with her: the same he had detected in the apartment of Sanjak Sanbura in Eastminster.

Munzari was waiting for him inside the compound. "Did you find anything?"

When he looked at her, all he saw was questions. "Tell me again why you're here?"

"My task is to open doors for you," she said. The words sounded rehearsed.

"As long as you remember that, we won't have a problem."

Dhaka went up onto the roof terrace to survey the city. Winking eyes in the sky warned him that surveillance was continuous, all-pervasive. The Caliphate knew everything. Sirens sounded constantly.

Armoured *Hyenes* buzzed through the smoke in a haze of red and blue lights, heading to one trouble spot or another. In the old days, he'd been one of those paramilitary officers, rappeling down to clear out radicals' cells, bands of *kuffar* terrorists, each one more dangerous than the last.

Now it was hard to believe there was anything here but despair. The war had never really ended. The Endless Jihad had turned inwards, and the Caliphate had been consuming itself ever since. The pathetic inhabitants shuffled around dressed in rags, barefoot, pushing their meagre belongings in handcarts, shopping trolleys, on the backs of bicycles. His memories were blurred, tinged with the narcotic excesses of those times. Drugs were the only way to deal with the madness. Most of those he knew were dead by now, but the disease was the same. The craving, the hunger; the moth, drawn towards the flame that it knows spells its annihilation. He had not wanted to come back here, but he had had no choice.

His armband buzzed and Kara Murat's face appeared before him. He was eating, in his usual sloppy way. It still disgusted Dhaka no matter how many years went by.

"Where are you?"

"You have something for me?" Dhaka ignored the question. Kara Murat grunted, wiped something from his mouth with the back of his hand and spoke, but was obliterated by a break in the connection.

"What?"

"The hologram. They managed to reconstruct it." Dhaka stroked the wristpad and the image floated before him. A human skull studded with rubies, emeralds and precious stones set inside what looked like a maze.

"Any idea what it is?"

Kara Murat sighed. "You know how it is with historical stuff. Our technical guys are hopeless."

Anything before the Great Victory was taboo. The past was a dangerous area that had been banned from educational courses for decades. Anyone caught dabbling risked being denounced as an unbeliever, or a worshipper of idols.

"So, they don't have a clue?" Dhaka asked.

"The best they can come up with is Al Andalus, Moorish Spain. It seems there is some connection to a messiah they called the *Duende*, which means 'spirit', something like a *jinn*."

"That's the best they can do?"

"I'm afraid so." Kara Murat sniffed. "I sent you a file. Where are you again?"

"Never mind where I am. How are you doing with the iridium?"

"Oh, lucky you reminded me. They traced the source to a location just northwest of Hurriyet." Kara grunted "You might have known it would come from some shithole like that. I wonder who they'll send out there."

"Some poor sucker, I imagine," said Dhaka. "Look, do me a favour, keep this to yourself for the moment."

"Can't do that," Kara Murat sniffed. "They'll be on to me in no time."

"There's a chance we have a security leak, we need to keep this under wraps. Blame me. You can say you're waiting for confirmation."

"Twenty-four hours, no more," Kara grunted. Dhaka broke the connection. He studied the image again and then headed downstairs for something to eat. Munzari was waiting for him. Dhaka wondered if she had access to all traffic to and from his coder. She fell in alongside him as he walked.

"Did you eat?" Dhaka stared through the doorway at the canteen.

"Yeah, it's not bad, but stay away from anything with meat in it."

Dhaka chose a plate of vegetable tagine. He pressed the panel and watched the infrared beam play over it until it was steaming hot. His time was limited. He was beginning to understand Munzari's role in this setup. Why he was here. Why Colonel Asgari had picked him.

Munzari trailed behind him to a bench in the corner. The window offered a view down into the central well of the barracks. They were five floors below the surface, and the air had a tinny, metallic smell.

"Tell me a bit about yourself."

The question seemed to take her by surprise. "Me?"

"Yes, you must have excelled in some way for Colonel Asgari to choose you for this mission."

"I simply dedicated myself to becoming a good militia officer."

"When did you join?"

Munzari lifted her chin. "As a child I joined the suicide brigades."

The Angels of Death, as they were known. Dhaka's blood ran cold at the memory of children running towards enemy lines and detonating explosive charges in their vests.

"You're too young to have been in the War."

"That is correct. I never had the chance to make the supreme sacrifice."

"Something you regret?" Dhaka pushed something around his plate, trying to work out what it was.

"The supreme sacrifice is what we all dreamed of."

"Only you never got the chance." Dhaka studied her face. She seemed to really believe what she was saying.

"I was found to have a strong affinity for intelligence work. I was offered a chance to join the ISD."

Dhaka washed the food down with a slug of mint tea. "Why do you think they asked you to accompany me here?"

"May I speak frankly?"

"Certainly."

"There are gaps in your service record, and a history of insubordination. I believe they wanted someone who could keep you in line."

"Are you good at that, keeping people in line?"

She frowned, as though she didn't get it. "I'm going to try."

"The hologram. You know what it represents?"

"*Duende* is Spanish for a supernatural spirit," said Munzari. "It's a corruption of the Arabic word *jinn*. In the time before the Caliphate there were those who worshipped such idols."

Dhaka pushed aside his plate. "There used to be a sect of radicals operating in this area. They were planning a revolt against the Caliphate."

"How long ago was this?"

"About fifteen years. Sanjak Sanbura was heading an investigation into them."

"Is that why he was killed?"

"It's possible."

"What happened to them?"

"The cell was broken up. Most of them died." Dhaka watched her reaction. "A small number of them got away. They settled in a cave in the Zarbek mountains. They worship the gem-studded skull of a former leader, a messiah from another age, a *mahdi* they call the 'Duende 2077.' The figure in the hologram."

"None of this is in the file."

"No," Dhaka shook his head. "It wouldn't be."

"How is it that you know these things?"

"Colonel Asgari chose me for a reason. When I was stationed here, I had some dealings with the cell."

"You infiltrated them." Munzari's raised her chin slowly. "The gaps in your record."

"I was undercover for almost three years."

"What happened?"

"Undercover work is complicated."

Her eyes narrowed. "What does that mean?"

"It means it was a long time ago," Dhaka shrugged. "Their leader was never caught. Nobody's heard of them for years."

"Until now."

"Until now." Dhaka fell silent. He sat back and studied her for a moment. "How does it usually happen?"

Munzari understood what he meant. "The Rapture, we call it. It used to be manual. The *shahid* would trigger the detonator themselves. Nowadays it's remote controlled, like everything else."

"So, how does that work? You go through life never knowing when you're going to explode?"

"That is a simplistic understanding," she smiled. "It means you live every moment as if it were your last in this world. It's the most intense form of life there is."

Which is why so many people dreamed of nothing more than joining the suicide corps. At least now he had an idea how they were planning to get rid of him.

"I need to go out there," said Dhaka.

"My orders are to stay with you at all times."

"It's not going to be an easy trip."

"I'm tougher than you think," she said.

* * *

THEY LEFT THE city at dawn in an unmarked Hijazi 4 cruiser. They made good time and by noon they had reached the ghost town of Masdar. Munzari had been busy while Dhaka drove.

"This messiah, the one they called the Duende 2077, did you ever meet him?"

"Why do you ask?" Dhaka brought the cruiser down alongside an old service station. The desert wind blew through broken windows. A half-dome shed stood to one side, one panel of rusting corrugated iron flapping in the wind. "It's just that the messiah disappeared around the same time you left the group."

"Coincidence." Dhaka powered down and stared out through the windscreen.

"Is it?" She looked out. "Why have we stopped here?"

"We have a technical problem."

Munzari frowned. "The cruiser was fine when we signed it out."

Dhaka smiled. "I told you it was going to be tough."

She was still tapping the control panel when he stunned her. He figured it would take her a couple of hours to call for help; by then, he would be long gone. He slipped his communicator under the seat alongside her. Who knows, she might still get her wish of martyrdom, but he wouldn't be around to witness it.

The jet skiff was a vintage turn-of-the-century model, built out of a Bugatti Veyron chassis that still had the old police paintwork on the sides. It had lasted well in storage. He rolled it out of the shed and used the cruiser's batteries to start her up.

The warm air whistled mournfully over his head. If he listened carefully, he imagined he heard voices speaking, drawing him in, speaking his true name. The desert flew by below. Already Masdar was a dark smudge in the rearview mirror. To the right, the silver shimmer of the sea beckoned, and within minutes he was skirting the line between sand and water. The sun was sinking towards the western horizon. Ahead of him, the Zarbek mountains rose from the flat ground like a ripple of bruises.

It was written that the messiah would return from the east, and so he corrected his course. He had always known this day would come; he just hadn't known *when*. Now that it was here, he felt a calmness settle over him.

Now the real work could begin.

THE RIGHTEOUS GUIDE
OF ARABSAT
Sophia Al-Maria

FRIDAY AFTERNOONS, KHALID went to sit with his mother in the women's parlour and watch Ulama TV. Even though there was an entire constellation of satellite channels since they had a dish installed, Ulama was always on. And in spite of the fact it was a program for women, Khalid found Sheikh Safar's *Right Guidance* series deeply compelling. It wasn't the histrionics or the drama he enjoyed, it was the Sheikh's judgement. Sheikh Safar was the channel's premiere agony aunt, and the lines were ever lit with distraught housewives seeking righteous guidance in matters personal. Every day they called to air their woes to a silent jury of viewers. And on the daily, the confessions became ever more shocking and the questions more embarrassing.

Today, a young caller was phoning in asking why she wasn't pregnant after two years of marriage. She coyly described her marital relations before the

Sheikh shook his head, interrupting her, "Dear sister, I fear you are engaging in anal congress."

He stated this with the frank confidence of a family doctor diagnosing chicken pox.

"What?" The caller sounded a little shaken. The sheikh held the camera's gaze. "You and your husband have not been practicing the correct manner of sexual union."

"Stakhfarallah!" Mother exclaimed. "That poor girl."

But Khalid could see glee glimmering behind the pity as she leaned in towards the new flatscreen Samsung, ears pricked for the sound of sobbing.

Sheikh Safar continued. "It sounds as if you are both innocent of knowing any better and you must bear in mind you may save many others from committing the same sin out of ignorance by sharing your story." Then there was a quiver of dead air before the Sheikh barked, "Next caller!"

KHALID ENJOYED COMING to the women's side of the house, but was only allowed on Fridays, when his cousins would be out visiting anyway. There'd been an incident, when he was ten, that had sent him into exile for the rest of his life. *The Pink Panther* had been playing on the old antennae TV. He remembered how the slinky, suggestive saxophone triggered something abstractly pleasurable in his child-self.

He remembered hiding behind a pile of cushions and covering his eyes with his hand. The next thing was his sisters' shrill disgust: "Just because your eyes are covered doesn't mean we can't see you!" Both girls ran from the room to tattle on him. He was never allowed back but for Fridays with mother after that.

Khalid was cringing in the throes of this memory when his mother rose from the floor cushions with some difficulty, shifting her bulk onto a metal cane and hobbling towards the women's side of the house to perform her ablutions before prayer. "When do you plan on having a home?" she asked, as casually as a mother *can* ask a question like that.

"Do you want to share me with another woman?" he teased and catching her in the doorway, he held his mother's henna-limned hands in his own.

"If she brings me grandchildren… yes." And she removed her hand from Khalid's and headed to the ladies' side of the house, yelling, "Girls! Prayer!" before shutting the door.

In spite of himself, Khalid began to think about marriage.

KHALID'S UNCLE SAEED was a bombastic man. He regularly led convoys to Bahrain on paydays with a box of condoms and a thirst for Johnny Walker Red Label. He had once offered to take Khalid with him on one of these jaunts, but Khalid had shrunk at the thought. Now Saeed had found Khalid a different kind of girl. Not a Russian or Filipino in a hotel bar, but a real Bedouin girl. Saeed could be lewd about sexual encounters and was famous for his dirty jokes, but the moment coitus with a Saudi woman was involved, he turned into a po-faced, paranoid prude. As such, Khalid's uncle was parsimonious with his wedding night advice. "She's a Bedouin girl. Lay her face-down in the dark, so your eyes won't meet. Eye-contact will embarrass her."

But Khalid's nuptials did not go according to Saeed's advice.

The night of the reception, Khalid entered the rented hall. Its thin carpet built up a charge under all the shuffling greetings. Khalid's nickname as a child had always been 'the bear' for his portly size and stomping gait, and he had worked up a froth of sweat on his way down the long hall to the ladies' section of the wedding. Now he was confronted by his own face, projected on a silk curtain billowing above the wedding stage. A Filipina photographer with a light-mounted camera was flitting around, "Look to me, sir. Look to me!" she hissed from behind the blinding light. But Khalid couldn't bring himself to do it. He was dimly aware beyond the camera's light of the hundreds of women rowed around the stage, shrouded in a communal swath of crepe and silk. From where he stood, it was a shifting, fleshy gloom.

The bride's male entourage of brothers and father

minced beside him onto the catwalk, brandishing daggers, with their black and beige *bishts* gathered up around them like skirts. He thought he looked like a lumbering beast hosting a flock of long-beaked birds. He felt dizzy from the cacophony of hundreds of mouths ululating all at once. Their gaze was heavy on him—eyes all colourful and kohl-rimmed and following him like the glowing eyes in a cartoon haunted house. The only female face exposed in the room was his bride's. Khalid focused all his attention on the odd little figure sitting on a swan-shaped bench at the end of the dais. When he reached her, he couldn't tell what she really looked like. An opaque mask of *makiaj* obscured her features and a golden green haze hung beneath a pair of acutely angled eyebrows.

Her painted expression was one of shock.

She might as well have been wearing a *niqab* for all the clues her makeup gave, but she was smiling. At him. The first thing he asked her that night, when they'd arrived at their new home, was to remove her false face.

"But it's the fashion," she replied. "They call it kabuki."

"I want to see what you look like." It had been an expensive makeup job and Aneeza had only gotten to wear it for a few hours. The effervescence in her smile went flat. "As you like," she said, defeated, rising glumly from the bed to the en suite.

Khalid glanced around the room at her bridal trousseau, which had exploded from a pearlescent Samsonite. Beside the coat rack, where several abayas hung like sullen shadows, was a rack of weights. He disliked this; it meant she was vain about her body, and why should she be vain about her body if no one was going to see it?

"Is this better?" Aneeza appeared behind him in the mirror. Without makeup, she looked like her brothers. He wondered mildly to himself if he might look like his sisters in makeup.

Khalid lied. "Yes." Now Khalid saw that Aneeza had oddly wide-set eyes and had plucked her eyebrows to high points.

"You shouldn't pluck your eyebrows. It's *haram*."

"Who says?"

"Sheikh Safar."

"Okay, then. I'll stop."

She lay down beside him, the feather trim of her apple-green negligee tickling his nose.

"I'm sorry," she whispered.

"For what?" he asked and allowed her to rest her head on him.

"My cycle started."

A cold shiver of nausea ran from where he felt her ear pressed to his thigh like a cold shell.

"Oh," he replied, noticing the glitter from her hairspray had shed onto his *sirwal* like dandruff. "Never mind."

Khalid was rafting on an internal river of doubt when her approach sent him down a tributary of dread. He needed to get away from this. He slid her off of him by getting up to go to the en suite. He didn't intend to look, but saw a rumpled pink package of Always hidden behind the toilet seat. A coil of padded paper rimmed with a bright spreading red, wrapped in a teal blue sachet. He felt sick, admonished himself for looking. Did he think it would be blue like in the commercials?

When he went back he lay on the far side of the bed staring at the ceiling. Aneeza lay opposite, staring at him with her head propped on the palm of her hand. It was tensely silent between them for some time.

"Have you ever loved before?" she asked, to break the stand-off.

He was taken aback by the directness of the question. He gave it real thought.

"I had a cat once." She gave him a look, encouraging him to explain further. "I left her on the roof. She was a white Persian. I remember her fur was all matted with sweat on the side she died on."

Aneeza sat up straight. "I didn't mean *that* kind of love, silly." And she slithered across the sheets towards him. Silk on silk.

A vivid disgust rose in Khalid's heart. He protested. "But your period."

"Shh." She cooed. "There are other ways." And she tended to him with efficiency, as if he were a doll she'd practiced on before. As if she'd had some education in these matters.

The fluorescent overhead light set off the ashy freckles under her skin as her eyes flickered up at him and then back down to a crescent of expressive lash. Khalid had to close his eyes, but there she was inside his brain too. Staring, grinning, licking her teeth, reaching across his body.

He soothed himself with a mantra—*We're married. We're married.*—and tried to concentrate on a vague goal slowly coming into focus. First it appeared as a silvery hole, aglow in his mind's eye. Now it was black as a cave and throbbed pink at the edges where the ceiling lights penetrated his eyelids. He was sinking into a soft, rocking movement.

"Hey!" he leapt up out of the bed like a cat scrambling from a bathtub. "What are you doing?!"

She slipped her tongue back into her strange little mouth and withdrew her hand from his *sirwal*. "I thought you'd like it."

"Why would you do that?" he said, sitting up.

He turned the TV on urgently, like a cook opening a window to fan smoke out of the kitchen. He stood there blocking the screen, hand on one hip, remote in hand. On it were ponderous shots of the new Masjid al Haram building, all white stucco columns and rotating fans. From above, the marble tiers of Mecca. Twelve cranes studded the edge of the site as if marking the pilgrims' progress around some great hourless clock.

"It looks like City Centre Mall now," Aneeza piped up from the bed.

Khalid's nostrils flared. "How can you compare Mecca to a mall?" Aneeza shrugged. "I'm sleeping in the majlis," he announced. There he turned on *Right Guidance* and fell asleep, feeling safe under Sheikh Safar's watchful, muted gaze.

AFTER KHALID'S FAILED wedding night, a seed was planted.

But it was not the kind of seed his mother looked forward to spoiling.

Khalid was an exquisitely sensitive man, and he was convinced his wife had some experience of 'love' previous to his own. Why else would she have behaved that way if she hadn't learned it somewhere? And although he didn't particularly *want* Aneeza, he couldn't bear the thought anyone else would either.

The next Friday he went to visit his mother. As usual, Sheikh Safar was on. Mecca was keyed in from on high and Khalid could see all the tiny pilgrims gathered around the Kaaba in a cosmic twist. The backdrop of the holy city provided him with a calming image in the midst of all the emotional turmoil and lurid circumstances. This Friday, a tearful woman was on the phone, worried about her effeminate son. "He steals his sister's clothing, and every time he does, his father beats him. It hurts me to see them fighting. But he just goes back. Last week, he refused to remove nail polish from his toes."

The voice on the other end of the line sobbed.

"Dear lady, your problem is very simple. The boy is possessed by a female djinn."

"But how?"

"Please sister, just take him to a mutawa, who can help you to exorcise the demon. Do not attempt to exorcise the child yourself. It can be a very dangerous procedure. Especially when the possession involves sexual deviance. Do you promise?"

"Yes." A sniffle of gratitude. "God bless you, Sheikh."

Khalid took the momentary pause in programming to broach what was bothering him.

"Mother, how did you choose Aneeza for me? I mean, what do we know about her family?"

She answered without looking away from Sheikh Safar. "I told you, they're our cousins' cousins." Khalid knew much of the exiled family, but had never heard of Aneeza or her brothers before meeting them on the night of their engagement.

"Alright. But what do you know about *her*?"

"Why? What's happened?"

"There is something not right about her behavior. I think she might be possessed."

His mother scoffed.

"She and her sisters are all from a second marriage. Good girls."

"Good girls?" Khalid caught a derisive side-eye from his mother.

"Stop being so childish. She's your wife, ask her what you want to know yourself!"

And with that, she thumbed the volume button to maximum in welcome of Sheikh Safar's return from a commercial break.

Khalid rose with a petulant sigh. Mother turned her attention back to him.

"Just talk to the girl! She's probably more afraid of you than you are of her."

Khalid smiled a sad smile. "That's the same thing you told me about spiders."

And as he bent to kiss her goodbye on her forehead, his mother saw an unnameable absence behind the eyes where her son used to be.

EVERY MORNING SINCE the wedding, Aneeza had woken up after dawn prayer and put on a pair of white trainers. She'd then slip into her sport *abaya* and apply her *niqab* in a few swift tugs and ties, before going out to walk with the neighbor lady Um Rashid. Both pledged that after Ramadan, they were going to stop wasting away in front of the TV and 'do something'; by which they meant, get some light exercise and have a good gossip. Khalid found himself watching her from the roof as she left, and waiting there amongst the clutch of satellite dishes, giving the hawk-eye to every tinted car that passed through the neighborhood until she returned.

One morning when Aneeza left the house, Khalid went into her bedroom in hopes of finding proof of the sordid scenes he had comped her into. Her makeup was color-coordinated in its case. The limp shadows of her Abaya wardrobe were all hung neatly in the closet. Pastel-flannel pajamas and paisley *jalabiyas* were rolled and stacked on shelves like colorful fabric loaves. He found no incriminating journal, no photos of other men and no mobile phone to look through. The worst thing he found was a stack of *Archie* comics hidden in a shoebox at the back of the closet, and he used to read them himself, so he couldn't blame her for that.

He lay back on the bed and stared at the plush bear holding a heart she kept propped at the center of their bed. He picked it up; it was heavier than he'd expected. There was a zipper at the back. He unzipped the animal from anus to nape, and out popped an oddly-shaped knob of metal, as if a piece of molten mercury had solidified tumor-like inside the stuffed animal.

But then he discovered that it had a pink rubber button at one end. He pressed it. It vibrated. Although he'd never seen one, he had heard of vibrators from friends who had managed to circumnavigate the government censors and were more widely-travelled on the internet than him.

Khalid took care to put the device back into the bear's stuffing and leave the room as he'd found it.

He fell asleep around midday to the voices on an Egyptian expose about Christian and Muslim exorcisms. "Your mother may have told you that djinn wear their feet backwards or that they prefer the magic hour of *maghrib*! She may have told you as a child that if you awaken paralyzed, a djinn has been sitting on your chest. But black magic is very real."

It cut to a respectable looking religious man with a thick black bruise in the middle of his forehead. The name *Doctor Zaki Abdallah* zipped across his chest as he answered questions of the interviewer. "Some of the most common signs that present in those who come to me are heavy menstruation, erectile dysfunction, excessive interest in sex, or *lack* of interest in sex, and often there is a psychotic element such as seeing movement under the skin or encountering a double of the supposedly cursed or possessed person—" The list carried on while Khalid silently tallied how many of these indicators Aneeza was suffering form. The symptoms leapt across his dozing mind, piling images of his wife up in the superstitious furrows of his subconscious mind.

The same subterranean place where he went to dream of Mecca.

Khalid was small and could not keep up in the tide of other pilgrims, so his father carried him the final perambulations of the Kaaba. Each time his father reached a hand out to the black stone as they passed it, Khalid could see the cornerstone through the crowd, framed with a vulvic sterling border. A wide kind of fear spread through his chest and he felt as if he were paralyzed as they spiralled down in a drain towards the centre where that vertical mouth waited. They passed the event horizon of the *hajj* and Khalid's father lurched through the crowd to the ancient meteorite. He then hoisted Khalid into the curved silver gullet against his will. He cried out and it echoed back to him from the metal frame. It was black inside. "Kiss it!" his father yelled.

There was urgency in his voice as a guard wrestled with him. The others were pressing closer, all fighting to touch the silver lips of the casing or peck the black stone buried inside the opening. The guard shoved Khalid's father away and he was swept away in the crowd. Khalid was sucked inside and the opening clamped shut like a parrot's maw. Inside was not a black stone, but a hematite cave filled with a strange mercurial crystal. Then, from within the crystalline womb of the Kaaba, he could see the crowd churning by when, without warning, something peered in.

The great slit eye of a mantis.

Khalid awoke from a sleep paralysis. He looked out the barred window. The sun had set, but the sky was still pink outside. He could get up to pray *maghrib* still. He rolled over on the couch to see the TV was still on, glowing blue in the darkening room.

It wasn't the channel he'd fallen asleep to. The satellite frequency must have changed.

It took Khalid a few moments to understand what he was seeing on the screen, but as he did, a strangely satisfying shudder of disgust rippled through his insides.

It was an orgy.

Khalid froze in a dilated sort of fear: ears open, breath sucking in a litany of prayer. He wanted to watch and wanted to turn it off, fearful of the consequence. Impossible bodies were sliding all over like a tumble of shameless lizards all licking and splayed. Men and women alike bore gaping holes like wet mouths. All open, all staring at Khalid. And then Khalid saw it entering one of the bodies—the silver knob of metal with the pink button. It moved beneath the skin of a taut belly like a beak seeking exit from an egg.

Aneeza's toy.

Right there in the TV. And among the slapping and flapping and moaning and groaning in a wash of liquid crystal ripples—Khalid thought he saw her. The double of his wife, Aneeza—transported impossibly to an over-lit studio somewhere in Europe then off some stray satellite that might be hurtling towards him even now in punishment for watching this. The words of the Egyptian doctor returned: "Seeing movement under the skin or encountering a double."

"Habibi?" a voice whispered from somewhere.

Khalid hadn't noticed the room had become so dark. He couldn't see her, but he knew she was here.

Khalid peered at the corner beneath the air conditioner.

A shadow darker than the others.

She stepped forward, her movements oddly liquid and her body moving into the bluish light of the TV, looking like a column that might collapse.

"What are you watching?"

Khalid looked beyond her to the flat reflection of the TV. It had gone to static. And now his wife's body was lit with strange, brief shadows casting across her in the flickering light.

"Habibi. Did you go into my room?"

Certain he was dreaming, Khalid shut his eyes, hoping she might go away and he would wake up. He wished some kind of immaculate miracle might occur and save him from contact with that unknowable, inhuman other: the infinitely twisting insides of a woman.

"Habibi," she repeated. This time her voice sounded as if it came from some cavern behind her throat. And her tongue flickered at her lips as she bent over him in the dark. And then, looking up into her face, he saw a flange of amphibious fingers pull her blue lips apart. It was a bright thing, sizzling with light. Its eyes wide-set like Aneeza's, but red like a mantis. Khalid could feel the prickling of electric hairs stinging his belly. "Look to her," the creature lisped from behind the blinding light. "Look to her." Khalid looked, and let her swallow him up. The miracle and the horror of her body finally revealed and the marriage finally consummated.

THE NEXT MORNING Khalid knew he had his answer. His wife *was* possessed, and by a very powerful, lustful djinn at that. What else would cause her to keep sex toys in their marital bed? What else would make a nice girl behave this way? How else would he have seen her in that pornographic film?

While she was away visiting her sisters and mother, he prepared. He watched YouTube videos of exorcisms and testimonials on technique. By the time Aneeza had returned, he had a pretty clear idea of what had to be done. He downloaded mp3s of several *ruqayas* and put them onto his player. Then he went to the pharmacy to buy rose water, a crate of Nestlé Pure Life and the most expensive bottle of Oud he could afford in a crystal decanter.

The next morning, Khalid watched Aneeza on her return from the day's walk, sneakers pouncing out from under her abaya one by one like little white kittens. As she unlocked the metal gate to the house he ducked behind the rooftop's wall and squatted amongst the satellite dishes until she was safely inside.

On entering, Aneeza found that the house was oddly silent and filled with the smell of cheap rose water. She followed the scent into her room to find it filled with candles. Ulama TV was on in the background and the water for the bathtub running, steam billowing from the open door.

The stuffed toy on her bed had its back flayed open.

She saw Khalid in the mirror before she felt the plastic ropes around her middle, holding her arms down to her sides.

"God have mercy, God protect us," he said as he gagged her and laid her down gently on the bed, but when she kicked at him powerfully, he tied her ankles too. She thrashed and struggled, glaring at him. "You have to listen to this," Khalid said as he slipped headphones from his iPod over her ears. She continued to thrash. "This is proving beyond any doubt that you are possessed, Aneeza. We must take further steps to relieve you of your djinni. Now don't scream." He ungagged her and spitting air into a bottle of water with three swift whistles, he poured it down her throat. She choked.

More proof. After this, he followed all the steps prescribed. A steaming rose water bath. A liter of holy water down the throat. But she did not recant and there was no change in her behavior, even when later that night she had grown too tired to kick anymore. Checking her binds, Khalid let her have a rest with the Verse of Fidelity playing from the ear buds he had planted like seeds in her head and covered over with her *shala*.

He had begun to feel more for her in these few hours than he had in all the months of their marriage.

Khalid thought to himself, with some surprise, that he was happy. Sitting her up as if she were his baby and rocking her, Khalid thought he could feel himself dissolve into her and simply disappear there. Aneeza's eyes were shut now. She was unconscious. He had to keep her awake or the djinn might bed down even tighter to her. He ran a bath and placed her in, dousing it with what was left of the Zamzam water.

It was then Khalid heard a familiar voice and poked his head from the en suite to look at Sheikh Safar on the bedroom TV.

"How can I help you sister? You're on the air." The sheikh asked, patiently tenting his fingers beneath the wiry curtain of his beard.

"It's my son," Mother said. "He's afraid of his wife."

Back in the bathtub, bubbles rose in a shroud around Aneeza's face. She kicked and struggled still, but the surface of the hot water only peaked and jagged in quiet laps.

"He thinks she is possessed. I don't know how to help them."

"Dear sister, you must try not to worry. Perhaps your son is right and she is possessed. Trust that God will show him the right path."

"InshaAllah," Mother said and Khalid agreed, staring down at the drowning woman on the bottom of his dull pink tub. He went to the threshold of the bathroom and looked back. "InshaAllah."

THE SPITE HOUSE
Kirsty Logan

I GO OUT most nights. There's always something new
to find. Always something unneeded that I need.
The evening smells of green leaves and frustration
and burnt sugar. This last thing confuses me, until I
notice the grumpy guy in the corner stall dropping
doughnuts into a portable fryer. Usually he does
coffee and sandwiches, which don't interest me. Fried
sugar, on the other hand… I'll stop back later, see
if any doughnuts are going spare. The city is quiet
tonight, so they probably won't all get used, which
means they're basically already mine.

Guys on bikes shout to each other; trucks *kwa-thunk*
over potholes; clusters of friends tumble out of bars,
checking their hair in the darkened windows. I turn
off the main drag and down one of the quiet alleys
that bisect the raucous streets. Without thinking about
it, I've hunched my head down into my shoulders—
my ears ache with cold, and I realise I forgot my hat.

Stupid, I know—the hair is a dead giveaway. And it's not that I'm ashamed, but sometimes it's nice not to have people immediately know what you are, you know?

The bars close, and the streets get louder, then go quiet. The night stretches and contracts around me. The guys on bikes are replaced by foxes slinking between the shadows. I'm far from home, labyrinthing through unfamiliar alleys, before I find the right house.

I know it's the right house because there's nothing separating the end of the garden from the start of the alley. No wall, no fence. Even the edge of the grass is ragged, no clear lines at all. And more importantly, stuff. Loads of it. There's a green vintage telephone and a plant pot full of foreign coins and a clear plastic crate of Happy Meal toys and what looks like a motorbike under a mucky green tarp. And most of it is technically in the alley rather than in the garden. It's all flecked with rain and dotted with leaves and it is definitely, definitely not being used. So I step forward, and—

Okay, look, maybe you're thinking I'm some kind of tragic bin-raider. That I rip open bin-bags, wipe carrot peelings off broken toys, steal credit card statements to buy shit online. But it's not like that. This isn't rubbish, out here behind the houses. The bins don't even go in the alleys—they go out the front of these houses, see? Lined up along the pavement every week for the bin lorry to collect. And I—

Look, I need to get on with this before someone comes, but there's some stuff you need to know about who I am and where I come from. You have time right now, and I don't. So go and get a book and look it up. It won't take long. I'll still be here in the alley when you get back.

Spite houses are buildings constructed or modified to antagonize neighbours or landowners, usually by blocking access or light. They have one purpose, and one purpose only; although technically 'houses', these buildings are often symbols of defiance rather than genuine attempts at a home. When building a spite house, the comfort and safety of someone living inside are secondary considerations at best. What does it matter if the bedroom is too narrow to fit a bed? What does it matter if there's no electricity or gas or running water? What does it matter if there's no ventilation or natural light? If the house is awkward and dark and damp, if the house rattles in the wind or leaks in the rain, if the house presses its bare walls to your shoulder as you walk through the rooms? If the house is not, in fact, a usable home—then the spite burns all the stronger.

From *Spite Houses: Architecture as Emotion*
by Kaite Caskey-Sparks
(University of Summerhayes Press)

* * *

THE BACK DOOR slams open and there's a woman silhouetted in the light from the kitchen.

"What are you doing in my garden?" she says, bold into the night. I wish I could say there was a shake in her voice, but there isn't. The kitchen light gleams on her pale hair, on the silk covering her shoulders.

"I'm not actually in your garden," I say, and I make sure to keep my voice sweeter than the doughnuts I can still smell on the air. "I'm just outside it."

"And taking things that are in it."

I spread my hands wide. I've barely got an accent any more, and that makes a difference. I'm doing everything I can to be apologetic, friendly, so super-fucking-nice you wouldn't even believe. "I'm sorry," I say, "I didn't realise you were using them." She's not using anything in this garden, I know she's not. And she knows it too.

"I—well. Not right now. But I will be."

"Ah," I say. "Sorry. You're right—I store things I will definitely use at the bottom of my garden too." I pause for her to speak, to argue with me; she doesn't. I grin and carry on, still sugar-sweet. "In the rain. And the dirt. With mice running over them and foxes peeing on them."

I try not to flinch as she marches down the garden towards me, out of the light of the house, joining me in the dark. Maybe I went too far this time. Not everyone goes for the cheeky act. Now she's closer I can see that the slinky dress I thought she was wearing is actually a dressing gown, and I can see her faded floral nightdress through the gap where she hasn't tied the gown properly, and somewhere in the garden she's stepped in a puddle and now there's dirt on her slippers too. I make sure that no part of me—not the tip of my boot, not a strand of my hair—is trespassing on her garden. She looks at me and she narrows her eyes.

And I can feel her looking at the red of my hair, at the red of my eyes, and even in the dark I know she can see the blue tinge of my skin.

"Oh," she says. "You're…"

"Yeah," I say, keeping my head high. "I am." For a moment I think she's going to run back into her house, or phone the police, or open up that plastic box of Happy Meal toys and throw them at me one by one.

She doesn't do any of those things. Instead she says, suddenly softly, "What's your name?"

"Esha," I say. Why lie? I'm a lot of things, but I'm not a liar.

"I'm Lexy," she says. I take her at her word, though I have no way of knowing if *she's* a liar.

"It's nice to meet you," I say, which I know is weird but I'm a stranger who's suddenly appeared in her garden and she's in a dressing gown so, really, what's *not* a weird thing to say?

"Okay, Esha," she says. "You've got me. I'm not using any of this, not now and not ever. They're not even mine. My husband—my ex-husband… it's complicated."

I say nothing, so she can assume I'm feeling whatever emotion she wants me to feel. Lexy isn't giving me the usual reaction from a person who's just found me about to take their stuff, and I'm not sure how to proceed. Best to keep it vague and non-committal.

"He won't clear his stuff out, but he won't let me sell any of it. Honestly, he's a fucking—he's such a fucking—"

I still say nothing but I try to make my expression more thoughtful, more angry, more sad, more— whatever she wants to think.

"I just wish…" she says.

That word. Oh, that floors me. It's years since I've heard it spoken. My djinn half is from my father's side, if you're curious, and my childhood was rich with the stories he told me about when he was younger, before the Emancipation. He told me about being given the spite house—the house where I now live alone. He told me that my whole life only happened because I got things that other people weren't using, and since he's been gone I've lived my life on that same principle. He told me a lot of things, and the most important of those things is never, ever to use the word *wish*.

But Lexy is totally unaware, her words flowing up like she's struck oil, like she's been holding in the words for years, like she's just been waiting for the right person to speak them to.

"I wish…" she says, and that's when everything changes.

Your history books will tell you that the Djinn Emancipation occurred seven years after the fall of the Iberian Empire, when thousands of djinn were made corporeal. They will tell you that a djinn is a supernatural creature, confined to a magical object, that can shapeshift and grant wishes. In your history books you can see archive photos from the time of the emancipation. Placards scrawled with NO SNAKES IN OUR NEIGHBOURHOOD, NO SNAKES NEAR OUR CHILDREN; HUMAN RIGHTS CAN'T BE WISHED AWAY; OUT BLUE DOGS.

What your books will not tell you is the answer to this question: what is a djinn that is no longer a djinn? When it is no longer supernatural, no longer confined to a magical object, can no longer shapeshift or grant wishes any more than anyone else?

Initially it was expected that the main problem would be the outcry over lost wishes, but in fact the situation was much more mundane. It all came down to housing. The djinn were smokeless fire; now they were bone and blood. Thousands of new bodies, needing thousands of new homes. The djinn have existed since antiquity, moving near us but always hidden, always tucked away until we needed them. No one minded them when they stayed in their little coffeepots and lamps and jewel-boxes.

We accepted that they would always be among us.
We just couldn't accept that they would be us.

From *While in the Woods I Stumbled:*
An Oral History of the Djinn Emancipation
by Julie Sloma (Jackalope Press)

"I WISH…" LEXY says, standing at the bottom of her garden in her dressing gown. "I wish…"

"Just say it," I say, and I don't even understand what's happening at that point. My voice is only a whisper, but it carries, it has power, and I'm leaning towards Lexy but I'm taller than her too. I feel like my body is stretching tall, up past the trees and the houses, my shoulders among the stars.

"Say it," I say.

"I wish," says Lexy, her voice so soft, so unassuming, "that he'd never existed."

I am tall and my voice carries and I have power, so much power, I can feel it in my fingertips, at the base of my tongue, with every throb of my heart.

"Wish granted," I say.

As I'm standing there, overwhelmed by power and confusion, Lexy whips the mucky green tarp off the motorbike—the keys are in the ignition, for fuck's sake, she was *desperate* for someone to take it—and with bungee cords she ties the plastic box of Happy Meal toys onto the back of the bike, and she motions for me to get on, and I turn the key and turn the key again and finally the engine catches and I roar off down the alley, and what the actual fuck just happened.

THE NEXT NIGHT, I go back to Lexy's house. She's still got a lot of things she's not using, and she seems willing to let me have them. I've already listed all the Happy Meal toys on eBay. Nothing yet on Grimace, but the Hamburglar has three bids. And the city has been so empty lately, and I know I said I wasn't hungry, but come on. Everyone is hungry.

A walk that took over an hour last night takes ten minutes on the bike. It chews up the streets and spits them out behind me, and I feel like the tallest, fastest, fullest thing I've ever been.

She's waiting for me at the bottom of her garden. As the bike's headlight approaches her, I see the ratty dressing gown has gone; she's also wearing a pretty floral dress and her hair is shining pale as opals.

I pull the bike in where the grass meets the alley. There's no plant pot full of foreign coins. There's no vintage plastic telephone or mucky green tarp. There's nothing at all. I step off the bike and lean it on the kickstand.

"It's gone," I say.

"What's gone?"

"The rest of your husband's stuff."

"My what?"

"Your ex-husband, I mean."

"What are you talking about?" She lifts the torch and shines it in my face. "I was never married."

I stand there at the bottom of the garden, squinting into the torchlight, and I think: *well, shit*. I granted a goddamn wish. I can't even tell you how many times I tried to make wishes come true as a child. Even though I knew that word was dangerous, even though I knew it was a word only ever used against us. I wished and I wished and I wished, and not a single one of those fuckers ever came close to true. But Lexy made a wish to me, and now it's come true, and that means I—that means *she*—

I have no clue what it means.

"Nice bike," Lexy says.

"Yeah," I say, not sure whether to laugh. "I got it from—I mean, you gave it… Wait, why are you here?"

"It's my house."

"Why are you here, waiting for me?"

"I thought you'd come. I wanted to give you something."

And that snags in my brain, of course it does. She wished her ex didn't exist, but if he didn't exist then he wouldn't have left his stuff in her garden, and then I wouldn't have stopped at her house to take the stuff, and then I wouldn't have been there for her to make the wish. My head is spinning, and I don't know what the fuck is happening, but I know it's something, so I don't climb back onto her bike—*my* bike—and leave. Maybe I should. But I don't.

"My neighbour," says Lexy. "She's got a lot of stuff she's not using. It's all in a caravan, just sitting in her driveway. I think she'd want you to have it."

"Maybe I should ask her," I say.

"Oh, don't worry. I already checked with her," says Lexy, her voice breezy-light. "And I was hoping that afterwards, I could ask you for something. Just a small thing."

And I think: *well, I guess this is how it works.*

"Okay," I say.

I follow Lexy down the alley and around to the front of the houses. It's not late enough for the stars to be out, but it is early enough for the streetlights to be on, and half the houses are dark. From the front, Lexy's house looks a lot like all the others, except that Lexy has plastic flowers in her window boxes and an incredibly shiny red car parked in the street outside. The neighbour's house has plenty of flowers— real ones—among the weeds and overgrown grass and a brightly-painted bench and a kid's bike on a kickstand. Wind chimes made of sea-glass clink in the breeze, and beside the neighbour's front door, three pairs of walking boots stand on the doormat. There's a light on in an upstairs window. Lexy's house and her neighbour's house should each have a narrow but usable driveway, but there's a caravan parked in it, which means neither house has a usable driveway.

"Here you go," says Lexy cheerily. "She says she's not using anything that's in here."

Inside the caravan the bed is pulled out and piled with brightly-coloured blankets and duvets and cushions. There's a teapot on the unlit stove and an empty wine bottle with two glasses on the tiny chipboard table. Everything is cramped and cheerful and covered in a light layer of dust.

I emerge clutching a full box, piled so high I can't see over it: cushions (my house is too narrow for a proper bed, so the more padding between me and the floor, the better), a vintage picnic set (for eBay), retro versions of Scrabble and Monopoly (for eBay), and two full bottles of wine (for me).

Together Lexy and I walk round to the back of her house. She pulls bungee cords from her pocket and fastens my box of things to the back of the bike. I know I must seem like an idiot, standing there silently, carrying some woman's abandoned possessions around, but did you miss the part where I apparently granted a goddamn wish? I'm finding it hard to figure out the right thing to say.

"I wish," says Lexy lightly, fastening the final bungee cord, and at her words I feel the power flare up in me. "I wish that grotty old caravan wouldn't block the light into my front room."

I clamber onto the bike and roar away from Lexy, and I can taste the power on my tongue, can feel it filling my lungs, sparking in my mouth, throbbing along with my heart.

* * *

The current generation will grow up finding it logical that djinn and spite houses would go together. A large number of small, useless houses. A large number of useless people used to small spaces. But some of us will remember a time that the djinn—like spite houses—existed for one reason: to piss someone off. And while that's fine for a house, for a person that sort of baggage is difficult to shake.

When they first emerged, all solid limbs and mouths that needed feeding, the newspapers used words like 'swarm' and 'invasion.' It was agreed that we should help the djinn, and that quite frankly the economy needed them. Who else was going to make things for us and then clean up after? But not so many of them, not all at once. And what were we supposed to do when they had no birth certificates, no formal education, no real job history? We all wondered: now that they were corporeal, how much of their own ways would stick? Would they still eat animal bones and dung? Would they still twist each one of our desires into something dangerous and new? What did they want from us now? And what did we want from them?

From *While in the Woods I Stumbled: An Oral History of the Djinn Emancipation* by Julie Sloma (Jackalope Press)

*　　*　　*

THE NEXT NIGHT, I go back to Lexy's. I tell myself it's the last time. Yes, she has lots of good stuff and yes, it's easier to keep going back there than to scour an increasingly cold and empty city. But I know that there are more important things in this world than having a full belly. I know the power of that word she keeps saying, and I know it can't be good.

I've barely swung my leg over the bike when Lexy's pulling on my hand, leading me round to the front of the houses.

"Ta da!" Lexy says. "My wish came true!"

And true enough, the caravan is no longer blocking the light into Lexy's front room. In fact, the caravan isn't there at all. Instead there's a mess of blackened metal and rubber, caked with a layer of melted white plastic. In the yellow glow of the streetlights, it looks sickly and ruined. Looking at it makes me feel bad and wrong and small.

"Would you just look!" Lexy says, so proud, so happy. "Look at all that light flooding into my windows!"

"It's dark," I say, and I can't keep the shake from my voice.

"Well," sighs Lexy. "I mean, during the day. I'm sure you can imagine. Isn't it so much better this way? I'm so glad we made this deal."

"Deal?" I say, and I know I sound like an idiot but give me a break, I'm in shock here. I'm a little slow on the uptake, but now that I look I can see that the neighbour's house is empty; the kid's bike has gone from the garden and all the lights are off.

"I wished it," says Lexy, slowly like she's talking to a child. "And you granted it."

"I didn't," I say. "I didn't do this."

"Oh, come on, now! You don't have to be coy with me. I'm not going to tell anyone. It's our little secret."

"But I didn't do anything. It was a fire, anyone can see it's been set on fire. And I didn't do that. I wouldn't."

"Didn't you?" she says.

I want to snatch my words back, and then snatch Lexy's too. Because I don't want to be a liar, but I think I might be lying. How can I say I didn't do it if I don't know what I did? If I don't know whether I did anything at all?

"Fine," sighs Lexy at my silence. "Have it your way. You keep pretending that you didn't grant my wish, and I'll keep knowing that you did. I don't mind how we do this as long as you keep granting my wishes. I have lots more things to give to you in return."

"I've changed my mind," I say, "I don't want this." But she's not listening.

"I think," she says, "that I should make a wish for someone else. Because I'm sweet and kind. Don't you think I've been kind to you?"

"I said I've changed my mind. I don't want anything."

"But *I* do. My neighbour, you see. She's very sad. She doesn't say it—she doesn't say anything at all to me, now—but I can tell. I see it in her eyes. I think I should make a wish for her. And I think you should grant it. Look, I brought you some things in return."

She picks up a cardboard box from her front step. It's taped shut, but as she holds it out to me I can hear its insides shift and clatter.

"I don't want…" I say, backing away from her. "I can't…"

"I wish," says Lexy, standing there outside her darkened house, holding a box in her arms, her voice so soft, so sweet, like a powdered doughnut fresh from the fryer, "I wish that my neighbour could be put out of her misery."

I forget about the bike I've left at the bottom of Lexy's garden. I start to walk away from her. And then I run.

Spite houses exist in dozens of forms in dozens of countries. And it's not just houses—in the west end of Glasgow, a landowner raised ground level by two storeys just to disrupt traffic. In Vancouver, a developer built a six-foot-wide commercial building to stop the city from widening the street. A spite house, in short, is any structure used by one person to antagonize another. Spite is everywhere, in every city. It is built into the very bricks.

From *Spite Houses: Architecture as Emotion*
by Kaite Caskey-Sparks (University of
Summerhayes Press)

* * *

THE NEXT NIGHT, I don't go to Lexy's house. The night after that, she comes to mine.

I know she's not a monster, or an axe-wielding murderer, but it's hard to fight the urge to scream when her smiling face appears at my peephole. I open the door, wishing I could put it on a chain. Instead I hold my boot against the half-open door, holding it firm so she can't push it further.

"How did you know where I live?"

"Hey, Esha," she says, her tone light. Like we're friends, like I've invited her round. "Are you sick? Why didn't you come over last night?"

"Listen. We can't do this any more. I lied to you, and I'm sorry, but that's the end of it."

"When did you lie?"

"Not out loud, not in words, but I—by not saying I couldn't grant wishes, I made it seem like I *could* grant wishes. Which is ridiculous. You know it is. I can't grant wishes, and I shouldn't have lied about it, but I wanted… I just wanted…" The sour aftertaste of power is still under my tongue, and I ache to spit it out.

"It's okay," Lexy says. "I believe in you."

"No, I don't…" I shift my foot, opening the door a little more, but still not inviting her in. "Listen. This isn't about self-confidence. It's a fact."

"Come over, Esha. I have so much more to give you. There's so much more I want from you."

"But I don't want anything from you."

"No? But there has to be a give and take, Esha."

"Stop calling me—" I say, and I stop, because even in my head it sounds ridiculous that I don't want Lexy to call me by my name. But I don't like the way she's saying it. Over and over, with emphasis, like it's a magic spell. Maybe I can't grant wishes, but words still have power. And I don't want Lexy to have power over me.

"There's still plenty left for me to give you, Esha."

"I saw the caravan. I didn't burn it. It was you. Why would you do that? Why wouldn't you talk to your neighbour?"

"Good riddance to that filthy thing. We both got what we wanted, didn't we, Esha? See, that's how it works between us. I give you things, and you grant my wishes. That's how it's always worked between us and you."

"What's that supposed to mean?"

"That's how I knew where you lived. Come on, you don't think everyone knows? It's clear what you are and where you belong. Look at this nasty place. What kind of home is this?" She motions at my house, and I don't need to look at it to know what she means. The awkward shape, the shallow depth, the useless chimneys, the bricked-up windows. The way it blocks the view for the house behind, the way it juts out over the pavement so people have to go onto the road to get past. It was built in spite, and it was spite that put me in it.

"You know something, Esha," says Lexy, and before I realise what's happening she's slid her foot between the frame and the door so I can't close it, leaning close enough that when she speaks I feels the warmth of her breath on my cheek. It smells sweet, like powdered sugar. "My husband used to fuck my neighbour in that caravan. She wouldn't let him fuck her in the house in case her kid walked in. So every lunchtime he'd leave work and go to that caravan and he'd fuck her for an hour. And then every evening I'd complain that the caravan blocked the light from getting in our window, and he'd agree with me. And then he left me to live in her house, and he fucks her in her bed, and that caravan was still sitting there, blocking all my light. Isn't that funny? Isn't that the funniest thing you've ever heard?"

"Go away," I say. "Don't come here again."

"Esha, wait," she says, and I think we've already established that I'm an idiot because I do wait.

"Don't you want to know?" she croons, the way you'd soothe a dog. "Don't you want to know if my wish came true?"

I kick her foot out of the way and slam the door, but nothing stops her voice creeping through the cracks in the door and into my ears. "I have another wish. Are you listening, Esha? It's for my husband this time. My darling sweetheart husband."

"No!" I shout through the door, but she doesn't hear me or she doesn't care. She keeps talking, and her voice is smooth as oil.

"I've left a lovely little box of things here for you, Esha. And in return, here is what I would like. I wish—"

The memory of power swells up in me, making my head spin, making my stomach lurch, and I run into the bathroom and shut the door and clamp my hands over my ears and hum as loud as I can. I keep going until my throat burns. I don't dare stop. I stay there until I see the light of dawn slipping under the door.

Later that day I buy a chain for my front door. I move the box that Lexy left on my porch onto the street, and by the next day it's gone. Every night I sleep with earplugs in. During the day, I always have loud music in my earphones. The sudden hard burr of a motorbike makes me flinch.

It's been two months, and I haven't seen Lexy. But she's left me with something. Every time I come back to my awkward house with its useless chimneys, its narrow rooms, its smallness, I realise that my home doesn't make me feel small. My home doesn't make me feel awkward or useless. Every time I think of Lexy, of how huge she made me feel when she said that word, I feel tiny and trapped. I realise that one of us lives in a spite house. But it isn't me.

EMPERORS OF JINN
Usman T. Malik

"THERE ONCE WAS a jinn who wore spectacles," Zak tells the room, tugging at his sunglasses. The sunglasses are rimless, tinted blue. The blue washes the hollows below Zak's eyes. The twins think his eyes look trapped in an aquarium. They could laugh, but they don't. Zak doesn't like being laughed at. Zak doesn't like much of anything. Sometimes he punches. He likes that.

"Jinns don't need spectacles," Saman says. She raises a slender golden-haired arm (the twins have heard she has white blood, on her father's side) and scratches the nearly invisible scar that slithers above her left eyebrow. She must have taken a bad fall once.

"Do too. Remember Zakoota?'

Saman snorts. "*Ainak Wala Jin*? Does it even run these days? What a baby. Ammi says it was boring twenty years ago, must be *awful* now. Which channel?"

The twins look at each other. They decide they like her.

You do too.

They are sitting in wicker chairs on the verandah behind Zak's house. The verandah overlooks a perfectly green lawn that stretches westward until it nudges a black metal fence, beyond which are fields and pastures and lots of tilled, fallow farmland. Two peacocks strut on the lawn past a squatting gardener who is weeding beds of jasmine, marigold and yellow rose. It's a nice view. The sunsets are smog-free.

The house sits at the end of a driveway that curves through poplar-lined lanes past a mosaic of gardens. The house is colossal—the biggest the twins have ever seen, or will. It has three floors, five kitchens, twenty-two rooms, one elevator, and two taxidermied lions flanking the landing of a balustraded staircase winding up from the marbled front hall. Zak's uncle shot the lions on a hunting trip in South Africa. It was a real battle to the end, Zak said; his uncle nearly lost a guard.

"His spectacles have nothing to do with his vision, dumbass," Zak is saying. "We're talking enchanted glasses. Take 'em off and he loses his magic. Put 'em on and he can see the unseen world again. Like a reverse Superman."

"Why is the jinn on Earth?" Saman says. "Banished from Mount Kaf, I suppose."

Zak is thirteen, Saman is fourteen, the twins are eleven. They're all related on their mothers' side. Their mothers have arranged an end-of-summer weekend at the Saigol farmhouse on the outskirts of Lahore. More like a farm estate, the twins think. They've read about sprawling English estates in books written by authors with important-sounding names like Blyton and Montgomery. Their mother used to insist on buying them.

As, I'm sure, does yours.

Zak's real name is Zakariya, but no one calls him that. If you call him Zakariya, he will get mad. 'Zakariya' isn't cool, he will explain before he punches you in the stomach. Or in the face. Which isn't cool either, of course, but really, what can you do?

"No, he's here of his own free will," Zak says, patiently. He occupies the only rocking chair on the verandah, and rocks it back and forth, back and forth. "He has fallen in love with a spectacle-maker."

Saman rolls her eyes. The twins coil the hemp strands in their armrests around their fingers. They think of the cottage at the bottom of the garden.

"He's given his glasses to the spectacle maker as a token of his love. He will stay on Earth until he weds her." Zak twists and rotates his shoulders, and the rocking chair speeds up. "He has chained her to his soul."

"That's a terrible story," Saman says. "Can I see your grandma's book on jinns?"

*   *   *

WHAT FOLLOWS HAS been researched thoroughly. The twins understand it and you know it to be true as well.

1. There are thousands of stories about jinn possession in human history.
2. According to the *Journal of the Royal Society of Medicine*, most victims are likely to be of South Asian, Middle Eastern, and African backgrounds.
3. The *Kitab al Jinn* was compiled by many people. They are all dead now.

THERE ARE TWO places on the Saigol farmhouse you're not supposed to go.

One is the Drawing Room—a steel-reinforced door tucked next to the servant quarters at the end of a long hallway in the basement. It's a strange room: you can't hear anything even if there are a dozen men inside, and sometimes there are. Saman knows because Zak told her. Occasionally his father and uncle go in there with their guards and lock the door. They stay in there for hours. Not a peep.

The other is the cottage at the bottom of the front garden.

A jinn lives in the cottage at the bottom of the front garden. Saman has seen the place on a previous visit to the Saigol farmhouse, but she's never been inside.

She wants to go see the jinn, but she's too proud to ask Zak—and a bit intimidated. The jinn sleeps under Rukhsana Apee's skin. Has been hibernating in Zak's sister for ages. Everyone knows that, though you're not supposed to know.

You are not supposed to know either, but now you do.

He must be so old, Saman thinks.

Saman follows the twins up the staircase and into Zak's room. It is huge, a boy's room with boy bedsheets and boy clothes thrown on the floor. The mantlepiece is littered with cricket and hockey trophies, action figures—Wolverine, Batman, Loki and Thor petrified in death grips—and two jars filled with polished stones and marbles. Posters of the Rolling Stones, Usher, three girls in bikinis, and Salman Ahmad wearing a beige Peshawari cap, long fingers riffing on an electric guitar, glisten on the walls.

"Your dado lets you take the book to your room?" Saman says.

"Uh-huh."

"Didn't you say it's real valuable?"

"Uh-huh. It's real old. Four centuries or some shit like that. After Apee got sick. Dado said she saw a shadow seated in a chair on top of a tree near the cottage. Shortly after, Dado bought the book from a peer sahib. Paid a lot of money for it. She keeps it in a glass case but sometimes she misplaces the key. So..." Zak tosses his sunglasses on the bed. He yanks a drawer from his dresser, rummages, pulls out a thick tome.

Saman and the twins gather around.

The book is leatherbound, the cover art contained in a transparent book jacket. A twin-horned creature with a goat face, fangs, and tufts of black hair on its corrugated head looms in the foreground. Its umbilicus bulges from its belly like a pregnancy and its hands are raised, plucking peacocks with serpent tails from midair. At its feet crouches a girl sketched in mid-laughter. She has maddened red eyes and is licking the creature's toes. The creature and the girl are surrounded by men with dog, shadow, and raven faces.

Saman smiles. The twins shudder. Zak scowls at no one in particular.

"*Kitab al Jinn*," Saman murmurs.

"What does that say?" The twins point. Arabic words swirl across the cover in gilded letters. There is a golden smudge where the name of the author should have been.

"I read a bit of it last time I was here. I think it's a book of spells," Saman is saying. "It also has descriptions of the many kinds of jinns you can banish. I wonder if you can summon them as well." Saman reaches out a finger and taps the cover.

"Does it have jinn stories?" the twins say. This is the first they've seen the book, although Zak and Saman have been talking about it since they got to the house.

Zak scowls some more. "No summoning anything."

"Why? You scared?"

Zak balls up his hands into fists. "No one is summoning anything."

Saman and the twins ponder his fists. This is odd, you must think. You've surmised that Zak's a daredevil. "Can I take a few pictures of the pictures in the book?" Saman says finally. "With my cell?"

"Why?"

"Because they're nasty," she says brightly, "and I like nasty things."

Zak looks at her. The twins look at them both. Zak's fists open. He fiddles with the book cover, taps the edge of his dresser. "Fine," he says, then reluctantly, "We could try a seance or something, if you want."

"What's a seance?" the twins ask.

"Ooh, yes," Saman says. "I'd love to talk to something which isn't there. Should we do this by the cottage where your jinn lives inside—?"

"No. We will do it in Dado's study. It's quiet." Zak says. "I've got some skull candles I can bring, and the Ouija board Mother brought me from USA."

Zak doesn't say 'America', like most people. It's always 'USA', and he enunciates it so seriously.

"What's a 'weejah board'?" The twins ask, but Zak is already walking out the door.

They go to Zak's Dado's study.

*　　*　　*

IN NO PARTICULAR order, the *Kitab al Jinn* teaches the following truths. You need to memorize them. The twins have.

Here:

1. Jinns are made from smokeless fire.
2. Jinns are souls blown into winds.
3. Jinns try to eavesdrop on the heavens and are repulsed by meteors.
4. Jinns have the power to take on any form.
5. Jinns inhabit darkness, cemeteries, caves and ruins.
6. Evil jinns are repelled by goodness and prayers.
7. If those are not an option and you run into a jinn in a deserted place, pulling your pants down also works.

ELEGANTLY LINED WITH mahogany bookshelves, the study is on the ground floor. A small window cracks open onto a side garden. The bay window faces east and at sunrise, its stained glass paints flame and icicles on the hardwood floor. You adore the colors, you do. Overhead, a crystal chandelier sparkles. It trembles in the breeze from the ceiling fan, sends slivers of light and shadow skittering across the round table on which Zak has splayed out the jinn book.

Pensive, Zak says, "I don't remember this picture."

The twins glance at each other, then back away from the table and go to the side window. Outside, it's late afternoon. The sun is a yellow splash between the leaves of the oak framed by the window. Beyond the tree you see primrose beds, a blue-green pond, and a chicken wire coop. Its door is open.

The two peacocks from the back garden have made their way to the pond. Silently they stand at its bank. Their blue backs glisten. One peacock's train of feathers—the male's, you think—fans out and above it gloriously. Shimmering in the sunlight, the feathers seem to vibrate. The twins contemplate the feathers; the eyespots on the feathers contemplate the twins. The bird lowers its train and cocks its head. Majestically, the peafowl raise their feet and saunter inside the coop.

The twins think of the hatchery. They don't know anyone who owns a hatchery besides the Saigols. Zak's father is fond of double round crested parrots, gray francolin teetars, peacocks, and partridges. The twin's mother told them so. The twins have always wanted to visit the hatchery, but now is not the time.

They put their hands on the window, feel the glass. It's warmed nice by the sunlight. The twins feel the stirring of a comfortless sadness they cannot explain. You feel it too, but it passes quickly.

The twins return to the round table.

Saman's gaze is riveted on the pages. Her fingers play with the end of the green scarf wrapped around her neck. Propped on her elbows, she leans in, a smooth mechanical motion, as if drawn by strings. She breathes on the illustrations, the calligrams and magic boxes that ripple and shutter like an optical illusion, as Zak turns the pages. The twins watch Saman's eyes, fascinated. Her pupils seem star-shaped. A brown lock of hair drops past the scar on her eyebrow; she blows it away, but it returns. The twins discover they want to play with that lock. They would, too, but Zak is frowning.

"Seriously, this picture..." he says.

Saman takes the book from him. She flips back to the calligram that has caught her eye—a verse in Arabic, its curlicues and flourishes twisting to form a horned beast with myriad eyes and twin humps. Saman reaches out a finger and traces the beast's outline, caressing its eyes of *noon*, its humps of conjoined *laam*. Her heart is pounding. She glances at the bottom of the page, sees the numbers in the magic box drawn there quiver in time to her heartbeat.

This is the moment you need to remember. When the stuff hidden and in-between turns into a looming. The twins know this all too well.

Saman tries to speak, stops, clears her throat, says, "Is that a spell right next to it?"

"I have no idea." Zak takes the book, shuffles the pages, and murmurs to himself, "This wasn't there before."

"Oh, move on already." Saman snatches the book back, finds what she's looking for. "*How to Conquer the Emperor of Jinns*. There are several stations of fear in this one."

She reads out loud, words rising like vapors from her lips, her voice soothing, honey on a sore throat. Her wonderful eyes follow the words. "The emperor of jinns," she says dreamily.

"Sounds like an asshole, doesn't he?" Zak says.

The twins look at each other. They miss the peacocks already. They miss their mother too. When did she say she'd be back?

Commotion outside in the garden. Shouts. The sound of running feet.

Zak is already at the window, peering out, his fingers clinging to the glass. His neck is flushed. He turns to face them.

Saman has closed the book. "What?" she says.

Zak's eyes are gleaming. "There's a killer on the property."

STOP ME IF you've heard this one.

"There are several stations of fear in this. The procedure goes: in a place of desolation, draw a circle and apply perfume within. After *isha* prayer recite *Chapter of the Jinn* seven times and *Chapter of the Shrouded One* sixty times. Impart blessings upon the Prophet at the beginning and end of the *amal*. Do this daily for forty days. Fast with a purified intention while you do this, to draw power against Demons and Horrific Faces.

"At the end of forty days, the Emperor of Jinns will come to you.

"NOTE: for a lesser jinn, read the spell on the next page aloud ten times and walk through a red doorway. Repeat this thrice.

"BE WARNED: without a pure heart and trained tongue, you will not be able to control the manifestation that appears."

This excerpt from *Kitab Al Jinn* is from the chapter on magic and dopplegängers. The twins have read this carefully. The twins cannot stop talking about it. They're still talking about it, if you listen. You should listen closely.

Here's how this next part goes.

HE IS A scrawny broomstick of a boy in dusky shalwar kameez with holes—filthy wild hair, bruised lips, skulking face. He can't be more than eleven. Trapped against the peafowl coop, he trembles like a weed, white wakes of tears on his face. A gardener holds his right arm, an armed guard the left.

He stinks like a servant, you think.

"What did you do, asshole?" Zak asks softly. He nods to the guard and the guard's hand swings. The full-palmed slap sounds like a brick falling on a steel sheet. The boy wails. "You thought you wouldn't get caught?"

"Suh... sahib, I didn't mean to," says the boy

between sobs. "I swear on my mother's name I was just looking for food."

"In the coop, chootiyay?" says the guard and kicks him in the shin. The boy screams. "Your mother left her pussy for you to eat?" The guard looks at Saman, face turning apologetic. "Sorry, baji. These bastards bring out the worst on my tongue."

Saman is bored. It is a beautiful day and yes, this was exciting for a moment or two, but she wants to get back to the jinn book now. She can feel the tug of the summoning spell. She thinks of the calligram situated by it, the eyes, the humps. Her skin is moist. It is a hot day. She wonders what would happen if one read half the spell, or, say, did twenty days of *amal* instead of forty. She thinks of the second spell for calling lesser jinns. In her mind she can still see the words glowing. Serpentine they curl, mystery upon mystery, nebulous, a-blur. It is a gorgeous, golden day, really.

Saman begins to mutter the words.

"Please, sahib," the boy is moaning. "Let me go. Forgive me this once. I... I was so hungry. I just wanted some of their feed. The bird attacked me, bit my leg. I didn't know what else to do." He tries to point to his leg where the shalwar is torn, soaked with blood, but the gardener jerks his arm out again.

The twins look at each other. Together, they go to the coop, where on the straw-covered ground a peacock lies, ugly in death, eyes bulging like marbles. Its crushed head oozes red-gray. An iron rod is trapped under its body. The other bird skitters at the far end of the coop, its foot leashed to a ring in the wall by its handler.

You sigh. The twins pretend not to hear. They exit the coop and glance at the drama unfolding by the pond. Saman has vanished. The boy is being dragged to the back of the house by two guards. "Teach him a lesson. Keep him there for a night or two," someone shouts. "Make the police wait a while."

Zak is shaking out the stiffness from his right hand. His face is florid.

"Where'd they take him?" the twins ask.

Zak shakes his head. "Bahan-chod," he murmurs. "Damn sister-fucker. Murdered our bird."

And as Zak finishes, the air fills with a smell, a mix of sweat and musk and dirty underpants. The shadow of the oak flickers across the primrose. The bushes and pond water ripple. The twins back away from Zak. They find themselves backing away from each other.

What's happening out there is Saman summoning something, something is happening out there, the twins think, but already their thoughts are drifting apart. The two are thinning out, molting, the link between them quivering, tenuous, as they float away from each other, slipping and cascading, still carrying each other afloat, but all the while sundering.

Before they could come apart, they rush to see what Saman is about.

You follow them.

*   *   *

THE TWINS UNDERSTAND—and by now you do as well—the duplicity of the *Kitab Al Jinn*. If you don't, here is a powerful example—an example of power:

1. Sheikh-al-Akbar Ibn Arabi believed the word *angel* hides a dozen mysterious interpretations.
2. The word *jinn* is mysterious too.
3. The word *jinn* means hidden, other, secreted away.
4. The word *jinn* is not mysterious at all.
5. The entity jinn is a lie. It wears spectacles.
6. Mystery is power, the bearer of mysteries most powerful of all. That which precedes is Secret. That which proceeds is Empire.
7. Power is the secret of jinn. If you don't believe it, that's because you smell like a servant.

THE TWINS ARE watching Saman. You stand watch over them both.

She stands by the gray structure that is the hatchery, holding the jinn book to her chest, the green scarf wrapped around her left wrist. She studies the path that winds by the hatchery past the rose bushes and disappears in a grove of poplars. Tugged by gusts of garden wind, Saman's long white kameez shivers. Her shoulders hitch. Cold in this weather, you wonder.

The twins move close to her.

You follow.

The cottage is a quaint, low structure with three chimneys, white walls, and cedar shingles undulating across the top. The stacked roof edges roll under the eaves. Its faded red door is flanked by jasmine bushes. No windows. Ivy creeps across the walls and over the door's casing and sash. It looks like one of those fairy tale houses Saman has seen in books—magical, secret, impossible to glimpse from the drive or really any part of the farmhouse.

Saman stops by the jasmine. She stares at the red door. He sleeps in Rukhsana Apee's skin, she thinks. Chained to her soul, madly in love with his prison. A band of heat builds in her belly and inches its way down. Saman stares and stares. After forty days, she thinks. He must be so old now.

She doesn't have forty days on the farmhouse.

Quickly Saman kneels on the grass. It is freshly sprinkled and the muddy coolness seeps through her jeans. She takes off her scarf, shakes it out on the ground, and places the *Book of Jinn* on it. From the pocket of her jeans, she pulls out a piece of chalk. She draws and draws and after several minutes manages a faint white circle on the grass around her. She sits and rifles through the book's pages till she comes across the calligram, the sinuous curves of it heaving as she flips the pages one last time.

There! The spell to summon the lesser jinns, written

in Arabic. She can read the Arabic script, even if there is no translation, no means to discern meaning, and no need.

The twins try to read along, but the page darkens before their eyes. They cannot see the spell. For the first time, the twins are afraid. You can sense the fear thicken and rise like a curtain around them. You narrow your eyes, concentrate, and the spell is there, the words secret and powerful, nestled against each other, rooting you to this place you now call yours.

Saman finds the words different from what she remembered by the pond. She is sure she didn't misremember before. She is sure something has changed in the order of words. In the arrangement of pages that build the world of jinns.

She begins to read the spell out loud.

The leaves of the jasmine turn.

The white flowers redden.

The petals start falling off.

Enthralled, Saman chants. There is a presence behind her. She can feel it, you can feel it, the twins can see it. The presence is growing, a crackling blackness hovering, churning, unfolding above her, like the wings of a monstrous bird.

The twins are terrified. They've always wanted to go to the hatchery and now they turn and dash. They race between trees smothered by shadow, leap over tombstones exploding from the ground, sharp moss-covered teeth that grow and grow, encircling them, hemming them into a knot tightening into itself. The twins are panting and crying, the hatchery is so close, it's right *there* if only they could—

In the corner of their eyes, the building appears. Only it isn't a hatchery anymore. It is a thatched shed. A sword, an axe, something metallic, is buried in its door.

It glints.

And the curtain stiffens, enwombing the twins, drawing them into the embrace of a deep, dark, unsatiated mother.

You watch the twins disappear. You feel strong, curious, strangely loquacious, even if your vocabulary hasn't quite flowered yet. You turn and walk back to where Saman is kneeling within the circle, hugging herself, rocking back and forth, sighing out the last of the spell. Dead leaves swirl in the air. Inundated by presence, the grove hums. The cottage breathes. Last glimmers of daylight or wetness on Saman's cheeks? Her hair is disheveled, her lips look swollen. She looks so small from where you stand, or she has receded into the distance.

"Please?" Saman whispers.

It is all right, you tell Saman, and the leaves above her head coagulate into a wreath that sinks and settles around her slender body.

Saman begins to shake. The red door of the cottage stays shut.

* * *

ZAK LURKS BY the cottage at the bottom of the front garden.

The evening is moonless, a celebration of shadow in the grove, but little electric lamps have popped alight along the path, a trail of mushrooms leading to and from the cottage. The smell of jasmine doesn't fill the air tonight. Zak fiddles with the brass keyring he is holding. They clink and slide.

The grove listens. It is still breathing.

One by one, Zak counts off the keys.

Behind him, the white circle made by Saman's chalk has faded. Saman left a couple hours ago. She looked dazed. Forlorn, Zak thinks. Dragging her feet as if hobbled by iron chains. She didn't hug him goodbye. He doesn't think he will see her anytime soon.

Zak slips the key inside the lock. He turns it, pushes. The red door gives way, swinging open to a narrow corridor. Zak's blood pounds in his fingertips. The hand that holds the keyring is trembling. The cottage is dark; his sister hates light. Soon their mother will make her last rounds and turn on recessed lamps to get her daughter through another summer night.

Zak takes a deep breath, bracing himself for the familiar hateful odor—musk and sweat and dirty undergarments. How many times has he seen the servants emerge from this hell hole, carrying soiled clothes and cutlery? Bent plastic spoons, tineless forks, warped tin plates, chewed bits of styrofoam. There has been blood on them over the years. Blood and filth have shaped Zak's understanding of Rukhsana Apee, but lately there has been something else.

You cock your head and read him: curious, dread-filled, a bit elated. You wait patiently because Zak is pissed. Zak is thrilled. Zak is feeling things he doesn't understand ever since he followed the filthy boy into the basement after his uncle told the guards to throw the bastard in the Drawing Room. They did as ordered. Zak had wanted to stay and watch, but his uncle shooed him away. Zak crept back and put his ear to the steel-reinforced door. Not a peep.

That fuck, that murderer. Killed what was ours. Sister-fucker. He'll get his tonight.

You notice that Zak is warm from top to bottom. His skin is sweaty. The warmer his skin, the stranger his heart.

Shuffling. Snickering. Clinking of metal against metal. Sounds that make up the world of the cottage.

Zak begins to tremble.

And now because he's afraid, afraid of the jinn, his heart is hammering, his pupils are dilating, Zak unbuckles his belt. He drops his jeans and moves into the shadows to inhabit the darkness in his sister's room.

YOU ARE WROUGHT. You are abrim.

And now because you are converged, you rise. Through the eye of the narrowest tangle of root, shoot, and branch, past the tallest emerald treetops, up and up, gathering strength. A curlicue of mystery, a calligram of power, you wrap yourself around yourself and tornado to the Saigol mansion, quaking that mausoleum of a hatchery in your wake—where a long time ago, when it was a horse shed, a clutch of lesser relatives and their children were beheaded with scythes and secreted beneath the floorboards for transgressions no one remembers, or deigns to remember. Down the smoke vents, up the stairs, past Zak's bedroom, a titanic wind known by one secret name, you howl into the depths of the house, where behind a steel reinforced door, surrounded by a grinder of guards and thugs, a young murderer hangs from the ceiling fan by his roped feet. Blood drips from his nostrils onto the concrete floor.

Zak's uncle is seated on a cedarwood chair before the hanging. In one hand he holds a Cuban cigar, in the other a cellphone. "The one by the canal, yes, yes, that one. Two hundred acres." Before him, the stinking boy screams as iron rods descend on his arms and bare feet. Zak's uncle waves away the smoke and screams with a flourish of his iPhone and lazily drapes one leg over the other.

Tenderly, like the gentlest lover, you drape the young murderer. He exhales. You cup your hands and breathe yourself into him. You lick his marrow, settle into his blood. Enthroned, you fasten his skin across us, like the slide of a curtain. You tauten it around us, mystery around mystery. Layer within layers.

The pages of a book. The membranes of a womb.

HISTORY
Nnedi Okorafor

HISTORY WAS A powerful witch who didn't know what the hell she was doing. However, few laughed at or gossiped about her. She was too glamorous, too enchanting, she was too entertaining. Plus, many were waiting for the right time and the right place. Tonight was both of those things, but History wasn't aware of this fact; she was just there to dance and sing and be the superstar that millions so loved.

As she inspected her face in the mirror, she half listened to the TV mounted on the wall behind her. "The woman was in labor when she stepped out of her home," an excited anchorwoman said, staring into the camera. "She was alone and she'd planned to catch a cab, but, well, the baby refused to wait. We're right at a crosswalk here on East 68th Street and 3rd Avenue, and she's in the *process* of giving birth! The news team just happened to be in the area, so we're covering this miracle live!" History turned to take a look. The anchorwoman laughed giddily as the camera turned to show a group of people crowded around paramedics. The woman in labor was barely in sight.

"Wow, that's bananas," History whispered, decreasing the volume and turning back to her mirror. "Good luck to her."

She shut her eyes and took a deep breath to clear her mind. She was here, now, almost ready. When she opened her eyes, she stared at herself in the large round mirror. Her dark brown skin glittered with the make-up her crew of artists had applied an hour ago. They'd used broad strokes of mascara to make her almond-shaped eyes sharp and piercing, and red, red lipstick to make her thick lips like cherries. She looked garish, but on stage she'd be the image of a queen, and that's all that mattered.

"One-two-three, one-two-three, one-two-three," she whispered. Counting soothed her nerves, as long as she didn't count too high. When she got past three, she always began finding it difficult to think and her discomfort would cause things to fall off tables and shelves. She glanced down at the turquoise mat her bare feet rested on and wiggled her toes. She smiled. The tattered old thing was the most valuable object she owned.

"Your toenails are so long you'd cut the grass if you walked barefoot," a nasal voice said. The bush baby snickered as it flattened itself on the top half of the large round mirror. It mashed its body against the surface, pressing until its white bug-eyes bugged out even more. History tried to ignore the creature inside the mirror. "Stop it," she eventually said. "I'll be on stage in minutes, you're distracting me." She paused, admiring the sound of her own voice. She hadn't even applied the juju, yet already it was like honey.

"That is my greatest wish," the bush baby said, stretching itself into a thin line, against the rounded top of the mirror. "You're a thief, and thieves don't deserve any peace of mind. Only annoyance and distraction."

Though not so much now, over the years the reward for tolerating its insolence was far greater than the satisfaction of shutting it up forever. Twenty years ago, she'd stolen the bush baby's mat and then lived through the seven-day ordeal it enacted fair and square; when the constant banging and screeching was over, silence had never been so sweet. Even an eleven-year-old needed silence at some point.

Surviving the bush baby's ordeal meant that she became its lord and master. Also (and most importantly to History), the creature's powerful juju blessed her with great wealth as she grew up. Still, though she could have, she didn't hurt the irritating squat onion-shaped earth spirit; she'd never had the heart. She'd toted the bush baby-inhabited mirror with her across the United States, across the sea and there and back again so many times, he'd become a kind of companion to her.

She plumped up her bushy blonde wig, tilted her face to the side and smirked. She'd been dancing since she could walk, dancing well. She'd been singing since before she could talk, humming sweet melodies her mother imagined she must have heard in her head and her father thought she learned from the local birds. History was *born* amazing, but it was the bush baby's mat that got her where she was today. Stealing it was fate.

HISTORY HAD GROWN up in a large Eastern Nigerian village surrounded by dense forest. Her parents were African American researchers from Jackson, Mississippi studying Cross River State's glorious butterflies. One day, they came home from a long day of research and found their five-year-old daughter singing like an angel and dancing like a goddess for the captivated audience of her caregiver's market women friends and local passersby. Right then and there, her parents knew her destiny.

Little History was never very gifted in academics, and her mother often laughed at her daughter's lack of critical thinking skills, but History was born with the power to mesmerize. And five years later, a year before they left Nigeria, some of the local women (with the permission of her parents and her caregiver, who was like a second mother to her) took her to Abassi, a local woman who was both the best farmer and the oldest person in the village. Abassi was also—quietly, unassuming—a sorceress.

"Don't take her back to America until I am done preparing her," Abassi told History's parents after spending two hours talking to the ten-year-old girl. "Someone like her will cause a lot of trouble. If she's taught a few things, the world will be better off."

And teach her Abassi did. Over that year, she groomed the ten-year-old to become her successor. Little History was to take her gifts wherever she wanted, be it into the forests of rural Nigeria or back to her parents' hometown in Mississippi. One fateful night, weeks before she and her family were to leave, little History saw something and made a choice that changed her life. She was eleven and restless. Thus, she was up that night gazing out the window, dreaming of what America would be like. And that was how she saw the bush baby.

A short onion-shaped creature, standing upright, with beady blue eyes and soft pig-like skin, the bush baby looked nothing like the cuddly furry animal one would find under the name 'bush baby' in the encyclopedia. The bush babies of Cross River carried lanterns that glowed a soft orange in the night, and rolled-up mats made of a straw-like turquoise material. History remembered Abassi telling her about them. Their peculiar look, and the fact that if you stole a bush baby's mat you could become rich, were easy enough for History to remember.

She crept outside and crouched behind the car in the compound. When the bush baby walked by, she leapt and tackled it, pressing it to the ground with her weight. She was a plump child, and this served to her advantage.

"Are you *crazy?*" it screeched. Then it spit some of the worst obscenities in the Igbo language that History had ever heard. Still, she and the creature wrestled and eventually she won. Right before her eyes, the creature farted loudly and then disappeared. That night, there it was, inside her mirror, leering and rudely gesturing at her. And it continued to do so when her father entered the room to get her ready for bed, to her father's horror.

Now, twenty years later, History still had the mirror and mat, though she didn't need the mirror anymore and could afford elaborate mirrors plated with gold and diamonds and free of annoying forest spirits. She was deep into her career as the top performer and singer in the world.

During that pivotal year of learning with Abassi, History developed what Abassi and everyone in the village called 'four eyes'. Thus, now as an adult, she could see and shove away the large, oily, green ghost-hopper sitting on her red leather juju bag. The insect was big as a stapler, but light as a pencil. It flicked her hand with its powerful yet ghostly legs as it jumped to her table, knocked over her capped bottled water and proceeded to walk up the wall. History righted her bottle of water and reached into the bag again.

She brought out a brown leather satchel filled with sand and poured a hand-sized pile of it on her cleared dresser table. Then she spread it over the surface with an open hand and drew two lines in it at 45-degree angles with her index finger. At the tip of each line, she did the same. Then she did the same to those lines. With each repetition, she drew shorter and shorter lines, branching out in a way that always reminded her of a tree she liked to gaze at back in Nigeria. She'd never known the name of that tree, but with her 'four eyes' she had seen that every part of it was inhabited by coin-sized spherical spirits that bloomed into flowers at night. Only certain bats saw them, and those bats liked to eat them when they were ripe. *That tree was so strange,* she thought as she drew.

When she finished, she reached into her bag again and grasped the long glass neck of a large bottle and slowly brought it out. It was like a wine bottle, except the body of it was round instead of cylindrical. Inside was what would make this particular concert the best of her career. She held it to her face. Last night when she'd summoned the jinni, it had been in the form of a tiny, angry, periwinkle dragon. Tonight, it had decided to take the form of something like her bush baby, round like the bottle with soft dimply flesh and so fat that it filled almost every inch of it. The folds of fat that would have been its neck waggled as it cocked its head, smirking slyly at her. Then it opened its mouth and stuck its pink bumpy tongue out at her, pressing it against the glass. "Blaaaaah!" it said, and then it laughed wildly.

"Nonsense," History softly said, resting a hand on her table. She touched the tip of the fractal image she'd drawn in the sand. "It is well, Ne Ikomm. You will reach deep, but save one hand, which shall remain outside. This way all who watch may see and be in awe of our power," she recited. It was always best to speak inclusively when dealing with even small djinn like this one. Their voracious powers came with voracious egos. Abassi would have told her to use a more local spirit, or at least one who had known her closest ancestors. This could have meant a ghost, fairy, forest spirit or even an immigrant masquerade. However, History wanted to go exotic, distant, and wasn't Arab magic more powerful than African? Who had told her that? She couldn't remember, but it seemed true.

The media, her label, her fans, everyone had high expectations for tonight's performance. HBO was filming this one for a documentary that would bring together her life's work. And though she couldn't read it, she could *feel* it, deep in her bones. Tonight was especially special. Yes, a jinni would do.

It giggled, belched out a foul stench of brimstone and turned around so that its ample backside was facing her, pressed obnoxiously against the glass. "You think you can dance, and maybe you can, but you are a fool," it said in its rumbly, bumptious voice.

"I've seen a Sudanese girl half your age dance the fire dance, washing her whole village in flames. Now *that* is real dancing."

"I never said I was the best," she said coolly. "But I'm damn good at what I do."

The creature sniffed dismissively. "Yes. That's why you need me, right?" The creature was not imprisoned; the glass bottle was of its own choosing. And it would have as much fun tonight as she would. *So why is it being such an ass*? She wondered. *Literally.*

Regardless, as she looked at its backside, she couldn't help but admire its lovely periwinkle glow. Its wonderful light filled the room and its touch made her sit up straighter, inhale more deeply, deliciously flex all her muscles. She would dance for *all* the spirits and demons this evening. They would see her.

With its jiggling jowls and butt cheeks, it made crass faces and gestures at the bush baby in the mirror (who laughed raucously at its antics). This, along with its lovely periwinkle color, made History feel both naughty and gorgeous. She put the bottle down and took a deep breath. Then she sang for the jinni in the glass. The jinni, the bush baby in the mirror and other spirits hanging around her dressing room listened. Her voice was like the most precious palm tree nectar, slowly pouring over everything in the room, warm, sweet, clear and thick. She smiled as she sang and closed her eyes, enjoying the vibration of her voice, harmonizing every part of her body.

When she felt the soft tingling in her fingertips, she opened her eyes. The jinni was turned to her and it had changed into what looked like a spherical yet recognizably female stone figurine sitting in the middle of the glass bottle. It had large breasts, no face and meaty thighs and it blazed an electric periwinkle. The bush baby in her mirror was shading its eyes, the ghost hopper was flying joyfully about the room, there were two humanoid spirits sitting on her white couch, rolling as if they were underwater. She grasped the bottle and turned it upside down.

"Aaaah," the jinni breathed as its stone body plunked to the opening of the bottle, melted like plastic, stretched and then slid out of the bottle's long neck onto the dresser's surface. The fractals in the sand shifted as if to catch the jinni as it poured over them.

There was a knock on her door. "Two minutes," Sheila said.

The light became a thin vapor. History even felt it enter her lungs as she inhaled. She glanced at the TV, where the woman on the street was still trying to give birth, and then used the remote to turn it off. She straightened her golden dress, checked her hair one last time and opened the door.

"Break your legs," the bush baby laughingly called from behind her. She shut the door without a glance back. The periwinkle light flooded the hallway as make-up artists rushed at her with brushes, powder puffs, and pencils. No one was allowed in her dressing room right before her shows, so they'd waited there like obedient dogs. Now, they descended on her like seagulls to abandoned French fries.

As she walked, they perfected. She glanced around and saw that the hallway was packed with all sorts of pot-bellied imps, floating soft-fleshed ogbanjes, bush souls, and many other named and nameless spirits. They always gathered at her performances, but never so many. The arena could pack thousands, and from what her manager told her, it was near capacity tonight.

When she stepped onto the stage the audience went wild. The noise was near solid, and she squinted as she smiled. Now her fingertips were throbbing and every surface of her skin tingled. *Breathe*, she thought; but what she saw was breathtaking. The lights were still low and she could see over the heads of thousands; they were like a swarm of ants—powerful and unified. These people had come for a show. And tonight, there were all *kinds* of people. Near the center, on the lawn, she saw what resembled a giant transparent bale of dry hay. It bounced and undulated amongst the packed people, spraying semi-transparent straw. Some of the human audience members wiped at their faces, necks and arms, as the straw showered onto them.

She saw the great Nigerian Igbo masquerade whose spoken name was Ijele. It hovered above the audience near the front, all its figures—the mother, father, child, police officers, everyone—standing on their bright ribbon woven platforms. History had always thought Ijele looked like a giant erector set monster made by one of those autistic kids. She spotted Mako jumbies walking amongst the people, as well. They were like stilted blue, yellow and orange spiders, gracefully prancing over unsuspecting human audience members.

Even on stage, she saw a shadowy figure standing on the far side, watching her and her band. He was old, brown-skinned, and leaned on a cane. Legba. So there were not only powerful spirits and demons here tonight; there were gods and probably goddesses, too. As if to solidify her realization, she saw lightning flash in the bowels of looming clouds that no humans seemed to notice... except people like her, who had 'four eyes'. Shango the Yoruba God of Thunder was here.

So many were present and for a moment, she frowned and thought, *What's going on here? Maybe I*—But then she saw glowing periwinkle and her voice swelled in her chest. She brought the microphone to her lips and hummed as she walked to the center of the stage and the lights came on. A unified shriek of joy burst from her audience. The vibrations hit her and she was in her own ecstasy as she began to sing her favorite song. Yes, today, she decided to start with her favorite, which happened to be her most popular. As she sang, the audience sang along, too. And then it took her and she was both gone and there.

*   *   *

HISTORY WAS SINGING the soulful song that made her grandmother cry. This was when she came back to herself. She had not written the song; she did not write any of her songs. However, when she sang this one, the tune always forced her to dig deep within herself and remember a vision she had in Nigeria when Abassi had asked her to remember her past life.

It had been when she was ten, a month after she'd begun training and Abassi had made her stay awake for four days in a row. On the fourth day, Abassi asked History to remember her past life. Without effort, her mind rushed back to a time when she'd also been ten years old. She was standing in the bush as a young boy crying. Before him, his father fought two men, as another two destroyed his stone gods and knocked down their shrine. History did not fully understand what was happening, but she felt the same deep sense of loss as that boy had, so long ago. The feeling was so deep that when the vision stopped, her heart was beating irregularly and she passed out.

She felt that anguish now, standing before the audience, her mouth open as it poured out a melodious vibration. Even though her eyes were unfocused, she could see it sweeping over the captive audience, a soft periwinkle vapor. The vapor was glowing. Poison or perfume, History didn't know. But as she sang, her back arched and something flew from her chest. All went black.

SHE WAS LOOKING up. The clouds above rumbled as they churned, lightning flashing within. Someone was screaming. Then there were more screams. Something was happening. The ground began to undulate and she brought her head down to see her audience was no longer unified, as people tried to flee in different directions. The stage quaked, making her stumble. Behind her, she heard a cymbal hit the floor. One of her backup singers yelped as she fell. The stage quaked again and History fell to her knees. She breathed into her chest, warm sweat beading from her brow. She wiped it away, smudging her make-up.

When she looked up, she saw that where her audience had been, there was now only trampled dirt. In the center, near the front of the stage, blazed a quivering ring of fire. Above, the sky opened and released torrents of warm water. As raindrops hit the ring, they hissed and steamed out of existence. History frantically wondered if she were witnessing a slow explosion. Someone was tapping at her shoulder. She looked up and met the face of the old man who'd been standing on the side of the stage. "Stupid, stupid witch," he said, but he was smiling. His teeth were worn away and his gums were a dark brown. "What a mess you've made."

"Me?" she asked. "I didn't—"

"Get up," he said, holding out a hand.

She allowed him to help her up and walked quickly after him. She wiped at her wet face; even her clothes were soaked through. When had she torn off her wig? The air felt cool, so close to her wet scalp. She chanced a pause and a look back, and saw the ring burning now, white hot; the rain coming into contact with it instantly vaporized. A blue light was forming at the center. There were only a few people left in the stadium now, slipping and sliding on the mud as they fled… few *human* people. The others were still around. Not far from the fire ring, something was undulating beneath the muddy ground, and Ijele was dancing wildly on top of it. On stage, a *tungwa* exploded, the resulting jumble of teeth and tufts of black hair immediately pounded down by the rain.

Suddenly, there was a great *CRACK!* and the blue light shot out of the ring and zoomed up out of the stadium, and into the stormy sky. A great cacophony of noise burst from all the great peoples still hanging around. Ijele's many life-sized characters whooped and hollered, its police officer held up its gun and fired shots into the air. Several smoky humanoid spirits did cartwheels. An ogbanje hovered by and slapped its plump brown baby legs together as it gleefully giggled and rolled in mid-air. Noises of elation came from all over the stadium. History wiped water from her face and frowned. If she had to describe it, she could have only described it as... applause? Yes, she knew a standing ovation when she heard it.

The man pulled History away. Expertly jogging in her six-and-a-half inch heels, she followed him closely, but as he pulled her along, he disappeared. She kept running. She met two security guards, who ushered her into her tour bus.

Two of her back-up dancers huddled on the couch in the back. Both were pulling towels tightly around their bodies, and they stared at her with stunned eyes. Her manager and hairdresser leaned against the side windows; they too stared at her as if they were sure their lives were about to end. The bus door opened and her cousin climbed on, soaked to the bone. Her hand shaking, she held a waterproof cell phone up to History. "Here," her cousin said, looking up at her.

"Did they bring out my mirror?" History asked, taking the phone.

"Yes, and it's safe." Nicki turned to leave.

History grabbed Nicki's shoulder. "Hang on. Nicki, what... what happened?" she asked. "I don't remem—"

Nicki shook her head, pulling away from her. "I don't know. I don't know. It was so scary!" She stepped backwards off the bus and quickly walked away.

"Wait!" History called, stepping down. But Nicki kept going, entering a car behind the bus. There was smoke rising from the stadium. Was the stage burning? Why?

The cries of a baby made her jump. The television mounted on the bus wall was on and it was tuned to the channel covering the woman in labor at an intersection in New York. One of the kneeling paramedics held up a wet brown crying baby. The child's eyes were open as he wailed. History shivered, her eyes locking with the child's, as if she stood right there on the New York street. Then there was a burst of applause from the people standing around the scene. The anchorwoman turned to the camera with tears in her eyes. "Wasn't that just... wow. Oh, the miracle of life..."

History sat in the empty bus driver seat. She shut her eyes and shook her head. "Ugh," she breathed. She held the phone to her ear. Behind her, her manager asked the girls if there was an emergency exit in the back. She heard the emergency door click open.

"Uyai," Abassi said. History pressed the phone to her ear. This was the name only she called History, when they were alone, during History's apprenticeship. No one else knew the name, not even her mother. It meant 'beauty' in Efik. Abassi said all names were juju, powerful spells that everyone was foolish enough to speak every day.

"Mama Abassi," History said.

"Do you know what you've done?"

History paused. If she spoke too soon, the poor connection would clip her words. "How do you know?"

"Because flowers are blooming on all the trees here, all around my compound," the old woman said, switching to Efik. "The village children are looking around with wide eyes like she-goats." She laughed so hard that she coughed.

"I don't know what I have done," History said.

"That's because you are a creative force. You open doors. To do one's duty is to eat the prized fruit of honor. You are a channel. But you don't pay attention to maps and calendars, you barely read books," Abassi said. "You don't understand ley lines, you don't know the names of those around you, or the flap of the butterfly's wing."

"Come on, Mama Abassi. Today was just a show," she said. "I wasn't doing—"

"Nothing is just nothing," Mama Abassi said. "But your work is done. You even had a chance to bless him. We'll take care of him from here."

"Mama Abassi, stop speaking in proverbs and circles. I don't get what you're saying?"

"Power doesn't always come with the gift to empower, not even for witches," Mama Abassi said. History could hear her suck her teeth in annoyance. "Women like you will always be used, but it's good because you are around good people." She began to recite the cleansing song she always recited on the phone with History whenever they talked after a performance, but History wasn't really listening. She was falling deep into thought, and her temples ached with the effort.

Abassi never minced words with her and those words always left History feeling as if she were floating in the sea of her life, with no control or understanding of where she was going. And tonight, Abassi's words kind of hurt. History had come to give her audience something wonderful, and instead everything had gone up in strange flames and panic. Now here Abassi was telling her that she'd been 'used', as well.

She humphed and frowned quietly, an old irritation creeping up on her. The bush baby had said it one evening when she was about sixteen and she'd never forgotten. "You treat that Mama Abassi like your second mother," it had said. "But don't you ever wonder if she's just keeping you under control? Or even making *use* of your talents?"

History had gasped at his words and slapped at the mirror. "*Tufiakwa!*" she hissed. "God forbid! You say such evil things sometimes."

It snickered darkly, sitting heavily on her reflection's head, looking her in the eye. "Well, it wouldn't be anything new. Didn't *her* people use *your* people as currency in order to buy nonsense from the white man? Isn't *that* how slavery started?"

She scoffed angrily and rubbed the mirror, muting his laughter and any other evil words he spoke. Still, the bush baby had succeeded in planting that tiny speck of doubt. And hadn't Abassi just come close to stating the bush baby's words herself?

The sky was still churning, but the clouds were

breaking. Whatever had happened was passing now. Abassi was right... most of the time. This time she was only mostly right. Maybe people did use History, and she was certainly around plenty of good people, but this time she *would* empower. She rubbed her forehead, trying to massage away her headache. Her mind grasped the image of the freshly born baby on television. She would give her mat to that child. "And the mirror," she whispered to herself.

"Eh?" Abassi asked. "Is the connection going bad?" She'd finished the cleansing song and History had been so deep in thought that she'd forgotten to say the expected, "Thank you."

"No," she quickly said. "It's fine. Thank you, Mama, thank you."

She heard Abassi cluck her tongue. "You are most welcome. Oh, do not worry, Uyai. You are perfectly safe and your bush baby is truly good luck. Your fame will grow from this. When you clear your schedule, come home."

"I will."

FOR YEARS, HISTORY remembered that evening as the evening when the stadium she performed in was struck by lightning and burned down. And she quickly forgot the abundant presence of different people—from human to spirit to deity—that night. After finding the location of the woman who'd given birth on the street and sending the child the turquoise mat (with her signature on the edge), the mirror, and a year's worth of diapers as a gift, she didn't think twice about the child... except in her deepest dreams, when she saw his piercing eyes. And never in her long and prosperous life did she realize that this street-born child was the one who became the man that the world called the Conductor. It never ever crossed her simple mind that she'd gifted him with a lifelong friend who brought him the financial stability he needed to quiet his mind and invent.

History was not a smart witch, but she was a very, very powerful one.

ABOUT THE AUTHORS

Sophia Al-Maria lives in London, where she writes for film and TV. Her first book, *The Girl Who Fell to Earth*, was published in 2012 and has been translated into Arabic. Douglas Coupland said of it, "This book could easily alter the way you see the early twenty-first century." She is credited with coining the term 'Gulf Futurism'. In 2016, she presented a solo show at the Whitney Museum in New York called *Black Friday*, shot in nighttime shopping malls in Qatar—it was very loud and very scary.

Monica Byrne is the author of the Tiptree Award-winning debut novel *The Girl in the Road*. She's also a playwright, artist, futurist, activist, traveler, and the first speaker in TED's history to deliver a work of science fiction as a talk. She is supported entirely by her patrons at patreon.com/monicabyrne and is based in Durham, North Carolina.

Neil Gaiman is the author of over thirty acclaimed books and graphic novels for adults and children, including *American Gods, Stardust, Coraline*, and *The Graveyard Book*. His most recent novel for adults, *The Ocean at the End of the Lane*, was highly acclaimed, appeared on the hardback and paperback *Sunday Times* bestseller lists and won several awards, including being voted Book of the Year in the National Book Awards 2013. The recipient of numerous literary honours, Neil Gaiman's work has been adapted for film, television and radio. He has written scripts for *Doctor Who*, collaborated with authors and illustrators including Terry Pratchett, Dave McKean and Chris Riddell, and *The Sandman* is established as one of the classic graphic novels.

Hermes is the pen name of Mohamed Magdy, a Cairo-based Egyptian poet, writer and translator who left medical practice shortly after completing his training as a doctor and finishing his military service. He currently works as a freelance writer and editor following a two-year stint as an editor at Egyptian publishing house Kotob Khan. His publications include two poetry collections, *Chirping in Braille* and *My Beloved Kalashnikov*, as well as Arabic translations of three novels. He was featured in *The Tahrir of Poetry: Seven Egyptian Contemporary Poets* which was curated and translated by Maged Zaher. His latest poetry collection, *Evasions,* will be published in Cairo in January 2017.

Saad Z. Hossain lives and writes in Dhaka, Bangladesh, for a minuscule audience of five to ten people. He started writing fantasy and science fiction type stuff to avoid having to research anything. His novel *Escape from Baghdad!* was published by Unnamed Press in the US, and Aleph in India. It is available in bookstores, libraries, bonfires, Amazon and Kindle. *Escape from Baghdad!* was included in the *Financial Times*' Best Books of 2015, and the Tor Reviewers' List 2015. It has been well-reviewed by *Vice, Kirkus, NPR, Library Journal, Wasafiri, Times of India*, amongst others. He is working on his next novel, *Djinn City*. The djinns are not pleased.

Maria Dahvana Headley is a #1 New York Times-bestselling author & editor, most recently of the novels *Magonia, Aerie, Queen of Kings*, and the internationally-bestselling memoir *The Year of Yes*. With Kat Howard, she is the author of *The End of the Sentence*, and with Neil Gaiman, she is co-editor of *Unnatural Creatures*. Her short stories have been included in many 'year's best' anthologies, including *Best American Science Fiction and Fantasy*, and have been finalists for the Nebula and Shirley Jackson Awards.

Catherine Faris King is a Lebanese-Irish-American writer. She has always known that Los Angeles, her hometown, has magic in it. When not writing, she enjoys blogging, cooking, and globetrotting. She is currently working on her first novel.

Kirsty Logan is the author of short story collection *The Rental Heart and Other Fairytales* (2014), which was awarded the Polari First Book Prize and the Saboteur Award for Best Short Story Collection, and debut novel *The Gracekeepers* (2015), which won a Lambda Literary Award. Her most recent book, *A Portable Shelter* (2015), is a collection of linked short stories inspired by Scottish folktales and was published in a limited edition with custom woodblock illustrations. Kirsty also works as a book reviewer, writing teacher and editor.

Jamal Mahjoub once studied Geology. He has since worked as translator, librarian, chef and freelance journalist. He has published fiction and non-fiction. His work has been widely translated and awarded various prizes. As Parker Bilal, he writes the Makana crime fiction series, the latest of which is *Dark Water* (2017). He currently lives in Amsterdam.

Usman T. Malik is a Pakistani writer of strange stories. His work has won a Bram Stoker and a British Fantasy Award and is a finalist for the Nebula and the World Fantasy. He resides in two worlds, but you can find on Twitter @usmantm.

Kuzhali Manickavel's collections *Things We Found During the Autopsy, Insects Are Just like You and Me Except Some of Them Have Wings* and e-chapbook *Eating Sugar, Telling Lies* are available from Blaft Publications, Chennai. Her work has also appeared in *Granta, Agni, Subtropics, Michigan Quarterly Review* and *DIAGRAM*.

Amal El-Mohtar is an author, editor and critic. She has received the Locus and Parsec Awards, been a finalist for the Nebula and World Fantasy awards, and won the Rhysling Award for poetry three times. Her fiction has most recently appeared in anthologies such as *The Starlit Wood: New Fairy Tales* (Saga Press), and magazines such as *Uncanny, Strange Horizons,* and *Lightspeed.* She regularly contributes criticism to NPR Books, edits an online poetry quarterly called *Goblin Fruit,* and lives in Ottawa with her partner and two cats.

Claire North is a pseudonym for Kate Griffin, who is actually Catherine Webb. All of these people are a London-based fantasy and science-fiction writer with a fondness for urban wonders and Thai food, who also works as a theatre lighting designer. Recent books include *Touch, The Sudden Appearance of Hope* and *The First Fifteen Lives of Harry August,* and *The End of the Day* is released early 2017.

Nnedi Okorafor is a Nigerian American writer of speculative fiction and an associate professor at the University at Buffalo, New York. Her works include *Who Fears Death*, the *Binti* novella series, *The Book of Phoenix*, the *Akata Witch* series and *Lagoon*. She is the winner of a Hugo, Nebula, and World Fantasy Award and her debut novel *Zahrah the Windseeker* won the prestigious Wole Soyinka Prize for Literature. Learn more about Nnedi at nnedi.com.

K. J. Parker was born in London in 1961. Having worked as an auction-house porter, coin-dealer and lawyer, he started writing full-time twenty years ago and has fretted incessantly about money ever since. He writes at night and spends the day tending a very small smallholding in the west of England (100% organic and 100% carbon neutral, but only because he can't afford any proper gear). He won the World Fantasy Award for novellas in 2013 and 2014, and has been nominated twice since. He averages 92.7 in the SSBSA winter league. Parker also writes under the name Tom Holt, but has long since lost track of which of the two he really is.

Sami Shah is a writer and comedian from Pakistan, now living in Australia. His memoir *I, Migrant* has been nominated for multiple literary awards, and although it didn't win any, that still counts for something. *Fire Boy*, his first novel about a half-djinn boy growing up in Karachi, is steeped in Islamic mythology and real-world politics. Saladin Ahmed described it as, 'Bold, compelling fantasy', and he knows of what he speaks.

Kamila Shamsie is the author of six novels, including *Burnt Shadows*, which has been translated into more than 20 languages and was shortlisted for the Orange Prize for Fiction, and *A God in Every Stone* which was shortlisted for the Bailey's Women's Prize for Fiction. Three of her other novels (*In the City by the Sea, Kartography, Broken Verses*) have received awards from the Pakistan Academy of Letters. A Fellow of the Royal Society of Literature, and one of Granta's 'Best of Young British Novelists', she grew up in Karachi, and now lives in London.

James Smythe is the award winning author of *The Machine, No Harm Can Come To A Good Man*, the Anomaly Quartet and the Australia Trilogy, amongst others. He lives in London and teaches Creative Writing at Roehampton University.

E. J. Swift is the author of The Osiris Project trilogy, a speculative fiction series set in a world radically altered by climate change, comprising *Osiris, Cataveiro* and *Tamaruq*. Her short fiction has appeared in anthologies including *The Best British Fantasy* and the digital book *Strata*. Swift was shortlisted for a 2013 BSFA Award in the Short Fiction category for her story "Saga's Children" (*The Lowest Heaven*) and was longlisted for the 2015 Sunday Times EFG Short Story Award for "The Spiders of Stockholm" (*Irregularity*).

Helene Wecker's novel *The Golem and the Jinni* was published by HarperCollins in 2013, and won the Mythopoeic Award, the Ribalow Prize, and the VCU Cabell First Novelist Award. Its sequel, *The Iron Season*, will appear in 2018. Her short fiction has appeared in the *Catamaran Literary Reader* and *Joyland Magazine*. Helene grew up in suburban Chicago, and received her B.A. in English from Carleton College in Minnesota and her MFA from Columbia University in New York. After many years spent bouncing around between both coasts and the Midwest, she's finally settled in the San Francisco Bay Area, where she lives with her husband and kids.

Neon Yang is a lapsed scientist, former practicing journalist and master hermit destroying SFF one queer story at a time. They live in Singapore and received their MA in Creative Writing from the University of East Anglia in Norwich. Their Tensorate novellas, *The Red Threads of Fortune* and *The Black Tides of Heaven*, came out from Tor.com Publishing in 2017.

*

Mahvesh Murad is an editor, critic and voice artist from Karachi, Pakistan. She is the editor of the award-winning *Apex Book of World SF 4*, host of the interview podcast *Midnight in Karachi* for Tor.com and the voice of many international radio and TV commercials, as well as multiple short stories.

Jared Shurin has edited or co-edited 11 anthologies in partnership with Tate Britain, the Egypt Exploration Society, the Royal Observatory and others. He has been a finalist for the British Science Fiction and Hugo Awards, and twice won the British Fantasy Award. Jared is the editor of the award-winning geek culture website *Pornokitsch*.

FIND US ONLINE!

www.rebellionpublishing.com

/rebellionpub

/rebellionpublishing

/rebellionpublishing

SIGN UP TO OUR NEWSLETTER!

rebellionpublishing.com/newsletter

YOUR REVIEWS MATTER!

Enjoy this book? Got something to say?

Leave a review on Amazon, GoodReads or with your
favourite bookseller and let the world know!

"EXQUISITE AND AUDACIOUS, AND HIGHLY RECOMMENDED"
THE NEW YORK TIMES ON *THE DJINN FALLS IN LOVE*

The Outcast Hours

EDITED BY

MAHVESH MURAD & JARED SHURIN

INCLUDING STORIES BY

MARINA WARNER · CHINA MIÉVILLE · FRANCES HARDINGE · SAMI SHAH
S. L. GREY · OMAR ROBERT HAMILTON & MANY MORE

⊙ SOLARISBOOKS.COM

SINOPTICON

A CELEBRATION OF CHINESE SCIENCE FICTION

Featuring Stories by Jiang Bo, Bao Shu,
Regina Kanyu Wang, Anna Wu and more

TRANSLATED AND EDITED
BY XUETING CHRISTINE NI

FOREWORD BY XIA JIA

⊙ SOLARISBOOKS.COM

Tales of
Time Crossed
Romance

SEANAN McGUIRE
JEFFREY FORD
ALIX E. HARROW
ROWAN COLEMAN

SOMEONE
IN
TIME

THEODORA GOSS
ZEN CHO
ELIZABETH HAND
AND MANY MORE

Edited by
Jonathan
Strahan

⊙ SOLARISBOOKS.COM

NEW SUNS

ORIGINAL SPECULATIVE FICTION BY
PEOPLE OF COLOR EDITED BY NISI SHAWL

WINNER
OF THE LOCUS,
WORLD FANTASY,
BRAVE NEW WORDS
AND IGNYTE
AWARDS

INTRODUCTION BY **LEVAR BURTON**
INCLUDING STORIES BY **INDRAPRAMIT DAS**
E LILY YU, REBECCA ROANHORSE, ANIL MENON,
JAYMEE GOH AND MANY OTHERS

⊙ SOLARISBOOKS.COM